TOUCH

TOUCH

CHERYL KAHN

CONTENTS

"Where there is sensation, there is also pleasure and pain,
and, where these, necessarily also desire."
—ARISTOTLE, *On the Soul*

1

SLEEPING BEAUTY

THE WORDS ON THE PAGE BLURRED, AND I BLINKED AWAY the dangers of sleep. Jerking upright against the headboard, I cursed myself for reading in bed again. But reading on the attic floor meant stiff muscles the next day, and stiff muscles made defending myself hard. Since waking in the river, I'd learned I needed my body at its best.

I yawned.

I should move to the floor. Much less temptation to give in to exhaustion when I wasn't so comfortable. It wouldn't even be cold down there tonight. Warm air seeped in from the low attic window. A rare muggy night in northwestern Colorado. I'd even pushed off my top sheet and comforter, my skin sticky, my hair clinging to my neck and chest. Not even a gentle summer breeze to stir the needled limbs of the blue spruce growing right outside. If only I had the energy to move. I scanned the page, searching for where I'd left off:

What do you think, would not one tiny crime be wiped out by thousands of good deeds?

The next line swam before my eyes, and I sank deeper into the mattress. I finally gave in, clicking off my light. If rereading my favorite book off the AP English summer list wouldn't keep my mind from shutting down while my body rested, perhaps nothing would. How many days since I'd slept? Two?

Three?

My book fell and landed with a soft thud.

I'd pick it up later. Maybe I could get some rest…

Wet. Cold. Numb. I floated on icy, fluid fingers.

My head throbbed, pounding over the roar of water battering my ears. Where was I?

No! Not again. My conscious mind tried to take control of the dream—the memory. I knew where and what this was. I didn't want to be back in this river.

A drifting tree branch dug into my side. Blood swirled into the lapping currents, mingling with the red waves of my hair. How did I get here?

I remembered a light. A flash of light, and… nothing.

Help.

I needed help. I couldn't move. I could barely think. My legs ached, bobbing like driftwood. My arms prickled, ice cold.

Clouds rolled by above, their shapes changing with time. A dog dissolved into a fanged man. The man became a dragon.

Deep voices rumbled over the water.

Thank God. Soon I'd be warm. Safe.

A smooth baritone said, "I'm risking my job for this. You'll have to pay me more. A lot more."

He appeared above me, his jaw shadowed with stubble, a phone to his ear. A U.S. Forest Service badge hung on his shirt.

"My God," he murmured, scanning my body. He hissed at the person on the line, "You didn't do this to her, did you? These burns."

Another muffled voice called from behind me, and the man looked up, ending the call. "Thank God, man. You're late. I need help."

As someone else splashed toward us, he reached for me. Fingertips stung my arms. Palms clamped down, sparking with heat. The burning built to an excruciating peak, robbing me of breath and thought. My skin was boiling! My vision fuzzed, distracting me from the pain. The blue sky dissolved. The man remained, but a white ceiling replaced the clouds. A room. A sofa. A woman. Tear tracks marred her concealer as she bore down on the man—the same man touching me. He was slouching in a recliner. She clutched a paper in her fist and shook it at him.

"You keep telling me it's fine, it's fine, then this shows up on the door?!" She wrung the paper in her hands. "We're going to lose this house if you don't do something."

The man kept his head low as his hands formed fists on the armrests. "Do something?" he said in a low voice that made my neck prickle.

I tried to shout a warning to the woman, but I had no voice, no form. I was an observer to this vision in my head.

The woman shrank back, but her scowl remained as she held out the paper. FORECLOSURE was splashed across it in bold red letters. "We have to get this money," she sobbed. "You've been putting it off for months. Get off your ass and do something!"

The man sprang up like a wild beast. "Oh, I'll do something!"

The woman screamed and stumbled back, eyes fixed on his raised fist. His other hand caught her arm as she fled, and the fist came down with a thud.

"Is that doing something for you?"

I thrashed in the water and fought to wipe the image from my mind as someone lifted my head out of the current. The house dissolved, the ceiling turning blue. Sky above me.

"Gentle. Mind the burns on her legs," a new man's voice said.

Mud smeared my back as the men pulled me out of the water. Fingerprints set fires on my elbows and shoulders. Pain spread from their touch, and my body came to life. Kicking. Struggling to escape. Their skin, their fingers, their softest grasps were hurting me. Agony.

I woke to a piercing scream.

Mine.

While hands touched my arms in my mind, I bit off the scream and tried to wipe out the image. As pain swept down my arms, I clenched my teeth against another cry, but feared it was too late. It was. I'd been heard.

"I'm coming, Cassandra!" Gram called. Her ancient spring mattress squeaked.

Damn. Why couldn't this be a night I'd woken before the screams? Probably hadn't been asleep long enough, maybe not even an hour this time. It wouldn't make any difference if I told her not to come—she'd come anyway.

"It'll be all right." Her metal walker scraped across the wooden cottage floor.

I wanted to spare her the climb up the steep, narrow stairs, and go down to her instead. But I couldn't. Pain blazed from my arms, burning across my chest, down to my feet tangled in my sheets.

I struggled to block it out, searching for a distraction. My cheek hit my pillow, and my Sleeping Beauty nightlight glowed in front of me. Defenseless, helpless, safe, the smiling princess slept in her pinker-than-pink puffy dress, waiting for her prince to come. Her happy expression, her hopeful future, reminded me I wasn't like her. I wasn't trapped in a dream. I'd woken from it. And the pain would slowly recede. My flesh hadn't been burned by real flames. It would not actually melt away.

But my body didn't know that. My jaw loosened, and a scream exploded from my mouth. Short. Sharp. Finding nothing to absorb it, the shrill noise bounced off bare walls, my small single bed, and my battered cedar trunk, housing everything I'd amassed in the two years since surviving the river. Another scream swelled, but I swallowed it back down.

I gulped, managed to turn my head up, and looked to the largest of the cracks in the old plaster ceiling put in by Gram's husband before he left for the front lines of World War II. The attic could have been planned as a nursery—the cottage had only one bedroom below, and an antique crib had sat collecting cobwebs when I moved in—but I would never risk upsetting Gram with questions.

The cracks in the ceiling splintered and fractured in

haphazard directions like a black widow spider's web. I traced their outline. It soothed me, following the twists and turns in the plaster, ruptured over time without purpose or plan. Maybe many things in this world weren't meant to have direction. Or even meaning.

Gram's slippers made a soft shuffling sound as she reached the top stair. The pain eased just enough for me to wiggle my fingers back to life. I tried to wave, but my hand shook, clenched, and fell. Gram peered in, glancing toward the bed, hidden in shadows, then down near the open window. Moonlight streamed in from the higher window, causing her short white curls to glow. She felt for the light switch, and with a sharp click, everything swam in brightness. My eyelids flinched shut. With sight gone, sounds intensified. Crickets chirped in the distance, the floorboards creaked under Gram's footsteps, her breath wheezed in and out, sounding more strained with each step.

"I'm here." Gram sounded out of breath. Had I reminded her to take her pill? Of course. I must have. My body relaxed slightly through the pain. I'd never missed a night since discovering she was prone to forget taking her medication. But Gram's real problem wasn't asthma. If only I were a better girl. A normal girl.

Gram inhaled with another wheeze. "Are you okay?"

"Yes." I opened my eyes to her wrinkled face, pulled tight with concern. "No need to worry."

"Same nightmare?"

"Yes." I looked away.

"You don't think what happened in the grocery, you keeping me from falling, brought this on?"

"No." I met her eyes, ignoring my shame. "You didn't even touch me." I was just afraid she might. "Tonight… it's just a nightmare. It happens sometimes." If I were being honest, I would tell her it happens almost every night, and it's more than a dream— it's the memory of the morning my life began, seared into my psyche—but that would just worry her more.

"But you bit your lip so hard." She brushed her fingers over her own bottom lip, a subconscious gesture of empathy, then winced. "You must have hurt or been terrified of getting hurt again. All because I'm so clumsy."

"It was nothing," I said quickly. "And anyway, who cleans the floor without telling anyone? You're not clumsy, Gram."

I called her Gram because she insisted on it, but I wished Anna Rose Merritt were my grandmother. Instead, she was the only one in the tiny town of Meeker who'd stepped forward to take care of me after I was found in nearby White River without clothes, memories, or anyone to claim me. One of the men who rescued me, the first on the scene, said I'd been raving about being in danger, mumbling, "They'll kill me if I show up without it."

So Social Services didn't publicize my appearance. Gram heard about me needing a foster home from one of her friends, Betty, who volunteered at the hospital. Once it became clear they weren't going to identify me, and my memory showed no signs of ever coming back, the social workers had been reluctant to leave me with Gram. Thankfully, she was persistent. Since they guessed I was sixteen, the social workers probably figured I'd soon be old enough to take care of myself.

Luckily, Gram was still going strong. Despite her difficulties walking, she was surprisingly resilient for her age. When I first met Gram's friends—before I'd scared them away—they had whispered enviously that she hadn't aged in years. Betty had even hinted Gram was older than most people in town suspected. Her age didn't matter to me, so long as no one used it as an excuse to take me from her.

Gram scanned my body, taking in my clenched hand, my tangled feet. She gripped the side of the headboard and eased onto the edge of the bed. The subtle scent of her lavender hand cream helped calm me but couldn't dispel my pain. "You look so pale. Are you sure you're okay?"

"Better now." My voice only cracked a little as the lie came out. Another wave of pain washed over me, and I flinched, squeezing my eyes shut.

Her lavender scent drifted closer, as if she'd leaned in. "Really? I swear the nightmare comes more and more. And tonight you screamed louder than ever—"

"I'm fine."

"But your face." She shifted on the bed, clearly worried.

I forced my eyes open and my face to relax, lying again. Everyone lied, even to those they trusted. I'd learned that long ago. But what if they trusted only one person?

"You know they were trying to help you, right?" she asked. "They were being as gentle as they could when they pulled you from the water. You need to keep telling yourself that. Maybe you can get over this fear."

"Yes, Gram."

Gram didn't understand why that morning still haunted me. Because she, like everyone else, thought the sensations I felt were all in my head, some sort of psychological condition brought on by the burns and other trauma I'd suffered. They'd found a few charred strips of material and evidence of a campfire upriver. Strangely, they'd found nothing else, no supplies, but they suspected I'd been camping, and when my pajama pants had caught fire, I'd run to the water. The doctors who'd worked on me said I probably got pulled under and swept away where the rapids were strongest, as the river cut south outside of town into White River forest. I had burns on my legs, and several broken ribs. The doctors agreed I had been lucky to survive at all, and it would just take time and therapy for my mind to heal, to stop what they called "the delusions and confabulations"—the second being an actual technical term for memory disorders.

The doctors were clueless. My mind fabricated nothing. I felt actual pain every time I dreamed of that morning. I also felt actual pain any time anyone's skin touched mine. It was real.

Thank God—if there really was a God—I never told anyone what else happened when I experienced human touch. The doctors thought I was crazy enough. If they found out about the visions, they'd surely fit me for a straitjacket and make good on their threats to take me from Gram.

I shivered at the thought.

Gram pulled up the comforter, tucking it around my chest, keeping her hands away from the flesh above my camisole. Fresh sweat broke out under my hair, but I forced a smile in response.

"Maybe we should try the therapy again." Gram rubbed my forearm, the comforter acting as a barrier between us.

"It doesn't work." I shuddered, wiggling into the bed.

"But the doctors keep recommending it for home. We haven't tried in ages. I hate feeling like I'm hurting you."

I burrowed my face in the soft flannel of my pillowcase and finally peeked at her as I lay on my side. "Gram, do you think I could've been born this way?"

"Like a skin sensitivity? They tested you."

"Yeah." Testing? More like torture. "I just wish I could remember something from before. Maybe my condition comes from something before. My childhood."

"Maybe. We still have to try making things better." Gram patted the flannel above my hand. "We'll try the therapy again soon."

"I guess." I grimaced.

"Good." Gram patted my covered hand again. "Now rest. You push yourself too hard. Every day at the animal shelter. Extra shifts at that burger place. It's too much. Summer's almost over. You need time to relax."

"Sure." Relaxing sounded nice. It just wasn't going to happen.

The wrinkles around her mouth tightened. "I also want us to drive to Glenwood Springs." I frowned, and her expression tightened further. "I mean it. No protests. We're going to the mall."

"Why?"

"It's your senior year."

I wouldn't let Gram waste money driving over an hour to the nearest mall to buy new clothes for me when the second-hand store in town worked fine. But I'd already upset her enough for one night. So I gave in. "Okay. Night, Gram. Sorry about waking you."

She gripped the headboard and pulled herself up. A soft thump sounded from the floor, her foot finding my book. It was thick: *Crime and Punishment*. Bracing herself on the edge of my trunk, she bent and picked it up. "This. Again?" Her voice filled with pain.

How could I respond? All summer, she hadn't understood my obsession with reading about a murderer.

She opened and closed her mouth, then drew in a jagged breath as her shoulders slumped. She set the book on the trunk and made her way to the door, her lavender scent fading, warm air replacing it with spruce and pine. She mumbled something to herself. It sounded like, "Good things take time." Gram pivoted at the top of the stairs. Her face, even with all its creases and crinkles, relaxed into a hopeful expression. "You'll see. We'll work hard, give it time, and it'll all work out, angel."

Her angel. It made me want to be a better person. When I was a nameless patient in the hospital, the nurses thought I was asleep and joked I was their demon patient, with red hair and claws that would come out if someone tried to touch me. But Gram told them I was her angel. She'd called me angel ever since.

"We'll have you feeling better and back to normal in no time."

She clicked off the light.

I buried my mouth into my pillow and sighed. Gram might be the only person I'd learned to trust in two years, but I couldn't trust her with this. I had never felt even close to normal since the morning my remembered life began. The best I could hope was for the nightmare to give me a break. Or maybe for the pain to lessen, or at least stop getting worse. As for the rest of it? The hell. The darkness. The things I saw when people touched me…

Maybe I'd get lucky and they wouldn't drive me insane.

I turned onto my back and focused again on the cracks in the ceiling, keeping my eyes wide open the rest of the night, counting each splinter lacing through the plaster, willing myself not to sleep, not to dream. I wouldn't even risk glancing toward the pink glow of the Sleeping Beauty nightlight. I couldn't be tempted to be like her, drifting into dreams.

Sleeping Beauty could dream for both of us.

She was the one who would never burn.

The only one who'd ever touch someone.

The one getting a fairytale ending.

2
BURNING

THE NEXT MORNING, I RACED TOWARD THE ANIMAL SHEL-
ter on my bike, squinting through the early morning sun.
Warm in my shorts and t-shirt, I enjoyed the wind ruffling
my hair. As I turned into the parking lot, I barely missed hitting a
sparkling black BMW SUV parked in a reserved volunteer space.

I skidded to a stop, eyeing its expensive lines and bumper
sticker that read Meeker Bulldogs. Just my luck. A classmate. Worse,
a wealthy one who probably lived outside of town in one of the
huge houses dominating White River. They were probably sent
here to do community service for texting while driving, or drinking
or smoking pot at one of their summer parties. Despite their small
numbers, these offspring of Colorado mining magnates somehow
always managed to ruin my life.

Like Stock Boy, a spoiled rich kid from school whose parents
forced him to take a job at the local grocery after he was caught running a test-cheating ring.

Did he know I'd turned him in? Unlikely, unless Principal Cook
let it slip. Revealing their secrets seemed fair, especially since I only
learned them because they wouldn't keep their hands to themselves.
After discovering during gym class that I would scream or moan if
someone touched me, they began torturing me with a brush here, a
reach there. They accused me of faking pain, but they sure acted like

they knew it really hurt. Things got bad because of who had made the discovery: the most popular boy in school.

I'd pretended my ribs still ached from the river so I could stay home, until Social Services forced me back to school. Fortunately, by then, I had an advantage. One more thing I owed to Gram. When I'd ripped up a flyer I picked up at the martial arts studio, realizing I couldn't pay for classes or risk being near other students, Gram sold the old crib in the attic to pay for private lessons. My first day there, I perfected my first move. I rushed home to thank her, unable to suppress my smile. Gram stared, and her eyes widened. She'd never seen me smile. She didn't say a word. I finally blurted out, "Learning how to defend myself was the best gift ever!" She tilted her head, blinked, and scooted into the kitchen with her walker. When she baked three loaves of banana bread and two batches of oatmeal cookies we couldn't possibly finish, it was a sure sign I'd somehow said the wrong thing. So, I never commented on it again. But secretly, I loved being able to protect myself from pain.

I refocused on the SUV and shifted on my seat. Maybe I should head to Burger Boys, see if I could pick up an extra shift? I gripped my handles. But there was no one else to bother me. The only other car in the lot was Dr. G's. I glided to the bike rack, closer to what I wanted—the delicious warmth of the new husky puppies in my arms, wet licks of affection on my hands, the soft rub of a head nudging my leg for attention. Most importantly, seeing Zoe. Zoe should be with the pups. The tiny creatures were abandoned outside the shelter last month, so sick that Dr. G had warned me against naming them, but they were doing better now.

I took a deep breath, chained up my bike, and raced to the door. Two steps in, I froze. A hulking someone bent over the counter, reaching for the new volunteer paperwork. Even with his body hunched to fill out the form, his head almost reached the top of the nearby file cabinet. I had to stand on my toes to see inside the top drawer. My whole body tensed at the imposition of his physical presence in my workspace. His tan forearms bulged, and his biceps reshaped his light blue, short-sleeved polo. He was trim for his size, sure, but he would tower over any other high school student. Still, he had the school's mascot on his bumper. Must be a new student.

Not that it made any difference. I started to back out the way I came.

He raised his head and looked at me.

I knew I should turn and walk out, but my whole body seemed suddenly uninterested in my opinion and refused to budge.

His gaze held mine, and I lost my breath.

He was beautiful, in a grotesque sort of way.

I allowed myself a moment to take his strange beauty in. His features were perfectly formed. A strong, chiseled jaw line, straight white teeth with full lips, deep blue eyes framed with thick lashes, and wavy dark brown hair. But the perfection was spoiled by a thick scar slicing from his right temple to his right ear, across his cheekbone to his mouth, straight down the right side of his chin, widening across his neck, and disappearing under his upturned collar. The left side of his mouth curved up at the corner, as if he'd just smiled at me, but the right side was dragged down by puckered red tissue, as if he were cringing away. The damaged skin didn't look like the rubbery burn marks on my legs. More like the scars on my stomach, only worse.

His left cheek lifted, his crooked smile widening.

What had happened to him? God, if it was anything like my injuries after I woke, it must have hurt like hell.

I answered his half-smile by meeting his eyes in what I hoped was a sign of strength. (And I didn't like people staring at my scars, so I didn't want to stare at his.) A deep pink hue creeping up the damaged skin stretching across his neck made me drop my gaze, only to take in—again—the massiveness of his body. He took a deep breath. His chest grew even bigger. I lifted my right forearm, palm out to warn him to stay back. He cleared his throat, stepped around the counter, and started toward me with powerful—yet hesitant?—steps. He rubbed his right hand on his form-fitting, dark designer jeans and extended it.

Oh no, had he thought I meant to shake hands? Was he so new in town he hadn't heard about me? Was this some sort of trick? I raised my palm higher, warding him off.

"Hi, I'm Gabriel." His large hand loomed closer.

"Oh, hi." I retreated toward the door until my heel then my back thudded against it.

He hesitated, took a glance at my legs without actually staring, and kept walking until he stood a foot from me with his hand still extended.

"I'm a new volunteer here. You must be Cassandra."

I wrapped my arms around my waist protectively.

His lopsided smile dropped a fraction, but his hand persisted. "I actually used to volunteer here before, but it's been a while. Dr. Garza told me you're always in early. To ask you any questions."

My arms loosened. I bit my lip. This new guy seemed okay, but I'd been fooled before. He'd also caught me off guard. I was wearing my Burger Boys t-shirt and my cut-off shorts with no leggings underneath to take advantage of the short time I had before school started again. Worse, I'd left my gloves at home.

At least I had my sneakers on, and I was a good runner.

I scooted over, feeling for the door handle. He finally let his hand fall to his side but shifted over too. We continued to stare at each other, dutifully ignoring each other's scars. He was enormous up close. My hand found and gripped the door handle. A subtle scent wafted around me and caught me in place. It somehow soothed me, reminding me of the woodsy aroma of my trunk tinged with something richer, headier, like the forest on a fall day.

Cedar and cloves.

"You'll be a senior?" His deep voice jolted me, but not in an unpleasant way.

My hand released the cold metal, my heart racing but not with fear. Odd. I managed a nod.

"Then you probably know my cousin, Cameron Knight?"

Of course I knew the most popular boy in school.

I shivered but didn't respond. This guy was even taller than Cameron, and bigger, but thankfully didn't remind me of him.

"Or maybe one of my younger brothers, Aaron?" The eyebrow on the unscarred side of his face rose. "He's homeschooled but plays football for Meeker." If his brother was anything approaching his size, football was no surprise.

But Aaron Knight? No, I didn't know him. I did know the rumors about the Knight family's tragic house fire. A woman and child had died. Since he'd disappeared right afterward, Cameron's dad had been blamed for starting it. Although the police couldn't prove it.

Not knowing this guy's brother wasn't a surprise either, if he didn't attend classes and only played football. I didn't particularly care about sports. I only joined track because Coach had seen me running home from the forest once and convinced me to do cross country. At least being involved in an activity pleased the social workers. It was maybe the only thing they approved of, from what Principal Cook reported about me.

Gabriel still stood much too close, staring. I wanted to tell him to back off. Nothing came out. I was too startled by his gaze. He waited politely for an answer, but it was more than that. He seemed to search for something. His eyes questioned me, but without malice or disbelief. More like… he wanted to know me. Whatever he found broadened the unmarred side of his smile, making him appear even more misshapen as the rest of his skin remained locked in a perpetual grimace. Slowly his eyes widened and brightened, eclipsing any grotesqueness with gentleness and warmth—an open expression so unlike his cousin's.

And it seemed he really didn't know anything about me.

Maybe I could act normal. Maybe we could engage in a bit of meaningless chitchat like I'd seen the kids at school do a million times. Maybe he'd even want to help me out with the animals. Maybe, just maybe, he might like to…

Another deep inhale expanded his barrel chest. My heart raced, this time with that familiar friend, fear. My eyes darted, seeking an escape from his bulk. Sweat broke out on my neck beneath my long, loose curls.

My thoughts had been nothing more than a daydream. The desire to flee swept through me, right down to my sneakered feet.

"Don't get any closer," I practically shouted.

He flinched and backpedaled, his hand drifting to his scar.

I hurried around him toward the door leading to the back wing where the dogs were housed. Once I had the safety of space between us, I spun to face him. He watched me but made no move to follow.

His hand had traced the scar to his neck, and when our eyes locked, his looked down. With insecurity? That couldn't be right. He must've been eying me strangely, given my unusual reaction, and then just lost interest. That made sense, and yet, for some reason, it bothered me.

"Yes, I'm Cassandra—Cassie." My voice sounded high-pitched, shaky.

He looked up, his cheeks red.

I rolled my shoulders back and started again. "I'm here mornings. Evenings during school. I take care of the dogs. Feed them, groom them, clean their cages, that sort of thing. Um, maybe you can talk to Dr. G about working with the cats." I mumbled the last words and flew through the door, racing to the dog cages.

Wagging tails and a chorus of yips and barks greeted me. I whispered soothing words, promising to pet them soon, and scurried to the end of the far row. I opened up Zoe's cage, sank to my knees, wrapped my arms around her, and buried my face in her plush, golden fur. I absorbed Zoe's warmth. Nothing else mattered. I didn't even care if it was pathetic to substitute closeness with her for developing real relationships with people. Animals had never hurt me. *And our relationship was real.*

I took in every ounce of comfort I could until Zoe squirmed out of my arms and wiggled her rear end and her lone rear leg out of the quilt Gram had made for her. Zoe showered my hands with kisses, until they felt damp and a bit sticky, and the awkwardness of that encounter with the new guy melted away. Humiliation still burned in my stomach, but Zoe's sticky affection helped ease the silly longing to be the kind of girl who could've smiled back. Flirted with a guy like him. As if that was ever happening.

I rubbed Zoe's favorite spot behind her ear. She leaned into my hand. This was love. Right? Of course, I cared for Gram too, but that was different. My existence would never force Zoe to change the way she lived. Though some people would say Zoe was just a dog, a mutt at that, she was also a fighter. A survivor. She'd never given up after she'd been found in a ditch along a back road, blood covering her thick, golden retriever-like coat. Not even when she'd lost a leg or when infection ravaged her big body. She'd maintained her sunny temperament through it all, worming her way into Dr. G's heart. And that, combined with my pleas, was how she'd really survived—making it past the short time frame when the animals had to be claimed or adopted before being put on the "kill list."

Zoe lifted her head and licked under my nose, causing me to inhale a bit of her slobber.

"Eww." I rubbed my face and sputtered.

Zoe licked my hand, then turned to press her nose to the adjoining cage where Dr. G had moved the pups last week. They whimpered for our attention. Trust Zoe to know how to distract me from thoughts of animals that hadn't been adopted, hadn't made it. At least Zoe would never have to worry about the kill list. This or any other week. I almost had the money saved for the adoption fee and everything else she would need, thanks to the extra shifts at Burger Boys.

I opened the cage and cuddled B.B. and B.G.—short for baby boy and baby girl (I hadn't been able to stop from naming them just a bit)—then quickly lost myself in the routine of filling food bowls, replenishing water, and letting all the dogs out to the shelter's fenced-in yard for some playtime. Even Zoe, since she was now strong enough, just not fast enough to get to the toys first. I snuck her a chew rope, but a little terrier stole it away. She curled up in the corner, letting B.B. and B.G. snuggle her when they got tired.

It was almost thirty minutes to noon—when adoption hours started and I raced to my shift at Burger Boys—when I herded the last group back inside. I saved Zoe and the pups for last, giving Zoe a few minutes practice wearing her special harness designed for three-legged dogs. I gave her a farewell rub and the pups another cuddle, loving their downy-soft fur as they nuzzled under my chin. Their soft warmth shot straight to my chest, doing something funny to my heart. Did everyone feel sensations of touch this strongly? No wonder people were always buying the softest sheets, paying more for cashmere, and holding hands. I settled the pups in their cage, being careful not to brush against the cold, sharp metal.

A crash in the storage room startled me. A clang followed. Dr. G was usually busy until adoption hours, treating the sick animals he kept in the clinic by his office. It must be that Gabriel guy making a mess. You'd think he'd be a bit more capable of being left to his own devices if he really had volunteered here before.

Another crash resonated down the hall. I supposed I should check on him. First, I finished tucking a blanket around a sleepy B.B. He nibbled my fingers, then closed his eyes with a little sigh. Then I did something I almost never did.

I searched for my reflection. In the glass running between the room and hall, I found it. For some reason, today I didn't want to look like how I felt. Like a misfit. I licked my fingertips and rubbed at the muddy paw prints on my chest. I smoothed down my black, v-neck work shirt. There was nothing I could do about the tattered ends of my shorts. And certainly nothing to do about my legs—Gram had convinced me to stop caring about them long ago. The dark smudges under my eyes, the redness around my green irises, and my sleep-deprived skin couldn't be fixed either. I pinched my cheeks to add a bit of color.

Ugh… my fiery hair flying around my face didn't help with my crazy-girl look. Most people seemed to think only cartoon characters had hair this color, but even if I would waste money dyeing it, Gram said no—I was perfect the way I was. To save money on haircuts, I left it long, falling almost to my waist. The best I could do at the moment was a big, messy ponytail.

I'd wasted my time though because it wasn't Gabriel.

Kaylee Cook stood in the middle of the storage room with not a highlighted hair out of place, surrounded by a fallen shelving unit, scattered sections of cage, and dozens of metal food bowls still wobbling on the floor. Her eyes homed in on my legs, finally glancing up to meet my gaze.

"Stop staring, Freakenstein. Get over here. Pick these up." She kicked a bowl with her sandal.

I refused to budge from the narrow hallway, just outside the small room. I made a deliberate effort to keep my voice calm. "What are you doing here? You know Dr. G said to start later." *After I'm gone.* Kaylee didn't live in the fancy houses outside of town—not on her dad's school salary—but her friends did.

Her lips pursed, as if considering how much to say to convince me not to go to Dr. G. "I heard Gabriel's home—finally—snuck back weeks ago. Ree ran into him yesterday, buying roses of all things."

"So?" What did Gabriel being home, from wherever he'd been, and buying flowers have to do with her breaking rules?

"I know he used to hang out here."

"But—"

"The roses don't matter, who they were for. It's about time I dated a college guy. And just, well, a boy like him." She nodded, as if we were friends, or I had a clue what she was talking about. Or cared.

I shrugged.

"Even after what happened to him." She wrinkled her nose in apparent disgust. "I mean, he's still Gabriel Knight, right?" She sighed dreamily, like she was talking about the latest pop star.

I mean, he did seem pretty nice, but what was with that sigh?

"So, I'm going to be here whenever he is." She flipped back a lock of her perfectly sleek, flat-ironed hair, and put her hands on either side of her tiny waist, like she was striking a cheerleading pose. I almost laughed. This was one place she didn't have influence.

"I don't think so. Dr. G will keep you away. Permanently, if I ask." Though bothering Dr. G would be my last resort.

She frowned, and her hands strayed to the pink scarf she'd tied as a belt around her sundress. She smoothed a frayed edge, and her fingers tangled in a clump of loose thread. I saw it. And she saw me see it. For an instant, her face crumpled.

She'd never admit it, but she must have gotten that scarf at the second-hand store. I'd seen one just like it there last week, tattered on one end (though not as bad as my shorts; that probably wasn't the look she was going for).

I softened my tone. "Listen, I don't really care if you come in early or what you do with the new guy. Just stay away from me, or I'm going to say something to Dr. G."

She rearranged the scarf, concealing the frayed edge. "It's not like I actually hurt you before," she protested with a sparkly, pink-lipped pout. "You make things up."

"Just keep to the cats. That's where I told him to help out anyway."

"Yeah, whatever," Kaylee mumbled, and her gaze shifted up. She gave the top of my head a bright smile and started stepping around the mess she'd made, with no intention of cleaning it up. Surely that was my cue to get out of there.

I turned and almost ran smack into Gabriel.

He'd walked up right behind me. Only a few inches separated my chest from his stomach. My momentum carried me forward, heading into him. As if in slow motion, I swayed and fought the instinct to reach out to him.

Gabriel lifted his hand to grab my arm. "Whoa, steady there, just coming to check on the noise."

I was too close. Everything was happening too quickly for me to stop him. As his fingers reached for my flesh, I braced myself for pain.

The burn started as usual, a scalding handprint on my upper arm, shooting heat in all directions. Then the worst part began.

The vision appeared.

Gabriel's mind showed me some sort of… animal? A massive brown bear reared on its hind legs, in front of a large opening in a sheet of rock. Its eyes—beady, surprisingly deep blue orbs in a broad, domed head—locked onto something in the distance. The animal lumbered forward, tottering closer to Gabriel but not looking at him.

Breaking through the vision, Gabriel's distant voice echoed, "Are you okay?" The blistering grip around my arm tightened.

The vision shifted, scanning across a clearing of rock, settling on a cluster of trees. Something huge and white parted the branches. An ox of a man. Starkly bald and gigantic—even larger than Gabriel. Wider. His chest a battering ram. The giant man plodded forward, his skull lighting up inch by inch in the sun's bright rays. His head shone almost as brightly as the glint off the two knives that he pulled from leather sheaths hanging at his sides.

"Sorry I startled you, Cassie." The distorted words intruded into my thoughts before the vision reasserted itself.

"Who sent you?" Gabriel shouted across the clearing.

"You should know," the giant said in a soft, accented voice. "You couldn't keep it hidden forever."

"You'll have to get through us if you want it."

"We"—the giant motioned his knives to another bald, monstrous, knife-toting man under the trees—"can do that."

"It won't be easy." Gabriel looked beyond them, to a second bear, darker than the other, trailing the large men.

"I know." The giant glanced to his friend, and they charged.

Gabriel moved back, closer to the first bear, still on its hind legs. He raised his arms. I braced myself for something horrible to happen. For the real darkness to start. For this to be about something disastrous Gabriel had done. But the vision faded away before I could see what happened next.

I returned fully back into my own consciousness. I barely felt any pain. How could that be?

I gasped and teetered.

Gabriel's firm grip steadied me. His touch stung like a scalding hot bath instead of a branding iron. My teeth weren't clenched. There was no scream to suppress. No anguish to imprison in my lungs. And strangest of all, beneath the pain I felt what I could only assume was his palm.

Silky and warm.

Soft and smooth.

My mouth opened. For several seconds, I forgot to breathe. I felt… actually felt… Gabriel's hand on my arm. *Gabriel's skin on mine.*

I froze. So did he.

He stood perfectly still, with that same searching gaze.

I was too mesmerized to look away. His attention was different… almost gentle on my face, rather than the harsh, judgmental looks of others meant to cut and sting.

His hold on my arm wasn't so distasteful either. Actually, I kind of liked it. Really liked it. The suppleness of his fingers. The intense heat radiating from his palm. His skin gripping mine. Touch. *Human touch* unadulterated by excruciating sensations.

I tried to enjoy it, but a familiar pressure raced along my arm, throbbing. Like my skin was still burning, even as I felt the contact of his hand. His touch was at once like having my glove yanked off at school, burning pain shooting up my arm from gropey fingers, and receiving a soft lick from Zoe.

Finally, I couldn't bear the intensity—the intimacy, the mix of sensations—any longer. I closed my mouth. My jaw tightened. "Let go."

He blinked and released me.

For an instant, the soft heat lingered. Then vanished. All the painful sensations vanished too. How odd. No lingering pain to bear, no fire to slowly dampen and fizzle out.

"I didn't mean to startle you." Gabriel took a small step back. Not far enough. I searched for space to squeeze by. But he was too big, the hallway too narrow. "You seemed shaky. I didn't want you to fall."

"It's okay." Kaylee's dress swished behind me.

"Okay?" Gabriel asked her, his eyes on me.

"Yeah. But don't you know? You can't get near her." She kicked a bowl into the corner.

My heart pounded in my ears. I was frantic to flee.

"She'll tell everyone you hurt her, cause all sorts of trouble." Kaylee's sandals struck the floor with a harsh click-clack.

Gabriel still blocked the hallway. My hairline dampened with sweat.

"What are you talking about?" Gabriel looked over my shoulder at her.

"You're lucky she didn't scream her head off."

Gabriel frowned.

It seemed to embolden Kaylee. "She's some sorta weirdo. She usually screams." Kaylee's breath brushed my ear, uncomfortably close.

"Um, can you please move?" My gaze darted to either side of him. A trickle of sweat ran down my cheek. "I need to get out of here. I—I only stay till the shelter opens for adoption hours." The bead of sweat picked up speed, heading for the vee of my t-shirt.

Gabriel's chin dropped, his eyes tracing the physical manifestation of my unease down my neck. "Yes." His gaze lingered on my flushed chest for an instant. His lopsided face quickly tipped back up. "Um, of course."

"So move." I prepared to push him away. It didn't matter if he knew about me or not. I wasn't going to stand around to be touched again or listen to Kaylee gossip about me.

"Yes, yes. Sorry, again." Gabriel pressed his back to the wall.

I slipped past, dashing down the hall, feeling his eyes follow me. I stumbled, but kept running toward the lobby, my chin trembling.

I didn't dare turn back. I couldn't risk seeing how strangely Gabriel looked at me now. His eyes would shout what I already knew, what Kaylee had pointed out. Awkward! Antisocial! Weirdo! And she hadn't even told him the nickname his cousin, Mr. Popular, had given me. Freakenstein.

My chest tightened.

I raced into the lobby, threw open the door, darted to my bike, and fumbled with the chain.

"Cassie?" a deep voice called from the door. "Can I help? What's wrong?"

I glanced up.

Gabriel stood by the door, and to my dismay, his expression was creased with concern instead of contempt, reminding me of what I'd never have. Closeness. Companionship.

Kaylee would explain to him what was wrong with me, I was quite sure. With shoulders hunched, I freed my bike and hopped on without looking up. There was only so much pain a girl could stomach in one day, and the pain radiating through my chest as my feet found the pedals was the most dangerous kind.

Physical pain would fade.

I started pedaling.

But loneliness…

I pedaled faster.

It'd burn you up from the inside if you let it.

3

BLAZING

THE FOLLOWING AFTERNOON, GRAM AND I STOOD OVER HER husband's grave in Meeker Highland Cemetery. The sunset blazed golden orange, smoldering along the jagged line of distant mountains, lighting up the sapphire sky.

Gabriel's piercing blue eyes and haunting smile invaded my head. Again. I blamed it on the mystery of the vision I'd received from him and the bearable nature of his touch.

I shivered, even with the sun's last rays caressing my arms.

It wasn't too surprising Gabriel's mind hadn't revealed anything as heinous as the visions I'd seen during forced trips into Glenwood Springs and Denver, being touched by doctors and social workers, or when bumped by strangers while running errands for Gram. Of course, you could never tell just by looking at someone, but Gabriel didn't seem the type to hit his girlfriend for talking to another man, corner a woman taking a shortcut on the way home through a back alley, or break into what he'd thought was an empty house in the middle of the night. No surprise, either, that Gabriel's mind wasn't like those of my nastiest classmates. One boy's touch had shown me several visions of him abusing his young stepsister, leaving me nauseous as well as burning. Another had raped a girl in a back room at a party. Several seemed to like pushing uppers and other pills on friends. From his conduct, Gabriel didn't seem the sort.

But what was the meaning of what I'd seen inside him? It didn't seem like he'd done anything wrong, but he must have, because that was the common thread of all my visions. What did Gabriel have to feel guilty about in what he'd unknowingly shown me?

Everyone had secrets. Everyone had sins. Failures buried deep within. Even Gram. Weaknesses and mistakes, or desires so dark they made me wonder why so many people believed humans were divine creations.

So why was Gabriel tussling with huge guys with the knives, and the bears? What might have brought him to such a strange, violent moment? Why not something mundane in its cruelty, like a memory of him bullying a weaker kid to feel better about himself, peer pressuring a friend to do something stupid, or cheating on something—or someone? Like his girlfriend. A guy like him must have a girlfriend at college. Or a boyfriend. Maybe the men, the knives, the animals were some sort of symbol? A repressed desire to hurt someone? But that didn't make sense. I'd learned visions like Gabriel's, so clear and viewed through the person's eyes, were actual memories, not just bad thoughts or desires.

With everyone else I'd touched, it was always so transparent. I was transported to their darkest deed, sickest fantasy, or whatever guilt gnawed away (or should have been gnawing away) in their subconscious. The more contact I had, the more I saw, until I was stuck cycling through all the basest moments of their life. Maybe there was a piece missing to Gabriel's vision? Something I didn't understand?

"You seem distracted, angel," Gram said.

I shrugged.

Gram bent to place her weekly offering on the gravestone. Sometimes she left a note. Other times, a bit of needlework. One time, on their anniversary, a copy of their wedding photo, which was framed on Gram's dresser.

This week, lilies from her garden.

Releasing the long stalks with one hand, she kept the other gripped on her walker. The soft light of sunset smoothed the rubbery skin above her knuckles until I could almost imagine her hands were the same as I saw the rest of her, as perfect as any person could be. In reality, an injury suffered long ago had left them burned and almost as rubbery as my legs.

I stared at her gnarled hand while she focused on the ground. I'd visited the grave so often with Gram, I didn't need to look down with her to picture the inscription carved in the stone.

Richard Merritt, 1922–1944, Loving Husband to Anna Rose, who gave his life in service of his country and the defeat of Nazism and Fascism. May we forever stand against the forces of evil in this world.

It was my favorite inscription in the cemetery. I liked the idea of fighting the bad things in this world. I just felt incapable of doing it myself, most of the time. And yet, in such a solitary, peaceful place, with white gravestones laid out in neat rows, it was almost possible to imagine that one person could make a difference, bring order and justice to the wickedness I'd seen. I knelt by Gram and traced my fingertips over the grooved lettering, finally resting my palm on the cool, smooth stone.

Gram bent her head and closed her eyes for a few moments. She then lifted her face and stood stock-still, but her eyes searched the clouds. The sun dipped below the horizon, its rays lingering on the mountains, reflecting into the deep blue sky. She looked so peaceful, bathed in the remaining pink and orange light.

Gram's hand found the chain under the collar of her cardigan and blouse, which held her wedding ring near her heart. Her fingertips played with the thin strand, and she murmured under her breath. Gram often ended her time at Richard's grave with a few whispers to the sky, but half of what I caught never made sense. Sometimes it was clear she thought she was talking to Richard. Other times it was silly stuff, as though she spoke to a child.

One, two, three bright flashes of light jumped at the corner of my eye.

I stilled. Nothing was there. I turned. Nothing appeared. A white animal darting between graves? Sunbeams? My mind playing tricks on me?

I tried to ignore it, looking back to Gram. She hadn't moved, but a small smile lifted her wrinkled face.

She was such a positive force in a world that needed more of it. It really was a shame she'd never remarried and had children. She claimed the bond she'd had with Richard only came once, and she wouldn't waste time with someone else when it was still possible to be with him one day. I didn't really understand all of what she said, but I guessed it had something to do with heaven.

I'd recently discovered Gram loved Richard so much, even after so many years without him, that she'd chosen my name based on one of his interests in life, not hers. I'd originally thought Gram had insisted the social workers dub me Cassandra because of her love of all things Jane Austen, and Jane's friendship with her beloved older sister, Cassandra. I was relieved when I learned that wasn't the case. I hated all things Jane Austen—too many happy endings for my liking. No matter the conflict, the flawed-but-lovable heroine and the strong-usually-wealthy hero always ended up together.

Real life doesn't work that way. Heck, Jane Austen's own sad and solitary existence was proof of what a letdown life can be. Unfortunately, that didn't stop Gram from having me read Jane Austen out loud every free evening we had at home (which were many). Gram had trouble reading the small print herself, and said it gave us something productive to do, rather than turn on one of the million reality TV shows.

So, I always assumed I'd been named after that Cassandra. Instead, my namesake was one of Richard's favorite heroines of Greek mythology, Cassandra, the daughter of King Priam, the last king of Troy. Her beauty caused the god Apollo to give her the gift of prophecy. However, when she refused the god her body, Apollo cursed her, ordaining that none of her prophecies would be believed. Cassandra accurately predicted events like the fall of Troy, but her warnings were ignored, her home ravaged as she'd foreseen.

Had Gram somehow known from the moment she first met me that I, too, was cursed?

"Cassandra." Gram raised her voice. "You're definitely distracted by something. In fact, you've seemed distant ever since you got home yesterday."

"Sorry, Gram. Just some things at the shelter got me thinking." More bright flashes zipped closer, skirting a tree to the side of our row. The moment I faced the light, it was gone.

"What at the shelter?"

I turned back to her. "Just a new volunteer… Oh, and Zoe's better and better. I'm going to talk to Dr. G about bringing her home."

"That's good, angel. About Zoe." Zoe had won Gram over too, during Gram's weekly visits. "Now this new volunteer, they're friendly?"

I glanced back to the tree as a blurry beam leaped behind the trunk. But it had hovered several feet off the ground, higher than most animals could jump. I searched the branches. Nothing climbed them. Not even a rustle of leaves.

"I said, this new volunteer is friendly, right?" Gram coughed. "And will you please look at me? Your head's in the clouds this afternoon."

"Um, yeah. The new guy seems friendly enough." I turned.

"Are you sure?"

"Don't worry. He used to volunteer several years ago. He just wants to help out. Nothing like the kids who are there for community service."

"So he's nice to you?"

I nodded. "This morning he even helped me clean out the dog run. Usually no one wants to help with that mess." What I didn't say was I'd left Gabriel to do the smelly job himself after he'd joined me outside. When he came back in, I'd felt him staring at me as I brushed and petted a blind lab who'd been picked up wandering across Main Street the night before, and I almost left early for work. I'd been saved by Kaylee, bouncing down the hall, calling for him.

"Good. You need to tell Dr. Garza if he starts bothering you. I just don't understand why the other kids can't leave you alone."

Gram gripped her walker and stepped away from Richard's grave. She paused to rest a hand to the side of her cardigan, near her heart, and finally took another step away. "Now, we need to get moving if we're going to make it before the stores close." She glanced at her watch, a well-worn gold bracelet with a small timepiece Richard had given her before he left for the war. "In fact, we're already running late. Maybe we should go tomorrow." She readjusted her purse strap and gripped the walker again.

"I wanted to talk to you about that. I don't need new clothes."

"You do." She squared her shoulders. "All those torn shirts, pant legs. My mending is really starting to show."

"Mended clothes are fine."

"But I want you to look nice and I—"

"Okay, okay… maybe extra leggings and another pair of gloves would be useful," I said.

She'd only press the matter, and I'd give in completely or admit what she already suspected—I'd been lying when I claimed most of the tears were accidents.

I took off across the grass in the direction of Gram's car, hoping the conversation was over. I think Gram knew that when it came down to it, I could never refuse her anything.

Gram muttered something about how stubborn I was, following behind me, but I kept walking, thinking of Gabriel again and his eyes that matched the sky.

His hand on my skin… that brief bliss of soft skin against mine. Warmth. Pleasure. Could I even let myself hope that I could experience it again? That I could be normal?

No. No hope.

Hope—misplaced hope—could destroy you.

But maybe, if I tested things out first, subjected myself to physical contact with someone else… Gram was clearly my best bet, especially since she wanted me to give the doctors and their therapy another chance. We'd tried twice, both times at home, but Gram had been as shaken by my reactions as me.

I stopped, waiting for her to catch up. We were in the middle of the back section of the cemetery. A good place to do this. Secluded, and a place where I actually felt a sense of peace. "Gram, why don't we work on that therapy? It has been ages."

"Good idea. We'll do it back home, since clearly we're not going shopping."

"Let's do it now." I'd lose my nerve if we waited, and I had to know—despite the worsening nightmares and the increasing agony with each new stranger's touch—could things finally be getting better?

"But the doctors said you need to be in a comfortable place, somewhere you feel safe."

"I feel safe here." I swept a hand over the grounds. Not a person in sight. Besides, what the doctors said was garbage. The pain had nothing to do with where I was or how I felt.

"If you're sure…"

"Yes."

"Close your eyes, then." Gram stepped stiffly toward me. "Now, you know I'm going to touch you over your clothing first. It's okay for someone to touch you."

"I'm ready."

"Just stay calm. Keep your eyes closed."

I closed my eyes and took a deep breath.

Her lavender fragrance tickled my nose.

I waited.

A light pressure brushed my shoulder. Covered by my work shirt. No pain. A pressure on my back. Covered. No pain. Gram was clearly taking this seriously because I felt three more points of contact. My other shoulder, waist, and thigh, above my jean shorts. All covered. No pain.

She touched my left wrist.

The fire sparked instantly. I screamed out, pulling away with so much force I backhanded Gram's face. *I hit Gram. Oh God.*

And the pain. Worse than ever before. Was this how it'd felt when the campfire burned me? Oh God. The blaze gained momentum, sweeping up my arm, back down to my fingertips. I couldn't stop screaming. I collapsed, convulsing on the ground with my arm trapped underneath me. The vision was a bit delayed, but sure enough, it came.

A youthful version of Gram, with radiant skin and flowing black hair, yelled at Richard while he held her close. The vision was clear, but I wasn't seeing it through her eyes. Likely a guilt-ridden memory she'd replayed and reworked in her mind. She struggled away from him and pounded on his chest.

"…hate you. I really hate you for this," Gram cried out.

They were in the kitchen of her cottage. The cabinets glistened with fresh paint. A brand-new porcelain sink I'd never seen before gleamed in the sunlight streaming through the window.

"You can't volunteer. You can't leave us! I don't care if you're serving your country, fighting Hitler. I don't care about children over there when *my* child could be slaughtered, burned here." She swept her hand around the kitchen, but she seemed to mean "here" as more than their home.

"They've never discovered any of our family. Not here."

"But if they do, they'll come. You owe her more than dying in a ditch." She pounded his chest again with her delicate fists.

Richard overpowered her, wrapping his arms around her. He squeezed her tight as his arms expanded unnaturally, extending longer behind her. Dark brown hair sprouted and quickly covered both forearms. "I have to do this. You understand, right?"

"I don't care if it's the right thing to do. You can't die."

He rested his head on top of hers. "You and the little one are my everything," he whispered into her hair. "The love I have won't be destroyed by death."

"We'll never forgive you if you die." A broken sob slipped through her teeth. She finally pulled away from his chest, fumbling with her watch. She ripped it off, its gold flashing. "I should've realized, with what it says. What it means."

Richard stepped close and stroked her back, his arms now completely covered in dense hair. No, thicker and darker than hair. Fur. Like the bears' fur from Gabriel's vision. *Was I adding that? Blending visions? Was my condition deteriorating into insanity?*

Richard kissed Gram's forehead, and she didn't seem at all disturbed by the fact that his arms were that of a bear, not a man. "Remember, if I die, I'll always be watching over you. Watching over you both. And I won't rest until I find a way to reach out to you. It's possible I could come back to you one day."

"None of that matters." Her voice fell flat. "If you leave us, I'll never forgive you."

Richard shook his head. His bear arms tightened around her.

She jerked away and dropped her watch in the sink. It clinked against the bottom. "Its words mean nothing. Nothing without you."

He pulled her back, kissed her one more time, then released her in one swift motion and walked away.

4

DESIRE

CLOUDS CHURNED ABOVE. BLADES OF GRASS TOWERED OVER my face. Free from the vision, I lay on my back, my arms loose at my sides.

I'd stopped screaming, but fiery agony still blazed along the side of my body where Gram had touched me. I was helpless to stop it. Helpless to even sit up and see how badly I'd hurt Gram. My mind whispered poisonous words to me: *You're weak. Useless.*

"You're burning! My god." Gram gasped. "Your skin is actually bubbling and burning." Her face appeared, staring at my arm in horror.

My body shook. I had no control over my movements.

A large tear rolled down Gram's cheek, hung on her chin, and fell. It sliced through the air, heading for the bare skin of my throat. It disappeared from my sight, but I didn't feel it hit. All I felt was pain, radiating from my left hand and through the left side of my body. The clouds churned faster, and all I could think was *Rain is moving in. We can't get stuck in the rain.* Last time we had, it ended in disaster.

My body shook harder.

"Help," Gram yelled. "Help!"

She muttered something like, "This is why people need cell phones."

My body shook even harder, rocking my head.

She yanked off her purse, pressed it to the back of my head, and looked up to the sky. "Do something," she pleaded to the clouds as she tried to still my head. "I can't lose her. Not her too." Her chin dropped to her chest. "Please, Richard."

I was pretty sure Richard couldn't hear her. No one else was likely to hear her either. The grounds were usually deserted when we visited late afternoons. Burial services happened in the mornings, and those left behind—alone in their final resting place—rarely had company. Gram kept adjusting the purse, but my head kept shaking. She started to sob.

It's okay, I wanted to say, but words wouldn't come. Trying to block out the pain, my mind wandered off to the last time we got stuck in the rain.

Gram's car was in the shop, so we walked to visit Betty, Gram's oldest friend, who'd just gotten home from the hospital. When we arrived, Gram rushed into the living room to see her. I went to the kitchen to put away the soup Gram had made. Betty's granddaughter washed dishes. Betty's great-grandson colored at the table. Apparently even the younger kids had heard about me. The moment I turned, the boy touched me. I screamed, instinctively pushing him away. His chair rocked back and clattered to the floor, spilling him in a heap on the tile, and then his screams had mingled with mine. His mother flew to his side and cradled him, and I saw the odd angle of his arm, the bone pressing against the skin. Betty asked us to leave as the clouds swelled. They burst before we got home, the violent wind whipping raindrops against us, soaking Gram to the bone. She didn't leave her bed for an entire week afterward.

That couldn't happen again.

Slowly, the burning eased a bit, and the shaking turned into a twitch. Maybe I could stand, get Gram out of here. Wishful thinking. A tremor threw my head to the left. My nose pressed into the grass. I inhaled its earthy scent, and something else that smelled vaguely like bacon cooking. Rancid bacon. Nauseating and sweet.

My arm.

My stomach lurched. I dry heaved.

Blades poked my face. My left eye closed, but my right eye took in the view. No two blades of grass were the same. They crisscrossed in haphazard directions. The beautiful form mesmerized me, and my mind seized on it as a distraction from the pain and nausea. There is so much beauty in the simple things. My eyes blurred, and the green lines danced in a watery haze. Small miracles all around me, even amid the ugliest part of my existence.

A crunch in the grass brought me out of my daze. My right eye slowly focused on a large leather loafer planted inches away.

Someone helped Gram stand, lifted her purse strap back over her shoulder, and spoke. A deep, male voice. His breath came fast, like he'd sprinted over. I tried to concentrate on the words.

"…going to be okay. I'm calling 911." He sounded familiar.

"Th-thank you," Gram sputtered. "Thank you. I've never seen her…never seen her…this bad."

I moaned softly, trying to get control of my voice. I needed to show Gram I'd be okay. And no hospital. No doctors. Not unless Gram needed help. All the doctors already thought I was crazy. I didn't need them to think I was getting worse and take me from her.

I moaned louder. A toned, tan leg, half bare in khaki shorts and lightly dusted with hair, bent down in front of my face.

"Are you sure it's just her arm?" he asked, his breath surprisingly steady now. "She keeps shaking. Maybe I should check her—"

"No!" Gram cried. "She can't be touched. Her skin is very, very sensitive."

Trying to explain my problem wasn't easy even in the best of circumstances.

"Waste of plastic." A large hand gripping a thin, black cell phone fell against the tanned leg. "I'm going to have to run to the road for a better signal."

"Hey," I managed. It was barely a whisper, but as much as I could get out.

"I think she said something." The leg shifted, moving into a crouch.

Gabriel's misshapen face appeared nearly nose to nose to mine. "Cassie, it's me. Gabriel. From the shelter." The pulse point above his upturned shirt collar beat faster when I didn't reply. "Where does it hurt?"

Darkness fell over him, the sky seeming to have skipped twilight.

"Is Gram okay?" My voice sounded faint.

"She's fine. I meant you. Where are you hurt?"

"Get Gram out of here. Don't call anyone."

"We're calling for an ambulance. You need help."

"No," I said as loudly as I could manage.

Gabriel blanched, turning to Gram. "I think she's in shock."

"No." I moaned again. "Don't call. They'll take me away."

"Oh goodness." Gram took a wheezy breath. She must be thinking of the same thing as me—the last meeting with the head psychiatrist and social worker. They'd told us that they were having serious doubts about my placement, especially with the continued reports from school. All the fights. They'd even threatened to place me in a clinic and get an order from a judge saying I wasn't ready to be legally on my own if things didn't improve.

A beam of light illuminated Gabriel's hair. A break in the clouds?

Gabriel's eyes returned to survey me. "But we have to do something." He ran a hand through his hair, and the light vanished. "I have some first aid training. I could probably deal with the burns, but she's in some sort of paralysis. Did she have a seizure? She'll also need pain meds. Her arm is going to hurt so bad."

Gabriel's gaze locked with mine. A puzzled look flickered across his face. "How did this happen?" he asked Gram.

"It's her skin. She can't bear being touched, though the doctors say we need to keep trying. I should never have done it here." Gram rested a trembling arm on her walker. The metal squeaked as she shifted and tried to catch her breath. "I've never seen it cause something like this, but the pain and weakness, they've always gone away once she has time to recover. So let's just wait a few minutes." Gram twisted her watch back and forth. "If she doesn't get better, we'll call."

"Okay, but we're not waiting long." Gabriel's pulse still beat fast, but he seemed to digest all of that with ease.

"My neck hurts turned like this," I choked out, my voice steadier. The twitches were a little farther apart now. I pulled in a deep breath, feeling a small sense of accomplishment.

"We can't risk touching you." Gram's voice sounded steadier too. "You'll have to—"

"Could I touch her if something was covering my hands?" Gabriel asked.

"Yes, that's fine—At least, it always has been before," Gram responded for us both.

Gabriel moved above me. Something soft pushed between the ground and my head, until my cheek rested on a makeshift pillow. I inhaled into it and smelled cedar. Cloves. Gabriel had taken off his shirt to support my neck. I inhaled again, deeply, and my body calmed. The twitching stopped completely. The scent evoked not only my cedar trunk or the forest, but the feeling of coming home after a long day at school to be greeted by Gram's cinnamon-spiced hot chocolate. It helped me forget about the acid taste in my mouth, slowly overshadowing the smell of my burned arm.

In my new position, I could see more.

Sunlight still reflected in the atmosphere and broke through the clouds. Maybe it wouldn't rain? Gram's peach and cream-toned makeup ran in several streaks down her cheeks. While her chin must hurt, where I'd hit her, all her attention was focused on me. What had I ever done to deserve her? How would I ever make this, and everything else, up to her?

Gabriel gazed down at me too, as earnestly as Gram, with a concerned expression. He looked even bigger with his chest bare. And less at ease. His hand fidgeted around his scars, fingers spreading wide over the raised marks, as if wanting to hide them. But they covered too much of him. The jagged scar didn't just drop down to his neck; it continued all the way through a light dusting of brown hair to below his right nipple. Two thick, ugly scars slashed across the left of his stomach and ribcage, marring the perfection of his toned abdomen. A bit of lighter skin peeked out above his shorts, the rest darker, as if he spent a lot of time outdoors without his shirt on. But he certainly seemed uneasy with it off now.

Gram and Gabriel standing over me had distracted me from the pain. It was still there but no longer controlled me. I focused on moving, starting with wiggling my toes and fingers. I rolled my neck, turning my face away from the comforting scent of Gabriel's shirt.

"Good, angel. That's a start," Gram encouraged. I tried to lift my head, but pain cut down the left side of my body. I swallowed a whimper.

Gram turned to Gabriel. "I know this sounds strange. But sometimes when she's in pain, it helps if I rub her arm, if it's covered."

"It doesn't sound strange at all." He coughed awkwardly. "But are you sure she wants that?"

"Angel, would it be okay if we rubbed your shoulder, through your t-shirt?"

A distraction from the pain. Sure, I could use it. Maybe Gram could too. "Yes."

But instead of Gabriel helping Gram down to me, she nodded at him and Gabriel knelt. Seated in the grass, his eyes widened when they found mine, seeming to ask for permission.

I found myself giving it. "Just be careful."

He reached his hand out tentatively, then gently rested it on my shoulder. His large palm warm through the cotton, he deepened the pressure. His fingers found the tension running to my neck and started to knead, massaging it. Every nerve ending came alive, heat blossoming along my skin, feeling nothing like when Gram soothed me after the nightmare.

I hissed. "That's enough."

His neck turned red. He jerked his arm away.

"I mean, thanks. Just give me a moment."

"Oh, okay." He jumped to his feet.

I refocused on blocking out the pain. When I had command of my arms, I lifted my left one, assessing the damage. In a way, it wasn't surprising to see the red and bubbled skin. I was so used to feeling on fire; it kind of made sense it would come to this. The burn looked the worst around my wrist and the back of my hand, gradually improving from there.

Gabriel cleared his throat. "How are you doing?"

"Better."

"Really?"

"Really."

"Can you sit up now?"

"No."

"I'll carry you." His gaze swept my body.

"Be careful," Gram cautioned.

"Of course." He looked over his shoulder to reassure her. Did a look of understanding pass between them? "We'll cover her as much as we can, Rose."

And when had she told him her name? The one only her friends used?

He helped me sit up, asked Gram to take off her cardigan, and carefully slipped my unburned right arm through one of the arm holes, leaving the burned one uncovered. I was too drained, too worried about Gram, not to follow his lead. He shook out his shirt and slipped it over my sneakers, up my legs to my shorts. He asked me to bend my knees, then lifted me into his arms, fitting my covered right side snugly against him. That arm instinctively wrapped around his neck. His movements were easy and effortless as he stood up straight.

Too tired to keep my eyes open, I closed them, and absorbed his warmth. Wow, was he on fire too? His chest radiated heat through the material separating our skin. I didn't have much experience being this close to someone, especially not in a situation where I could actually assess the sensations, but he was so hot. Was he feverish? Sick or not, my body sought his heat.

I resisted, forcing my eyes open. I didn't need a burned ear too. But still, his warmth was so comforting.

So inviting.

He carried me slowly across the cemetery, matching Gram's pace, and I strained my head away. But with each smooth step of his legs, the desire to melt into him grew. It had to be the pain talking, my body aching for a comfortable place to rest. A cool breeze swept the grounds, seemingly pushing me closer to him, nestling me into his hold. Longing stirred in my chest. A sprinkling of fat raindrops pelted us as we neared the gate, and I finally gave in, burrowing into him, tucking my chin so my head was protected by Gram's cardigan. His scent mixed with the lavender clinging to Gram's clothing, helping to relieve the lingering tension. My covered arm shifted, squeezing his shoulder. He squeezed back.

We finally reached his SUV, parked across the street from Gram's car. He shifted me higher with one arm and reached around me to open the door. He eased me in, settling me into a sitting position on the cool leather backseat. When his steadying hand finally left me, first trailing along my lower back, I almost convinced myself the craving to be close to him was indeed just my overstressed body asking for a break. A break from what, though? The pain imparted by every touch? Yes. But also what came with it. The isolation. And the burden, which could never be put down, of maintaining the isolation. Because isolation wasn't natural and had to be worked at, however necessary. And I was exhausted.

I knew though, deep down, exhaustion couldn't account for everything. Because as Gabriel carefully belted me in, his scent stirring around me, and then helped Gram into the passenger seat, glancing back at me with concern creasing his face, I couldn't escape one simple truth. A truth that summed up my existence.

I couldn't remember ever wanting to get close to anyone—ever wanting to touch anyone—before this moment.

5

SAFE

GABRIEL GOT US BACK TO GRAM'S STREET QUICKLY, BUT NOT fast enough to beat the downpour. The cottage peeked through the haze, and rain drummed against the SUV's roof. I had to get Gram and myself to the door. We needed more help. Strangely, I trusted him to give it, but I hated having to ask.

Gabriel parked as close as he could to the cottage. On the street by the mailbox, next to the long walkway curving up to the porch.

Gram placed a hand on the rain-streaked window. "I'm sorry. Richard would've… I just never got around to…"

She'd never added a garage or driveway. While the lot was big enough, all she and Richard had managed was a small flower garden and a soaring blue spruce, probably little more than a sapling when they'd planted it, both barely visible in the storm. Before I could muster a word, Gabriel gave Gram a half-smile and hopped out. He hurried to the trunk, retrieved her walker and a golf umbrella, and circled around to her side. He popped open the umbrella, holding it over her as she gripped his arm and slid down. With his large body stooped next to hers, they walked slowly and carefully to the porch.

I fumbled with my seatbelt. At last it clicked open, and I fell into the door. I opened it with my unburned arm, still wrapped in Gram's cardigan, and got as far as staring at a puddle on the pavement. Perched on the edge of the seat, my legs twitching slightly, still covered with Gabriel's shirt—how would I get down? The next moment, Gabriel was back, water dripping from his hair, no umbrella. He scooped me up, rounded his shoulders, shielding me with his bulky frame, and jogged toward the door. When he leapt up the porch steps, my head jolted toward his chest. My cheek nearly grazed the raised scar below his collarbone. I flinched.

"Oh. Sorry." He brought us into the open doorway and jerked to a stop inside. My knees bumped the coat rack, my feet knocked into Gram's purse hanging off it, and my hair brushed the wall. "Oops, just let me…"

"Let you?" I prompted when he just gawked at me, pupils dilating.

A drop of water ran down his cheek as his gaze traveled to my mouth.

"Um, let you?"

He shivered, but his palm was hot against my side.

He laughed awkwardly. He'd gone from uncertain to… nervous. Why?

"Please, Gabriel." Gram waved him toward the living room. A gust of cold wind pushed into the cottage behind us. Gram's shoulders trembled in her thin blouse, and she closed the door. "I'll be right back, dears."

Gabriel carried me to the couch and settled me across it. "I'll get your shoes, okay?"

"Okay," I said without thought. There I was, trusting him again.

He tugged off my sneakers, gripping the sides and heels, and took a small step back, bumping into the coffee table. "I, ah…" His words trailed off when I shivered, cold without his heat. He eyed the small quilt on the back of the couch, but instead of reaching over me for it, he studied my burned arm pulling at the vee of my t-shirt. He scooted around the table, taking several more steps back, like he didn't want to be near me now.

I shivered again, but this time from a wave of unease.

Shouldn't I feel *more* at ease with the distance between us?

I didn't. My hands shook. My head throbbed. Like I'd misplaced something I'd been holding moments ago. Such a confusing feeling. There was only one thing I could compare it to. The time Cameron and a friend surprised me in the school parking lot on a frosty winter's day. I'd been stripped of both my fleece jacket and sweater, Cameron hanging back as his friend circled me. When the cold hit my arms and the sensitive flesh around my waist, it wasn't the layers of warmth I'd missed the most. It was the layer of safety.

I took a deep breath, pushing out the strange thought, and my shivers subsided. Gabriel sighed and straightened to his full height, shaking water from his hair and brushing it from his neck, looking around. What must he be thinking of Gram's tiny home? The house was the smallest on the street—the only one built between the start of the Depression and World War II—and the living room was barely big enough to hold the low coffee table laden with Gram's latest splurge of quilting books, a small cart holding an outdated TV on the top and Gram's Austen books on the bottom, and the worn plaid, two-seater couch I lay across with bent knees. Gabriel's head almost touched the light fixture dangling from the ceiling. He looked out of place in his smooth khaki shorts and leather loafers.

"Um, just give me a sec, and you can go." I started to scoot my legs out of his polo.

He took a deep breath, broadening his tanned shoulders.

"I mean, thanks for all your help, but we'll be fine now." He really needed to put his shirt back on, so I could stop staring at his chest.

He wrapped his forearms around his ribcage, seeming aware of his bareness too. "I'm not leaving," he said as I struggled to untangle my legs. "I'm going to take a look at that arm. Then you have some questions to answer."

"No, really. Gram and I'll be fine. We really appreciated your help," I said, the thanks foreign on my tongue, "and it'd be great if you didn't mention what happened to anyone." I finally wiggled my way free and instantly felt exposed.

His loafers dripped onto Gram's oval braided rug, and he

slipped them off, setting them on last week's paper Gram had forgotten by the couch, then wrapped both forearms around his midsection again, covering the lowest of his scars. "I know you'll be fine, because I'm staying until I make sure, and you tell me what happened."

God, he needed to drop the Boy Scout act. "Listen, my arm will heal, and I'm not much for conversation anyway," I snapped. "So feel free to wait for it to clear." I jutted my chin toward the window. "But then go." I tossed his shirt at him with my good arm. I shot him a cynical smirk. "You can talk to Kaylee Cook or anyone else in town, and they'll tell you all about me."

"Kaylee already told me a bit, and she's got a nasty habit of posting things about others online." Gabriel tilted his head as his eyes met mine, the shirt dangling uselessly from one hand, not covering nearly enough of his insistently bare chest. "But clearly what you're going through is real. And serious."

I finally tore my eyes from his hypnotic stare and stared stonily at his scarred face instead.

"I think maybe I can help, or at least that I know someone who can." His deep blue eyes called mine back, trapping them as he said, "And I'd like to get to know you better."

I ogled him in disbelief for a second, wishing it could be true. But in the end, I snorted. "Really? Well, let's get this over with if we must." I lifted my left arm. "See, it's already looking better."

The red, raw skin was gone. All that remained were several large blisters around my hand and a bit of pink skin creeping up my arm.

The eyebrow on the unmarked side of Gabriel's face rose. "Hmmm." Amazement slowed and deepened his voice. "It does look better." He captured my gaze again, his look acknowledging how unusual this was, though he thankfully didn't verbalize it.

Gram walked stiffly into the room, without her walker. She carried a first aid kit in one hand and a roll of white gauze in the other. A fresh cardigan—one of her extra chunky ones—was buttoned up to her chin. "This is what we have to work with." She stretched out her arms as Gabriel stepped forward to take them. Her hands free, she turned toward the hallway to her room. "I'll be right back with ibuprofen."

"I don't need it." I protested so loudly she stopped in her tracks. I shifted on the couch, eager to regain more strength so I could retreat to the attic. I didn't want to hurt Gram's feelings, but most of the time it was best to recover upstairs on my own. "But maybe you should take one, Gram. It must hurt, where I hit you."

"You're a real trooper, aren't you?" Gabriel said.

Real trooper? If someone at school heard him say that, they'd call him a dork… at least behind his back. It was actually kind of cute.

He flashed his half-smile as he set the supplies on the table, on top of one of Gram's quilting books. "Just take the pills. It'll make us all feel better."

Gram didn't wait for another protest. She left the room. Gabriel stayed close, looking down at me with a thoughtful expression tugging at his puckered cheek. I squirmed. Usually, if someone came near, it was by accident or with malicious intent, and they never stayed long. But here he was, just hanging out. He shifted, and one of his knees brushed the edge of the cushion where my arm rested. I inched it away.

"So, what were you doing at the cemetery?" I asked, more sharply than I'd intended, perturbed that I couldn't find it in me to ask him to step away. No one had ever interacted this casually with me before. The normalcy of it was intoxicating, like getting a sneak peek of a dream life.

His eyes shut tightly, breaking our gaze. When he finally opened them, his blue irises scanned his own torso, as if my question had caused him to inventory his scars. What could I say to ease the sudden tension?

"Visiting my mom's grave."

Oh no. Was his mom the woman from Cameron's family who'd died in the house fire?

"Leaving roses, more roses," he murmured.

Tense silence filled the room—again.

"I'm sorry," I said at last.

More silence. Rain tapped against the window. Gabriel's gaze dropped farther.

"That is, I'm sorry for your loss. I mean, I won't pretend I know what's it like, losing your mom… but if it'd be anything like losing Gram, it must be rough."

"Thanks." He looked back up, his warped mouth setting in a grim, jagged line.

"I think you can put your shirt back on." I forced a smile. Not only was it getting much too hard to look away, but he seemed to need distraction from whatever memories were causing his dark expression.

"Oh yeah, right." He gave a quiet laugh. "I don't normally forget." He held up the shirt, seeming to realize for the first time it was in his hand. "Although it is warm in here." He smiled awkwardly and pulled the fabric over his head. When his head popped through the collar, his eyes caught mine moving over the muscles dancing under his skin. He tugged the polo down hard.

"Sorry. I forget how I look now," he choked out.

"Um, there's nothing wrong with you—it's me," I muttered, my neck flushing. I picked at the balling couch fabric. "I mean, I don't spend a lot of time around guys. You're gorgeous." My fingers froze, horrified when the thought slipped out, almost in a whisper.

But he'd heard. Every bit of darkness fell away, allowing his mouth to lift into a blinding smile.

My cheeks and chest burned. My skin probably matched my ridiculous hair. I raised my unburned hand to my chest, as if that would hide it.

Gabriel's smile widened, his demeanor more confident.

I was so thankful when Gram returned, I gulped down a glass of water with the ibuprofen. Gabriel slipped on a pair of Gram's kitchen gloves, and I let him take my hand. His movements were sure and swift as he disinfected the area and bandaged it up, all the while rambling about the differences in degrees of burns and how he'd been sure I had at least a second-degree burn at the cemetery, but now it looked like a mild first-degree burn at worst. It was best not to respond.

He probably thought I'd burned myself. Of course, he did say something about it not being made up, but he was probably trying to appease the psycho girl. Like everyone else, he probably assumed I was doing things to get attention and had taken it to the next level. He was just more polite about it. Gram had even witnessed the burn happen, and so far, she didn't seem to be processing the scope of it either.

When Gabriel finished, I managed to sit up, and he settled Gram's cardigan over my shoulders. The rain had cleared, but Gram invited him to stay for the pea soup she'd put in the crockpot that morning, delaying my escape. Though my weak, dangling legs were delaying it too.

Gabriel moved the quilting books to the floor and helped Gram set the ceramic crockpot liner onto a trivet on the coffee table.

She was back a few moments later with two bowls and two spoons. "Share the couch. I'll eat in the kitchen."

"I'm good on the floor," Gabriel insisted, waving her to the couch. He retrieved another bowl and spoon, and sat on the other side of the coffee table. The guy clearly craved eye contact. He stared at us through the whole meal, and for some reason, I kept looking back.

Gabriel ate rapidly, heartily, spooning mouthfuls of the piping hot soup into his mouth. I ate more than I'd planned, surprisingly hungry. Gram only took a few small sips from her spoon, glancing sidelong at me all the while. She finally abandoned her bowl and retreated to the kitchen. I was frustrated she hadn't eaten more, but she didn't eat when she was worried, and if she was worried… The rattle of measuring spoons, the clinking of Gram's flour and sugar canisters, and the whir of her new mixer confirmed my suspicions. She was baking again. I'd have to entertain our guest all by myself.

"You know she's not my real grandmother, right?" I lifted another spoonful and blew on it.

"Yes, I know." Gabriel pushed away his empty bowl—his fourth serving. He leaned back to rest on his bent elbows and stretched out his long legs until his bare feet disappeared under the low table, almost reaching my socks. "Kaylee told me you were found in White River. Somewhere along where it runs through the forest."

"Oh, okay."

"And actually, I've known Rose my whole life."

My hand jerked, sloshing soup down my shirt. Thankfully, it had cooled. I set the spoon down and dabbed at the mess with my napkin. He relaxed farther back on his elbows when my eyebrows wordlessly questioned him.

"Rose and my dad, they go way back. We visited off and on, until I left for college. Two years ago."

I blinked, processing. "Well, if you guys have the time to visit Gram when you're home, she could really use the friendly faces. Taking me in, it's been…" Emotion clogged my throat. I tossed the napkin on the table, glancing down at my feet and catching sight of the book Gram had asked me to read (again) to her last night— *Pride and Prejudice*. I found the strength to push the offensively happy love story under the couch.

"It's been what?" Gabriel asked.

"Hard on her." The fat lump in my throat kept me from meeting his eyes.

"I haven't been back since I left. That's why I haven't visited Rose in ages. And my dad's been, well, distracted. Now I regret being away for lots of reasons, especially since it was over a fight with him."

I looked up and tried to read him, his lips tight and crooked. What kind of fight would make him stay away that long? Of course, all kids resented their parents for certain things, but I'd always thought if I could just know mine—know they'd loved me—I'd forgive them anything.

"And it turns out the fight was stupid. My dad was right all along." Gabriel's expression darkened. "But that's all in the past." He gave a short, firm nod. "I won't be burying myself in classes, living like a hermit. I'm putting classes on hold. I'm home for as long as needed now."

He transfixed me again, looking *into* me somehow. Again, I could've sworn he was searching my green irises for hidden truths, invading my private thoughts.

"Now, I want to know more about these skin issues. How bad is it? When did it start?"

I dropped my bowl on the table with a clatter. I fought against the hope that sprang up, unbidden, *Maybe he'll believe me.* "What is this? An interrogation?"

I wasn't used to answering so many questions without things going sour.

"I care, Cassie." He patiently ignored the flash of anger in my voice.

My jaw tightened.

"If you don't tell me, I'll just ask Rose."

Gram would tell him all about me too. It was already obvious she liked him.

"Leave her out of this."

A familiar soft pounding reverberated from the kitchen. The sound of Gram kneading dough on her wooden pastry table. She must be baking up a storm in there.

"Start talking." He made a small move like he was going to get up and ask her.

"There's not much to say." I squirmed on the couch. "I've had this problem with touching people ever since I was rescued from White River. That's as far back as I can remember. I probably hit my head on a rock or something, and it wiped out everything, all my memories."

"How long ago was that?"

"About two years."

"That's strange. Aren't most cases of amnesia temporary?" He crossed his ankles, reminding me how close he was.

"Well, yes, that's what the doctors said. So, it is a bit unusual," I acknowledged.

"Do you remember anything? Anything at all?" Gabriel reclined even farther on the rug, continuing to make himself at home, without ever breaking eye contact.

I tried to read his intentions. They were impossible to gauge. But I did remember something.

"A weird light."

His eyes widened.

The sharp flash of light had come right toward me, half blinding me as it materialized from the trees. I'd eventually dismissed it entirely, burying the memory because dwelling on it never helped explain anything about me. It only brought back the pain of waking in the river that morning.

"Can you describe it?"

"Just like a lightning bolt or something, before the water."

Gabriel frowned, looking perplexed.

I might as well recount that whole morning for him, since I'd gone this far. "And one of the rescuers said I was raving about needing to find something. How I'd get killed if I showed up without it."

"What!?" He sat up ramrod straight.

"I don't remember anything about it." I just remembered the vision from the rescuer who'd arrived first, whispering into a phone about risking his job. "Actually, I think one of the rescuers might've been involved in something shady." I bit my tongue. I couldn't tell Gabriel why I suspected that. So, I quickly added, "Social Services thought it might be drugs or money that I was raving about. I might be mixed up in something criminal." I pulled my knees into my chest, wrapping my arms around them.

He tilted his head. "Well, if that's true, I'm sure you were a victim." He eyed my curled form, and his eyebrows drew together. "Everyone else must've thought so too. Kaylee said when you started school, they were warned not to post or talk about you, that you were trouble—" He broke off with an apologetic wince.

He didn't need to. I heard it all since Cameron had singled me out. People hide a lot in their heads; they rarely speak their nastiest thoughts, unless prompted. But Cameron had prompted everyone.

"I mean,"—he cleared his throat—"it sounds like the police thought you might be in danger?"

I nodded, gripping my knees tighter. "The police tried to keep my presence here quiet. They investigated missing child reports. Nothing added up. They said sometimes runaways or child victims of human trafficking get wrapped up in gangs. Maybe I'd escaped."

He gulped, as if digesting the possibilities of my past. "But I don't see how that has anything to do with your skin condition. Rose said today was the first time you've suffered any visible marks. So you're getting worse?"

"Um, I guess. Don't say anything to Gram."

"Oh, I think she can tell on her own. She was pretty upset when I found you guys." He took a deep breath, making himself impossibly broad. His eyes seemed to vibrate as he looked even deeper into mine. "You didn't seem in so much pain when I touched you at the shelter."

"Well, um, it still hurt. A little." I loosened my hold on my knees and picked at a loose thread on my shorts, wondering if I'd recovered enough to move upstairs. If he wanted to stay, he could watch TV.

He stared back expectantly, waiting for a better answer.

I released my legs and flexed my aching calf muscles. My legs were still too weak. If I couldn't escape, I had to redirect his focus off me. "Let's play a game."

He smirked, like he saw right through me.

"I know Gin Rummy. It's Gram's favorite," I said with a shrug.

He cleared the bowls and the nearly empty crockpot liner, then fetched the cards from the kitchen table where Gram and I normally played. He offered them to me gingerly, holding the very end to keep our fingers from brushing, then sat back on the rug. I shuffled and, as I usually did before dealing, rubbed the top card between my fingers, loving its waxy texture. He watched my fingers move, and I stopped. He scooted in close.

We made it through two hands of cards. But when he asked if I remembered anything about the fire that had burned my legs, when the answer was obviously no if Kaylee had blabbed the whole story, I'd really had enough of talking about what had gone wrong with me.

I blurted out, "How did you learn so much about first aid?"

He set down his cards. "Oh. Well, I've been doing paramedic training. And I finished my sophomore year, middle of my pre-med classes, before I came home to fix things with my dad."

"So you want to be a doctor?" Maybe Gabriel would make a good one. Despite his inquisitiveness, I already liked him a lot more than my doctors, but that wasn't saying much.

He nodded. "I want to do research, on genetics. Inherited diseases actually. I've also thought about a vet degree. Maybe I'll do both."

"Both? Really?" And how had he already decided on a specialty? He wasn't even out of college yet.

"Yeah, I've got plenty of time." He smiled at me over the cards littering the table.

Wow. He thought he had all the time and opportunities in the world? Wasn't that nice. The surge of bitterness rose unbidden, but I reminded myself I'd thought about a vet degree too. If I could somehow save the money and stay sane long enough.

Locked in his gaze, again, it struck me that he was probably only being nice and acting interested in me because of my peculiarity. Like a scientist who'd discovered a new species of fish or a doctor who'd discovered a new genetic disease.

A scraping sound from the kitchen broke our locked gaze. Gram moved into the doorway with the support of her walker, wearing her favorite faded pink apron with an embroidered lily on the front pocket—her own handiwork.

"Cookies are almost ready. Maple oatmeal. Just don't eat them all on the way home." She winked at Gabriel. "Share with your father too. He liked these especially."

"I'm sure we'll love them. Once I make a little room." Gabriel patted his stomach, then settled back down, clearly in no hurry to leave. "I'll even share with Aaron and Cole. And Cameron. He's living with us now. Anyway, you shouldn't have gone to so much trouble."

"I wanted to do something to thank you for today, and it isn't any trouble. It isn't near enough. The cinnamon rolls aren't even in the oven yet." Her smile was light, mischievous, making her look years younger. Her eyes flickered back to the kitchen, then to me, then to Gabriel. "I don't know what I would've done if you hadn't—" She didn't finish the sentence, but pulled a crumpled handkerchief from her pocket and dabbed at the corner of one eye.

I studied her chest. Thankfully, she was breathing normally.

"Who's Cole?" I asked, hoping to distract Gram.

"The baby Knight brother." Gabriel gave a crooked grin. "Although he's bigger than Cameron, almost as big as Aaron now. You know them?"

I'd never answered him yesterday. "I, ah, know Cameron. Not your brothers. But I don't get out much."

"Well, no surprise you haven't met. They're homeschooled, like I was." Gabriel's eyebrows tightened together, as if his thoughts were elsewhere. "But Aaron played football last year and insists on taking classes now. Aaron will be a senior, like you and Cameron. You should come over and meet him. And my dad." His face tensed further, wrinkles appearing at the scarred corner of his mouth. "You need to meet my dad."

"Okay." I tried not to sound dismissive.

His expression relaxed.

Too little sleep caught up with me, weighing me down and fogging my head. I yawned.

He uncrossed his legs and stood. "Now, time for bed. You look exhausted."

"Wow. Thanks." I flushed, embarrassed and a bit annoyed that Gabriel had seen me at my worst today. Then I got annoyed at myself for even caring.

I began to stand, slowly testing my weight. I swayed, and Gram's cardigan slipped off my shoulders. Before my sleep-deprived brain could even think to retrieve it, Gabriel was there, wrapping the couch quilt around me, leaving my bandaged hand resting on top. He got an arm under the backs of my knees and swept me up against his chest.

Without prompting, he headed for the hall and stopped by the attic door, like he was familiar with Gram's home layout. "You're upstairs?"

"Yes," Gram answered for me.

"I can manage." I protested, although damn, it was a pretty weak protest with my cheek pressed against his chest.

"Of course." He tightened his grip. "But I want to help." He shifted me higher in his arms.

Any possible response eluded me. Only inches separated our faces, my lips hovering right above his. He looked down at my bandage and pressed his lips together, deepening their slant. Looking at him, the fog in my head cleared. Did his damaged skin feel like mine? Did it still hurt? Mine didn't. But he seemed more sensitive about his. He caught me staring, and his fingers tightened against my thigh. We both looked away. I tucked my chin, my cheek resting back against his warm polo.

Gram opened the door to the stairs and flipped the light switch. The bulb hanging in the middle of the tiny corridor lit the way up into the darkness beyond.

"Thanks," Gabriel said, his deep voice strained and unsure again.

I recovered my wits enough to remember what was important. "Gram, you need to take your medicine."

"Yes, I'll do that now."

"And leave the dishes till tomorrow."

"I will. Love you, angel." Gram turned down the hall toward her room.

Gabriel carried me up, much too slowly for my liking. Or so I told myself.

I opened my mouth, fully intending to say, "Speed it up, would you? I'm not going to break," but the complaint caught in my throat. He'd done nothing to deserve my rudeness, and I found myself in foreign territory without a plan of action. My heart raced with each steady step, uncomfortable only with how comfortable I was, curled in his arms. It felt impossibly nice, and the slower he went, the longer I had to study and memorize the sensation. It was a hard feeling to label, baffling in its newness. He finally stepped into my dim room and carried me to my bed at a snail's pace. When he paused to give a curious look at the wooden ramp I'd installed at the end of my bed for Zoe, it finally occurred to me.

Safe.

I felt safe with Gabriel. His presence in my personal space was unobtrusive, inoffensive. It didn't make any sense. I'd learned from experience that 99.9% of people—and especially guys—couldn't be trusted. But it was an oddly pleasant feeling nonetheless.

When he reached my bedside, Gabriel paused again, but this time, it was me he studied.

Cold, damp air swirled around the attic from the window I'd left open, but it couldn't chill me as I relaxed into him. My limbs meshed with his form. I let go, let them do as they pleased, not just from exhaustion, but from the sense of calm his now-familiar gaze created.

He shifted toward my pillow, slowly lowering me.

My eyelids fell shut.

"Goodnight, Cassie." His breath fluttered a few tendrils of my hair.

"Night." I sank into the mattress and rubbed my bandaged hand against my face, brushing his chin like a caress. Oh well.

For an instant, he squeezed me a bit tighter. Like a hug? I swallowed hard. My mind instinctively screamed, "Danger!" but my stomach did a happy little somersault. Which of them was right? Should I say something? But he didn't linger. He slid his arms out from under me, and I rolled away onto my side. Cold air moved into the space between us.

I trembled.

"I'll get the window." He carefully adjusted my hand to lie between my stomach and bent knees, tucked the quilt in all around me, and pulled up my comforter, which felt like a layer of ice. The wind gusted again.

"So cold," I said through chattering teeth. It was impossible, but I wished someone could… "Hold me." The words slipped out, in a mumble to myself.

Gabriel coughed.

I yawned, too tired to fight off sleep a moment longer, even with my feet numb under the covers. I tried to thank Gabriel for all his help and being so nice to Gram, but I was so tired, I wasn't sure if I actually said the words.

The window snapped shut.

Maybe I could get a bit of rest before the nightmare claimed me.

It had been such a long day. I rubbed one foot against my other calf to warm it, then the other. "So—so cold." I trembled harder. In that last flicker of consciousness, caught in limbo on the edge of sleep, a warm weight dipped the bed. As if someone were lying against me. Wrapping their warmth around me. Holding me. Comforting me. How strange, but nice. I sighed, a contented sound.

My mumbled wish had come true. If only in my dream.

6
EVERYONE'S HIDING SOMETHING

I WOKE TO SUNLIGHT STREAMING ACROSS THE ATTIC. I FELT hazy. An intoxicating combination of relaxed and disoriented.

I rolled over and looked up at the Burger Boys kid's meal watch I'd swiped from the trash at work and strapped to the bedpost.

Damn. It couldn't be right. Twenty minutes till noon?

I'd slept the whole night through. Without a trace of the nightmare or any pain. Incredible. How had I managed to sleep so deeply, so peacefully, for so long?

"Ugh." I threw back my comforter and the quilt wrapped around me. The extra sleep was needed, and I was thankful the nightmare had skipped a night, but Zoe would've missed me. I also needed to talk to Dr. G about bringing her home. And I was due at Burger Boys and needed to clean the kitchen for Gram. But first, before it got towed, I needed to get Gram's car—a 70s VW Beetle, too small to fit my bike so I'd have to jog there.

"Ugh." I hopped out of bed in yesterday's clothes, slid across the floor in my socks, and raced downstairs to shower, already totally over this day. I was going to be late, and my greasy, grabby-handed supervisor took sadistic glee in docking my pay for such insults to his tightly run domain.

I stripped off my clothes, stuffed them in the hamper, and paused in front of the shower, peeling away Gabriel's bandage. The blisters were gone. Gabriel had said to cover my hand with plastic to keep the burn from getting soaked, but my skin was as good as new, as unexplainable as the burn itself. I didn't want to think about what those things meant—about what sort of freak I really was—and shoved the thought out of my mind. I was an expert at that.

In and out of the shower, I wrapped my towel around me, and scurried back upstairs to my trunk for the fresh clothes I'd forgotten to grab in my rush. Reaching under my pillow for the key, I noticed the latches were open. My stomach dropped. I always locked it.

The old, cedar-paneled chest contained all my possessions—everything I called my own in my short life as I remembered it. Another gift from Gram, and I was absolutely obsessive about locking it. Another weird thing about me, maybe, but when you don't have a lot, it makes sense you value what you have that much more.

Clutching the towel to my chest, I opened the heavy lid. The piles of clothing were still folded and seemed untouched. The books I'd borrowed from the library—several off the AP English summer reading list, and Dante's *Divine Comedy* in three volumes, *Inferno*, *Purgatorio*, and *Paradiso*—were stacked by the clothing where I'd left them. But my loose pages of notes on the *Inferno* looked shuffled around. My shoulders tensed. My own books, purchased at my favorite used bookstore in Denver—*Frankenstein*, *Wuthering Heights*, Aristotle's *Ethics*, Kant's *Groundwork of the Metaphysics of Morals*, Nietzsche's *Beyond Good and Evil*, and the Bible—were out of order. The tension radiated through my body.

In the corner, the equipment for a summer project was where I'd left it: a battery, charger, and two tapes for an old video camera. And nearby, three envelopes I'd labeled to save money in: *Zoe*, *Gram*, *Future*. I'd taken out cash last month to replace Gram's broken mixer and buy Zoe her harness and a few things for around the house, and hadn't recounted the totals carefully then, but as I flipped through the bills, the new amounts appeared right. No money gone.

I tossed my towel over the nearest bedpost and hurriedly dug to the bottom of the trunk. I'd been too afraid to look for it first, the item even more precious than money. When my fist closed around the cold stone of my locket, my body relaxed.

Losing my locket would be like losing part of myself. It was my only link to whatever life I'd had before. Luckily its short braided chain had kept it from being washed away in the river. That chain was the only normal thing about it, though that was no surprise given its owner.

The locket pendant was a fat, egg-like stone of swirled reds and oranges. It opened like a locket should, but there were no pictures inside, just a peculiar engraving—*Πάντα ῥεῖ καὶ οὐδὲν μένει*. Thanks to the library's computer, I knew it was Greek and said something like *Change is the only constant*; or *Everything flows, nothing stands still*. The ridiculous quote was attributed to an ancient Greek philosopher, Heraclitus, whose works only survived in fragments quoted by Aristotle and other Greek philosophers. No wonder since he was dead wrong.

Change wasn't the only constant. Plenty of things never changed; it would violate their essence. Like my oddity.

Hoping for change was also a waste of time. As much as I'd wanted normalcy in the past two years, to experience human touch without pain, nothing had changed, only expounded, the agony multiplied. Well, until I'd touched Gabriel at the shelter. Yet the very next day, Gram's touch had blistered me. The milder reaction to Gabriel's touch was a fluke, a momentary aberration before my life continued to spiral downward.

How much longer before my body and mind cracked under the steadily increasing strain? I shivered and pushed the bleak thought away. Another thing I couldn't bear to think about. I tucked the locket back under its pile of clothes. Its reddish coloring complemented my hair, but I hadn't been able to bring myself to wear it since I'd first woken in the hospital bed with it lying next to me, its presence providing comfort, but no familiarity—unlocking no memories.

I took a moment to let the trunk's woodsy scent calm the

remaining tension from my panic attack, then snatched a clean work shirt and pair of shorts to throw on. The kitchen at Burger Boys was always sweltering. I'd almost passed out my first shift in long sleeves under my t-shirt. I shut the trunk and triple-checked the latches were secured. As a precaution, I slipped the key into my pocket. Maybe I'd left the trunk unlocked, but there was evidence of someone digging in there. Digging in my things! And Gram had never done that before, which meant… what exactly? Gabriel was a snoop? Or I hadn't shut up the trunk completely, and I was wrong about things looking shuffled through.

It was possible I'd left a few things out of order.

I hadn't gotten a lot of sleep recently.

Key pressed against my right thigh, I shelved the thoughts and got on with my day. I reached for a pair of short gloves and slipped on the special running shoes Gram gave me our first Christmas together, in anticipation of a nice run to the cemetery. I ran down the stairs, shouted out a goodbye to Gram, and flew out the front door.

There was Gram's VW, parked outside. I came to an abrupt halt and stared at it, then went back inside.

Gram was in the kitchen, rolling out pie dough. A huge bowl of apple filling and two pie tins sat on the counter behind her. Buttermilk biscuits sat cooling by the stove, tempting me with their buttery smell, and showing how busy (and worried) she'd been already today. And there were only two mixing bowls in the sink. The dishes from last night had been washed. She looked up from her pastry table, raising an eyebrow. "Weren't you going to check in before leaving?"

"I was just going to run out, bring your car back." I nodded toward the sink. "And check in when I did the dishes before work."

"I fret about you, you know that." She took a wheezy breath. "I was concerned when you didn't come down. I went up, you were sleeping so soundly. It's about time you got more rest. I thought you'd at least check in." Her lips pressed together.

"I know, I'm sorry. And so sorry about yesterday." I collapsed into a chair at the kitchen table, accepting the fact I was going to be late.

"It's okay." Her voice grew strained. "I just worry." She cleared her throat.

"I know, Gram." I sank further in the chair, wishing I could make the worry go away.

"Now, your hand. Does it hurt very badly?"

I stood. "Doesn't hurt at all." I gave her my best smile. "Looks good too." I flipped back my glove.

"You shouldn't be wearing that. Gabriel said the burn should breathe."

"But it's better." I stepped close, lifting my arm.

Her mouth fell open. "Oh my." She looked between the pristine skin where my burn had been and the aged burn marks on her own hands.

"See, everything's fine." I lied, hoping she wouldn't ask questions I didn't want to think about, like *How did your skin heal miraculously?* or *Why did your skin burn in the first place?* My skin might be fine, but I was messed up like always. "No need to worry." When Gram still frowned at my arm, my avoidance instincts kicked into high gear. Redirect. "Hey Gram, can I have a biscuit?"

"Of course."

"Thanks."

"How'd your VW get back?" I asked, scarfing the buttery treat. The question was as much a distraction as it was pure curiosity. She couldn't have done it herself, and no one in town helped us out since that incident at Betty's.

"Oh, Gabriel jogged over to the cemetery after he came down last night. Drove it back. Can you imagine? How nice."

"I guess. How long was he up in my room?"

"Oh, I don't know. Maybe an hour or—"

"What?!"

"Long enough for the cinnamon rolls to get out of the oven. Then he did the dishes, even though I told him you always do them, and went back up to check on you after bringing back the car, so I'm not exactly sure when—"

"What? No way." Of course. This is what I got for letting my guard down. Now I was sure I hadn't been dreaming. Gabriel had sat beside me, making sure I was asleep before going through my things. Dammit. Talk about invasion of privacy. God! If I'd been conscious I would've… The threat died in my head. Would I have kicked him out? Or would I have relished his overwhelming warmth, his impossible proximity, too much to do the smart thing, as I had each time he'd held me before? I couldn't answer that question, but the snooping was unforgivable… if he had snooped, that is. With an internal growl of frustration, I tried to shove those thoughts aside with all the rest, but Gram made it difficult.

"I left the cookies and cinnamon rolls for him before I went to bed. I assumed you must be staying up late again. Didn't want to interrupt if you two were getting along." Gram's creased cheeks pulled up in a small smile. "It's about time you made a friend. He comes from a wonderful family too. Such a nice young man. Reminds me of my Richard."

"Gram," I said, stern enough for her to take me seriously, "don't get any ideas. Gabriel and I aren't going to get along. He's way too nosy." Not to mention always gawking and asking personal questions. "Something's off. I'm pretty sure he's hiding something."

"Everyone's hiding something."

"Of course." I kept my voice soft. Gram had no way of knowing I knew that better than anyone. "But what Gabriel's hiding seems big. Like he knows something. Something I don't."

"What do you mean?"

"Well, he said something about maybe knowing someone who could help me—that I needed to meet his father. It was strange. Then with everything else"—like him going through my things!—"I don't think I can trust him."

"You don't trust anyone. We talked about that." She started to turn back to her dough but hesitated. She reached for her walker, gripping it tightly.

"Gram?" I stepped in, reaching for her. "Is everything okay?"

"I don't know." She shook her head. Her knuckles turned white around the metal bar. "What Gabriel said to you… what happened at the cemetery… oh goodness. It can't be." Gram paused. "It just can't be." Her breath quickened. "Seeing the burn appear, and Gabriel there, I thought it then but didn't want to believe it. If it's true, it's too much for me." Her chin trembled. It seemed like there were questions she didn't want to think about, either. My gloved hands hovered, ready to help her into a chair. She paused until she had recovered a bit. "Just promise me you'll be nice to Gabriel when you see him again," she said in one strained breath. "And let him introduce you to his father if he thinks that might help."

"Um, I don't know." I dropped my hands.

"But his family, it hadn't occurred to me before, maybe they can help you."

"What?"

"I have to think about this." Gram rubbed her chest. "But you should know the Knight family can be trusted."

"Trusted?" I asked, voice hard. What was it with the Knights that made everyone think they wore halos? I'd seen plenty of evidence to the contrary.

"Yes. I've known Gabriel's father, Bernard, for ages. Richard introduced us. Richard, Bernard, and one of Bernard's cousins— Jesse—were like brothers." A flash of sorrow clouded Gram's eyes, and her hand fell. "They grew up together." She stared past the kitchen entry, toward the living room wall where several old photos from her (and Richard's) youth hung. "Richard trusted them implicitly. So did I, as soon as I met them." She looked back to me, lifting her chin.

I rolled my eyes. I couldn't help it.

Gram frowned. "Cassandra, you can't keep closing yourself off. You've got good instincts. Stop doubting them. Bernard seemed a good person from the moment I met him. He's proved it over the years. He's been a good friend."

"Good friend?" It didn't seem right to hurt more of Gram's friendships by revealing Gabriel had gone through my things, at least not until I knew more.

"Yes. I was even one of the few guests at his wedding, when Bernard finally found his love, Lillian"—Lillian? Where had I heard that name before?—"and married her. And I still remember the births of the boys and—" she broke off, shaking her head, then straightened. "How special it was. There aren't any other young ones left."

"Left?"

"In their extended family." She coughed.

"Well, there's their cousin, Cameron, right?" And Cameron… why did "Lillian" make me think of him? "And if you guys were so close, then why hasn't Bernard visited?"

"He hasn't been himself. Not since Lillian passed a couple years back."

Oh no, maybe Gabriel's mom really had been the woman in the fire. It had happened when I was in the hospital. When I'd started school, the kids were still whispering about it, and Cameron's father.

Gram wheezed and paused for a breath. "You know, Bernard hasn't called in ages. We should stop by and check in on him."

"Yeah, maybe." I swallowed hard. I had to ask what had been on my mind since the vision yesterday, but I hoped it wouldn't upset her. "Gram, what does your watch say?"

"Hmm? Oh. How'd you know it says something, angel?"

"Well, Richard had it specially made…"

"That's right." Gram's face softened. "It is engraved. The band. All the way around, inside." She swiveled it around her wrist. "It says—no matter the time, my love will be with you. I will always find a way back to you." She turned away from the pastry table, her eyes seeking the sink.

I wasn't sure what that told me—besides reconfirming the

strength of Gram and Richard's love. What I did notice, for the first time, was something about the kitchen. It was so modern, compared to Gram's vision. And while much of the cottage showed its age, there had been other small remodels over the years too. How had Gram managed them? It was no secret her life had been hard. The Depression hadn't been easy on anyone, and during the War, she'd worked on a ranch outside of town, only to lose her job when the men came home. She'd once told me about her struggles to find good work again, eventually securing a position at the bakery, where she must've gotten the burns to her hands.

Thinking of Gram's struggles made me sad. She wouldn't want me to be. She never seemed saddened by her tough circumstances. Only by the loss of Richard.

She turned back to me and I monitored the rise and fall of her chest. Once I was assured her breathing was better, I tried not to worry and glanced at the singing bird clock mounted by the fridge, ready to chirp noon any minute. "Time to head off. I should probably take your car, if that's okay?"

"Sure. It's as much your car as mine." She gave me a wrinkled smile—finally—and I was happy to see her back to her normal self. "Take another biscuit. We'll talk more about visiting the Knights over dinner."

"Okay." I grabbed another biscuit, still warm in my hand. "But I might be home late. I'm going to stop by the shelter to talk to Dr. G about bringing Zoe home." Should've done it last week—she hadn't been sick in a while—but with the check waiting at work today, I'd have the money for the adoption fee and everything she'd need.

"Late dinner it is. Love you." Gram waved a goodbye as she shuffled back to the table for her rolling pin.

Hoping more baking would work out whatever was troubling her, I watched her another moment to make sure she didn't need me to stay. Her brow furrowed but her hands were steady on the pin. I took a bite of the biscuit and finally backed away. Why did Gram think the Knights could help me? Sure, Gabriel probably thought I was a wildly interesting medical anomaly, but could he and his reclusive dad *do* anything about my condition?

I only knew one thing about Gabriel for sure. In just two days, I'd let him drop deeper into my life than I'd ever planned, and I was already paying for it. He was a problem, disrupting my makeshift existence with his meddling and, if I was honest, by tantalizing me with that one troublesome feeling I could never afford: hope.

7
DISAPPOINTMENT

GRABBY-HANDS HAD MADE AN UNFAIR CUT TO MY WAGES—A full hour instead of the quarter I was late—but at least handed over my two weeks' paycheck without bothering me. I didn't need to see more fantasies of him forcing himself on me when I was alone restocking the kitchen pantry.

Now, I sped across town and parked in my usual spot, as far from the reserved volunteers' spots as possible, even though Dr. G's battered truck was the only one in the lot. I burst into the lobby. Empty. I tore off my gloves, shoved them in my back pocket, and sprinted to the dog cages. My arms felt itchy. I needed to hug Zoe. Just a few moments in the presence of a being I didn't fear might help temporarily convince me everything was okay.

Zoe's blanket lay by the door of her cage.

I reached my fingers through the metal links. The soft blanket stung my fingertips, like touching frost in the forest in spring. Zoe's covering was cold as the concrete beneath. I raced from cage to cage, then outside to the dog run, and back again, sweat soaking into my t-shirt. "Zoe. Zoe-bug, where are you?"

The other dogs barked back in confusion. B.B. and B.G. looked at me with wide, sad eyes. I'd never seen B.B. and B.G. so forlorn. I opened Zoe's cage and lifted her covering to my cheek. My hand went cold. Then numb.

Where was she? I stifled a scream with the quilted material.

Calm down. Think this through. She hadn't been sick in several weeks and looked good yesterday, so it didn't make any sense for her to be back in the clinic. Dr. G knew I wanted to adopt her—and no one ever wanted the less-than-perfect dogs anyway—so it didn't make sense that she would've been adopted. Her harness and leash were gone. Maybe Dr. G had taken her on a walk? But he never had time for that. Had he even realized I'd bought them?

Oh no. No, it couldn't be.

When I'd missed my time at the shelter this morning, I'd forgotten what day of the week it was. I forced myself to breathe deep. Dr. G wouldn't do that to Zoe. Right? He wouldn't put her on the kill list. I needed to stay calm, find Dr. G.

He was in his office, frowning over what appeared to be several large stacks of bills. He shuffled together a few stamped "PAST DUE" in red ink and ran his fingers through his dark hair, leaving trails where it was already stuck up. Tousled. Dreamy. That's what women in town called his look, but I'd learned it was from exhaustion and stress. I knocked on the door frame. He looked up, and his glasses slid down his nose. "Ah, Cassandra, good to see you."

It took everything in me not to scream Zoe's name. I tried for polite. "Hey, Dr. G, sorry about not making it in." I shifted my weight from foot to foot.

"It's all right. You do so much. You're allowed a day off."

"Is there anything left that needs to be done?" My sneaker tapped an impatient rhythm on the linoleum.

"No. Actually, the new volunteer took care of everything." I opened my mouth, and Dr. G rushed on. "Don't worry, Gabriel knows his way around. He used to volunteer when I started, gets along great with the animals, like you. Kaylee was here too, but we both know what a help she is." He gave a small smile.

"Oh, well, I guess that's good." I tried to slow my tapping. "So, Zoe's not in her cage."

"Oh." He startled and then sagged, looking resigned.

"Her harness and leash are missing." I prompted, tapping away.

"Oh, of course." He cut his eyes up at me and adjusted his glasses.

"What do you mean?"

"I've got good news."

"Okay…" My foot stilled, hovering.

"Zoe was adopted."

"What!" My sneaker planted on the floor. Relief washed over me, but agitation followed. "I told you I was going to adopt her. I was saving for it."

He tugged his tie. "I'm sorry. I knew you'd bonded with her and wanted to adopt a dog, but, well… It's been weeks." Weeks because she was recovering. He shook his head. "We always need to make room for the new ones—too many stray and abandoned dogs. You know that."

"Dr. G, it can't be too late to fix this." I swallowed my panic, determined I could still make this okay. "Don't you check out the new owner's place before letting them adopt a special needs dog? So Zoe's still here, somewhere, right?"

"No, she went home with Gabriel this afternoon."

"What?" My stomach plummeted.

"Gabriel met Zoe this morning and asked me how she lost a leg."

I gave him a hard stare, waiting for a better explanation.

He squirmed and his glasses slid back down. He pulled them off and met my eyes. His looked a bit bloodshot. I tried to soften my expression. He did work so hard. And my fear and anger wouldn't get me what I wanted—Zoe back with me, where she belonged.

He sank further into his chair and the old frame squeaked. "Gabriel said he was looking for a dog now that he's home. He and Zoe hit it off right away. I saw no reason not to let him take her. She's recovered. Anyway, you should be happy for her. The Knights live in one of those nice houses by the river. They can provide everything she needs."

I ignored the punch to my gut at his not-so-subtle inference about my financial standing, and bit back a sharp comment about privilege and riches being poor qualifications for a good home.

"Can't you just tell him you made a mistake?"

"I would prefer not to. That is, Gabriel just donated quite a large sum to the shelter." His posture eased. "Quite a large sum," he repeated, smiling. "In Zoe's name, no less. I think he was moved when I told him about everything she needed, how much we did to save her. You know things are tight around here. We'll still be in debt, even with the donation." He motioned to the bills on his desk. "I know I'd sort of promised she was yours, but the check…"

Sort of? You literally promised me! If I was taking too long, you should have talked to me!

But it wasn't that I took too long to save up the fee, which Dr. G had offered to waive but I'd insisted I pay because I knew the shelter needed it and I'd have time to save while Zoe recovered. It came down to him needing a much larger sum. Money I didn't have. Money people like Gabriel had plenty of. My vision went hazy. So many things came down to money. "I understand." My cheeks grew hot. I understood what was really going on here, all too well.

It was great Gabriel had made the donation, but it sent him to the front of the line. Where people with lots of money always went.

"What about one of the pups? They're almost ready. No fee. I insist." He cringed with guilt.

"Um, I have to go." I blinked, trying to clear my vision, and raced away.

My body shook, but my feet carried me down the hall. I collapsed against the door to the women's restroom, stumbling inside. My hip hit the sink, my back hit the wall. I slid down until the backs of my legs hit cold linoleum. My arms found their way around my knees, and I dropped my head onto them, trying not to cry out. Tears slipped through my closed lids, and I bit down on my trembling bottom lip. Signs of weakness.

I choked out a laugh.

Maybe everyone was right. Maybe "Freakenstein" was fitting. Maybe I wasn't strong enough to be normal. I'd always be an oddity who cried out when anyone drew near. Shedding tears—*stupid tears*—because I never wanted to be touched and would never let myself trust, really trust, someone to never hurt me.

Pain radiated from my chest, more violent than the burn in the cemetery. I felt weaker than when I'd been lying among the gravestones. I'd never have much. But I'd always thought I'd have Zoe.

How much longer could I endure this solitary existence?

My heart constricted with the loneliness that never left for long.

How much worse could things get?

I laughed. Much worse. Depression. Self-mutilation. Self-starvation. Irreversible psychological harm. Everything the tortured monkeys in touch deprivation studies suffered through. In researching what was wrong with me, I'd learned some scary things. The results of forced isolation, without physical contact of any kind, were horrifying.

I wrapped my arms around my chest. What it would be like to have someone else's arms around me? To hug without fear? Nice. Soothing. Comforting. Words seemed inadequate. Maybe it would be something like the safety and warmth I'd felt with Gabriel? But so much better if I could throw caution aside and touch someone freely in return.

I brushed my fingertips across my chest, allowing another moment to contemplate it. I wiped away the new tears that escaped despite my best effort. "Stop crying," I mumbled, rubbing my nose against my shirt sleeve. I didn't cry. *I never cried.* I scrubbed my cheeks until all evidence of my weakness was gone. Self-pity never did any good.

I forced myself to my feet and into the hall. I staggered back to give B.B. and B.G. the cuddle I'd missed this morning, then scurried out into the brisk air of early evening.

Sliding behind the wheel of the VW, I squared my shoulders. I resolved to leave my last sliver of foolish hope back on that bathroom floor. Normal things like a pet were not meant for me.

Maybe Zoe should be with someone who had friends and places to take her. Someone who could plan and count on a future.

Tomorrow I'd deal with Gabriel. I'd figure out where he lived from Gram, and not leave until he'd convinced me beyond a shadow of a doubt that he'd take care of my friend better than I could. Zoe deserved the best. If Gabriel didn't make the grade, I'd figure out what to do then. I always figured things out and managed to get by. Somehow.

I started the engine. I had a project to catch up on. I usually went every day, but I'd been incapacitated. I shoved my feelings about Zoe into that big aching place in my chest and headed out.

I drove to the far edge of town, surrounded by tree-lined streets and middle-class houses, and parked two blocks from my destination. I checked the VW's mirrors. No one approached. I hurried to my target: my hidden camera.

At the start of summer, I'd discovered a monster living in this quiet subdivision. No. Correction. Mike lived here. Calling Mike a monster dehumanized him, and real "bad guys" were very much human.

I shivered and raced across the street.

When Mike first touched me last year and imparted a vision of him raising his fist to a young girl, I got worried and dug for information. The girl was his ten-year-old stepsister. Mike was a bully and big for an upcoming senior, not surprising since he'd failed a grade and been suspended the following year because of a prank that had put another kid in the hospital. I'd discovered more after I practically encouraged Mike to touch me on a few later occasions.

Mike had a troubled past. People would talk, even around me, and I'd seen some of it in the visions. Growing up, he'd seen his dad yell at, beat on, and generally make life miserable for his mom. Mike had even joined in on some of it, with his dad's prompting, calling his mom a bitch after she'd made friends with a new male neighbor—a widower—and the widower's daughter. Eventually Mike's dad died in a car accident on his way home from a bar. While all of that might explain a lot of why Mike ended up as he did, none of it was an excuse for how he treated his new sister.

As far as I could tell, the trouble started the year before, when the girl's dad—the widower—married Mike's mom. I feared the girl was too young, too scared, to say anything. I'd tried approaching the school counselor and sent anonymous letters to the police and child welfare. The counselor brushed me off, saying Mike was "such a nice young man" since returning from suspension. If the police or children services did anything, it hadn't been effective, because there were new visions. Worse visions.

If they needed proof, I'd get it for them.

I checked for anyone watching me. Neighboring lawns and nearby windows clear, I scaled the tree outside the girl's bedroom window. A streaking white flash near the road—like at the cemetery—startled me. I clung to the trunk, scraping my ear along the bark. Nothing was there. I cursed my nerves and climbed higher.

I sighed. The old video camera I'd bought with some of my Zoe funds (*don't think about Zoe*) was still secured to the branch. I pulled it from its nest of leafy camouflage and plastic bag wrapping, cradled it in one arm, and scrambled back down.

I tried to stroll casually along the dark street, but I ended up racing over the pavement. My free hand shook as I neared the VW. When I got behind the wheel, I was too anxious to wait until I got to a safer place. I pressed rewind. I flipped open the small side-screen so I could view the pre-programmed hours of nighttime footage in fast-forward. The camera beeped and turned off. Battery dead.

Had I brought the spare? Yes. I swapped it and tapped my left foot by the clutch pedal until the rewind completed. It started to play.

Just like the other videos I'd recorded, the girl's bedside light was on. The butterfly cut-out lampshade emitted a soft glow. A sad sign she was waiting for trouble, but at least it allowed me a better view of the pink and purple, flowery room.

I hit fast-forward. Then pause. Then play.

Her covers shifted and quivered several times.

More fast-forwarding. More covers shifting. Pause, play, and fast-forward again. Was it another wasted effort? Nothing moved, except for the quaking lump under the pink covers. The girl got as little sleep as me, but she warded off more than a painful nightmare. She waited for a bump in the night. For someone coming to get her.

I saw her door crack open and released fast-forward.

A ghostly image emerged.

I got him. Finally.

Satisfaction and sorrow warred within me. Sometimes it felt awful to be right, to realize that looking for the good in people always ended in disappointment. Evil lurked, carefully hidden, beneath friendly faces.

In several hurried steps his short, muscled frame stood over the covers. Within seconds he had her pinned in a practiced wrestler's hold. He pressed himself over her, the bedside lamp lighting up his hard face. Then his dimly lit figure jerked into action.

My stomach lurched. I hit the fast-forward button, not wanting to see any more of my visions confirmed.

He should be dipped in a river of boiling blood and fire.

I'd started playing this game after reading Dante's *Inferno* last winter. After each vision, I'd assign that person to one of Dante's nine circles of hell, to be tortured in accordance with their crime. After witnessing so many evils, their horrors compounding inside me, it was oddly cleansing to imagine there was justice.

Some people, like Gram, showed a tolerable, probably unavoidable level of human failing and escaped my imaginary sentence. Dante had other, less well-known realms for those with mostly good hearts.

Unrepentant and habitual sinners received the punishment they'd earned in the *Inferno*. Mike was so lost that Dante's classifications couldn't even hold him. Not only did he deserve the outer ring of the seventh circle for violent sinners, swimming in boiling blood and fire, but also the ninth circle, frozen up to his head in ice, for betraying the special relationship he should have shared with his new stepsister. Rather than protecting his younger relative, he preyed on her instead.

In Dante's world, sinners got what they deserved, but in the here and now, deserving didn't seem to have much to do with it.

But I intended to change that a little. I drove to the office supply store and bought a mailing envelope, wrote a block letter address, a few words so they'd know what they had in the package, and dropped it in a mailbox on the street. When it reached the police's hands, the girl would be safe. I wore my gloves, in case they checked for prints. I was sure the police wouldn't believe how I knew so much about Mike, and of course, trespassing and videoing someone's house without their permission was against the law.

On the drive home, I realized I was smiling. I felt almost happy. Even proud of myself.

At least for this brief moment.

I shared a late dinner with Gram, enjoying our usual chatter across the kitchen table, except when she brought up Gabriel.

"He took Zoe." I pushed my meatloaf around my plate. "I'm not in the mood to talk about how wonderful he or his family is right now."

I don't think she understood why I was so upset—she thought things would work out somehow—but she'd written down his address while I washed dishes, mumbling something about how she was glad she'd told Gabriel about "that thing." She seemed lost in her thoughts, much too happy (relieved and overjoyed, really) that I was going over tomorrow. She insisted she'd call Bernard before I left and wake early to bake more cinnamon rolls for me to take. She'd already baked the biscuits, the pies, and more cookies—ginger this time—decreeing it was "fate," since now they wouldn't go to waste.

How much could these people eat?

Back in my room, I tucked the scrap of paper with Gabriel's address on it into one of my running shoes.

I loved the area he called home. It was nestled against the forest where I liked to run. You couldn't find a more beautiful landscape. Rushing water sweeping through a valley, dense woods, lush wildlife, a small mountain range sheltering it all. But on your way, you had to ignore the huge homes on the private land bordering the forest. You also had to ignore their residents, who thought they were better than everyone else.

Morning could not come soon enough. A book would pass the time and stave off sleep for a while. I dug for the key in my pocket, then stopped dead with it in my hand.

No.

The latches of my trunk were pried open, mangled. Someone had violated my things. Again. I threw open the lid and sorted through the clothes, the books, the dollar bills scattered around their envelopes. All shoved aside in a hurry. To get to something else. The object I valued most in this world—stolen.

My locket was gone.

I raced downstairs, catching Gram before she climbed into bed. "Gram, what was that thing, that thing you told Gabriel about?" I struggled for air.

"Oh." She pulled back her quilt. "We were just talking about when we met—you and me."

"In the hospital?" I racked my brain. "You didn't tell him about my locket, did you?"

"Well, yes." She hesitated. "I mean, I remember it laying there. Of course, I would've forgotten all about it, but—" She didn't have to say it. In the early days, when the nightmare came, I'd felt so lost when I woke, I'd ask her to get it out of the trunk for me. I used to hold it close, to fight the loneliness. She'd probably told him about that too. "The more he knows about you—us—that's good, right?" She bit her lip. "I mean, if he's our friend?" Her hands shook as she eased herself onto the bed.

I swallowed my anger. "It's okay, Gram." She hadn't done anything wrong. I couldn't blame her, or risk upsetting her. "Night. I'll be off early tomorrow."

She called out to me as I swung back the attic door and marched up the stairs. "Okay, just not too early. Love you, angel."

This was all my fault. I should've known Gabriel was no different than his cousin, and everyone else. He'd just found different ways to torment me for being the odd one out. Kill her with kindness. Figure out what makes her tick and rip it all away just to watch her writhe and wither. Clever bastard. My eyes stung, but I bit my cheek rather than shed tears over him. I'd make him pay. For hurting me without provocation. For making me believe, even for a second, that… we could… I ground my teeth.

I stumbled toward my trunk, leaning on its edge. I forced myself to straighten it up. I refolded the clothes, restacked the books, then stuffed the bills back in their envelopes, erasing the reminders of the pain. Finally, I pulled out *Crime and Punishment*. Reading about so-called "good men" performing bad deeds seemed especially relevant tonight.

Strange I hadn't seen anything dark inside Gabriel when we'd touched, but his actions spoke clearly enough. Odd he hadn't taken my locket the first time around, when he'd had the key, but then again, he hadn't known what to take yet, what was most special to me.

I bet Kaylee had given him the idea to take Zoe—or Cameron. They were probably all laughing together now.

My chest throbbed. I rubbed my palm over my heart, trying to soothe the pain with a gentle, healing touch, like Gram had taught me each night she soothed my nightmare pains.

I gripped the edge of my trunk and stood. I settled into bed, propping up the book, and took a deep breath.

There was no reason to feel this way. The loneliness would ease again. Zoe was coming home tomorrow. Whatever it took, I was bringing her home. Let Gabriel try and stop me.

8

THE KNIGHTS' HOME

A T MIDNIGHT, I DROPPED THE BOOK ON MY TRUNK, TIPTOED downstairs, and downed two mugs of coffee. I couldn't risk sleep. The nightmare was sure to return after taking a night off. I wouldn't be able to handle it in this state, feeling sick over the abuse of that girl, anxious over Zoe, agony about my locket. I lay awake in the dark.

Well before sunrise, my Burger Boys watch flashing 4:05, I dressed in a pair of full-length black leggings, a black tunic shirt with three-quarter-length sleeves, and this time, elbow-length gloves. Anyone who didn't know about me gave this outfit a strange look, but I didn't care. It covered me, and I liked looking retro. For the final touch, I pulled on one of my best investments: knee-high, black, faux-leather boots with spike heels. They'd proven an effective weapon, helping me fend off Cameron's friend that day in the parking lot. After Cameron watched me kick his friend in the gut, he didn't seem to want a bruise of his own. I hoped I would only need them for confidence today.

I tiptoed downstairs, but my effort was in vain. Gram yawned as she shuffled into the kitchen and filled a bag with two pies, two dozen ginger cookies, and a dozen biscuits. "I wanted to bake more." She glanced at her singing bird clock. 4:45. "And to call, let them know you're coming. Please don't knock until after sunrise." Her frown flipped as she tied a pink bow around the handles of the bag.

"Hopefully someone will be up." She presented the bag to me, and I grabbed the joined handles. "And try to get along with them." Her high-pitched plea followed me as I stormed out, the pink bow flopping at my side.

I barely noticed the world around me as I drove to the Knights' house, rehearsing what I would say and do. I parked Gram's car halfway up the Knights' expansive brick driveway, where it looped to an oversized garage in one direction and a massive front porch in the other. It seemed the safest spot for a quick getaway. I walked past a large fountain in the middle of a circular turnaround on the way to the porch, pausing to admire its sculpture of Poseidon spearing an octopus with his trident. Strange. A camera above the porch swiveled in its dome, tracking my movements. Strange and creepy. A dozen more hung under the eaves. I shivered. As if the cameras weren't intimidating enough, the house was impossibly huge. Three wide stories with an attic. A mix of rustic brick and natural stone, with two chimneys and rows of white-curtained windows flanked with black shutters. Even the window glass looked dense.

I hurried up the porch steps and to the front door, then dropped the bag of sweets at my feet, waiting for the sun to finish breaking over the horizon. Recalling the mangled latches of my trunk, Gabriel's violation of my trust, my stomach churned. "Please don't throw up," I mumbled, pressing a gloved hand to my belly.

Sunlight finally spilled over the forest. I took a deep breath and rapped the brass knocker, shaped like a roaring bear's head. An incredible work of craftsmanship, but disturbing when I thought back on Gabriel's vision. Maybe the Knights were hunters, and I was about to enter their armed fortress. Whatever the reason for the design, the knocker boomed against the thick door, echoing on the other side.

All I got was the cold welcome of a security camera, in the corner of the overhang. Lot of good all the cameras were doing if no one was watching them.

I reached for the bear's head again.

Footsteps approached behind the door, and my hand fell.

A heavy deadbolt shot back, the oak slab creaked open, and an exceedingly tall gentleman with a tired, haunted-looking face greeted me with a smile. A smile as gentle as Gram's, and as apparently sincere as I'd thought Gabriel's.

The resemblance to Gabriel was obvious in his strong build and wavy hair, the chocolate tone dusted with grey around the temples. "Cassandra." His smile widened. "Sorry to keep you waiting."

I stumbled back a step. "Um, that's okay?" I coughed out.

"Gabriel described you perfectly." He chuckled. "Come in, come in. Glad you came. I just wasn't expecting you so early."

Gram had called then? I reached for the bag and edged past him into a foyer. A life-sized sculpture of a man and woman drew my eye, lit beneath a twinkling chandelier. The smooth lines of the stone couple looked alive, his hands reaching for her as she twisted away, her forearms transforming into bark and tree branches. Just as I'd recognized Poseidon from Richard's old books on ancient Greece, I knew this was Apollo, chasing the river nymph he was cursed to love after being struck by Cupid's arrow. Were all rich people this eccentric in their décor?

"I'm Bernardus Knight. Please call me Bernard."

I tore my eyes from the stone. I'd expected Gabriel's dad to look much older, with everything Gram had said about him marrying and having kids late in life. But he looked not a day past fifty, if that, though he was clearly exhausted. Or maybe it was sadness that dimmed his blue eyes and deepened the small lines around his mouth.

He motioned to my gloves. "Looks like we can do a proper introduction this morning." He extended his hand. "How's the burn doing? The new one?" So Gabriel had told his dad all about me. Had he told him he'd stolen my dog and locket too? Probably not.

I ignored his question but shook his hand, trying to hide the fact that both of mine were shaking. Bernard squeezed my trembling fingers through the glove and released them with a sigh. I backed away quickly, moving farther into the foyer. He followed, moving to swing open a set of doors into a gloomy, unlit room. He looked back over his shoulder. I mustered as much confidence as I could and strode after him, my boots clicking on the hardwood floor.

He flipped a switch and two narrow beams pierced the center of two shuttered bay windows on a far wall. He folded the shutters, and the illumination spread to Monet-like landscapes on the other walls. Outside was a stone patio bordered by a flower garden overgrown with unkempt rose bushes. White River glittered beyond the broad lawn. The only imperfection was a patch of dirt near a lopsided crabapple tree missing its lower limbs. Mismatched, charred wood beams rose from the dirt like jagged teeth.

Was that where the fire had happened? And they'd left it like that? A reminder? An ache swelled in my throat. I turned away from the windows.

There were certainly no signs of damage in here. Elegant vases centered on white doilies sat on uniform, delicate tables, but none contained flowers. A sewing machine hid in the corner. The room's centerpiece was an arc of dainty sofas circling a low table bearing a tarnished silver tea set. The whole place was coated in dust, but not a footprint in sight.

"Please, sit," Bernard urged.

"I'm actually here to see Gabriel, but thank you." I remained standing.

"Hmm, well, we have a lot to talk about, but it can wait until Gabriel gets back. It's waited two years already." He sounded apologetic. Maybe he did know what Gabriel had done. But what did he mean by waited two years?

He motioned to the nearest couch. "Please, make yourself comfortable. This was Lillian's favorite room." Lillian. There was that name again, ringing some bell in my memory. I shook my head, refusing him again, and rubbed my arms. It was freezing in here. His shoulders fell. "Well, Gabriel will be home soon. I'll get refreshments."

"Here." I thrust Gram's bag at him, and the bow sagged. "These are for you. From Gram. I mean, Rose."

"How nice of her. I still need to thank her for sending Gabriel home with treats." He accepted the gift gingerly. "I don't see enough of her nowadays. That will have to change."

"Um, Gabriel brought a dog home. Zoe. Where is she?"

"She slipped into Cole's room after Gabriel left. I'll get her, and rouse Cole, Aaron, and Cameron too. You should meet the whole family—now that we've found you." Bernard's smile crinkled his crow's feet, but my blood chilled. Found me? Oblivious to my discomfort, he strode out with surprisingly lithe steps for such a large man.

I didn't want to meet the family. Didn't need a reunion with Cameron. I needed to grab Zoe, give Gabriel a swift kick in the pants, and get the hell out of this creepy place. I paced the crowded sitting room, planning my escape route when he brought Zoe to me, thinking I'd just have to apologize to Gram. I couldn't play nice if they swarmed me. I heard a door close and footsteps resound through the foyer. The footsteps quieted, and I peeked around the door. The broad, bare back of a very sweaty Gabriel raced up the stairs. My eyes latched onto his glistening, striking expanse of skin for several pounding heartbeats, then took in the rest of the picture. His toned calves flexing under his running shorts. His defined shoulder muscles bunching and releasing as his arms swung at his sides. No wonder Kaylee was after him. I ground my teeth, fighting back a confusing punch-drunk feeling.

"Hey!" I called.

He turned and immediately caught my gaze. The unmarked left side of his face lifted into a wide smile.

What was with all the smiles? This wasn't a friendly visit. If anyone should know that, it was Gabriel. "Cassie!" He walked back down, rubbing his palms on his shorts. He crossed his arms across the scars on his ribcage like he was trying to hide them again. His shoulders rounded, making his chest smaller. "You saved me a trip.

I was going to stop by your place if you didn't show up at the shel-ter this morning. We missed you yesterday."

"I couldn't make it." I softened my voice, keeping the anger out until Zoe was safe in my arms where she belonged. "I'll be there this morning. After we work things out here."

"Sure, just let me jump in the shower, get a shirt."

My eyes followed the beads of sweat down his chest. A shirt. Good idea. "Just the shirt." I needed to speed this visit up.

"Sure. Okay. Didn't realize you were in a rush."

He left and returned in a flash, a white t-shirt sporting a faded Meeker Bulldogs logo clinging to the sweat.

He motioned me back into his mother's sitting room. Neither of us sat. The moment stretched out awkwardly as some stupid part of me wondered if he had an explanation. Looking at him, and having him look back in his unabashed way, I couldn't fathom how my initial impression had been so wrong. Maybe he really could clear this up.

"I'd forgotten how nice this room is." He moved to one of the windows and turned back to me, tugging up his shirt collar. "Um, it's just so great to see you. But, ah, how's your wrist?"

I stayed by the door, wrapping my arms around my waist. "That's not why I'm here and you know it."

"Sorry. Didn't mean to be nosy. Just worried. I had my dad come to the shelter yesterday. We drove by your place too, but the VW was gone." Had Bernard been expecting me because of some-thing Gabriel said? It certainly seemed that way. He paced and swiped the back of his hand at new moisture glistening across his face. How could he still be sweating? My toes were icicles.

"I want Zoe back." I pressed my forearms into my belly to still them.

"What?" His shoulders stiffened. "Zoe? I didn't know she was yours—"

"Well, she is." I snapped my teeth shut so I wouldn't shout, then tried again. "I was saving up for the adoption fee. Dr. G promised her to me. She belongs with me." I needed her. "We belong together." My chin trembled.

"I had no idea," he said with an uneven frown.

Maybe I'd believe that, if my locket hadn't gone missing the same day.

"Maybe we can talk about this?" He offered his shy half-smile and motioned to the floral patterned loveseat across from him.

I held my strategic position inside the doorway. "There's nothing to talk about. She's coming with me." I squared my shoulders. "And you should let Dr. G keep the donation." And by donation, I meant bribe. Only Gram's words kept me from saying it out loud.

As if she heard me calling her, Zoe bounded into the room as fast as her three legs would allow and nearly knocked me over. I knelt and tried to hug her, but she squirmed, frantically trying to lick every inch of my face. I laughed, the sound dissolving into a soft gulp as the exhaustion and anxiety of last night melted away. I blinked back tears and dropped my head, hoping Gabriel couldn't see.

"Wow, I see you guys have a bond." Gabriel strode toward us, and I peeked up. His sneakers looked out of place on the fancy Persian rug in the middle of the room. They stopped at its edge, a few feet away.

Zoe finally calmed with a whimper and nestled into my chest. My arms tightened around her. A tear slipped out, and I buried my face in her fur.

Gabriel coughed. "I understand. She's pretty special. And she clearly adores you." He cleared his throat. "I also see you've gotten the wrong impression."

I cocked a brow at him, doubt curling my lip. A retort was on my tongue, but Bernard appeared in the doorway.

"Here you are." Bernard exchanged a serious look with his son. I stood and pressed my back against the wall so I wasn't caught between them.

"Did everything go well on the mountain?" Bernard asked.

"Yes. Finally got one of the others to wake up to give Grandpa a break," Gabriel said.

"And you left the elder a cell phone, gave him a refresher on how to use it?"

"Of course."

"Excellent. That will give us some time to chat. The boys will be down soon too. Maybe you should get cleaned up?"

"I was going to, but Cassie's in a hurry."

"Cassandra." Bernard turned, and I pressed Zoe's head into my leg. "I was hoping you could stay for breakfast." He gave another crinkly eyed smile.

Gabriel smiled again too. Clearly I wasn't getting my urgency across, but I wasn't sure how much Bernard knew and if I should bring up the subject of my stolen locket in front of him. I owed it to Gram to be on good behavior, but I was another cryptic conversation from booking it out of here. I'd had plenty experience feeling uncomfortable around people, but the feeling was usually mutual. I didn't know what to do with these hospitable smiles, and that uncertainty spiked my anxiety.

"I'll stay so long as everyone understands Zoe's leaving with me," I ventured with a shiver, testing the waters.

"Yes," Gabriel said and stepped forward to pat Zoe's head. She nuzzled his hand. "But maybe I can come visit you girls sometime? I'll miss her." He smiled at me in a tentative way, like I truly had the final say and he feared a rejection. But I couldn't trust my instincts with him.

What was he hiding behind that smile now?

I pinched my lips together until he stepped back, then addressed Bernard. "There's something else that Gabriel took from me. My locket. It's a red and orange stone—"

Gabriel's face darkened with a sharp inhale. Pleased I'd cracked his happy Boy Scout mask, I waited for Bernard, who looked pretty stormy himself.

"I know about the stone," Bernard said slowly. "I mean, I know about its existence. Gabriel told me. But he would never take it from you. Are you sure you didn't just misplace it?"

"I didn't misplace it." I held my chin high. "Gabriel was in my room one night. The next, it's gone."

"My dad's right." Gabriel looked shell-shocked. "I'd never take anything from you." He expanded his chest, and I straightened my spine, keeping my eyes level with his chin instead of his clinging t-shirt. "I can't believe it's gone," Gabriel continued. "And I can't believe you think I took it."

"Well, you were digging in my things, weren't you?" I hardened my voice.

"Um, yeah. I guess that does make me look totally suspicious." Gabriel dropped his head and rubbed at his neck. "But if you sit down, I'll try to explain." He caught my eye in that hypnotic, vibrating gaze of his. I couldn't move while he seemed to examine my soul. Whatever he found there made his mouth pop open in a dazed look of… surprise? His dad coughed.

"Please, sit." Gabriel cleared his throat, breaking the spell as he stumbled back into the middle of the room, bumping into the table, jostling the tea set. "I promise I didn't take anything. But you need to understand why I looked through your things."

I took a hesitant step, shaking off the fog, and tried to recover my anger. Gabriel was denying taking my locket to my face. He thought he could get away with it. But as much as I didn't want confirmation that I'd misplaced my rarely offered trust, it had to be him. No one else had even seen my locket since I moved in with Gram, and now suddenly he and his dad both knew about it?

"Please." Gabriel asked me to sit with a sweep of his hand.

Gram's voice echoed in my head, telling me not to close myself off all the time. She'd probably say that included giving people a chance to explain themselves. "This better be good."

Zoe followed my marching heels to a narrow, wing-backed chair hidden among the couches. I helped her up next to me and held her close, the two of us cocooned between two throw pillows hand-stitched with rose designs.

"I'm not sure where to begin." Gabriel looked at his dad. "How much can we say?"

Bernard gave him a pensive look, rubbing the short, grey-tinged scruff around his chin. "Hmmm."

Swift, booming footsteps charged the room, and two boys, almost mirror images of Gabriel except for his scars, strode in. It wasn't really accurate to call them boys, though, especially with their size. Big, but not quite as big as Gabriel. One looked about my age. He must be Aaron. One had a round, baby face. Cole.

Aaron had a sharp nose and intense look, like he was sizing me up and finding me lacking. He looked familiar, and after a moment, it clicked. I'd seen him at the diner before. I had a habit of looking in at the booths as I passed because that shady U.S. Forest Service guy frequented the place for his morning coffee.

Cole's doe eyes were a more startling blue than his brothers', reminding me of the husky pups. His smile, identical to his father's, broadened with each step he took toward me. Great, more grinning.

A moment later, Cameron slipped in silently, sporting his basketball jersey. He apparently lived in the thing, not wanting anyone to forget he'd taken the team to a state championship win as a sophomore. He turned his dark, closed-off eyes on me like a hunting predator.

Surrounded by Cameron and his hulking family, in their huge, isolated house, I tightened my arms around Zoe. Gabriel made introductions, though I didn't need them.

Bernard eyed my huddled position on the chair with a grave, almost remorseful expression. I was being weird in front of another friend of Gram's. I reluctantly unglued myself from Zoe and stood. Ignoring Cameron as he seemed to be ignoring me, I shook Aaron's hand and barely escaped a hug from Cole.

Zoe wagged her tail at Cole. He knelt down, scratched her

scruff, and fixed me with a broader smile. "There's no reason to be nervous. We're just so happy we finally found you!"

I swallowed hard, stiffening. There it was again. Found me? Cole jumped to his feet, and my heart galloped.

"Things are going to be so much better now. They already are. Dad hasn't opened this room in ages."

Cameron shot Cole a dark look. "And he shouldn't have." His hands tightened at his sides. "What if—?" He clamped his mouth shut and wandered to the window. I tensed harder, feeling flanked.

Cole ignored him and practically wagged his tail, whereas Aaron's brief smile had already faded. Even the homeschooled Knights seemed to know me. At least Aaron wasn't bothering to pretend he liked having me here.

I swiveled my head back to Cameron, but there was still plenty of distance between us. Surely he wouldn't touch me again in front of his uncle. Though he encouraged his buddies to torture me, he'd only touched me that once, in gym the first week of school. In his vision, he shouted at a woman with delicate features and honey-blond hair, calling her a horrible name, making her cry.

Bernard cleared his throat. "Shall we eat?"

I felt nauseous. Interrupted right when someone was finally going to give me some answers. Now we had to plod through more social niceties?

"Help me in the kitchen, Cole."

Bernard and Cole returned moments later with a gallon of milk, plastic cups, and a fancy platter piled high with ginger cookies, biscuits, and the last cinnamon roll they had left.

"We finished the maple oatmeal cookies," Cole piped up, then grumbled, "And Dad said we should save the pies." Bernard settled on a couch in the middle and passed around the platter. I mumbled a no thank you. But when Bernard and Gabriel kept trying to push a biscuit on me, I finally accepted a cup of milk from Cole, gulped it down, and broke off a bit of biscuit for Zoe. She gobbled it up and licked between my fingers.

Cole took a giant handful of cookies. Aaron seized the cinnamon roll and started poking Cole in the arm every few seconds. Didn't only little kids engage in that kind of horseplay? But then, how would I know? When the poking became a punch, Cole asked Bernard to be excused. Cameron, who hadn't eaten a thing, asked to be excused too and some of my unease lifted. Bernard nodded at them. Cameron raced off. Cole first bestowed another gentle smile on me. "I always loved having a sister," he whispered as he walked by.

My stomach flipped, and I hugged myself. What was all that about? I needed answers, or I was bolting, manners be damned. I crossed my arms, the frigid temperature more apparent than ever. "Somebody had better start talking."

Bernard, Aaron, and Gabriel turned toward me. I let out a loud breath, hoping it would settle my nerves, and tapped my boot not far from where Gabriel sat on the rug. He gulped down the last bite of his biscuit, coughed, and took a sip of milk. "So, um, back to what I was trying to say—about your stone. Your locket. You see, it's not really a locket. Not just a piece of jewelry. It's connected to something much larger." Gabriel eyed his dad, as though asking permission.

"Just spit it out." My arms tensed. Zoe jumped down to Gabriel and offered her belly. *Traitor.* "I don't see why this is so difficult." I patted my knee, trying to entice her back. Gabriel smiled crookedly and scratched her chest. Her eyes fluttered shut, and within seconds she was out with a snore. "I mean, you went through my things, which was bad enough, then my locket went missing the next day. I just want it back." I sighed. What else could I say to get him to fess up, so I could finally get out of here? "That necklace is the only thing I have from my old life—the life I don't remember. I know you know that. Gram told you."

"No, she didn't mention that part, but I'm sorry. I can't tell you how sorry I am for what you've gone through. When we could've been there, could've helped. But this is about more than a missing necklace." Gabriel shifted on the rug.

"Gabriel," barked Bernard, holding up a palm to silence his son.

I watched in disbelief as Bernard stood and walked to the corner table that housed the sewing machine, flicking on a lamp as he went, though it was plenty bright in here. He pulled a lighter from his pocket and lit a singular scented candle beside the machine, then stared at the dancing flame for several long seconds. Gabriel and Aaron watched it too, unblinking.

Bernard turned, his eyes darting over the walls and ceiling, his jaw severe. When he saw my expression, he softened. "I am sorry, but you see, even with certain… precautions, we can't risk going into the details here."

In their own house? What were these people into?

"But you're special. Really, truly special," he continued, and my heart skipped a beat, thinking of cults and horror movies. "And we think you were drawn here—by your stone, your locket—to what we're protecting. So you see, we can help you, and well, you can help us."

Help *them*?

"What are you talking about?" I leapt to my feet.

"Please." Bernard waved for me to sit. I stayed up, my heel tapping the rug. Zoe's nose twitched, but her eyes stayed shut.

Bernard's gaze darted to Gabriel, Aaron, the candle, then back to me. "I know this must be hard for you, especially since whatever was explained to you before is gone. I once knew someone who could help with things like that—drawing out good memories, making bad ones go away—and might've been able to help you with your memory loss. But he passed away long ago." Bernard's crow's feet deepened with fatigue, all his age lines drawing down, finally making him look like he really could have introduced Gram and Richard all those years ago. "So we're it," he concluded. "We're the closest thing you have to family right now." Family? "I know you want me to just tell you everything, but to do so would be to put you at risk. We have only one fail-safe way to ensure we're not overheard, and your connection to the—" Bernard's head jerked toward the candle. When I looked, the flame danced upright as before, but he narrowed his eyes at it and grew tight-lipped. "We'll take you someplace safe, tell you more. Then you'll see you can trust us. You have to trust us."

Acid bubbled up my throat. I swallowed it and unleashed on him, far beyond caring if I was rude at this point. "Listen, I don't know what you're talking about, but you're not my family, and I don't trust you as far as I can throw you. Unless you explain yourself, I'm done."

"Maybe," he said softly, "you need someone to trust."

"You and your family haven't earned it. The way you're talking, I'm sure Gabriel has my locket, and I want it back, now. It's sentimental, not magical"—I scoffed the word—"and you have no right to it."

"Cassie, I don't—"

I cut off Gabriel's denial with a seething glare.

Bernard shifted on the couch. "Try thinking about it this way." He eyed the corners again. "Your past is a complete mystery, which is unusual. Isn't it possible the truth might be unusual too, and not come out all at once, or be entirely known to those trying to help you find it?" More weird hints and beating around the bush. Infuriating. "Maybe even that some caution and discretion is needed." Was that an excuse? Or a threat?

He stood and moved closer to me.

I slipped around my chair to put space, and something solid, between us.

"I know, we're going about this the wrong way."

"You can say that again." I hurried to Zoe and petted her side, being careful not to get close to Gabriel. She woke. "Come on, Zoe. We're leaving." I stood, and she jumped awkwardly to her feet. She looked at me, then to Gabriel. Finally, she licked Gabriel on his scarred cheek and turned to me.

Gabriel pushed himself off the rug. "Cassie. At least know you need to be on your guard. Always. Especially if someone you don't know tries to get close to you."

"You mean, like you?" I tried to laugh but choked on the harsh sound. No one but stupid kids had bothered me before he'd shown up. Zoe hop-walked out of the room at her own speed. I kept pace with her, although I wanted to race out.

Bernard followed us. "We'll continue this next time. Someplace… safer. Until then, Gabriel and Aaron will watch out for you."

I ignored him. I'd be watching out for them. I fled as fast as Zoe would allow. Gabriel rushed around us, darting up the stairs.

"Thank Rose for me," Bernard called as I neared the door. "Tell her I'll be visiting soon." I reached for the knob. "Cassandra!" he exclaimed.

I turned.

His smile was gone. "Before you go, you need to know how sorry I am for not finding you sooner." Bernard's weathered features looked even more haunted than before. "If only I hadn't had to shut myself away recently, I might've realized it. You must've felt completely alone. You're not alone. Not anymore—"

"Stop." The word echoed around the foyer. Bernard and Aaron's eyes widened. Zoe looked up with a whimper. "Just stop. I don't need you. Any of you. Ask around town. I take care of myself."

"But there aren't many of us left. We need to stick together," Bernard said, coming to stand next me.

"Aren't many of us left? What does that even mean?!"

Gabriel rushed down with a small box as Bernard cringed against my outburst. A nervous glance passed between him and his father. Aaron too. A muscle ticked at the side of Bernard's face.

I let out a short, hard laugh. "When you're ready to tell me what's really going on, you know where to find me." I jerked the door open, relishing the warmth of the late morning sun. I tacked on a "Thanks for breakfast" for Gram's sake, then nodded a goodbye to Aaron, who'd walked up behind his father. He didn't move a muscle.

I flew across the porch, Zoe struggling to keep at my heels. We left the Knights, and probably my locket, behind.

9

CONNECTIONS

ETWEEN MY CLICKING FOOTFALLS ON THE DRIVEWAY, I heard the soft thuds of Gabriel's tennis shoes as I rounded the fountain. When Zoe and I reached Gram's car, I turned on my heel. "I don't know what's going on." I widened my stance like I was preparing for a fight. "But either explain yourself or keep your distance. I'm glad you understand about Zoe, but I don't like you."

Gabriel flinched.

A surprising flash of remorse tightened my chest. "I don't like what's going on with you," I clarified. "How you're being."

His scar tissue relaxed an inch, but he tightened his grip on the box. "I'm sorry I searched your room. It was wrong."

"Of course it was."

"It's just that you're special like us, and when I felt…" I dodged his intense gaze. "…and realized who you might be…" He inhaled sharply through his nose. "I had to know more. And the stone seems to prove you're here for us. That you finally found us." Were the Knights followers of some bizarre religion? They all seemed to recite the same lines. Gabriel's stare sent an uncomfortable tingle down my spine. I twisted away to unlock the car, my cold hand fumbling to get the key in the lock.

"You know," he said, behind me, "my dad's trying to help. So am I. Once you get to know us, we can explain, in a place where we can… um… it'll all work out."

"Hmph." I finally got the key in and turned back to him. "Seriously—and I want a straight answer this time—why do you think your father can help me?"

"Well, my dad's been around awhile, known several different people like us, seen several types, which is rare. What I'm trying to say is, while he doesn't know your family, anything about them, he knows about different kinds of people. So, if anyone can help, it's him." Gabriel nodded, but sounded far from confident. His chin dropped. "You must think we're nuts."

"Um, yeah. Types!?" I had often wondered what I'd endure to cure myself of this touch affliction, but ritualistic healing by nut jobs wasn't on my list of maybes. "I don't need your father talking like he has any responsibility for me. He doesn't."

"He just talks that way because he cares." Gabriel shifted the box to one arm. "We all do." He reached out slowly, tentatively, like he had at the cemetery, toward my covered shoulder.

"Don't you dare touch me." I instinctively raised my splayed hands in front of my chest. "There is nothing between you and me. We're not friends."

Gabriel's hand fell and the scarred side of his face quivered.

My heart clenched. My body swayed forward, as if wanting to ease his pain.

He leaned in too. "Don't you feel the connection? This invisible pull between you and me?"

I shook my head. Although I had felt something. I *did* feel something.

His eyes widened. "It's there for me." He stared right into me. "It's everything about you. I mean, of course part of it's because you're like me. But it's so much more than that." He sucked in a breath. "It's you. How wonderful you are. It's how you make me feel."

"Wonderful?" Everyone in this family spoke so intimately yet so obliquely. Maddening, yet I let his penetrating gaze hold me.

"You, um—you don't feel it?"

Was this a trick too?

I'd felt something for him, undeniably, but he'd ruined it. I could never trust him again.

Gabriel's dejected expression lifted into eager hopefulness as I pondered, then slowly clouded again when I let the silence drag too long.

My lips parted.

Zoe whimpered.

To see his hope dashed sparked empathy, and my first instinct was to tell the truth, say yes. The promise of his lopsided smile was a further temptation. But I was stronger than that; I could overcome my feelings, and I owed him nothing. I pressed my lips into a firm line. I wouldn't let his distress—real or fake—pain me. I had enough pain in my life. "I don't know what's left to say."

The box slipped in Gabriel's grip.

"I'm going home," I said as he fumbled with it.

Zoe whimpered louder.

I gave her a pat. "It'll be okay." I settled her into the back seat.

I got in the front, and Gabriel passed the box through the open window. "Please, take this. For Zoe and you."

I placed it on the passenger's seat. It contained a few cans of dog food, Zoe's harness and leash, and a small, damaged, pink-covered notebook.

"That was my sister's." He pointed to what was left of the pink cover. "It might help explain things. For now, until we can do better. I'm sorry again, Cassie."

"Thanks," I acknowledged and pulled away. I circled around the drive and didn't look in the rearview mirror until I reached the road. Gabriel remained there, watching, even as I turned the VW toward home and said goodbye to one of the stranger mornings of my short life—and that was saying something.

Squeak. Squeak. Zoe chomped on a plastic hedgehog, then dropped it suddenly like she'd had a brilliant idea, spun around on the living room rug, and pounced on a stuffed squirrel.

"Zoe-bug." I laughed. "They're yours. You don't have to play with them all at once!"

I'd found the hedgehog under the mysterious, pink notebook and bought the squirrel on the way home. She held both toys—one in her mouth, one in her paws—her tail wagging wildly. She finally scrambled to her feet and sniffed her way to the kitchen to say hello to Gram again. Within moments, she had sprawled out on the kitchen floor, tuckered out from her day of excitement and lots of love from me and Gram, and immediately began to snore.

Bedtime it was, then. I helped Zoe navigate the stairs, showed her the water dish by my trunk, and taught her how to use the wooden ramp at the end of my bed. Then I held her close by my pillow, tucking my comforter around her, making sure she was happily (and soundly) asleep, before slipping out the low window, down the blue spruce, to the VW. I headed to the one place I could find peace from the thoughts casting a shadow over what should have been the best of days.

To the one place I could run for miles, with no one to bother me: my favorite trail by White River.

My connection to the earth was the primary sense guiding me as my feet pounded the soft pine bed of the forest floor. The hazy night dispersed the moonlight, so only the largest trees on the edge of the trail were visible. I left my running light off and dangling from my neck. I didn't want to be walled in by the lamp's hollow glow. Tonight, I needed the comfort of losing myself in the familiar, dense landscape.

I knew perfectly well running alone at night wasn't safe, but sometimes I needed it. I limited my nocturnal excursions to days I knew I couldn't fight sleep, when my brain and body demanded exhaustion in order to shut off. Only exhaustion promised a bit more sleep before the nightmare claimed me.

Besides, if there was ever a night when I needed to be alone with my thoughts, it was tonight. I couldn't stop thinking about him. Gabriel, I forced myself to say his name in my head. I replayed his voice, working to determine if his apologies and his declarations of a connection between us were genuine.

I'd even opened the pink notebook the moment I got home, hoping it would answer questions and get him out of my mind. It just raised more questions. And it would take time to sift through. To my disbelief, he'd given me his sister's diary, filled with the ramblings of a young girl. Half the pages were blackened, and I feared she was the child in the fire. What I could tell so far was that she'd been scared. And very lonely. I would have to spend more time piecing together exactly why. She wrote constantly of "shadows," watching for them every day, hiding. But even now, surrounded by real shadows on all sides, I couldn't yet figure what these monsters really represented or where the fear of them came from.

What had happened to her? Why had no one mentioned her before?

And did her family have any idea how frightened she'd been?

I didn't want Gram to find the burned diary and worry, so I'd left it in my trunk.

With every stride, with every brush of cool night air against my arms, I let the significance of what Gabriel said earlier in the day wash over me. But none of it came together to form a logical puzzle. Visions of bears and giants; Gabriel's scars; snooping; stealing lockets and misappropriating three-legged dogs; an "elder"; mysterious goings-on up in the mountains; living in a high-security art museum kept at glacial temperatures; paranoia somehow tied to candles; smiling too much; Gabriel always trying to catch my eye; scarfing down piles of food; homeschooling three active boys; and a recluse who doesn't age for a father—those things I could deal with, and some I could even understand.

I stumbled over a mound of dirt and forced myself to pause by a rotting tree stump. A fern rippled in the breeze, and the moonlight cast the dancing shadows of its leaves over my arms. *Shadows.* Some small woodland creature snapped a twig, and I almost came out of my skin. That diary had given me the heebie jeebies. I shook it off, then refocused on my running and my thoughts.

The problem was, what Gabriel said this morning added two new elements of craziness. Frightening elements, because they hit too close to home. They'd kill any sliver of hope left inside me, if I somehow allowed myself to believe in Gabriel and it turned out it was all a lie.

First, Gabriel's claim that he and I shared some sort of connection called to the crushing loneliness I barely kept at bay, appealing to the part of me that desperately craved companionship.

Second, Gabriel and Bernard's hints that the Knights were also abnormal in some way beckoned to my most fervent, hidden desire that maybe there was someone else out there like me. Someone who could help me understand my plight. Someone who could make me understand my suffering, all the darkness I saw in people.

Someone who might know who I am or why I was this way.

That was a dangerous hope I couldn't allow Gabriel to nourish. I'd learned the hard way I was meant to be alone forever. I quickened my pace to my body's limit, making my own steady thunder with my feet, sending a charge through my erect spine. My heart pounded wildly. I had to shut Gabriel out. The Knights wanted something from me. "We can help you, and you can help us," Bernard had said.

Their bright smiles and promises of family masked an agenda.

The frantic thump of my pumping blood was deafening. An owl hooted nearby but I barely heard it. The trail cut in toward the river, not far from where my life began. The roar of currents hitting rocky banks swelled in my ears, raging along with my thunderous emotions.

I felt vulnerable, more alone than ever. Gram wasn't in a position to look out for me. I was supposed to look out for her, even if that meant leaving should my burns get worse or should my possibly shady past come to haunt me.

I reached a clearing along the path. The moon's dispersed reflection shimmered on the water. I stopped, catching my breath and trying to soak up a bit of the river's serenity. The water was content to have no purpose, not caring where it went.

I allowed the crisp air to settle in my chest and soothe all the rage I carried there, spawned from my fated role of unwilling witness, forced to face the sins of the world.

I longed for ignorance, longed for real contact free of visions and hellish rivers of fire flowing beneath my skin. If I had those things, I could care for someone. I wouldn't have to live the rest of my life alone.

Across the river, a bright flash of light jarred me. Electric. A beacon in the night sky. The light fizzled, then reappeared, flashing like a tiny lightning bolt zigzagging between trees. Getting closer to the water. Disappearing again.

My heart hammered.

Was I going crazy? As I'd feared? Or was someone—or something—following me?

I looked up and down the far riverbank, but the light was gone. Several minutes passed as I searched for traces of the light and its source. Was there any reasonable explanation for it? I listened for any sound over the rushing current. Nothing.

I turned away, then carefully looked back over my shoulder through loose curls escaping my ponytail. The lightning bolt reappeared, diving into the river. It glowed like a flare stick in the water, moving with purpose, coming right for me.

I took off at a dead run, racing for Gram's VW at the trailhead.

Faster. Faster. Not fast enough. I was flying down the path, exerting my body beyond its limits. A natural high lifted me, adrenaline pushing my pace. I slowed an instant, glancing back.

A light flashed between two trees. On my side of the river. *Chasing me!?*

Run. Run. After about a mile—just minutes later at my speed—I made out a large shape lumbering on the trail ahead. I skidded to a stop. The figure was wide, too large for a mountain lion. A bear? I blinked, praying it was a mirage.

The figure seemed to diminish in width as it drew nearer, but at the same time grew impossibly taller. More imposing. I tried to scream, but my throat was closed. I tried again. An embarrassing croak escaped.

I prepared to run back toward the water. Whatever the light was, I doubted it would eat me.

"Cassie," a deep voice called out from ahead of me. "Sorry I startled you."

Oh God. That voice had been haunting me all day. I must be hallucinating from exhaustion. The darkened shape I first saw had been too wide, too stocky, to be Gabriel. Yet, his solid form materialized out of the darkness. With each stride he took, a bit of my fear fell away. Whatever his issues, Gabriel wasn't Cameron. So long as I kept him out of my head, or my heart, he wouldn't hurt me.

He wore only a pair of running shorts and for once didn't seem to care that all his scars were showing. He stepped within inches of me, his chest more impressive than ever, and I could finally make out his crooked mouth, set in a grim line.

"This is ridiculous." I took a step back, glancing over my shoulder, but there was no light. "What are you doing here?"

"What am I doing here?" He swallowed up the space I'd gained by leaning toward me, locking his gaze on mine. "What are you doing here? Are you crazy? You don't even have a light!"

"You don't even have any shoes." I pointed at his bare feet.

"I do. I just slipped them off a bit ago." He shrugged awkwardly.

"You're the crazy one." I huffed. "And I do have a light." I motioned to the light below my neck. "I just didn't turn it on."

"You could hurt yourself."

"So could you." I spoke my next thoughts in a jumbled rush.

"Was that you before? With a flashlight in the trees on the other side of the river? How did you get over here so fast?"

"What are you talking about?"

"I thought I saw something, on the other side of the water. So you're saying it wasn't you?"

"We've been on the same trail. I saw you coming, going crazy fast." Gabriel searched my eyes, and his jaw tightened. "You saw someone on the other side?"

"No. Just a light." I shivered and glanced back again. He looked over me, down the trail, and rubbed the back of his neck. I knew I was making no sense, but he seemed to take my fear seriously.

He pursed his lips. "I'll have Aaron and Cole look for whatever it was. I'll follow you back to your car."

"Okay. Thanks," I said sincerely, even though it was probably my weary eyes playing tricks. "Now, care to tell me why you're here?"

"I've been following you, since you slipped out on Rose." His tone was matter of fact. Not even a hint of embarrassment.

"Following me all night? You've got to be kidding. Stalking's a crime, you know." My voice rose with agitation, and I searched the darkness one final time for the light. Maybe I really was going crazy.

"I didn't mean to scare you, but it's not safe here anymore. I would have asked to run with you, but you seemed to want to be alone. That last sprint was too much, though." His shoulders bunched up. "You'll hurt yourself."

"Don't worry. I run this trail all the time. And I don't need a bodyguard." I settled into a wider stance, placing my hands on my hips, like Kaylee might do, hoping I looked and sounded more confident than I felt.

"I do have to worry. And I care too much to stop worrying, even if I tried."

"You care?" My hands fell to my sides, and I couldn't summon the biting sarcasm I'd intended. The word was too pleasant on my tongue.

"I do. I do care. Like I said earlier. And I thought you did too after the other day." His voice lowered, turning soft. Hesitant. "I know I screwed up."

"Stop. You can't like me! Leave me be."

"I can't. Not completely." He sounded sad, and took a step back, snapping a twig. "If anything happened to you." He clutched an arm around his scarred ribs. "My family and I have made such a mess of things, but we'll explain. And then"—he gulped—"then maybe you'll have to leave," he said so softly I wasn't sure I caught the words. "Once you know how to keep yourself safe. But not yet."

"Whatever your family is mixed up in, it doesn't involve me. I'll be fine, and I can defend myself. Just get out of my head," I pleaded in a whisper, suddenly feeling tired and lightheaded, ready for this day to be over. "You have to get out of my head," I repeated to myself as I stepped around him on the path. My legs felt stiff, but I forced them into a jog back toward Gram's car. I felt so out of sorts, I turned on my light, to keep from tripping and falling right in front of him.

"You're going to have to admit you're special," Gabriel called after me, his voice rising with my strides.

I slowed and glanced behind me. My light flashed across his bare chest, and I remembered its warmth, how it felt to be in his arms. He wiped sweat off his collarbone. I inhaled sharply. "Wow."

He must have heard. "And you're going to have to admit you like me."

I laughed and, smiling despite myself, quickened my pace, ignoring my protesting limbs. I finally gained momentum and raced into the night, sensing Gabriel's presence behind me the whole way. At the last mile marker, my light flashed on a rock, a white t-shirt strewn across it, a faded Meeker Bulldogs logo imprinted in the corner. I sprinted the last mile. My legs stretched and churned, flying over dirt and gravel. I leapt over a boulder. Not sure what I was running to, I ran from Gabriel and everything I felt about him.

10

ATTRACTION

I SPLAYED OUT ON MY BED LIKE A BLOB OF DROPPED JELL-O AND counted backwards from one hundred. 99…98…97… I needed sleep after the sprint, no sleep last night, and no answers today. 3…2…1.

I stared at the ceiling and started over at 100. Sleep wouldn't come. Gabriel had made himself at home in my mind. The thought of his face made my heart somersault despite everything. The lure of someone interested in me proved greater than I could have imagined.

"Ugh." I curled myself into a tight ball around a sleeping Zoe.

Was the bright light a new symptom of my madness? Maybe. Maybe not… Unease prickled down my spine, every nerve ending firing. I jumped to the floor, and my legs wobbled. I steadied myself on the corner bedpost, raced downstairs to the door, and shot the deadbolt into place. I hurried to the living room, reached around the couch, and yanked the curtains shut. But I'd never seen the light around the cottage. The closest it'd come was the cemetery, then Mike's house. Too close for peace of mind. I called Burger Boys, then Dr. G's office, leaving messages saying I wouldn't be in. I needed to figure things out. I'd start with Gabriel and what he and his family wanted from me. I pulled his sister's diary from my trunk and crawled back into bed. Zoe stirred, snuggling into me. She cracked open a sleepy, questioning eye as I flipped through the blackened pages.

"Aaron wanted to go fishing. But I saw dark clouds above the mountain. I didn't think it was safe." Gabriel's sister had been traumatized, searching for danger in any sliver of darkness. She feared shadows lurked there, like boogeymen lying in wait. She fretted over what they'd do if they found her, what might happen to her mom. She never wanted to leave the house. I found bits of hope mixed in with her fears, tied to some sort of hero figure she'd conjured. "Someday a girl will come and save us." And later, "Everything will be okay when she comes. It has to be." She'd also idolized her oldest brother, thought Aaron was super cool, and that both Aaron and Cole were the best playmates in the world. Her only playmates, apparently, reading how much she longed to meet other kids. Cameron popped up once. Just something about how much time he spent with her mom. She seemed a bit jealous. Her mom taught her to sew. Her dad taught her how to build wooden derby cars. Someone called "CJ" visited, bringing books. She wrote irregularly, and only a few of the late entries were dated—the last over two years ago. "There's been a big change. Dad will figure it out. I told him about the light I saw floating outside my window, and the one that chased me into the house. But it didn't make scary shapes like the shadows. Maybe it's not bad. Please don't let it be bad." My heart plummeted into my stomach, and I closed the damaged cover. An aura of tragedy surrounded the Knights, and misery loved company. Maybe there really was a connection between me and the Knights. What if Gabriel's sister was like me? But she never mentioned burns or visions, just that light, chasing her. My head pounded.

Coffee. I needed coffee.

I downed the pot and rinsed my mug, not sure how long I stood there, water trickling down the drain. Gram shuffled into the kitchen. She bent to pet Zoe as I shut off the water and set my mug on the drying rack. "Don't skip breakfast, angel. Take a hardboiled egg and some berries with you."

I wiped my hands on a dish rag. "No need. I'm taking the day off."

Her thin lips pulled into a huge smile. She hummed her favorite song, *Singing in the Rain*, as she peered into the fridge. "Hmm." She pulled out eggs and a pot of homemade jam.

I slipped Zoe's harness over her head and started down the driveway, fighting paranoia, imagining a flash in every sunbeam. As we ambled onto the asphalt, the backend of a sparkling black SUV turned the corner. Gabriel's or a coincidence? A muddied pickup I didn't recognize revved up on the next street.

We meandered around the block. A neighbor shuffled outside in his slippers to get the paper. A rabbit darted across a lawn. My unease ebbed.

Back home, Gram poured Earl Grey into two porcelain teacups from her mom's set, the one she normally used for special occasions. I carried the delicate cups one at a time to the table where a plate of crumpets and the jam waited. As I set her cup down, Gram stared at my healed hand with a pensive look. Her brow stayed wrinkled as she spent the rest of the morning baking special dog cookies in the shapes of bones and feeding them to Zoe as soon as they cooled. What could I do to ease Gram's worry?

I was no good at baking. When Gram was recuperating from that incident at Betty's, I'd mixed up a batch of molasses cookies for her and burnt them to a crisp—so it seemed all I could do was wash dishes. I rubbed at a doughy spot, the water slippery on my fingertips, its warmth seeping into my hands, reminding me of being near Gabriel. Gabriel… so concerned about me last night. Apparently so genuine. His worry made a little more sense now, but fearing shadows and flashing lights was still crazy talk to a normal person. Besides, his concern was likely for his family. I couldn't help them out with their mystery task if I was injured in a running accident. Zoe sat on the rag rug by the stove, her tail thumping, waiting for the next batch to cool, and I did more dishes and thought of Gabriel's eyes. Gorgeous. Piercing. Get over them.

That night, Gram asked if I would read *Pride and Prejudice* again. I dug it out from under the couch. Zoe settled into her bed on the living room floor, and I flipped through the pages and thought of Gabriel's words. His words about *us*. But I couldn't even touch him. His pretty speech about a connection wasn't real.

The escalating pain I felt every time I touched someone, or had the nightmare, was real. My love for Zoe, whose warm licks staved off my looming insanity, was real. And my very real locket was still missing, likely by Gabriel's hand.

After another nightmare, I lay awake for hours and obsessed about Gabriel. Mid-morning, I finally left Gram and Zoe together and rode my bike to the library, sat at my favorite computer in a corner near the window, and looked up articles on the house fire Cameron's dad had been blamed for.

Gabriel's mom and sister had died in a gasoline-soaked storage shed full of lawn equipment. No one understood how they had gotten trapped inside. The news articles praised Gabriel as a hero. He'd broken through a window trying to save them, earning his scars. He and his father put out the flames with their sprinkler system before the fire trucks arrived. Apparently, the only reason Cameron's father had been blamed for arson was his sudden disappearance that day. More strange and haunting events surrounding the Knights. It didn't seem the news, the police, or anyone understood the full story.

I exited the library to the beep of a garbage truck backing up, forks ready to lift a dumpster across the street. I hopped on my bike, swerved around the truck, and pedaled toward the shelter. As I neared the end of the street, the truck honked. I glanced over my shoulder and a black SUV darted out from behind the dumpster. The SUV slowed and drove behind me at a distance. When I got to the shelter parking lot and dropped to my knees to chain up my bike, the SUV pulled into one of the spaces for volunteers.

Gabriel stepped out, wearing a teal polo and dark, crisp-looking jeans. I stood, my hand shaking on my bike seat. "You were following me. Again."

Instead of denying the obvious, he nervously rubbed the scar on his neck.

"Fine. I know you think you need to." I pulled at a loose thread on my seat and stuffed my other fidgety hand into my pocket. "But I told you, keep your distance. Unless you have my locket or answers, stay away from me—on the other side of the shelter with Kaylee and the cats." My voice was cold and strained from a throbbing exhaustion headache.

He gave a stiff nod, and I raced inside to feed the dogs. As I was setting down the last bowl, Gabriel walked toward the storage room, watching me intently. His eyes found me again as he came back with a bag of litter and returned to the cats.

From Kaylee's occasional high-pitched squawking down the hall, they must have been having a good time. Not long after, they walked to the storage room together. She glanced uneasily at his scars, but he ignored her. As I cuddled B.G. against my chest, Gabriel again paused outside the glass to catch my eyes. Kaylee grimaced at his marred profile, her upper lip curling with distaste.

Despite his scars (which weren't that bad, really, and nothing worthy of disgust), she was clearly obsessed with him.

I tightened my hold on B.G. and mouthed "cats" to Gabriel. He winced, grabbed Kaylee's hand, and hurried her down the hall.

As they returned to the cats, I overheard Kaylee whining about wanting him to drive her to and from the shelter the next day. Despite his initial protest, he must've agreed because the next morning a big fancy truck rumbled to a stop in front of Gram's cottage. Aaron's truck. He followed me to the shelter much more closely and obviously than Gabriel had. He met up with Gabriel and Kaylee in the lobby, giving Kaylee a huge grin and offering to help her carry a bag of cat toys her dad had donated.

Aaron and Gabriel disappeared with Kaylee down the hall, walking close enough to brush arms. Casual touch without a second thought. My stomach twisted, and I fled to the dogs. I cuddled B.B. and B.G., trying to ignore the bursts of echoing laughter from the cat kennels. Gabriel trekked up and down the hall all day. I caught him staring at me as I calmed a yippy poodle, gave an old dachshund its meds, and coaxed a timid Pitbull—a fight ring survivor—into a hug with a treat. Each time, I struggled to read his lopsided face because he immediately looked away.

Minutes before noon, I watered the lawn in the play yard, then hosed off the fire hydrant, eager to be off before adoption hours. Leather loafers sank into the yellow grass next to me. "Can I at least ask how you and Zoe are doing?" Gabriel's voice rose over the spray of the water.

My eyes ran up his dark jeans, his expensive coral polo, but avoided his face as I said, "You drop into my life, raising questions but no answers, rummage through my things, then want to know how I'm doing? Shouldn't you already know? You and your brother are stalking me."

He coughed. "I can't apologize enough for searching through your things." He chewed on his bottom lip. "It wasn't just wrong. I should've been more upfront with you. More honest from the beginning."

"Exactly." I turned off the spray.

"Can you forgive me?"

"I—I'm not sure." I tightened my grip on the handle. "Until you can explain more, please just leave me alone."

His mouth fell open. "Cassie, we have to talk." He motioned between us. "I can't leave things like this." He took a step forward.

I flinched.

He stumbled back, withdrawing as if I'd kicked him with one of my spike-heeled boots. I almost apologized as he wandered off with a mumbled goodbye. Did I care? I shouldn't.

But it was impossible to cast him out of my head when he appeared everywhere. First at Burger Boys that afternoon, then at the library after dinner. When I saw his car lurking in the lot, I cupped my hands around my mouth and shouted, "Exactly what kind of trouble do you think I'm going to get into here, huh?" I got no response and rolled my eyes, but as I slid a book into the return slot outside, I heard his door open. I whirled, ready to tell him to scram, but he wasn't looking at me. He stared over my head, at the streetlamp, and he seemed… scared. His face was pale, and his pulse pounded visibly in his throat. I kinked my neck trying to find whatever he was ogling, but all I saw was a moth circling the light.

"What's the—"

"I-it's not safe out here at night."

I snorted. "This isn't downtown Denver. I'm fine."

His eyes whizzed around me, darting between the lamp and the street, and then his shoulders relaxed a fraction. "Just be careful. Go straight home."

My jaw hardened. If he hadn't said it like that, like a command, I might have skipped my run, but I wasn't going to let him boss me around. He'd seemed genuinely freaked out, but there was absolutely no one else around. Maybe this was some kind of game to make me trust him again? He followed me to the trailhead for my second-favorite running route (far from the river) and then home after. It was starting to really piss me off. I didn't need his concern, real or fake. I wasn't a kid. I wasn't his sister.

The next day, I unchained my bike at the shelter, ready to leave, and he appeared again. He was practically hyperventilating. "I have to try one more time. Please, tell me how you're doing. Have you… No one's bothered you? Nothing weird happening?"

When I only stared back, thinking, *You're the only new weird thing in my life,* he said, "How's that last pitbull, from the fight ring?"

I swallowed. Dogs were an easy subject, and I rarely got to indulge in small talk. "He's getting used to being petted, but having his Golden buddy adopted before him set him back a little. He gets nervous without him."

Gabriel nodded. "You'll save him, make him adoptable like the others. You really care, and they can sense it. That black and white one, Bosco, is still in love with you, even with his new family around. He practically knocks down his fence when you visit."

I scowled. "How do you know about Bosco? He was adopted while you were gone."

"I…" He cringed and made a pained noise in the back of his throat.

I'd thought I knew each time he trailed me, making it obvious, like a bodyguard following at a respectful distance, but apparently, he was sneaky when he wanted to be. I checked on Bosco once a week, peeking into his new backyard to make sure he still looked happy and healthy. I felt particularly attached, since I'd been the one to report his original owner for dog fighting—a fact I'd learned through an unpleasant encounter at the local bike shop.

"You need to cut it out. You're the only thing bothering me lately."

"Cassie, I didn't… It's hard to explain."

"Yeah, so you and your dad keep saying."

"Let me make this right." He trapped my eyes, locking my feet in place.

I stared into his gorgeous, piercing blue irises. My heart clenched. I barely managed a reply. "I'm not sure what there is to make right." There could be nothing between us, nothing to repair. I couldn't bear seeing or hearing his response, didn't have time to ponder his intent. I hopped on my seat and sped off.

At least I escaped any physical contact that week, even Grabby-hands. He cornered me as I threw trash bags into the dumpster outside Burger Boys. Officer Fry, who'd been a regular customer of Gram's at the bakery in his youth, happened to be sauntering back to his patrol car with his takeout bag. He saw. He and his partner issued a stern warning to Grabby-hands that actually seemed to be working. But I couldn't totally avoid pain, even in my sleep.

That night, I woke to the familiar agony. After stifling my scream and calming Zoe, I found patches of red on my arms, where my rescuers had gripped me. The next night I slept, the nightmare left small blisters trailing up my shoulders and across my chest. Great. My condition was escalating. If a dream could leave a burn, what would happen if someone actually touched me again? I applied bandages and hid the burns with clothing until they faded, vanishing within a day. When I couldn't hide them anymore, making my presence in Gram's life an even greater burden, it would be time to take my Future envelope, leave the Gram envelope for her, and go before Social Services caught wind. The thought was so depressing, I shoved it out of my mind.

Too soon, the day I'd been dreading arrived. The first day of school.

I hopped out of bed, doubled over, and clutched my stomach. Worrying had gnawed at my guts all night. I popped two Tums and swallowed the chalky goo as I dressed in my best school outfit. What I'd worn to Gabriel's house. I tucked my long gloves into my backpack, threw it over my shoulder, and stormed into the kitchen with Zoe hopping behind. "Morning, Gram."

She nodded, flipping through a quilting catalog at the table.

I downed the Earl Grey in the mug across from hers, pushed away a waiting muffin, and grabbed a small nectarine from the counter. I slipped it into my backpack and caught Gram frowning. "You should eat." Her eyes narrowed. "And wear a skirt. Maybe some color?"

I glanced down at my all-black outfit. My stomach gurgled, and I wrapped an arm around it.

Her expression softened. "It's just you've been looking a bit Goth. I think that's what the kids call it. This is the first day, your senior year. It should be special."

Zoe rubbed against Gram's leg, and I backed out of the kitchen. I couldn't eat, but I changed into a white blouse and pulled a plaid, pleated skirt over my leggings. I kept the boots and slipped on the gloves.

I looked even odder, but anything to make Gram happier. She'd baked so much I'd had to give some to Dr. G, despite my lingering resentment at his betrayal.

Back downstairs, in Gram's bedroom, I tried not to fidget as she studied me. "Now, you know it's what's in here that matters." She tapped her chest. "But it's nice to dress appropriately when we can. Hmm…" She shuffled to her pewter trinket box on the dresser. "And some days are special." She pulled out her pearls.

I'd always refused wearing them before, but after last week, the cemetery… I gathered my loose curls into a messy bun and let her clasp the short strand around my neck, a task which seemed to take her much too long. She was overly cautious this close to me.

I grimaced into Gram's full-length mirror. At best, I could now be called prep-Goth. Mission accomplished, though. Gram smiled, reflected behind me. Her smile followed me to the front door and brightened when she handed me my padded lunch bag and waved me off with Zoe at her side. Zoe cocked her head and whimpered. She seemed to sense my nerves.

I trudged down the porch and unchained my bike. Could Gram's pearls slip off on the ride? I undid the clasp and slid them into a pocket inside my lunch bag. I stuffed my lunch bag inside my backpack and threw it around my shoulders with a sigh.

Aaron's truck followed me to school. Gabriel sent Aaron every day lately, apparently thinking my plea to leave me alone only applied to himself.

As I chained my bike up in the school parking lot, excited voices hummed all around. The medley of cars in the lot was a telling reflection of the span of wealth in town—a lot of old, beat-up American trucks, several new ones tucked in, and a scattering of expensive imports hiding between. So far, no one was paying any attention to me. They were too distracted, buzzing about a "new guy."

Apparently, he was "totally hot." That seemed sort of shallow, but lurking beneath my judgment was an ache. I wished I had someone to gossip with too.

I found my locker and put away my lunch. I banged the bent locker door closed with the side of my fist. The buzzing about the new guy got louder. A senior girl, hair twisted into a ridiculous top knot, whispered to her friend as they walked by, "He's in our class!" I almost stopped a sophomore who'd just started at Burger Boys to ask if they were talking about Aaron. But that didn't make sense. Most people would know Aaron from football already.

I slid into a chair in the far corner of Mrs. Merkle's first period AP English class. "I just *have* to be the one to show him around," Reese Jordan squealed to Kaylee in their seats near the front. I turned my back to the wall and stared idly at a No Means No poster by the whiteboard.

"I don't think so, Ree," Kaylee said, smoothing her skirt. "I'm the one showing him around.".

Kaylee's presence proved that getting into an AP class—and weaseling unearned As and Bs out of the teachers—was one of the perks of being the principal's daughter. Without a good transcript for college applications, she wouldn't be going to a fancy school like her friends. That, and a large scholarship. Principal Cook had raised her and older twin brother and sister on his own after his wife walked out.

Principal Cook looked so harried most of the time, I could have forgiven him for giving Kaylee an unfair advantage if she showed any sign of trying to deserve it. At least Reese was one of Kaylee's harder-working friends and belonged in the class. But she and her younger sister, Paige, who dated Cameron off and on, were two of my worst tormentors.

Desks filled with kids chatting or pulling out cells. I sized up several faces that reminded me of past struggles, kids I needed to dodge between bells.

Aaron sauntered in with a half-unzipped backpack, empty except for a Meeker football hoodie. He threw it down by an open chair across from Kaylee. After he tugged up the khaki shorts riding low on his hips, he looked around the room and over his shoulder at me. Instinctively, carelessly, I acknowledged his look with a nod. He jerked away.

My chest tightened. So he'd followed me around, but he wasn't even pretending to like me today? He leaned over and said something to Kaylee. I dropped my eyes to the worn desktop, a heart around *C + S* carved in the corner, and got angry at myself for even caring. I flipped through the notes I'd made on the summer reading assignments.

I glanced up when a tall, willowy figure wearing the yellow and blue t-shirt from last year's production of *Beauty and the Beast* slipped into the chair across from me. Mia. Dr. G's niece. She filed papers at the shelter sometimes. She sat ramrod straight, looking serious and uncomfortable, like me. I gave her a small smile. She returned it with a hesitant one of her own. "Hi, again," I said under my breath, trying not to draw attention to my pointless pursuit of friendship.

Her smile deepened, accentuating her high, dark cheekbones. "Hi, Cassie," she said, almost singing my name. She auditioned for Belle with that musical voice, but when the role went to Kaylee's sister, Mia played in the pit orchestra.

The room fell silent, all chatter halting midsentence. A cell phone clattered to the floor. I peered around heads, hoping to greet Mrs. Merkle with a wave. All I managed was a startled blink. *Wow.* I should've known they wouldn't quiet for Mrs. Merkle that quickly. He really was *totally hot.*

The new guy stood at the front of the frozen room, and everyone stared together. Kaylee finally glanced at Reese, jaw dangling. "Oh. My. God," she mouthed.

I understood why.

Hazel eyes were set off by olive-toned skin and long, black hair. Almost too long. He was tall, although not as tall as Gabriel, and trim. He looked like a model in his dark dress slacks and white button-down shirt, the first few buttons open at the collar, sleeves rolled up his forearms.

God, was I looking him over like everyone else?

Yes. Yes, I was. Kaylee motioned to the empty desk behind her, but he ignored her, walking towards the windows and down the end row, giving me no more than a glance. He turned quickly as he dropped into the seat in front of me, and I suspected he'd felt me staring. I blushed. My whole face felt impossibly hot. But strangely, my stomach had settled. I grabbed my nectarine from my bag and inhaled it in a few gulps.

The nectarine pit messy in my clenched hand, I found myself staring at the back of his head—ogling might be a better word. His hair curled around his neck, nearing his broad shoulders. I sighed, not feeling like myself at all. The new guy lifted a hand to stifle a yawn.

Mrs. Merkle entered the room with a commanding click of her thick heels against the tile. Her hair was piled into a huge beehive, and she surveyed us behind purple and pink polka-dotted glasses. She rapped a ruler against her desk. When conversation only dulled, she rapped again. Thankfully, my face cooled, and I focused long enough to tuck the pit into a scrap of paper and wipe my hand on my leggings.

"Good morning, everyone. Hope break treated you well." Mrs. Merkle's tone was strictly business but genuine, leaving no doubt she cared. Even about me, who brought trouble to every class. Her parents had been neighbors of Gram's before they passed. "I apologize for being late. A teacher's meeting. A lot more bureaucracy around here than there used to be, you know." She placed a hand on her hip, flashing a mood ring that looked like a genuine artifact from the 70s. "Now, I hope you're all excited about AP English. If you thought junior Honors English was fun, you're going to love this!"

The class groaned and I smiled, feeling more myself now that I wasn't staring at the new guy.

"You two, put your cell phones away." She pointed to two girls with bent heads near the front. "Now, let's see." She tapped her finger on her chin. "We have two new students joining us—Aaron Knight, who some of you probably know, and Vin Zephyrus. I thought we'd have each one say a bit about themselves—favorite book, hobbies, where they're from, that sort of thing. Aaron, if you'd start?"

Aaron shifted in his chair, giving Kaylee a cocky look. She played with a strand of her hair. "As most of you know, I've—"

"Please stand." Mrs. Merkle pointed to the open area in front of the whiteboard.

Aaron scowled. He stood by his desk and turned to the class, but his eyes kept flashing to Kaylee. "As most of you know, I quarterbacked the football team last year. Same thing this year, plus wrestling. I'm into most sports—I follow all the Colorado teams." Kaylee smiled at him, and his bravado dissolved into a goofy grin as he sat down.

"That was a bit brief, but I guess it will do." Mrs. Merkle turned to the new guy strolling to the front of the room. Chairs creaked as everyone shifted forward to stare at him.

His cool, almost bland expression said this was a chore and he'd rather be taking out the trash. His gaze slid over the gawking classroom, and, for an instant, it landed on me. Realizing I was mooning over him like everyone else, I was about to turn away in disgust, when something stirred in my chest. Something… strange.

I reached up to smooth back a loose curl that had escaped my bun, and his wandering eyes snapped back to me.

My fingers fell to my neck, rubbing the smooth skin under my ear. The longer I returned his stare, the more I felt the strange stirring tightening my chest until I could hardly breathe. My cheeks were too hot.

My lips parted as a name for the stirring popped into my head. *Attraction.* I gasped, raising a hand to mouth to smother the sound.

I was attracted to him?

Yes, that must be it. But beyond that, deeper in my chest, was an instant, aching pull. Uncomfortable. I squirmed, but our eyes were glued, snapping back no matter how hard I fought. His lips parted and softened. His throat worked, as though swallowing some sort of deep emotion. Then his face wiped itself clean, expression bland again. He cleared his throat and dragged his gaze from mine.

11
VIN ZEPHYRUS

"Good morning. I'm Vin Zephyrus," he said with an accent I couldn't place—definitely foreign, maybe European? Though that didn't narrow it down much. Judging from the just-audible sighs from several girls in the room, they thought it added to his hotness factor. I had to agree. My cheeks heated again as I drank him in.

Aaron huffed and Mrs. Merkle shot him a critical look. Vin waited like a severe guest speaker addressing an assembly. This time, his surveying gaze jumped over me.

Clearly whatever I felt was one-sided.

I bit my lip and dropped my gaze to the $C + S$ carved in the desktop.

"I apologize if my accent makes it difficult to understand me." A softness in his voice made me look back up. "I'm originally from Greece. We've moved around a lot. My father's work brought us to the states a few years ago." His voice was almost as musical as Mia's, but confident, as if daring anyone to challenge him. "As for a favorite English book, I've always connected with something…"— his eyes skimmed along the windows to the back, where for a split second, I swore our gazes collided again—"in *Wuthering Heights*." He looked away, out the window. "Catherine and Heathcliff. Tragic love… yet so enduring."

The girls in the class let out another sigh. I stifled a laugh. Sure,

I liked *Wuthering Heights* too—because it showed how vengeful and twisted human nature could be. Catherine and Heathcliff didn't just love each other. They tormented each other. In death, too, when she dies after giving birth to Edgar's child and Heathcliff is haunted by her ghost. The story might be laced with the supernatural, but it couldn't be more realistic in depicting the dark side of human emotions.

Vin paused again, pensive. "I don't really follow American sports teams. But I enjoy football—our football—soccer. And cycling. You'll probably see me out on my road bike. Anyway, I hope to get to know everyone better." His bland look begged to differ.

As he walked closer to me and his desk, I felt the pull again. This guy wasn't just appealing. I wanted… *needed* to get closer to him. For a moment, I didn't fight it, and with every step he took, I leaned forward, melting into the desk. Butterflies tickled my stomach. My cheeks burned so intensely that a dagger of panic pierced my chest, thinking for a second some asshole had poked me. Then something inside me rose up, resisted. I shook my head, gripping my chair to straighten myself out. He paused by his desk and brushed some lint off his dress slacks before sitting down, never sparing me a glance.

Thankfully Mrs. Merkle pulled a marker from her beehive and wrote "Crime and Punishment: Themes and Motifs" on the whiteboard. It distracted me from thinking about him, sitting so close. Even the strands of hair around his collar that were a bit too long were perfect. He was… perfection. I almost sighed. What was wrong with me!? I'd never had these sorts of feelings about guys before Gabriel's subtle appeal had snuck through my defenses. Now the electric pull of this guy. Get it together!

"Cassandra, please start us off," Mrs. Merkle said, startling me. "Tell us what about the book spoke to you and why." She turned to the whiteboard, poised to write down my answer.

The truth? I gulped. The clock above the door ticked off several seconds.

She spun to look at me. "There's no right or wrong. Just make it personal." I couldn't do that. "We need to connect with the characters, to appreciate deeper themes."

Kaylee glanced at Aaron and mumbled something about the dangers of penniless psychopaths connecting with each other. He gave her a startled look, but responded, "I doubt this one will kill us for our money."

Kaylee laughed.

"What? What did you say?" Mrs. Merkle slid between their rows.

"Nothing," Kaylee said. Aaron cast his eyes down.

"Well, unless you'd like to write an extra essay this week, I suggest you be respectful." Her beehive swayed as she looked to the back of the room again. "Cassandra?"

I sank deeper in my chair. The book raised questions that plagued me all the time—about right and wrong, self-denial, and guilt—but I couldn't reveal why.

Isolation.

Yes, isolation was something I could talk about. "So." I swallowed. "At first, Raskolnikov sees himself as separate from everyone else. Sees himself as superior to them, better than them. Sees them in terms of how they can serve him. It leads him to obsess about the pawn broker, to murder her for her money."

"Yes, good. That's right." Mrs. Merkle wrote, "Isolation from Society" then "Superman Complex" on the board. She looked over her shoulder. "And why did this theme connect with you?"

"I get why he was so depressed."

Vin drew in a sharp breath.

"I mean, don't we all want to withdraw from others at times?" I continued. "Have some time to ourselves, get away from even those people we live with? But that's no justification for what he did."

"Hmm. Were you surprised when he confessed?" Mrs. Merkle adjusted her glasses.

"No, I wasn't surprised at all," I lied. "The guilt was making him sick. Sonya's love was meant to bring him back to society, humanity, after he'd alienated himself." Even so, I'd been completely surprised by the confession. My visions had taught me people rarely acknowledged their wrongdoings and selfishness to themselves, much less confessed it to someone else or accepted punishment. I'd yet to meet a Raskolnikov outside of fiction. I had to keep that to myself, though.

Mrs. Merkle practically skipped around the room asking similar questions, sliding to and from students' desks and the board, revealing pretty quickly who'd taken the summer reading seriously and who hadn't. Near the end of class Mrs. Merkle asked Reese to pass out a take-home essay assignment on the symbolism in the book. I sighed. I didn't mind written assignments, but Mrs. Merkle wanted them typed. I'd have to use one of the computers at the library or school lab when no one was around. Reese took her time, pausing to whisper something to Luke, a boy with gelled hair and an affinity for skinny ties who lived near her along the river. As she walked down the last row, Reese grinned, a gleam in her eyes. One instant she headed toward Mia's desk with papers, the next she turned and stumbled, tripping on Vin's bag. She started to fall, reaching out her free hand for my neck. "Watch out," Mia whispered.

I twisted away and threw up an arm, but my elbow struck the desk, deflecting my shield. I shrank back in my seat and closed my eyes. *Don't scream. Don't scream.*

Nothing happened.

"But I was just… ugh, you stupid freak," Reese muttered close to my ear.

I opened my eyes.

From his seat, Vin gripped Reese's forearms, pressing them back into her stomach. She was bent over his arms, sneering at me, but Vin pushed her upright in one rough motion. He snatched papers from her hand and handed one across the aisle to Mia and one over his shoulder to me. For an instant, I couldn't move.

He glanced back at me.

My mouth fell open.

Vin's eyes swept over my messy bun and my gloved hands. I

finally seized the paper, and my covered fingertips brushed his. After he let go, his hand trembled. He flexed it and took a deep breath.

Reese drawled, "Sorry," looking at Vin, not at me. When he looked up, her voluminous false lashes fluttered.

He responded with a… smile? Could something like that even be called a smile? I'd never seen one so unfriendly—hard and cold as diamond. He leaned toward Reese and whispered, so low I barely caught it, "Never try that again."

I had no idea what to say or do. The new guy barely glanced at me all class, but then went out of his way to stand up for me? I figured, at the very least, I owed him a warning, in case he didn't want to join me in social exile.

When the bell rang, I already had my backpack over my shoulders. I stepped to the side of his desk. "Just so you know," I said, trying not to stare at his lightly haired forearms as he packed his bag, "I'm pretty low on the social food chain around here." He glanced up looking troubled, two creases between his brows, but a second later, they smoothed into a placid expression. God, he was hot.

I pulled my eyes away. Kaylee, Reese, and a gaggle of their newly arrived friends waited for him nearby, all quiet giggles and expensive shoes, all wearing the same celebrity perfume. "They're at the opposite end," I said, gesturing their way just as Kaylee pulled Mia into her group of gawkers with a cutesy little smile and whispered in her ear.

"Of the… social food chain?" he asked with a thick accent, but I swore he'd understood me.

"Yes. So you might want to keep some distance from me. For your own sake." I fled, jumping over a seat to avoid the girls in a mad dash to my next class.

I sat with my back flush against a tree in the school's side courtyard, slowly eating the turkey sandwich Gram had packed me, holding it with the hand I'd slipped out of its glove. A glob of mayonnaise fell onto my chin, and I wiped it off, scanning the lawn for anyone who came too close. I was starting to ease back into the school routine. But what had happened in first period? Not with Reese. I should've expected that, been ready. But the new guy.

Had he somehow learned about me and realized what Reese had planned? It seemed more likely he simply knew a bully when he saw one. Maybe he'd been picked on in another life or just felt sorry for me, like Mia.

I glanced to where Mia sat alone on a bench. Staring off into space, she peeled a strip from a string cheese and nibbled on the thread like she wasn't really hungry. I caught her eyes and nodded, trying to telegraph my thanks for her whispered warning. Her dark eyes flashed, and she made a move to stand, but one of her band friends rushed over. They soon scurried away together.

Defending me wasn't the only weird thing the new guy did. He'd also appeared in all of my other classes that morning, and despite my warning him off, he always sat nearby. It was a small senior class, though. I probably shouldn't make much of it.

But his proximity didn't help curb my attraction. I couldn't help looking at him, which spawned crazy thoughts about tapping his shoulder or asking him to drive me home after school.

It was so confusing, these moony thoughts. Maybe it was just teenage hormones? Even abnormal girls had them. And if there was ever a guy who was going to capture a girl's attention, make her wish she were something else—something less freaky—it would be a guy who looked like Vin. An urge to somehow make myself look prettier swept over me. I set down my sandwich, reached into my lunch bag for Gram's pearls, and put them on. Never mind that he'd still barely glanced at me.

He seemed pretty serious about his studies too. I respected that. He hadn't spoken more than two words to all the girls who'd tried to catch his attention. He didn't even bother to shoot back cocky grins like Aaron and several of the boys did, especially to Kaylee.

In fact, he didn't smile once all morning, unless baring his teeth at Reese counted.

Lost in thought, I didn't notice the movement around the tree trunk until too late. Kaylee and Reese appeared out of nowhere. I dropped my sandwich. Two beats later, they stood over me, each with a silly grin that contained very little humor. I scrambled away and rose to face them. I raised my gloved hand and widened my stance. Which defensive kick? One that would push them back, but not do too much damage?

"Let's see you get away now." Kaylee's white teeth flashed, but Reese's grin faltered at the prospect of trying to touch me again. "I think you need to learn a lesson about staying away from people," Kaylee continued as Reese took a step back, "especially Gabriel. His eyes on you. Yours on him. It's pathetic. I'm the one he's spending time with."

"You don't want to do this." I raised my palms higher. "I'm not going to let you touch me." I stepped back, hoping Kaylee would follow Reese's example and back off. I didn't need to end up in Principal Cook's office on the first day, and after hitting his daughter, no less. Kaylee was part of the in crowd because, though she couldn't afford designer clothes, it still paid to be her friend. Her enemies just paid.

"What are you going to do about it?" Kaylee flipped back a lock of hair.

"Defend myself. If I have to."

"You think you're so smart, don't you, Freakenstein?" She smirked.

A faint crunch in the grass signaled danger as Kaylee and Reese's eyes flicked over my shoulder. I ducked too late. Shooting pain devoured the back of my neck. The skin under my hair caught fire. Thick fingers looped my neck like a choker, disappearing under my chin, right above Gram's pearls. The hands pulled me back up, and the burn simmered to a full boil as jagged nails bit into my skin.

I twisted my head, and the nails bit harder, puncturing the soft flesh above my collar bone. I screamed, but the vise cinching my throat held back sound. The vision began to unfold, making it clear whose hands confined me. One of Kaylee's ex-boyfriends, the former captain of the wrestling team. Mike.

The images flashing through my mind were unspeakable. I tried to forget them as soon as they appeared, but I couldn't block out everything. (And I owed it to the girl to not just turn away.) Mike's short, muscled figure dwarfed her small body as he lay on top of her, his meaty hands tightening around her throat. Her strangled screams were devastating.

Mike's voice broke into the vision, his breath fanning my ear. "You're not just a loser. If you're leading men on, you're a bitch." His grip on my neck tightened.

The young girl's screams cut back in, then stopped. She lost consciousness. What happened to her next was even more horrifying. Horrifying and heartbreaking.

My stomach twisted. Boots slipping in the grass, I vomited up my lunch.

A stale turkey stench rose from the ground. I had no control over my body as I heaved twice more. The pain radiated down my spine, paralyzing me. It was agony. Not just the burning flesh of my neck, but the powerlessness.

I struggled to breathe, but couldn't get any air. I inhaled puke. Was I choking? I felt lightheaded. Faint. *Weak.*

So weak.

The hands released their hold. I sank to the ground. *So weak…* I slipped into darkness. Thump. My head landed on the ground, startling me.

Gram's pearls slid off my neck, coiling into a small white heap in the grass.

My eyes clouded.

Tears.

I blinked hard.

"Yikes. Is she having an allergic reaction?" Reese asked. "Paige has gotta see this. Her neck looks all bubbly."

My eyes rolled upward, past Mike's oddly soft, boyish features to the gliding, shifting clouds.

"Must be allergies. She looks awful. For once," Kaylee squealed. Kaylee and Reese stood several feet away, grinning down. Reese had clearly gotten over her second thoughts. Kaylee pulled out her cell. "I can't wait to post this." But she never got to angle the cell toward me. In unison, Kaylee and Reese glanced up, and their lips parted.

I drifted into darkness again…

For an instant, my eyes focused. The clouds seemed closer. I floated in a weightless haze, suspended in the air by strong arms.

"Agapi mou." A breathless voice sounded above.

"Oh, I didn't know you were looking for me." Kaylee's voice sounded far away. "Don't worry about her. A teacher will come. Just an allergic reaction."

A soft breath brushed my ear. "Agapi mou." My eyes focused one last time, on a white button-down shirt. White turned to grey as it faded away.

Everything went black.

12
DANGER

I STRUGGLED TO OPEN MY EYES, GLIMPSING WHITE CURLS, A pink cardigan. Gram hovering over me. Her comforting lavender scent surrounded me, restraining my cry of pain. My eyes opened wider.

"Thank goodness." Gram sighed. "I was about to call the doctor." Her hand fell from where it had been gripping my headboard. She took a step back. Suddenly I couldn't see her. My vision went hazy. My head pounded.

I took a deep breath, and my vision started to clear. I must've hit my head pretty hard after Mike let go. My whole neck ached, and I struggled to reach up and feel the damage.

"No, angel." Gram moved to stop my bare hand and froze. "It's looking better. Leave it be." She dropped her arm, and I obeyed.

Not a hard decision. I'd barely willed my hands off my comforter. This burn was the worst yet, if the pain indicated anything. I sputtered out a cough. My head pounded harder. My throat throbbed. When I coughed again, it tightened like a fist.

Beneath the searing sting of the burn, everything Mike had crushed felt bruised. "Water," I gasped.

Gram lifted a glass from the trunk, tilted it against my lips, and I guzzled as fast as my throat would allow. My chin quivered and droplets seeped out the corners of my mouth. When Gram pulled the glass away, I was finally able to lift an unsteady hand. I wiped my face, then gathered my strength to look into her troubled eyes. "Pearls okay?" I croaked.

"Those aren't the things I'm worried about." I opened my mouth, but she rushed on. "Yes, they're fine. Just a broken clasp."

"What happened?"

"A boy from school brought you home. Your stuff too. He said he didn't see everything, but someone was choking you—you fainted, hit your head," Gram said in a rush. "He was very concerned, but I told him he did the right thing bringing you home."

"Who?"

She looked at me with concern. "Maybe you should rest."

"I'll rest later. Who?"

"Did I do right? Should I have called a doctor? You've got a burn again and a nasty bump on your head." She leaned in, staring at a spot at my hairline.

I carefully reached up and felt a lump. "Who brought me home?" I insisted.

Gram's eyes glazed as she recalled the event. "Well, he says he's new to town. Vin Zepher something."

"Vin?" How had he even known where I lived?

The afternoon sun streaking in through the windows shone through her hair as she turned, staring at the attic entrance with a distant look. "Such a nice young gentleman, just like from Ms. Austen's books."

"Really?" I blinked. Vin made Gram dreamy-eyed too?

She pressed her hand over her heart and took a deep breath. "He couldn't have been more polite, although very serious. He acted more like an adult, I'd say."

"Like an adult? Vin?" I asked, still processing. He'd come to my rescue. Again.

"Yes, but I wasn't surprised." She stood straighter, clasping her hands like she had a secret. "When I asked about his parents, he said his father travels a lot, works in rare jewelry, fine art, that sort of thing."

"Okay." Sounded like Gram had gotten more out of him than the girls at school.

"They're renting a place out of town. Not far, one of those vacation cabin rentals between here and the mountains. He doesn't know how long they'll stay. And he has no other family. My guess is he's been forced to take care of himself for a long time." She tucked a short curl behind her ear and sat on the edge of the bed. "He's also very persistent. Insisted on getting the necklace fixed. And wanted to help clean you up. I politely refused. I had to remove your dirty blouse." Her gaze snapped to where the burn ended above my collarbone, seeming to refocus her attention. "I got all the buttons on my own—after I convinced him to go."

"Thanks, Gram." She must have removed my skirt, remaining glove, and boots too. I lay on my comforter in my camisole and black leggings. I still smelled vaguely like puke, but thankfully the blisters from the nightmare that had woken me that morning had already faded.

I wiggled my bare toes. I seemed to have control of my movements, but still felt drained. So weak. Pathetic.

"Zoe-bug?" I looked around the attic. "Where's Zoe?"

"Under the bed. She must be worried about you—she flew underneath it when Vin carried you up."

"Zoe," I called.

A faint whimper.

"Zoe-bug, it's okay."

She huffed through her nose but didn't come out.

"What else happened?"

"He actually apologized for not getting to you sooner. Kept mumbling something about too many silly girls in his way." Gram's smile was sly. "I could see why he'd have that problem. Such a handsome young man. He seems to like you a lot too." The curve of Gram's thin mouth widened.

"Gram, he's just a stupid boy!" My chest warmed, remembering how it felt to be near that "stupid boy.".

"I'm just happy you're making friends, stupid or not."

Vin must be really stupid to risk ostracization again. "Did Principal Cook call?"

"No. Vin brought you straight here, hoping I'd know what's best."

I groaned, happy Kaylee's father hadn't been involved but thinking of the mess I'd have to clean up with Vin, and Mike, Kaylee, and Reese too. Another fight couldn't get back to the social workers.

Gram misread my worry. "I think it's finally time we talk to the Social Services people about pulling you out of school." Her voice rose as the wrinkled lines of her face hardened into the most serious expression in her arsenal.

"Nooo," I pleaded in one long moan, not able to keep the edge of desperation from my voice. "I promise I'll be more careful. Mention that? They'll go ballistic."

"Ballistic?"

"I can't lose you." My fingers dug into my comforter.

"Okay." Gram gave in, a bit too easily. My body went limp. "We won't take you out of school yet." Her eyes narrowed. "But in exchange, there's something important we need to talk about. Something you need to do."

"Okay…"

"You need to let the Knight family help you."

"What?"

"You heard me."

I frowned. Maybe it was time to tell her my full opinion of her old friend and his sons.

"Bernard stopped by, and we had a long overdue chat."

Was he explaining things to her that he wouldn't to me? "What did he say?"

"Nothing I shouldn't have realized myself. I was just in too much denial to see it." She lowered her head. When she looked back up, her eyes swam with tears. "You see." The dam broke. "I can't talk about everything I know."

"What? Why not?"

"I promised Richard I would never reveal how much he'd told me, when it probably wasn't safe,"—a large drop rolled down her cheek, and I cursed Bernard for whatever he'd said that had brought up these memories—"but I can say you're in danger. And I hope, I think, Bernard can help."

"What do you mean?" I tried to keep my voice calm. It wasn't her I was upset with.

"I can't say too much." Gram shook her head, swaying her white curls. "You never know who's listening." She wiped her eyes, then looked around the attic, finally glancing out the low window.

More cloak-and-dagger secrecy, now from Gram. Baffling and utterly infuriating. "Okay...," I said, working to keep a growl from my voice, "so you can't tell me why, but you think the Knights can help with whatever's wrong with me?"

Gram nodded.

"But Gram, I don't see how they'd know anything about my problems, much less how to fix them."

"I'm not sure they know how they're going to fix things either, but they're in the best position to try. More important, they'll be able to protect you, at least as best they can."

"Protect me?"

She nodded again, moving closer to me on the bed.

"From?" I couldn't help my voice spiking an octave. "Why won't anybody just tell me?"

"From things we can't even see. That's why we have to be so careful," she whispered. "Richard said I may never know he is here, watching over me." She looped a gnarled finger through her watch's gold bracelet. "But if the bad spirits are near, they'll likely appear as shadows. They could be anywhere, hiding in dark corners!"

"Shadows?" My mouth dried. I'd thought Gabriel's sister had imagined "the shadows," thought they represented some other trauma, but... Gram thought they were dead people? Thought Richard was watching over her? God, being watched by ghosts?

That would really add to my paranoia. Was this really why no one would tell me what was going on?

Then again, a simple touch made my skin burn and bubble. Were ghosts and shadows really that hard to believe? But why would they care so much about me?

"I can't say anymore." She released the bracelet and glanced out the window once more. "You have to do this for me. I've been sticking my head in the sand, hiding my worries in my baking."

"But—"

"No. It's hard, but you have to trust me. I was blinded to what you are for so long because Richard said there were so few still alive, almost no girls."

"Few of what?" This secrecy was maddening. If they couldn't tell me all the details, why did they have to bring it up at all?

She shook her head. "And admitting it brought back too many old fears." Her voice lowered, thick with emotion. "Too many bad memories."

"Bad memories?" I pressed, cursing Bernard again. He'd clearly come over here and upset Gram with talk of bad things in the past. I knew she'd had some rough times, even more than what she'd let on.

"You should hear everything from Bernard, someplace it's safe."

"It's safe here." The attic was one of the few places it was safe.

"No." Gram shook her head harder. "I'm going to risk telling you this one thing though—because I think you need to hear it." She reached out her hands for one of mine. I quickly slid that arm under the comforter. She rested both hands on top. "Sometimes, when I think how proud I am of you, how strong you are, with everything you face…" She squeezed my forearm through the cover. "…I think of what my girl would've been like at your age."

I gasped, recalling the two hazy visions I had seen within Gram during therapy ages ago. Both of her on the street in front of her house, scolding a girl with rosy cheeks and pigtail braids. I'd wanted to believe they were tied to guilt over wrongly reprimanding a neighbor's child. Or maybe, considering the dusty crib she'd kept, they had something to do with a frustrated desire, an inability to have a child because Richard had been taken from her too soon. I'd denied the truth.

"I loved her so much, just as I love you." She paused, lost in thought. "The Knights would've said my girl wasn't special, not in the way you are, so she shouldn't have been in danger. But Bethany was in danger simply because of who—what—her father was. His family had stayed hidden here a long time, but they somehow discovered her, and I wasn't able to protect her."

"I'm sure it wasn't your fault. What happened?"

"I thought I was overreacting, trying to keep her inside with me as much as possible, when she fought against it." Gram frowned down at her gnarled hands, still gripping me through the comforter. "Bethany made it to her fifth birthday before she was burned." Her voice cracked, and Gram paused again, taking several strained breaths. "Before she was burned alive."

My free hand flew to my chest. "Oh, Gram." The horror of it was almost too much. "I'm so sorry." The vision from the cemetery made so much sense now. Richard and Gram had had a girl, a girl under some threat the Knights were somehow a part of too.

Gram's shoulders shook with each labored exhale, and I felt more and more useless. Her grip around the comforter loosened. I wished I was at least wearing more than my camisole, so I could reach out with my free arm. The risky, tangled mess of limbs would be worth it. Hugs made Gram feel better. And she needed to feel better. Immediately.

"Let's not talk about it anymore." Gram sniffled, reaching for a crumpled handkerchief on top of the trunk. "I never talk about it. It's better that way."

"Why don't we visit her at the cemetery too?"

"There's no gravestone. I couldn't bring myself to do it." She dabbed at her nose. "Richard had died in the War. My parents passed the year before. I pulled Bethany from the fire." Gram looked again at her scar-shriveled hands, turning them over. "But her burns… she died in the hospital—" Gram gulped back a sob. "Bernard eventually convinced me it was best to move on. Trying to get at the truth would've just attracted more attention. It seemed they'd only learned about Richard, didn't connect him to his relatives, thank goodness. He intentionally didn't act close to them, took a different last name. Best to keep it that way. And there was no hope of justice."

"But that must have been ages ago."

"It was. I told you because I wanted you to understand the danger you're in. I won't make the same mistakes again. Bernard will help us. He's helped me so much over the years. When I've let him."

"He has?" I pulled my covered arm out from the comforter and clasped both over my stomach.

"Yes, and those things weren't nearly this important. Not even fixing my wedding ring after the fire."

I'd never considered how her ring fit her burned hand before arthritis made her move it to a chain last year. How else could Bernard have helped?

I idly rubbed my chest above my camisole, my skin so sensitive after the incident with Mike that my nails scraped like sandpaper.

The remodels to the cottage. That must be it. The Knights must have paid for them. My wariness of the Knights faded slightly. Crazy or not, they now seemed well-intentioned.

"You have to listen to Bernard, you have to let Gabriel watch out for you, and you have to trust them. Do this for me. Try to trust them for me, if you won't do it for any other reason." She glanced down at her gnarled hands, then back up. "Will you do it?"

My mouth tightened. But if the Knights were ready to finally explain, I'd listen.

"Please, angel—you have to do it."

I looked into Gram's eyes, clouded with age and sorrow. "Yes. I'll give the Knights another chance."

The bed dipped, waking me from a light sleep. I'd told Gram not to tire herself out by coming back up today, but my protest died when my eyes opened on Gabriel. My heart raced. He sat with his hip by my bare arm, bracing a large hand near my neck to inspect my throat. My gaze wandered down a navy polo and his designer jeans, this pair well-worn. Threadbare pants or not, he was flawlessly put together, in true river kid fashion.

His eyes shifted upward, and I froze.

My heart gave a mighty thump when our eyes met.

"Oh, you're awake."

"Um, yeah."

"And you're speaking to me now?" His tentative half-smile did nothing to slow the wild pace of my heart.

"Yeah, but uh…" I tried to ignore his scent and heat as they swam around me. "Move away, okay?"

He blushed. "Rose asked me to check on you. Sorry I'm here." His hand flew to his collar, sweeping the upturned edges higher. He withdrew carefully, and Zoe scooted out from under the bed. She sat right next to him, and her traitorous tail thumped against the floor. He smiled.

"Listen." I edged as far away from him as I could. "I just told Gram I'd give your family another chance. So you can explain things. It doesn't mean I trust you."

His face fell. He sat back, and I released a breath I hadn't realized I'd been holding.

"Gram called you?"

"Well, no." He shifted to the edge of the mattress to pet Zoe. "I heard what happened. I wanted to make sure you're okay. Rose said you were. But are you?" He stared into me, vibrating irises searching.

"I'm fine. What did you hear?"

"Cameron and Aaron were supposed to be watching out for you. And after Cameron asked for more responsibility too. Unbelievable." He shook his head. "It should never have happened," he said gravely. His naivety was showing, and it disarmed me. He truly expected dutiful perfection from his too-cool-for-school little brother and his cruel, jerk cousin. He didn't see their flaws.

My temples throbbed. "What did you hear?" I repeated.

The doorbell rang. Gabriel paused at the interruption and finally answered. "Aaron noticed you were missing after lunch. He was supposed to take over from Cameron, but Kaylee told him you'd gotten into a fight, went home. Kaylee posted you started it, but I'm sure that's not true."

"Fantastic." My throat burned. I eyed the empty glass on the trunk. I just hoped Kaylee's father didn't find out—that was one story I couldn't straighten out. "Did Kaylee tell Aaron anything else? Did he talk to Reese too?"

"You don't have to worry about Kaylee or Reese," a melodic voice called out from the staircase.

Gabriel straightened with a start. Footsteps drew nearer. Gabriel moved as close as he could to me without actually touching my body. Who would Gram have allowed to come up, besides another one of the Knights? I found myself wanting to lean in toward Gabriel, anxious about the answer.

Of course, I should've known after Gram's reaction.

Vin appeared, striding into the attic like it was his room. His eyes homed in on the sliver of space between me and Gabriel. Two creases popped up between his brows.

"Great. You too," I muttered, trying to ignore his statuesque perfection. I shifted away from Gabriel and worked to affect a cool and collected expression even as my breath quickened. I felt every step Vin took toward me in my gut, constricting my diaphragm until I squirmed. Of course he'd be here right now, when I didn't even have the strength to stand. I'd never had guests up here before Gabriel and had certainly never imagined entertaining them from bed.

Vin paused in the center of the room. "I came to bring this back." He slipped his fingers into the pocket of his slacks and drew out a velvet pouch. He tipped Gram's pearls out into his palm. The gold clasp was shiny, brand-new. "And to check on you. Mrs. Merritt told you I brought you home?"

"She'd want you to call her Anna Rose. Or maybe just Rose—she seems to like you." I waved my hand at Gabriel's chest, which had drawn even closer to me somehow, trying to get him to stop crowding me. Vin's brows relaxed. "And yes, she told me." My voice weakened, hoarse. "Thank you. I guess I should say, thanks again."

"What do you mean—thanks again?" Gabriel asked, then turned to Vin before I could answer. "And who are you exactly?" His eyes bore into Vin like Vin was some sort of menace.

Vin ignored Gabriel and just smiled right at me. The force of it slammed into my stomach, flipping it over. Wow. This was the first time I'd seen Vin smile. Really smile.

It wasn't anything like the Knights' gentle smiles. This was so much more. So stunning. So intense. My limbs turned to jelly, and my cheeks burned. I couldn't look away...

"How do you know Cassie?" Gabriel's voice sounded distant. Zoe gave a muffled snort. Where was she?

"School." Vin's accent deepened. He kept his focus on me, his smile widening. Gabriel jumped off the bed and, in several quick steps, towered over Vin. Gabriel blocked my view of Vin's smile like an eclipse of the sun, and I regained control of my limbs.

Vin was nearly as tall as Gabriel, but when Gabriel expanded his chest, demanding Vin's attention, Vin looked like a bug about to be squashed.

Frankly, I was surprised Gabriel didn't growl.

Vin allowed Gabriel his staring contest. To my surprise, Gabriel stepped back first, his eyes wide as he messed with his collar.

"Gabriel, it's okay." I tried to dispel that self-conscious look that, to my dismay, always tugged at my heartstrings.

Gabriel pressed his fingers into the scar creeping up his chin, like he was trying to erase it. Despite the telling gesture, he glared more intently.

"Really, Gabriel. It's okay. Look at me."

He didn't.

I sighed.

Vin's eyes glanced between us with an odd, pondering expression, but otherwise he brushed off Gabriel's posturing. He calmly snaked the pearls back in the bag, stepping around Gabriel to set it on my trunk, and moved to the side of my bed. Vin's smile was gone, but his expression was still warm and tender. Like he was happy to see me, to be with me, regardless of Gabriel hovering over us like a concerned parent. "Feeling better?"

I nodded.

"No serious damage done today?"

I shook my head.

Vin's hazel eyes examined the lump on my head, the marks around my throat, then searched the rest of my body in methodical order. From the pale flesh of my upper chest, skimming along each bare arm, down my camisole and black leggings, to my ankles and the tips of my toes.

I stared back, giving myself over to that special pull—the attraction of this morning now impossibly heightened after that stunning smile. His flawless lips hinted at another, and my heart pounded until I was dizzy and butterflies swarmed my belly. I soaked him in, fanning the flames he lit inside me, relishing the pleasure of a rare warmth that raged but didn't harm. *Pleasure*. It was… addicting.

I barely noticed Gabriel watching at the end of the bed. Vin captured every bit of brain power, every nerve ending.

One side of his jaw was darkening with a bruise. "You didn't fight Mike, did you?" I managed to ask.

"You don't have to worry about Mike." Vin's smile fell. "Or Kaylee or Reese. They've already taken down their posts. Their lies. Nothing like this is going to happen again." He reached out and unhooked a loose curl from my headboard.

"Hey," Gabriel barked, and his distant voice helped me refocus. "Don't hurt her." But it wouldn't. My hair and nails—dead cells, not living flesh—were safe. But how could Vin know?

Vin stroked my hair between his thumb and finger, as if it were a substitution for a gentle caress of my face.

"Enough!" Gabriel broke through the fog. Though I registered what Vin had done was sort of creepy, considering we just met, I still just stared as he let the bright lock fall across my shoulder. Gabriel grabbed Vin's arm and pulled him away, and I was finally able to take in the whole room again. "I don't know who you are, but Cassie's none of your business. She's fine, you can just—"

"Let go." Vin forced an icy tilt of his lips, then shook off Gabriel as if it required no effort at all. "She's fine because I was there to deal with those imbeciles. You obviously seem protective of Cyn—um—Cassandra." Here I was mooning over this guy and he'd forgotten my name? His mouth twitched while he sized Gabriel up... and seemed unimpressed. "But you're doing a pretty poor job of actually protecting her."

Gabriel's face flushed. His mouth worked, but I interrupted before a fight kicked off. "I don't need anyone protecting me." I sat straighter on the bed. "I mean, I was tricked. It won't happen again." Both of them ignored me, the air thick with tension and testosterone.

"Why are you so interested anyway?" Gabriel asked, even the smooth side of his face distorting.

"I'm just looking out for her." Vin's flawless features relaxed. "A beautiful girl I—"

Gabriel inhaled sharply and stepped forward, a clear threat. Vin fell silent but didn't back away. They were both giving me such a headache, especially Vin with his "beautiful" comment. He must've said it to get a rise out of Gabriel, because Gabriel was acting like some sort of parental figure. Or jealous boyfriend, which he wasn't. Vin didn't know Gabriel was only here because of my freakishness, because I was supposedly similar to him in some way that made me a target. Vin shot Gabriel another strange, forced smile. "Why don't you leave, you big—"'

"Listen, both of you," I interjected before things could escalate, "I'm really tired. Could you both just leave?" I found the strength to rub my throbbing temples, wincing as my fingers brushed the lump.

"But—" Gabriel's protest died after one look at me. "Okay. We'll let you get some rest." He backed slowly toward the stairs, pausing to make sure Vin followed.

Vin gave me one last mesmerizing smile before waving good-bye. As soon as their footsteps faded down the stairs and the front door clicked shut, I gave into my exhaustion, turning toward Sleeping Beauty as my eyelids dropped.

Zoe scuffled her way out from under the bed. So that was where she'd disappeared to, again. Her three paws clicked on the wooden ramp and she settled next to me, curling into my side. I wrapped an arm around her, breathing in the sweet grassy scent of her fur, hoping for just a few hours of rest before the nightmare marked my skin.

I drifted to sleep, warm with Zoe against me and content enough on top of my comforter. Not thinking of Gabriel, for once, which surprised me after all my failed attempts to get him out of my head.

No, this time, I was thinking of Vin.

His gorgeous smile. The look he just gave me. The feelings it sparked inside me. How I wished I could be half as sure of myself as Vin seemed all of the time. How much I wanted to reach out to him, maybe even touch him. Just to see. The attraction was so strong, maybe I could dream that touching his flawless skin wouldn't hurt me.

13
FRIGID

I DRIFTED AWAKE, PULLED FROM SLEEP BY A SQUEEZE ON MY leg, and Gram's voice. "Angel, wake up."

My eyes cracked open, taking in the fractured lines of the ceiling in the dimness of evening. They fell back shut.

"Angel." She shook my leg.

"Hmm?"

"I couldn't wake you. You slept through dinner."

"Not hungry." I snuggled into Zoe. "I'll do dishes later."

"All right. But you could have a concussion. You need to tell me your name."

"Tired." I snuggled deeper.

"Your name. Then you can go back to sleep."

"Cassie."

"Angel, your full name."

"Cassie—um, Cassandra—Merritt."

"I'm still worried. Can you stay with her?" Who was she talking to?

I drifted, then was yanked back into half-consciousness by a deep voice asking me my address and the names of the shelter dogs.

I woke fully to sun streaking through the high attic window. The quilt from downstairs was wrapped around me, but warmth leeched from my back, leaving me shivering even though Zoe still slept on the other side of me.

I rolled over and looked at my Burger Boys watch. 8:25 am.

School. I'd be late. Should I bother dressing, going? I rolled toward my trunk. It still held the velvet pouch with Gram's pearls.

Vin. I wanted to see Vin. I grabbed fresh clothes and zipped into the shower. The lump on my head had shrunk. The burn from my Mike's hands had healed overnight. I ignored the stinging in my swollen throat as I dressed. I bounced back up to my room, helped Zoe downstairs, and into the kitchen. Gram sat at the table with the home phone to her ear.

"Morning," I choked out.

She squinted at my neck as she said, "Yes, Principal Cook's Office? This is Anna Rose Merritt. Cassandra's not feeling well. She'll be staying home today."

"Gram," I half-moaned and coughed. "I want to go."

"Rest. Just rest. Do you even remember me and Gabriel waking you last night?"

"Sort of." I flushed. "You let Gabriel stay here?" Again. Ugh.

"Yes. I didn't know who else to call. I couldn't wake you for dinner." Her eyes clouded.

Oh no. "It's okay, Gram."

"I knew you wouldn't want any doctors."

"Yeah, you're right." I took a deep breath, trying to let go of any thoughts of Vin. And Gabriel.

"Gabriel just wants to help. He did the dishes too." She blinked several times and reached for her walker. "I asked the Knights for dinner. Six o'clock." She gave me a serious expression which invited no argument. "Remember what you promised?"

I nodded and sat to drink the tea she had waiting for me, the warm liquid soothing my throat. The day passed quickly, resting in bed with Zoe, reading, daydreaming about Vin while attempting to help Gram cook. At 5:00, I washed dishes. At 5:30, I set the table. At 5:45, Gram glanced up from mashing potatoes. "Maybe you should wear a skirt?" I trudged upstairs. By 5:55, I settled on a full-length skirt and sweater. By 5:56, sweat dampened my brow. At 5:59, a knock echoed upstairs. I helped Zoe down. Bernard, Gabriel, and

Aaron crowded the living room, Bernard and Gabriel hovering by the TV cart, Aaron slouched on the couch.

Even without Cole and Cameron, we had to cram around the table. Warmth from the oven made the room cozy, but still, I shivered as I picked at a cornbread muffin. Bernard made small talk about the weather, Gram's cooking, school. He helped himself to a second serving of meatloaf, mashed potatoes, and green beans. Gabriel cleaned his plate except for a small bit of meat, which he not-so-sneakily fed to Zoe beneath the table.

Bernard cleared his throat. "So this will sound quite odd. But we need you in the forest with Gabriel this weekend." He rested a hand on Gabriel's shoulder. "You'll camp overnight. Close to what you need to see. Then head there in the morning."

"Head where?" I shifted in my seat.

"A special spot in the forest. You'll see." He speared a third piece of meatloaf. "I know we approached things the wrong way before. But it'll work out this time. Because after all," a note of wistfulness crept into his voice, "we can help you. And you can help us." He gave a soft smile and plopped the meat on his plate.

"But you can't even tell me what I can help with, so I can't be sure I want to help." My voice came out even harsher than I'd intended because of my strained vocal cords. No matter what Gram said, the Knights seemed as clueless as me about my condition. Bernard wasn't a doctor, to my knowledge. Gabriel didn't burn when people touched him, and he hadn't finished medical school yet. They wanted me to do something for them out in the forest, and they were dangling a carrot in front of my nose to get me there. But when Gram gave me a sharp look, I added, "At least promise me you'll finally answer some questions."

"Yes." Bernard stopped eating. "Where you're going, what you're seeing—Gabriel will have answers. He'll pick you up Saturday. Noon."

Gram nodded vigorously.

"Okay." My shoulders slumped.

Gram clapped her hands. "Food. I'll send them with plenty of food." As if that was our only worry. Everyone else dug into their peach pie.

I didn't sleep that night. The next morning, Aaron followed me to school. The teachers thought my hoarse voice was from a cold. Principal Cook seemed entirely oblivious. I only had one trouble: Vin. Had I dreamt his heated smiles?

He didn't smile at me all day. Or at anyone else, except an occasional hard, sham grin. Several times I caught myself staring at his aloof, perfect features. While I hoped I was a bit more discreet than the other girls, I wouldn't delude myself. I was drawn to him more than ever.

But why wouldn't he talk to me, or hardly even look at me?

It was okay. I hadn't believed he really liked me. Thought I was beautiful. He had clearly put on a show for Gabriel. But forgetting him was impossible when he was everywhere I went, sitting nearby in class, riding a fancy road bike around town, eating lunch across the courtyard, and reeling me in every time.

I didn't think I could sink any lower on the school's loser list, but crushing on the new Mr. Popular made me feel like I had.

Vin plagued my days and the new symptom of my condition plagued me each night, during the nightmares. I hid the red, blotchy marks and blisters on my arms, bigger and angrier each morning. Really, I didn't have much to complain about, because the skin healed itself so quickly, leaving me fresh and ready for the next time I succumbed to exhaustion.

At least there was one bright spot to the week. No one attempted to touch me, and no one, not even Cameron's closest friends, had whispered my nickname at my back. I actually enjoyed classes. Aaron's shadowing could be the reason, or maybe I was finally getting a reputation as a tough target. Or maybe it was because the girls were preoccupied with Vin, and the boys were caught up in some sort of sports recruiting rivalry that had started between Aaron and Cameron.

Aaron's group hung around the football bleachers during lunch, Cameron's pack behind the gym, smoking when they thought no one was looking. Only the few guys who played both sports or bounced between the groups, like Mike and the wrestlers, appeared conflicted.

During Friday's lunch period, Vin sat surrounded by girls in the sunny courtyard. And I was staring at him again. His flawless build. His flawless outfit: grey dress slacks, a striped purple button-down shirt with sleeves rolled up his forearms, and leather shoes. His flawless face. Even though his expression was still ice-cold.

I forced my eyes to my sandwich. *Stop looking at him.* I allowed myself small peeks.

Vin's ever-present flock seemed oblivious to his frigid dismissal of their squawking and giggling. Though I kept a more respectable distance, I was still one of those silly girls, waiting for him to turn his mesmerizing smile on me one more time. Like a junkie waiting for a fix.

Despite promising myself I wouldn't, I glanced directly at Vin and his groupies.

Vin glanced back and stood, breaking away from them, striding toward me.

Oh no. Had he finally gotten fed up with me gawking? I got to my feet and prepared myself for embarrassment. Butterflies took flight in my belly. Part nerves. Part Vin-effect.

He stopped within inches of me, eyes darting around… for eavesdroppers? At least he wasn't going to humiliate me publicly.

His search completed, his hard expression softened slightly. "I have to say something."

"Please do." My voice wobbled, and I braced myself for the tell-off I hoped would cure my obsession.

"Make sure Gabriel is the one before you get too close."

My lips parted in surprise.

"Do you understand?" He leaned in. A wave of heat swept over me, along with his fresh lime scent. My legs buckled, threatening to send me careening into him. I reached for the tree.

"What do you mean?" The tree bark scratched my arm, and I focused on its cool, rough texture to dull the heat in my face.

"Well, I'm pretty sure Gabriel thinks you guys are meant to be. That you have this… well…" I hadn't heard such an inarticulate string of words come out of Vin's mouth all week. "Just be careful—about trusting Gabriel, caring too much, at least so soon."

I straightened, releasing the bark. "Clearly you don't know me, Vin. But you don't have to worry about me trusting or caring too much about anyone. Especially Gabriel."

"I know you're going out with him. Going camping with him and—"

"How?" I questioned through the Vin-clutter in my head. "How did you know that?"

"Kaylee told me. It wasn't hard to get the details." Vin's cheeks tightened as he seemed to suppress a smile.

"Kaylee knows?"

"Aaron told her."

"Why would Aaron tell her?" Gram kept insisting we couldn't talk more about my cryptic arrangement with the Knights. Aaron surely got that same memo.

"I think Aaron realizes Kaylee needs to get over his big brother before he has a chance with her. I'd like to think Aaron would be more discreet than, um, to gossip,"—Vin must be feeling ill, to be stumbling over words this morning—"but he seems distracted, more interested in getting a leg up on Cameron. Who's the bigger man on campus." He shoved a fall of long black hair off his forehead, head jerking almost imperceptibly at the sound of a groupie calling his name. "But really, that stuff doesn't matter. What matters is that you make sure you know Gabriel. Know his motives. That he's right for you. Before you get too close."

"I'm not getting too close to anyone," I said, at the same time longing to be close to Vin. "But seriously, why do you care?"

"I'm your friend." He glanced all around the courtyard, looking uncertain, like Gram searching for things that weren't there or Bernard nervously scanning the walls of his own house. He didn't want other people to know how he supposedly felt?

"You don't feel like my friend." I cleared my throat, nervous about messing this up—a conversation with a boy I actually cared about. (Or did I just care about what he thought of me? Was there a difference?)

He stared back, totally silent.

"So why bother?"

"You are my both—I mean… new friend." His jaw tightened. "And I'm here for you, as whatever you need me to be—which, at the moment, is a guy who keeps his distance."

"Distance?"

"Just keep your guard up around Gabriel. That's all I wanted to say." Vin smiled tightly, an odd expression with his mouth closed but cheeks pulled up. My head clouded, but my body felt jumpy and alert. He said quickly, "Keep your guard up. The whole weekend. We'll talk after you get back." He strode back to his girls before I could think to respond. I stared after him the whole way, wishing he really were my friend. Maybe then I'd have an explanation for my insane yearning to leave my solitary existence behind and follow him wherever he'd take me.

I drifted through the rest of lunch in a brain fog, consumed by thoughts of Vin. What he'd said didn't help. I was dangerously close to thinking he was jealous of Gabriel. That two gorgeous boys were rivals. Over me. Two boys, one I didn't trust, and one I didn't know, neither one I understood, with me, the school freak, in the middle? It made me think of Shakespeare. That way madness lies.

Still drifting after lunch, through Calc and Physics, my head clouded with Vin, I burst through the door of the little-used bathroom across from the band room, almost tripping over Mia. Kneeling by her bag, she missed the impact, but I kicked the bag hard. Pens scattered. Papers flew. Her oboe case clattered away.

"Oh! I'm sorry, Mia." I scrambled after it.

Using the sink, she pulled herself to her feet. "It's okay." She eyed me uneasily as I set the case by her bag and started gathering up her things. "Just leave them." I kept moving. "Leave it." She bent forward, reaching for the tube of lip gloss in my hand, and even with my gloves, I flinched. She backed up. "I'm sorry."

"No, no." I stood. "I get it." I set the tube on the sink. "I'll go."

"It's not that." She sighed. "Listen, I'm the one who should apologize. I mean, my God, they actually choked you."

"What?" My whole body tensed, recalling Mike's hands on me. Mia didn't need to apologize. She wasn't like the other kids, even if she hung out with them sometimes. Or… how well did I know her? We'd been introduced by her uncle, said the occasional hello. I sometimes saw her helping her mom, Dr. G's oldest sister, at Garza's Flowers on Main. She kept to herself nearly as much as me.

"That morning." She shook her head. "I heard Kaylee and Mike planning something." Her shoulders sagged. "I didn't know what, I swear." She turned away toward the sink. "It's just they talk to me sometimes. Or at least, talk when I'm around." She ran her hands under the cold water, then shook off droplets, watching them scatter. "Like even though I'm a band geek, being friends with me is cool." She lifted her hands to either side of her face, frowning at herself in the mirror. "Because having friends like me is cool. They don't really care about me." She grabbed the tube of gloss and smoothed a bit over her lips. "They care what it looks like having me around." Her cheeks tightened, creases furrowing her dark complexion.

For the first time it struck me that Meeker wasn't the most diverse place. Dr. G's parents had moved here long ago, Gram had been friends with them, but the town hadn't changed much since. Maybe I wasn't the only one who felt like I didn't fit in?

Mia turned back to me. "I swear if I'd known anything definite, I'd have warned you."

There probably wasn't much she could've done. "It's okay. It worked out." Thanks to Vin. Butterflies flew again just thinking his name.

"I just wanted you to know. And um, sometimes, I think it's good not being like them." She offered a small smile that grew when I nodded.

Was Mia somebody I could talk to? Ask a few questions? I had so many. I thought of Vin's warning. "Do you know Gabriel Knight?"

She tilted her head. "Sure. Doesn't everyone?"

"Everyone?" Had their house fire achieved local legend status?

"Well, he could've been a bigger star than Cameron." I blinked. The papers had rightly labeled Gabriel a hero, but "star" seemed an odd choice of words. Mia glanced at her cell. "Listen, I gotta go, but if you want to know about Gabriel Knight, I'll tell you this— my sister dated him."

"What?" I coughed.

"Well, they went out once. She's older, almost out of college now, but he asked her to a dance her senior year. He was younger, homeschooled, but he seemed so nice, and everyone was still talking about him like he was some big celebrity." She shrugged, like I knew what she was talking about, but this must've been well before the fire. "And he was—nice, that is—but here's the thing. He never called her back. Ever."

"Oh?" And was I happy to hear that? I shouldn't be. He wasn't meant for me. Or me for him. Or whatever.

"She decided she was glad he didn't call. She said he was too serious. Intimidating." Not the word I would've used, but Gabriel was more imposing than most guys. Even his brothers. "Maybe he knew how she felt, and that's why he never called back. We don't know." Mia knelt, threw everything into her bag, and hurried toward the door. "Listen." She turned her head, accentuating her long, elegant neck. "Not sure why you're asking, but with the problems you have, I'd just"—she hesitated—"be careful. Gabriel seems like a nice guy. Really. He's great to everyone, even Kaylee. But Kaylee talks. Says they're friends, maybe more. And you know how mean she can be. Manipulative. If she gets him to do something, tricks him into it,"—her voice dropped lower—"it might be worse than Mike. Gabriel's a lot bigger than you."

14

CAVE CLOSED

Knock. Knock. Chirp. Chirp. Gabriel knocked on Gram's door as her clock sung noon. She glanced at my grimace and flew to the entry, gliding like a skater with her walker. "Gabriel! Hello!"

"Hi, Rose. Cassie." He wore a soft-looking, light blue pullover with an upturned collar, khaki shorts, and a hesitant half-smile. For Gram's sake, I tried to soften my grimace, then knelt by the coat rack and zipped up my backpack, stuffed with food Gram made, my favorite sweatshirt, and an extra change of clothes.

Zoe hop-walked into the hall and wagged her whole butt when she spotted Gabriel.

"Zoe!" Gabriel bent to rub behind her ears.

She did her return rub, which I'd thought she reserved for me.

His widening smile lit his face with genuine joy and a gentle affection that reminded me of Gram's expression when she told me she loved me.

He was so perplexing. Was he the person he appeared to be now, the person I'd thought he was after the cemetery? Or was he the person who'd violated my privacy, who Vin and Mia feared might trick and hurt me? Hopefully today, I'd get my answer. Although, if he were telling the full truth about himself and his family, that would mean some evil force was hunting me because I had a hidden purpose. And if he were just Cameron in disguise, I'd be trapped in the forest with him. There wasn't really a winning scenario here. I wiped a sweaty palm on my worn jeans.

"It's supposed to be cold tonight. Maybe rain," Gram said.

"I've got ponchos in our gear," Gabriel assured her.

"Take this too." Gram tugged the scarf she'd knitted me for our two-year anniversary together off the coat rack. She'd presented it with great ceremony, after a toast with her mom's teacups. It was black yarn, flecked with red and orange—an intentional color palette after I'd barely worn the pink and purple ones before it. "Love you, angel," she said as she handed it over.

"Gram, don't forget about your medicine." I'd never left her so long. "And if you need anything, call Dr. G." He'd probably help Gram regardless, but he owed me.

"Of course. Don't worry. I know this is all very strange but try to enjoy what you can. You'll be safe with Gabriel."

A sour taste flooded my mouth, but I nodded, tucked the scarf in the front of my backpack, and trudged down the porch. If the Knights were delusional or lying, that would mean they'd tricked Gram, too, in a time of great vulnerability, attributing the trauma of losing her child to evil shadows. As horrendous as that sounded, the alternative was outlandishly worse.

In Gabriel's SUV, I dropped my bag at my feet and scooted myself close to the passenger door. Silence built between us like a brick wall. He rolled down the windows, filling the interior with the breeze and birdsong. We drove out of town, then off paved roads, deeper into the forest than I usually went, parking at the end of a dirt forest service road that I rarely ventured to because it led to only one thing: the trailhead for Spring Cave.

I'd heard about Spring Cave but no one was supposed to go in because of some problem with a bat disease. Humans spread it throughout the bat population by tracking it through the cave on their equipment, shoes, and clothing. Rumor had it that even if you got past the layers of Forest Service fences, you couldn't get very far inside before being stopped by a system of underground rivers blocking the passages.

The gravel parking area was empty and eerily silent as Gabriel turned off the engine. He popped open the trunk and swung one of the two enormous packs laying there onto his back. Two large duffel bags lay beyond the remaining pack. "Need help?" I shifted my grip on my backpack.

"We're good. I'll make another trip, come back for the rest." He flashed me a hint of a half-smile, like that explained how he was going to carry all that on his own in one more journey. He shut the trunk, strode toward a clearing in the trees, and turned around by a narrow bridge spanning the river, waiting for me to follow. Halfway through our afternoon trek up the path, I had to break the silence.

"Um, why Spring Cave?" I took a deep gulp of the pine-scented air. "I thought no one was supposed to bother with it. And it's up the tallest mountain in the forest." I squinted up to the peak in the distance.

Gabriel looked over his shoulder. "You'll understand in the morning when you see it."

"That would be nice—to finally understand." I kicked a loose rock on the path. Each incline seemed to bring more wind, more chill. I stopped before the next switchback to pull on my well-loved Meeker cross-country hoodie—a gift from Coach.

At last we reached the fences surrounding the cave's entrance and a Forest Service sign: *No Entry. Cave Closed. Trespassers subject to fine and prosecution.*

I shivered, thinking about how isolated we would be up here, where no one expected hikers to tread. Yet, I shimmied around the far fence with him, deciding the promise of answers couldn't be passed up.

Gabriel dropped his pack. "We'll be setting up by the entrance." He pointed to a spot of packed dirt under an overhang of rock several yards from the black mouth of the cave. He handed me his cell. "Anything at all, call my dad."

"It gets a signal?"

"Strong. Dad's part owner of the cell company. They built a new tower, not far from here. I'll be back soon."

All I understood an hour later was that Gabriel better get back from his return trip soon before I froze to death. Why did we need so much stuff for one night anyway? I'd already put on my scarf and rummaged in the pack Gabriel had left, but there were just water bottles, two medium-sized metal tanks, some of Gabriel's t-shirts and boxers, two lighted helmets which must be for tomorrow, and two pillows. There'd better be a tent and some really heavy sleeping bags in those other bags.

"D-d-damn Gabriel," I cursed through chattering teeth. He never seemed to feel cold. Maybe he forgot other people did? My toes and fingers numbed first, the chill slowly creeping from there. I jumped around on the hard rock outside the ominous black hole, trying to keep my arms wrapped tightly around my chest to hold in every last bit of the warmth slowly seeping out.

Damn Gabriel to Dante's first circle of hell.

Actually, the first circle—merely a state of limbo for the un-baptized—wasn't such a bad place. Gabriel deserved something much worse right now. Maybe somewhere in the fourth circle for whatever sort of self-interested scheme he and his father had woven me into. The wind picked up, blowing through my sweatshirt, seeking entry and exit through every worn spot. I pulled up its hood and tucked my nose in my scarf, enjoying its softness caressing my cheeks, distracting me from the cold. I shuffled farther back into the large opening of rock surrounding the black hole, hoping it would offer a bit of protection from the biting wind. Every step into the opening swallowed a little more of the weak, late afternoon sunlight until I stood in almost complete darkness.

As I turned to face out to the valley, unease prickled my spine. I'd seen this view before. A flash of light above the trees caught the corner of my eye, stealing my breath. Another flash shot out near the trees. I forced a long, calming breath, shoving the burnt diary out of my head. It was probably lightning. Gram had warned us it might rain. The forest was silent. No crash to confirm I wasn't losing my mind… or being followed.

Gram had warned me about shadows, but I was afraid to ask her what the lights meant. Bad or not, she'd worry. I stared hard at the clusters of trees spanning the cave's entrance. When the light didn't reappear, I finally exhaled.

"Hey," Gabriel called as he walked into view, weighted down with the duffel bags in each hand and the other enormous pack on his back. Wow, he wasn't even out of breath.

"Hey." I stumbled back into the opening, and my hood fell. "How'd you get back so fast?"

His face lifted into an easy half-smile, and my heart raced. I forced my pulse to settle with a deep breath. No hormones allowed until I knew the truth. I shivered as the wind picked up again. "Let's get set up. You've got a tent? Sleeping bags? Can I help?"

He set down the bags and shrugged off the pack in one smooth motion. "I've got it."

I willed him to move faster as he sorted the gear. "I can help, you know." He kept rifling through folds of black material and what looked to be flippers you'd use for swimming, and my shivers returned in full force. My frustration grew. "Wh-what is wi-with so much stuff?" My teeth chattered.

He looked up from the bags. "Are you shivering?"

I gave him a hard look. "It's c-c-cold!"

Before I could blink, he was there, folding me into his arms. My cheek collided with his pullover, rubbing up against it. It was just as soft as it had looked. Softer than my flannel pillowcase. But firm and warm. The heat radiating from his body through the cotton was so intense, so welcome, it silenced any complaint I might have made. My fingers, pressed between our bodies, slowly regained feeling. I focused on remaining stick-straight, accepting his closeness without allowing my body to melt into his as it wanted to. *Damn my stupid body*. It deserved to spend some time in Dante's second circle of hell, for the lustful. As much as my mind had worked out all the reasons to stay away from Gabriel, there were moments—more than I wanted to admit—when my body demanded his presence. It didn't help when his arms tightened to quiet another shiver. My nose pressed into the pullover, inhaling.

Cedar. Cloves.

I sighed into his chest. Being this close to Gabriel was always the same, after my heart settled. Nice. Deliciously nice. Like racing home from school after it'd closed early on a snowy winter's day, to warm myself with a mug of Gram's hot chocolate. Home. A place of safety where I could drop my guard, relax. That was what he felt like when I didn't fight the sensations. Equally intoxicating, yet entirely different from the electric, breathtaking feelings Vin generated.

I stood immobile in Gabriel's arms for several minutes (although my nose may have nuzzled into his chest, but that was purely a matter of seeking his unbelievable heat). When I felt able to, I unglued my face, upper chest, and fingers from the cotton.

His arms tried to bring me back. "Please, Cassie. I just want to help. While I love—" At the sound of that word, that particular word, I jerked away and he broke off, letting me go.

"I'm warmer now." I lifted my chin in a stubborn gesture.

"If you say so." He shrugged, looking a bit defeated. "Sorry about not realizing you were getting cold. I don't usually think about that sort of thing."

"You're like a furnace." I gave up trying to look confident, warmer, and independent, and tucked my chin into my scarf.

"I can't help it," he said quickly, then turned, as if not wanting to see my reaction.

He got to work, much faster this time. He set up the tent below the rock overhang, rolled out our sleeping bags inside, threw in two pillows, then gently pressed a hand against my back, directing me in. He coughed and immediately withdrew his hand.

I crawled into one of the bags, thankful for its flannel lining.

"It'll be warmer if I close this." He zipped up the nylon opening of the tent, forgetting a sliver in the corner.

I scooted my cocoon over to that corner and watched as he built a modest fire and cooked the foil-wrapped packets Gram had put together for dinner. He paused several times to glance toward the tent, though I didn't think he could see in like I could see out. Each time, his face creased with an unreadable expression.

The draw of the fire and the smell of Gram's pot roast and butter beans pulled me back into the darkening night. I flipped up my hood, scurried to the fire, and rubbed my hands together over it. Gabriel motioned me to join him on his log. I looked around for another. "Is there anything I can do?"

"Just come enjoy the fire." He patted the end of the log. My only other seat options were cold rock and more cold rock.

"I don't know." I fiddled with my scarf, tucking the ends in my hood.

"Listen, we're both almost entirely covered. And that one time at the shelter was an accident. I'm so sorry, about that, really." Sincerity weighted down his face. "I didn't know about you then."

I did believe *that*, and I was strong enough to sit next to him without my body betraying me. Right? "Um, okay."

The log seemed too short. He seemed too big. Barely an inch separated us, and his body heat pulsed into me. At least the burning wood and our dinner masked his scent. I swayed slightly, leaning closer. Then away. Closer.

I scooted to the edge, half falling off.

"I know I've earned this. Made mistakes." Gabriel turned his broad shoulders and tried to look me in the eyes, which I made more difficult by staring into the fire. "Can we at least talk about it?"

I couldn't talk about it. I focused on the flames. I knew I was fighting feelings for him, but I had to protect myself. Focusing on the fire was easier. I was drawn in by fire. Even watching a single candle flicker mesmerized me. I never missed the town bonfires in the fall, despite the crowds. "You never answered me." I tried to redirect him.

"What's with all the gear and stuff? We're only out here one night. Right?" The flames sparked into the evening air. I'd always thought my interest in watching things burn was because my skin so often felt like it burned too. But that seemed backwards. I should fear fire, in that case. Maybe I could hope it was tied to some locked away memory from my past, a good one.

"Well, we're going to go pretty far inside the cave." Gabriel let me change the subject and shifted the foil squares at the edge of the fire with a long stick. "So I brought a bodysuit to keep you warm. And diving gear to get us through the passages closed off with water."

"Diving gear? How far in are we going?"

"Well, Spring Cave has miles of passages. There's hidden rooms that take up most of the space inside the mountain. Let's just say we're going pretty far. Farther than most have gone."

"This is safe?" I almost turned to look to him for reassurance.

"Perfectly. My dad made sure we knew the way when we were kids. How to use any equipment we might need. And there's less water sometimes." He sounded so confident. "But I got certified as a scuba instructor, just in case. I'll teach you everything."

"But aren't we supposed to stay out? I mean, the sign says we are. Aren't the bats sick?"

"That's just something Dad came up with to keep people out. There were other cave closures a few years ago, but the disease hasn't spread to the Rockies. They're pretty sure now people aren't a vector for the fungus anyway. We just made sure Spring Cave stayed restricted—fenced up good."

"Isn't that a pretty dirty trick to play on other cavers?" This devious side to the Knight family didn't increase my confidence in this trip.

"We had an incident, not long ago. The ban helps keep people away." He shrugged, seeming untroubled by their deception.

"And Gram knows about this deep caving business?"

"Not the details, but she knows it's important. You don't trust me?" His voice fell.

I didn't answer, but sighed, not bothering to hide my frustration. I'd thought he would've figured out by now that he didn't get trust until I got answers, and my locket. Any logical person would've figured it out. Or maybe I just wasn't very forgiving.

Gabriel sighed too, a pensive sound, then turned his attention back to the fire. When dinner was ready, we ate in silence, side by side. We finished at the same time. I jumped up. "I'll clean up. Secure trash over there." I pointed to a corner of the fence. "Wouldn't want it attracting animals."

"Great. I'll, um, just… check the area."

I guessed he meant for bears and, worse, mountain lions, who could be a real threat out here according to all the Forest Service's signs. But what was he going to do if he found one? He climbed the rock on the far side of the cave's entrance and disappeared into the darkness. My throat closed. *Don't worry.* I forced myself to breathe. *He's a big guy, and he'll call out if he needs help, right?*

I busied myself with putting things away and getting ready for bed. I scrambled out of my t-shirt and hoodie, changed from jeans to leggings, left my sports bra on, and pulled on the other top I'd brought, a thick wool sweater Gram had knitted me. I was almost ready to settle into the tent when the first crash of thunder erupted, followed quickly by several more, each one booming louder in the valley below. Dark clouds swirled around the mountain, then spewed a cascade of rain. A violent breeze swept around the entrance of the cave, saturating our shelter with damp air.

The fire was barely glowing, the few embers no help in combating the icy chill that seeped through my sweater as the moist wind howled.

I jumped into the tent, zipped it up, then zipped myself into my sleeping bag, but it did no good. It was too late. I was shivering again. And damn my stupid body, but it—*I*—didn't want to be alone this time.

What I wanted was Gabriel.

15
SHELTERED

I T MUST HAVE ONLY BEEN A FEW MINUTES BUT FELT LIKE FOR-
ever that I was alone, huddled under the sleeping bag, my limbs
numb but still quivering, my head buried under the bag's flannel lining. The beat of the rain picked up outside. My body shook
faster, as if adopting its rhythm.

The percussive pattern of sheets of rain striking rock was both
hypnotic and headache-inducing. Thin nylon walls were all that
separated me from the fury assaulting the mountain, and the rock
overhang all that kept it from pounding down on me. For a moment,
the pummeling reduced to a more sedate pitter-patter. I made out
the sound of someone rustling through our gear. The storm's rage
picked back up. "Gabriel," I tried to yell over it.

No response. Just the sharp beat of rain.

"Gabriel," I tried again, louder. "I need you." The last words
sounded small, but I wasn't going to pretend I didn't need his help
this time.

The zipper pulled back. The tent crinkled as he crawled in, re-
zipped the opening, and knelt at my side. "Is everything okay?" His
deep voice carried over a crash of thunder.

"I'm freezing again. Help. Please." Another shiver shook my
body, and I buried deeper, curling into a ball.

"Oh. The rain caught me. Give me a sec."

"What?" I peeked around the covering and cursed. Gabriel knelt over me bare-chested, water dripping from his hair.

"I'll grab a shirt." He wrapped a forearm around his ribcage and started to turn away in his boxer shorts.

"Um." The sound popped out of me, loud and insistent.

He turned back. The checkered material riding low on his hips did little to break up the expanses of skin. All tanned, except a strip below his belly button. "You don't need a shirt," I said, but what I meant was, "You don't need to be embarrassed by your scars." I just hoped I wouldn't regret it as I added, "It's just… why are you so tan?" I mumbled it into the edge of flannel, almost hoping he didn't hear me, but the storm quieted.

"I, ah, wasn't like this before coming home. But I like feeling the forest air on my skin, spending time on the mountain. Alone." He glanced down at himself, then over to me, like he was trying to figure out what I must be thinking.

God, he was beautiful. It had nothing to do with the shade of his skin—though it showed how much time he must've spent outdoors—it was just the sight of him. So much of him. The flashlight I'd left on by the other sleeping bag didn't help either, casting his hard legs and muscled torso into smooth lines and soft shadows. Even his scars looked less severe in the muted light.

Should I have him go back out, get dressed? But I was covered, and he had always backed off immediately when asked before—when it came to physical proximity, anyway. As if reading my thoughts, he said, "You know I would never touch you, without your permission."

"I know." The rain and wind picked up again, cold and relentless. I was so cold. I couldn't even feel my nose anymore. I had to get warm. I unzipped the sleeping bag, turned away, and with shaking hands checked that my leggings were tucked into my socks. I pulled my arms out of their sleeves, crossed them against my stomach under the wool, and looked back over my shoulder. "It's okay. Let's do this."

Gabriel scooted in behind me until his bare chest pressed against my sweater and his leg draped over mine, my leggings a thin but crucial barrier between us. His heat spread along my back and sank into me. "Ahh." The sound escaped my mouth. My legs jerked under his.

"Be careful." Gabriel's breath brushed my ear, warming it. "I know you're cold, but no sudden movements." He rested his head on the pillow and shifted to wrap an arm around my waist. It rested heavy, solid, strong. His hand lay below the line of my sports bra. We fit together immediately, naturally.

The shivers subsided.

"Thanks," I said. My calves rubbed beneath his leg of their own volition.

"Sure." His voice sounded muffled. A soft warmth pressed against my head, stirring up the vanilla scent of my shampoo.

"What are you doing?" Why was my voice so breathless?

"I'm sorry. I, um, rested my chin on you. I know your hair doesn't hurt, right, since I saw Vin—"

"Gabriel." To my surprise, I didn't want Vin invading this moment.

"I know you don't want to hear how I feel about you. But you have to know your hair… it's beautiful." His forearm flexed against my stomach.

"My hair's ridiculous." My voice rose over the wind howling outside. "And you really need to drop this fascination with me. I know I'm strange." My chin trembled.

He sighed into the curls bunched around my loose ponytail. "How can I explain?" He paused. "Your hair. It's special. Like the fire tonight. Like, almost like what we'll be seeing tomorrow."

More vague hints. Whatever. I'd gotten used to his family withholding information, promising explanations at some later and later date. "I need to tell you something, in case I fall asleep soon. I have these nightmares, and sometimes I can't control myself. I might scream. But no need to worry. I'll stop. If it happens, just go back to sleep."

"I'm not just going back to sleep if you wake up screaming, but we'll deal with that if it happens." He shifted against my back, and his arm tightened around me. "What are they about? The nightmares?"

"They're always the same. That morning I was found in the river." I tried to focus on what we were talking about, not how my body felt pressed against his.

"What happened?"

"I don't want to talk about it. Just wanted to warn you." Unfortunately, sleep seemed necessary, after our long hike today and before our plans for tomorrow. His warmth and the firm wall of his chest at my back lulled me, and I felt as though I was sinking into the pillow. Hopefully the storm would drown any sounds. The sweater should cover the burns.

"It might help to talk about it." Gabriel rounded his shoulders, pulling me deeper into the curve of his frame.

"It won't." I pulled back. A sliver of space between us filled with cold air.

"Please, I want to know." His voice barely carried over the rain, "What happened?"

"Fine." I pulled away further, needing more space to silence my body's desire to melt into him—a desire I would've bet money on not long ago that I'd never feel. I would've lost a fortune.

I tried to refocus on his question. "I'll tell you this." My muscles tensed. "I've suffered worse pain since. Like you saw at the cemetery, things have gotten worse." I curled in on myself. "But then, I had no chance to prepare, like I do now."

"At least tell me they were being careful—as careful as they could—when they got you out of the water?" Gabriel's voice was heavy with emotion. Empathy. Like he actually cared about me and despised the thought of me in pain. Nothing like a mildly curious med student observing an oddity, as I'd imagined.

"I have no idea. After just a few moments, it was too much. I blacked out."

His arm coaxed me impossibly, intolerably, close, yet I slid back to him without protest, my muscles relaxing enough to expand and contract with his chest. We breathed together, inhaling and exhaling as one for several long moments.

Wow, did everyone feel this synchronicity with people they allowed so near? I searched for the right word to describe this sharing of space, of movement, of emotion. It was almost… symbiotic.

"I'm so sorry for what happened." Soft weight pressed against my curls.

"I don't need your pity."

"It's not pity." He leaned forward.

"Okay then," I said, pausing him before his eyes found mine. "You have nothing to be sorry for."

"I do." His breath brushed my cheek. "Maybe I couldn't have prevented whatever happened when you first came here, but my family should've found you earlier. You shouldn't have been alone."

"I manage just fine on my own." My legs tensed under his.

"I know," he agreed easily, moving his head back. "I'll always regret not being there for you. But you're so strong. So much stronger than me."

"Yeah, no need for flattery. I know your family wants something from me. My point was simply that I make do. I don't need flattery, or pity."

"But," he sputtered, "you're incredibly strong. How can you not believe that about yourself?"

My cold lips pressed together. Nothing about my condition made me strong, but I wasn't about to admit out loud how pathetic it made me feel.

Gabriel released a long exhalation, his breath misting into the air. "I've suffered some painful things too… things I'd rather forget. And I ended up running away from my responsibilities and what was left of my family. Left for college early. Went farther away than

Dad and I'd planned too, even though I made myself go no farther than Denver. I was trying to escape any reminder of what happened, as if that was even possible. But you, Cassie—you're much stronger than that." His chest melded into my back as he took another expansive breath. "Stronger than me."

"I just didn't have a choice." If Gabriel had survived the loss of his mother, he must be pretty strong. Gram wasn't even my real Gram, and I couldn't imagine losing her. If I did have to leave her someday, if it was for the best, at least I'd know she was safe back in Meeker, back with friends.

"You could've let your condition beat you down. Instead, you found a way to deal with it, as best you could, and defend yourself. I really respect you for it. I wasn't that strong when it came time for me to be tested."

"What do you mean?" I started to turn toward him but was held down by his weight.

"When I was tested." He shuddered and tightened his grip. "I let the pain drive me away. As if I could forget the duty I will carry for the rest of my life, or at least until my family finds who we've been waiting for."

The cryptic talk had better stop tomorrow, as promised, but for now, I prodded gently. "Is this about your, um, scars? Do they still hurt?"

"No. But them being there bothers me a lot." The pillow shifted as if he shook his head. "In a way they're a reminder of how weak I've been and of what I lost. I was attacked, injured, in right about this spot, before I left for college." But weren't his scars from breaking into his family's storage shed?

"What happened?" Of course, if he was attacked here, I might know at least part of the answer, from the strange vision he'd shown me that first morning. That was why the view had seemed familiar. "It must have been horrible," I whispered.

"Knife wounds," he said simply. "Of course they hurt. But those things heal. I was speaking of something different." He shuddered again. "Something that eats away at me. Every day." His voice dropped so low it faded into the shrieks of wind. I moved farther back to hear him. The back of my head pressed into his shoulder, my hair rubbing between us, stirring up its vanilla scent again. It clouded around us in the humidity inside the tent. He tucked his chin around the top of my head and pulled me in tight, his subtle, spicy scent mingling with the vanilla. "I lost part of my family. My mom… my sister."

So it had been the day he lost his mom in the fire.

"Murdered."

"What?" I struggled to turn in the confines of his embrace, pushing at his arm and kicking off his leg. I wasn't thinking of protecting my skin, I just wanted to see his face. Free, I twisted in the sleeping bag, knocking my forehead against something warm and smooth.

Gabriel's shoulder. Muscled. Tanned. Entirely bare.

Oh no. I braced myself for pain. I kept waiting for it to ignite. It didn't. All I felt was the warmth, the suppleness of Gabriel's skin. The touch, the texture of it, but no pain.

No pain, I shouted in my head as a vision started. *No pain. No pain…*

A bare-chested Gabriel raced through the foyer of his family's home, then up the wide staircase carpeted in paisley, leaping three or four stairs at a time. He held a blood-soaked shirt against his rib-cage, and a sharp cry escaping his lips each time he jostled his chest. The right half of his face was a red, mangled mess of flesh. Blood trailed down his neck and chest.

He froze at the top of the stairs. "Mom! Sarah!" He looked down the hall, first left, then right, searching into the darkness beyond.

Silence.

"Mom! Sarah!" This time, he was begging.

"We're too late," Bernard called from below.

Gabriel turned and fell to his knees. He dropped the bloodied shirt, his head collapsing into his hands. "No!" he raged. Then again, so softly, his cry of grief was just for him. "No…"

At the bottom of the stairs, his father carried a small, blanket-wrapped bundle. Bernard's face was ghostly pale, his red eyes streaming tears onto the grey, nubbly-wool form in his arms. A limp hand protruded from a fold. Something fell from the blanket, landing with a thud.

A charred pink notebook.

"She had it with her, on a blanket, under the tree," Bernard whispered.

Gabriel lifted his head. "Under the tree?"

"Writing. Your mom wasn't far. Her tools were out of the shed, by her roses." Bernard's shoulders shook. The hand slipped from the blanket, revealing a thin, reddened wrist.

"No!" Gabriel wrapped his arms around his bloody midsection, folding into himself.

Bernard sank to his knees, curling his massive body around the small, bundled form.

The vision blurred, voices murmured indistinctly. Finally, a loud echo reverberated, "Dad! Cole's waking up." Aaron's voice?

"Stay with Cole, son. I'll be right up."

The visions swam into focus. Gabriel now stood stiffly in the foyer, his arms raised, as his father wrapped gauze around his chest. The blanket-wrapped form rested on a table nearby. The hand, like a toy doll's that had been held up to a lighter, still peeked out. On the floor at the foot of the table, a flowery bedspread swathed a larger bundle. Two tangled locks of honey-blonde hair spilled out one end. Gabriel's eyes flashed to them.

Bernard's gaze followed, his eyes welling. "I think they were strangled first," he choked out, "which means they were spared some pain."

"Spared?"

"I just mean…"

"Spared!" Gabriel roared, pushing away from Bernard. "They

were burned like trash. They can never come back now." Gabriel stumbled back, placing a hand on the huge sculpture in the middle of the foyer, struggling to breathe evenly. "Even if all the relics are found. Even if we somehow…" He leaned against the nymph. "Somehow bring back just the good ones." His chin fell, his shoulders dropped, his chest hollowing. "We should have been here, protecting them."

"We had to protect the relic. Right?" Bernard shook his head, as if banishing the doubt. "Of course. We had to protect it. You know that. If we hadn't, they still would have been targets. And if the Shadows found the relic, everything would be lost."

"How? How can you justify this?" Gabriel straightened away from the sculpture, wincing.

"I'm not justifying—" Bernard's voice cracked. "What happened… what happened to them." He gasped as if struggling to get enough air.

Gabriel stared back in silence.

"Your mother. She was my world—my whole life. And Sarah the sweetest, most precious—" Bernard glanced toward the table, taking another deep gulp that ended in a strangled sob. "We'll each have to find our own way. Somehow. To live with this."

Gabriel rubbed at dried blood on his neck. "But how did this happen? How were they discovered?"

"I don't know." Bernard shook his head, shutting his eyes. "I don't know."

"I'm not sure what you do know, having CJ patrolling the forest, the two of us up at the cave just because that thing lit up, while… No. This can't be happening!"

Bernard took several measured breaths, then looked at his son. "We have to find a way forward. We still have a job to do." He looked past Gabriel, to the sculpture of Apollo and his river nymph, then toward the door. "We have to protect it. They'll send someone else. As soon as you hibernate, the instant you heal, you and I are going to have to watch the entrance around the clock. Aaron, Cole, they're not ready. Cameron is no help. We may even need to wake the remaining elders."

"You can do that without me." Gabriel's voice was bitter. "As far as I'm concerned, they can have it."

"You can't possibly mean that." Bernard jerked forward, trying to wrap Gabriel in his arms.

"Oh, I do. I do mean it." Gabriel stormed past his father and slammed the massive front door behind him.

The vision faded, and I was back in my sleeping bag, the storm still howling.

A gust of wind snapped the dome of the tent, flapping the nylon with a sound like a gun shot. I jerked upright.

Gabriel knelt on the sleeping bag next to mine, caught in the full rays of the flashlight, staring at me with regret, clearly aware of what had happened—that we'd touched. We stared at each other in the dimness as a slow chill crept into the space between us. Several feet of tense, humid air. No longer so close our scents mingled, the space between our bodies now smelled of earth and rain. I would've demanded that space not even a day ago, regardless of having to be confined together, regardless of the cold. But now I wanted to leap across the chasm.

Instead, I pushed my arms through my sleeves, the wool scratching the backs of my hands.

"Oh God, please say you're okay." He leaned close to look at my forehead.

"I'm fine," I answered reflexively, and then realized with a shock that it was entirely true. The pain hadn't come at all. Even now, after the vision faded. Nothing. Absolutely nothing to indicate we'd touched besides my knowledge of the soft heat of Gabriel's skin. With nothing to obscure it.

What could I do to hold onto that feeling for the rest of my life? Gabriel's skin touching mine, even for an instant, had been bliss. Pure bliss. Could it happen again? If so, how long would it last? Especially before a vision started. Could a second try be just as wonderful as that first collision of skin?

I almost asked if I could touch him again but stopped short. Was it fair to pull another vision from him? Did I want to? With anyone else, the answer would have been a swift no, but the visions from Gabriel weren't so bad. Sad, more than anything. Which made them somehow more private. Intimate.

"Sure you're okay?" Gabriel asked in a rush. "You blacked out. I was calling your name, and you just stared up at me like you couldn't see me at all."

"I'm fine. I was just shocked to hear about your mother and sister…" This explanation, containing more truth than he knew, especially when I didn't understand how this vision fit in with news of the fire, didn't seem to reassure him.

"You sure?" Concern widened his eyes.

Maybe I should be more open with him. After all, Gram believed in Gabriel. And he was the only person whose touch had ever granted pleasure in place of pain. "I'll tell you something, but you have to keep it to yourself. No spilling. Not even your dad." Something told me I could trust him more than I'd been willing to.

"Well, I guess, if that's necessary." He swallowed hard and swiped his tongue over his bottom lip.

"Not anyone. People already think I'm crazy." I shifted onto my side and propped my head on my bent arm.

"You have my word." He breathed deep, expanding his chest.

"I'm not sure what that's worth." I kept my eyes glued on his scarred ribcage, afraid to look up into his soul-searching eyes, still not sure I was making the right decision. "But I'm going to risk the truth, since what's going on seems to be as much about you as it is about me."

"I'm not sure I understand."

"You will. The question is what you'll think of it." I sighed. "First, I didn't feel any pain when we just touched. Not one bit."

Gabriel made a sound of surprise. I didn't allow myself to look up.

"And the time you touched me before at the shelter, it wasn't so bad. Actually better than any contact has ever been for me," I said in a rush, as excitement momentarily overtook my hesitation. I barely caught his strained inhalation. I confirmed what he must be thinking. "I think it could have something to do with you specifically, since with everyone else the pain gets worse each time." My gaze moved between the scars on his torso. "But I know something's still wrong, because both times I still saw these visions… just now and at the shelter."

"What do you mean—visions?"

"I know this sounds crazy." I paused. "But when I touch someone, I see images. They form in my mind. Of bad things that person has done."

"Bad things?"

"Really bad," I mumbled to his chest, then dropped my eyes completely. "I see things that person might be guilty about doing or saying." I spoke more to the sleeping bags than to him. "But for most people, I think there is so much vileness in them, so much evil, guilt doesn't even play a part." My voice got softer. "When I touch them, their mind shows me something awful they have done, or thought about doing, and I see no remorse. And I can't explain how it happens. It just happens, every time." I looked back up but couldn't quite bring myself to go so far as his face, afraid of his expression.

"Oh, wow," he finally exhaled after a moment's pause, then moved in closer on his knees until I was forced to look up.

His smile was gentle. "Cassie, I had no idea. You should've told me. This explains so much."

"What could it possibly explain?"

"Well, you see, we're a lot alike." His crooked smile widened. "Well, actually, we're more like complete opposites." He laughed and lay on his side at the edge of his sleeping bag, practically nose to nose with me.

"There's nothing to laugh about." I scooted away and bent my arm farther back on my pillow. "Don't you understand? I see horrible things when I touch someone—absolutely horrible things they've done."

"I understand completely. Because when I look into someone's eyes, all I see is good."

My jaw dropped, and my head slipped off my hand.

"It's my gift from my mom's family. It can be a vision, like you spoke of," he explained. I curled into a tight ball and hugged myself. "But usually more like a mental impression or knowledge I get of all the best in that person… their best deeds, best thoughts, the kindest things they've done for others. It allows me to learn more about them, but even outside of that, it's a wonderful thing. It's almost like I absorb some of their goodness too. My gift allows me to share in their positive energy. It makes me… happy."

I recoiled further into my sleeping bag. Was he making fun of me? This couldn't be real.

Gabriel edged closer, keeping our gazes locked, letting me see his sincerity.

Slowly I relaxed, straightening into a more restful position.

He stared right into me, like always. "It's why I love looking at you. You're full of all that's good. And you express it in everything you do, in the most pure, genuine emotions."

"I don't believe you," I blurted out in a mixture of shock and disbelief. Shock that Gabriel could experience anything similar to what I did, and disbelief that he found anything good in me, or a lot of other people.

"I know you helped a young girl. You sent a video to the police."

My jaw fell open. Impossible he could know that. Unless… "You were probably following me."

"I know you've done similar things."

"Like?" I challenged.

"Like helping a shop owner clean up his store after it was vandalized. Like reporting that man who hurt Bosco, and working with

Dr. Garza to make sure he and the other bait dogs who survived ended up with you, so you could watch over them. Like encouraging a school counselor to talk to a girl who'd been raped. Stopping a bully at school who kept demanding money from another student. Exposing a classmate who was dealing to younger kids." His fingers combed his hair out of his face. "I could keep going, and that doesn't even include all the work you've done at the animal shelter day in and day out. Or the care you've shown Rose." He leaned in, and I mirrored him, drawn in by his magnetism. His fingers found a tangle of red curls that had escaped my ponytail and unraveled them. "But I could never figure out the motivation. Of course you're a good person. But how would you even know some of those animals or people were in trouble? Now it makes sense."

I sat up, the sleeping bag falling to my waist. All of my instincts told me to flee. That Gabriel knew too much about me, was up to some sort of trick. He was bound to hurt me. I knew that. I'd reasoned it all out before. He could know about the video I'd sent to the police if he'd started following me earlier than I'd thought. But how would he know about so many other things I'd done? Some when he'd been away?

For a moment I forgot I was trapped in a tent in the middle of a forest with a thunderstorm raging outside. Looking at him, gazing back at me with interest and care, even after I'd confessed the full extent of my abnormality, felt like a safe haven. A home. He felt like coming home. Acceptance. It warmed me, like the caress of Zoe's fur, the comfort of hearing Gram shuffling about in the kitchen. Exhilarating, to find it with someone my age, someone who claimed to be like me, but also terrifying. I had told myself so many times not to trust him. I had no idea how to respond to the confession of his "gift," as he called it.

"Have you seen things I've done from before? Before Meeker?" I decided to test him. Of course, I'd have no way of knowing if he was telling the truth.

He rolled onto his back, gazing at the shadows at the top of the tent. "No. And I'm not sure why. I've certainly tried. I would think if the memories were still there, I would be able to see them, even if you couldn't. But… no." He shifted on his side, facing me again.

I stayed silent, Gabriel's blue eyes never leaving mine. It seemed nothing fazed Gabriel. Nothing shocked him. Certainly not my revelation that I saw into people's minds. He accepted it without question.

Fine. I forced myself to breathe in and out, letting my knee-jerk moment of panic fade. The longer I stared back at him, the faster it disappeared. Along with most of my disbelief. I chose my response deliberately. For now, I would accept what he said was true. So Gabriel could see into people's minds too, specifically that part of them reflecting their morality—how they treated the world around them—like I did? *No big deal.*

And he saw only good things in people? Well, good for him. It was certainly better than what I saw, even if I doubted there could be much good in many people that wasn't born of self-interest and self-motivation.

The hair stood up on my arms.

I felt chilled again, and out of sorts, without Gabriel at my back. I sank under my sleeping bag, alone, blinking up at him, feel-ing lost. Mia had warned me that her sister had found him intimi-dating. Vin had warned me to not care too much too. I had plenty of other reasons not to allow myself to care. But I couldn't deny that something about Gabriel was special, especially to me. I could touch him. I wanted to touch him.

I rubbed my arms through the sweater. The thundering rever-berations of the storm crescendoed outside, swaying the tent and wafting in the sharp, mineral scent of wet rock. The temperature seemed to fall sharply. Gabriel's heat had been much more useful when he wasn't consigned to his own sleeping bag. It just didn't make sense to freeze all night, particularly now that there was way less risk of pain, if Gabriel accidentally touched me.

I didn't say a word. I simply pulled back my coverings, inviting him to join me. Gabriel turned off the flashlight and scooted into my small space. I slipped my arms back out of their sleeves, wrapping them against my cold stomach, and pressed my back into him in the darkness. He curved around me, one arm tightening above my stomach, the other resting above us. His fingers played with the ends of my curls.

I tucked my head under his chin and felt his prickly stubble through my hair.

Gabriel's chest expanded against me as he inhaled slowly, as if he were trying to breathe me in. He breathed out gradually, whispering into my hair, "It's going to be all right. It'll all make sense tomorrow. We're going to be just fine."

I took comfort in his words, even if few things in my life were ever fine.

I relaxed into his heat and slowly drifted toward sleep. I had a vague thought that it was so easy—simple and effortless—to let myself sleep tonight. I felt so safe and sheltered cocooned in Gabriel's warmth. Safe from the storm. Safe from pain. Safe from loneliness.

And as much as I knew I should fight those feelings, I didn't.

16
A LIGHT IN THE DARK

WHERE WAS I? I WOKE UP CONFUSED, ROUSED BY A GENTLE shake of my shoulder. Gabriel's voice in my ear. "Time to get up. It's an hour till dawn. We need to get moving."

Everything else happened in a dazed blur, in the dark of early morning. Gabriel directing me to put on a full-length bodysuit under my sweater and jeans, handing me an apple and one of Gram's oatmeal and nut bars for breakfast, helping secure the straps of the waterproof boots he'd brought along for me, putting a lighted helmet on my head, and loading us down with gear—a small day pack for me and a much larger one for him. I was still groggy, even as I crunched on the apple, and despite sleeping through the night in Gabriel's arms. I only had one coherent thought: This was the first night without the nightmare since Gabriel had stayed with me Monday night. And before that, since he'd carried me up to my room after the cemetery, staying with me hours then too.

I didn't want to think too much about that or what it meant.

The cave entrance was almost invisible in the faint glow before dawn, just a few feet of shadows, then a void. I yawned, actually wanting to go back to sleep, but following Gabriel's bodysuit-covered form inside. The lights on our helmets illuminated the coarse rock walls, revealing a spacious passage ahead. We walked quickly through it, silence and utter darkness surrounding us.

Cold, moist air hit my face, waking me up fully, and as the

chamber widened and sloped down, our footsteps echoed all around us. We passed a row of icicle-like structures hanging from the ceiling. A crowd of cone-like structures rose up from the floor under them. "Wow." I paused in front of what I'd only read about in textbooks. "Remind me what they are?"

"Stalactites, if they point down. Stalagmites usually form under them, and that"—Gabriel turned, pointing his light at a glassy, wave-like substance on the wall—"is flowstone." We kept walking past them, and other oddly-shaped cave formations, making me feel like I was walking through a statue gallery. We suddenly reached a sharp drop-off.

Gabriel grabbed my arm to steady me and I peered over the edge into a black abyss. My light shone down into a deep pit below, dispelling my hope that the way would be open and easy until we reached the underground rivers. Gabriel pointed to a ladder secured to the rock overhang by our feet, and we descended into the pit, then through a narrow, downward-sloped corridor.

My knees ached with the impact of hopping down from rock to rock. When the rock above us was too low to stand, we crawled on hands and knees, a rushing sound of running water in the distance. The space above us finally opened up, and the gentle rushing sound turned into a thundering reverberation. I paused, stooped over to avoid a cluster of stalactites. "We're hearing the largest underground waterway in Colorado," Gabriel explained over the gurgling pulsations. "The few adventurous cavers who'd made it this far named it Thunder Road. We'll catch a glimpse of it before following a series of passages much deeper into the mountain, to another series of waterways."

From that point on, Gabriel set a hurried pace, showing no hesitation about which passages to take, how to cross the channels of water we encountered, and where best to squeeze through the crevices where the walls narrowed to barely a body's width. At points the descent was so steep we used a rope system Gabriel devised to lower down our packs and then ourselves. We passed the edge of Thunder Road and finally approached another sizeable stream. "We've reached the first sump," Gabriel announced. "The first place where the passage to the next part of the cave is filled completely with water. We'll have to get in and use our scuba gear to swim through." We took off our helmets. He glanced at the quick rise and fall of my chest. "We can take a little break first, if you want."

I silently accepted by shrugging off my pack and sinking to the cold, damp ground.

My breath came in short, shallow gasps, gulping in the musty cave air, heavy with humidity from the stream running next to us. I felt like I'd just finished a long run through the forest. Gabriel looked as refreshed as ever. He knelt down and offered me a water bottle with a Bulldogs logo on it. "So," he said, "what did you see when we touched last night?"

"What?" I panted, grabbing the bottle from underneath, careful to avoid his fingers.

"I see only good things when I look in your eyes, or anyone else's for that matter, but what did you see last night... and the morning we met too?"

"Sure you want to know?" I struggled with the lid and took a small sip.

"Yes. I've thought a lot about what you could've seen. Was it really awful? Is that why you're struggling"—the scarred corner of his mouth twitched—"with how you feel about me?"

I took a larger draw from the bottle. "Well, that's the strange thing about what I saw. They were bad visions, but not bad in the sense I've gotten used to."

"What do you mean?"

After last night, I probably owed it to him to try to explain. "I think the first time I saw some sort of memory related to the time you said you were attacked outside the cave." Although I still didn't understand why the bears were involved. "And last night..." I lifted the water bottle to my lips and drained as much as I could to delay my answer. "I think I saw the moment when you found out that your mom and sister..."

"Oh." Gabriel looked away. His shoulders slumped.

A faint scuffling sound echoed from the passage we'd come through, mingling with the hum of the nearby water. Do bats get this deep into the cave? I shuddered, but reminded myself bats were actually really beneficial creatures, and refocused on Gabriel's distress. "But what I don't get"—I held up the half-empty bottle back to him until he took it—"is why I saw those things when we touched. Before, I've only seen things that reflect that person's dark side, things that person is sorry for or should be sorry for. How are your memories about anything you did wrong?" Maybe he'd explain why the memories were different than what the news reported too.

"Because I should feel remorse. I do. I feel guilty to this day." Gabriel finally collapsed to sit next to me, raised the water bottle to his drooping mouth, and finished what I had left in one long swig, drops escaping out of the slanted corner of his lips. "While my dad and I were outside the cave protecting what we'll be seeing soon, my mom and sister weren't protected... protected like they should have been. Like they would have been if I'd stayed with them." He wiped his mouth with the back of his hand. "They were being attacked." His hand lingered at the corner of his mouth, touching his scarred flesh, and his eyes focused on the swirling water nearby. "Burned. Burned until you couldn't recognize their faces." His hand fell and tightened into a fist in his lap. "And when Dad and I finally got back home, after, my dad made me out to be some sort of hero, to explain my wounds." His mouth contorted. "I was no hero." The tension fell from his hand, he rubbed the heel of his palm into his chest. "Especially when I let my grief drive me away."

My arm twitched at my side. "I can't imagine how horrible it was." I wanted to reach out to him. But stopped myself, shocked by the feeling.

"It was awful, but it was worse for Dad. He got home first. He found Aaron and Cole, out cold, brushed aside like they were trash.

He saw the fire on the lawn, just raging. Bodies, my mom and sister, inside…" Gabriel sighed. "Aaron came to, and helped get Cole to bed, but Dad had to handle the worst." His uneven features twisted into a grim expression. "Aaron was hard on himself for getting knocked out. He and Cole were ambushed. I tried to tell him if there had been a real fight, he and Cole probably would've been killed too. It would've taken Dad or me to have had a chance. Or CJ."

"CJ?" That name from his sister's diary.

"Cousin Jesse. My sister nicknamed him CJ. Dad's second cousin. Cameron's father." Gabriel's chin dropped to his chest.

"What happened to him?"

"CJ was also murdered that day, still in the forest, while my dad and I were racing to get home. Whoever got to my mom and sister… they, they killed CJ on their way out." Gabriel scooped up a pebble and threw it into the water in a hard yet graceful motion.

"But I thought Cameron's dad left?"

"No." Gabriel scooped up another pebble, but didn't throw it. He clenched it in his fist. "We had to bury his body, hide any evidence of what really happened, to keep our secrets safe. My mom and sister's deaths were hard enough for people—the police—to accept." He gulped. He paused for several moments, opening up his hand, rolling the pebble around in his palm, then whispered, seemingly to himself, "If only they'd stayed inside. Alarms on. I've never understood why they were outdoors." He dropped the pebble and rubbed his palm into his chest again, as if his heart ached, his voice falling softer still. "Maybe, in the safe room. Maybe even CJ…" His voice fell away.

I shifted, leaning closer. I didn't know what to say. How to comfort him. What might make Gram feel better? I reached for a bodysuit glove in the pack nearby, slipped it on and placed that hand on the cold rock near his. Several moments passed with just the sound of rushing water. At last he raised his chin. "Unlike Aaron, I left. Lost sight of my responsibility to keep guarding what's hidden here. I blamed my dad for caring more about some stupid object than protecting his family." He scrubbed a large hand over his face, as if he could erase the memory of what had happened. And, it seemed, how he'd reacted. His hand fell back to the rock, tensing again. "But we do have a duty. And Dad couldn't know we'd be attacked again that day, and how, after so many years, at a vulnerable moment. He did the best he could. I get that now."

"I'm still confused about how you did anything wrong." I shook my head. "How could you've seen such violence coming?"

"Because they were in the same danger you're in." His body stiffened as the tension in his fist spread. His muscles tensed, flexed and strained against his bodysuit.

I tensed too.

"All the females from families like ours are being hunted, killed, their bodies burned. So they can never come back to this world."

"Never come back?" I shivered.

Gabriel seemed lost in his thoughts. "And what makes it even more horrific—so ridiculously horrific—is that only one female even matters." He glanced at my hair spilling over my shoulder as his voice faded.

"Matters?" I prompted over the gurgles of the stream.

Gabriel sprung to standing, shaking his head. "Come on. I'll explain soon, where it's safe."

"Why does everyone keep insisting it's not safe to talk anywhere but in the middle of a mountain?" I bit my lip. "Is this about the shadows Gram's worried about?"

"Yes. The more layers of rock, and the closer to what we'll be seeing soon, the better."

"You mean safer."

"Yes. Time to move." He stepped in and reached out his hand to mine. Seeing that one was bare, with no fabric covering it, he snatched his hand back.

"What's the rush?"

"The sun's rising as we speak. You'll understand when you see it."

I gave in, curious to see whatever he was talking about, pushing myself to my feet. I removed my boots and outer clothing so I stood just in my bodysuit, and let Gabriel outfit me with scuba equipment—a second glove, head covering, a diving mask, pressurized dive tank, weight belt, diving booties, and flippers. I tucked a stray curl into the head covering and kept checking for stray hairs, as if getting my hair wet was my greatest concern.

Mercifully, Gabriel didn't point out my fidgeting, and instead seemed to know I'd never gone diving before, that I knew of. He explained several times how everything would work, patiently quizzed me to make sure I understood, then helped me into the water. We turned on our dive lights, swam toward the far wall, and finally submerged, swimming down, down, and down, to where it was cold, dark, and silent except for the hissing of our air. About 20 feet under, Gabriel waved away a cloud of silt and pointed to an opening in the rock. We swam through it, emerged through the passage, and swam up on the other side. We reached the top and Gabriel removed his mouth piece and directed us to the side where an expanse of dry rock jutted out above us. He pulled himself out of the water first, then lifted me out by my arms. "Good job, you're a natural," Gabriel praised then hurried us down a narrow path bordering the stream until we reached a dead end, and we repeated the same process of getting into the water, swimming across and down, through thick layers of silt this time, and passing through another underwater sump.

By the time we completed the third sump, the awkwardness and weight of the tank slowed me down. Whatever the Knight family had down here must be pretty special to warrant so much trouble. Whatever it was had a topnotch security system. Even if you knew it was in the mountain, how would you find it without knowing the location of all these underwater passages that the streams kept so well concealed, and made so difficult to pass through?

If all the work to get into the cave hadn't added to the question of what could possibly be hidden here, I might have given up when we reached yet another sump. Was it the fifth or sixth? I forced myself back into the water and once on dry rock on the other side, was rewarded with Gabriel's announcing "We're almost there!" We tore off our gloves and scrambled out of our equipment, leaving everything but our bodysuits and booties on a convenient, table-high ledge, with such a smooth surface—had it been carved into the rock wall? Before I could ask, Gabriel was off, striding down a descending corridor.

I raced to keep up. He abruptly turned to the side of the path, stopping beside a boulder. He pushed and struggled to move it. After several moments of effort, it finally slid away, revealing a low crevice in the wall. He dropped to his stomach, and wormed his way through the tiny opening. "Come on, Cassie," he called from the other side. "You're going to love this. We're not too late. It's glowing brighter than ever."

I crouched down and slithered through after him, wiggling my hips and pawing the cold, damp floor. The ceiling on the other side was low, but started to slant up. I crawled forward, and when there was room above, prepared to stand, but was rendered frozen by the sight.

The brilliant light, radiating from where Gabriel stood in front of me.

Gabriel had led me to a large chamber, crowded with the most spectacular natural wonders I'd ever seen. Immense stalactites hung from the ceiling, the largest where the ceiling rose impressively high at the far end of the cavern. Huge stalagmites stood in crowds across the floor, mounding up like giant roasted marshmallows. Wet, colorful flowstone surrounded us, shimmering in shades of brown, orange, and red. None of the other cave formations had been as breathtaking. What was even more remarkable was that I could see them all so well. Because of the light shining from the middle of the chamber floor.

There was so much light, it was if someone had dug a shallow pit and lit a bonfire in the mountain. Gabriel stood to the side of it, smiling down over it, the uneven planes of his face set off like they had been last night when we were sitting over the campfire. But there was no smoke. Just light. A small sun in the cave's core, its brightness illuminating the entire room, causing the flowstone to glow with golden hues.

Something about the light called to me, urging me forward into the absolute silence of the space. It pulled at me, warming my body, filling me with energy.

The desire to get closer to it grew.

My muscles twitched, ready to race toward it. My heart pounded loudly in my chest. At last I stood, and carefully stepped around the rock formations to join Gabriel. "Look," he said softly, almost reverently, and pointed down. "It's just like your locket."

I inhaled sharply. He was right.

The light radiated from a stone that appeared to be an exact replica of my locket—just fifteen or twenty times its size. A little larger than a football. This stone was also a thick oval, almost egg-shaped. And just like my locket, it had a swirled red and orange marbled surface. The similarities ended there, however, because this stone glowed so strongly it looked like it was on fire, giving off unnatural flashes like rolling waves of flames. The swirls in the stone itself took on a spectrum of colors, from the burnt orange of the sky at sunset to the vibrant red of the wildflowers in the forest, to the deep crimson of the pooling blood I'd seen once in a vision.

"What is it?" I continued to stare down. "And how the hell does it glow like that?"

"One thing at a time." Gabriel stepped closer until we stood side by side. "First, it only started glowing recently. My dad talked to Rose about when exactly you were found in White River, and we think it first started glowing when you came here." His arm, covered by his bodysuit, brushed mine and I inched to the side, but couldn't bring myself to move away from the stone. "And that was just days before I was attacked outside the cave and when my mom and sister—" he broke off and took a deep breath. "So we think your arrival, the light revealing itself, and the Shadow's discovery of it being here are all connected somehow."

"So because of some coincidence where I almost drowned in the river, you think this light has something to do with me?" It had to be more than a coincidence, but… I tore my eyes away from the flames to look up at him. "I mean, I know it's strange my locket looks like this thing." I turned back to the pit. "But what does that mean?"

"Well, in all the time this stone has been entrusted to my family, there was never any light reported. It's like it suddenly came to life when you arrived. Of course, we didn't know about you arriving. And worried it was a sign danger was near." Gabriel swallowed. "It glowed just a bit at first. My dad says it's gotten brighter since. And when I came home this summer, camping on the mountain, I spent a few days down here—um, resting—and discovered the light dims late at night, then brightens as the sun rises and right after." He rubbed his hand on his forehead. "It's weird though. When I've been back, sometimes it stays strong all through morning, other times not. Sometimes it glows more strongly in the evening. It's like it's a gauge, tied to the waxing and waning of something… something we're not seeing."

"But what makes it glow?" I knelt down and looked for some sort of power source where the stone rested. "What is it?"

"Well, from what we know, from what has been passed down through my family, the stone is simply a vessel. For what it holds inside. We call it a relic. The Fire relic."

"But if it didn't even light up until recently, how would you know what to call it? Or what's inside?" I rose to my feet.

"Because when it was given to us, my ancestors were told it's tied to the properties of fire."

"Hmm."

"Fire is one of the five natural elements classified by the Greek philosopher Aristotle." He looked at me expectantly, as if waiting for me to realize something important.

"So…" I did not immediately realize something important.

"So, somewhere other races stand guard over Earth, Water, Air, and Aether, and we were given Fire." Gabriel's large body shivered next to me, causing me to tear my eyes away from the light. "We were told to keep it hidden. Make sure it stayed safe. And to wait for a girl… to keep waiting, for however long it takes. And we have." He closed his eyes, breathing in like some sort of monk or yogi, stilling the shivers of his body. "My family has waited so long for her." Gabriel opened his eyes and gazed down at me, blue eyes bright with hope.

Before I could speak, could even breathe, a scuffling sound from behind us jarred us both. The sound was much louder than the one I'd heard before by the first sump. We spun to face the direction of the sound, at the entrance of the chamber.

A massive man—even larger than Gabriel—was writhing his way on his stomach through the opening we'd crawled through. He'd already pushed his bald head and half of his bare chest through, struggling with muscle-corded arms to pull the rest of his body in.

Gabriel stepped in front of me, blocking my view, drawing himself up to his full height. "Touch the relic," Gabriel called over his shoulder, his voice urgent, a tendon straining on the side of his neck.

"What?" I tried to see around him to catch a better glimpse of whoever—whatever—was trying to come in after us.

"The stone—touch it! Even if it burns you. Now!"

"But…" My voice trembled. I craned my head around Gabriel, finding myself needing to stare at whatever it was that had come after us. The giant had gotten stuck. He slowly scooted himself back out.

"Just trust me!" Gabriel pleaded, and shoved me back behind him.

I looked down at the glowing stone—so much like my lost locket—and felt the strong pull once more. The flames beckoned me, summoning me to the colorful surface below.

"Touch it!" Gabriel commanded, his deep voice rising with authority, and a hint of panic I'd never heard from him before.

I knelt down to the hollow in the floor, as much to appease Gabriel as to assuage my own yearning to get closer to the light.

Touch me. Touch me. The light seemed to sing in my head. I rested my hands on the cold edge of the pit, then scooted forward, reaching in. The flames parted for my hands as I got close, then dampened completely as I leaned down and touched the stone. It was hot, but not unbearably so, and a surge of energy shot up my hands. A jolt of electricity raced through my veins. Warm currents flowed up my arms, spreading like tiny sparks through my body. I tried to lift it, wanting to bring it closer, but it was heavier than its size suggested, and hardly moved. So I just closed my eyes, reveling in the contact, generating a glorious feeling, even better than the natural high after a long run through the forest.

Then—nothing.

The flow of energy vanished, the stone turned scorching hot. I let go with a wince and opened my eyes. The stone glowed back at me, taunting me with its mysterious light, the same as before. Maybe a little less bright? "Was it supposed to do something?"

"Yes," Gabriel yelled back. "Don't you feel different?"

"Not really." I stood and turned to face him, only to be greeted by his bare back, the upper curve of his glutes exposed, the top half of his bodysuit now dangling against his powerful legs. My breath caught in my throat. Even with everything going on, my eyes were glued to the sight.

"You held it tight, not just for an instant?"

"Yeah. It was really warm, almost hot."

Gabriel cursed, taking a small step back closer to me, and away from the entrance of the chamber. "That's not what we expected." Anything else he might have been about to say was interrupted by a pounding clatter echoing from the walls. The giant seemed to be trying to widen the opening before making another attempt to get inside. Gabriel continued to watch the giant carefully, slipping off his booties and removing the rest of his tightly fitted suit. "Pay attention."

His suit bottom fell to the cave floor with a soft thump. I started to look away, but something within me fought the instinct, fought the embarrassment, and I gave myself permission to look. I stared at

Gabriel's naked body from the back, taking in the soft tan lines around his glutes, watching his large muscles flex as he stepped away from the suit, glanced over his shoulder at me, and positioned himself in front of me. Knowing I was looking at him. Allowing me to see him.

"Cassie, you need to listen closely. I'm going to do something that might scare you. And I won't be able to talk to you once I do it. But as soon as that thing is clear of the hole and I have him pinned, I want you to go back through and run as fast as you can to the water. You'll need to try to swim back through—get out on your own. And if you get lost, or run into anyone, you need to hide. And—" Gabriel paused, as if he was just developing this stupid plan as he spoke, still deciding what came next. "And just keep hiding for however long it takes," he continued, "until you hear my voice, or my father, or Aaron. One of us will come for you. And if you run into any bears… well, they're old, they'll probably be asleep. And if not, you don't need to be afraid. Just make sure you stay hidden from anyone but my family or the bears," he exhaled the final words in one breath. "Understand?"

Nonsense. If Gabriel feared we were in danger, I wasn't going to just run and hide. I wasn't going to just leave him.

"So you'll do what I just said?" he asked over the rhythmic hammering now pulsing from the chamber's entry. "Cassie?"

"Uh-huh," I mumbled, and stepped out from behind his naked body so I could get a better view of what we were about to face. There was no time for embarrassment or nerves. A large pickaxe swung up and down in the hole Gabriel and I had crawled through. Chunks of rock fell around the entry, smacking the floor, striking up a percussive beat slightly out of time with the rhythmic pounding of the pickaxe. The echoes bounced around the chamber. A pummeling tempo like the rain last night.

With every sound assaulting my ears, my heart beat faster. Whatever this creature was, it was about to break through.

17

LAST ONE STANDING

T HE PICKAXE DISAPPEARED. THE PUMMELING STOPPED abruptly. The echoes started to fade and the giant exploded head-first through the enlarged opening.

Though silence descended around us, my heart still raced and a muscle jumped at the side of Gabriel's neck.

As the giant dove in, his arms circled out like he was swimming, making a breaststroke. He swept aside the chunks of rock, landed with a massive thump, and slid several feet across the floor. From a crouching position on his hands and knees he crawled forward, then unfurled his body, expanding to fill the low entrance of the cavern with a bulky mass of muscle and ungainly limbs, clad surprisingly only in wet cargo pants. He bumped his head into the rock above, and tilted his head to the side so he could fit. Surveying the room with his head tipped, his eyes passing over us like we were part of the scenery, he seemed in no hurry to say—or do—anything. He obviously knew exactly where he stood.

Between us and the only exit.

I waited for Gabriel to make the first move, since he seemed to know what we were dealing with. I took a deep breath, trying not to show any emotion as the intruder flexed his arms and shoulders like a wrestler warming up. He had no sense of urgency in his motions, as though he knew he had all the time in the world, and didn't have to rush anything. Because there was nothing we could do to stop him. His appearance made me recall the vision of Gabriel's memory outside the cave. *An ox of a man. Starkly bald and gigantic—even larger than Gabriel. Wider. His chest a battering ram.* Clearly, he was related to whatever that was in Gabriel's vision, big as an ox and armed with sharp knives. Removing any doubt, my gaze came to rest on the leather sheaths secured by a belt and hanging to either side of the giant's dripping cargo pants. One empty—missing the pickaxe—the other contained a wide blade with a curved hilt protruding from the top, ready to his hand.

He finally looked at Gabriel, giving him a cocky expression. "I'll spare you." His voice was soft, dusted with a light accent that made "spare" sound more like "sfare."

Gabriel's head snapped back slightly, as if he was confused by the giant's statement.

"You heard me right. I'll spare you, Cave Bear." Bear? And Gabriel had mentioned bears. Was Gabriel… related? "Just leave the girl and the relic, and get out." He stared at Gabriel, taking several hulking steps toward us and the light source. He canted his head to the side even more with a piercing crack, and straightened his neck once he had enough room above his head. His calm, almost lazy demeanor was even more frightening than if he had been in a hurry to get this over with.

"You don't need to do this." Gabriel raised bent arms in front of his chest, and the giant froze. "She's not the Una."

Una? The girl he'd been talking about?

"The Summum Malum says all the girls burn."

Summum Malum?

"So she's going to burn." The giant jerked his head toward me. "She'll burn just as soon—"

"But she's not the Una." Gabriel interrupted, closing the distance between us, his bare back blocking my view. "She touched the relic, nothing happened."

"He's right," I volunteered, stepping around Gabriel, wondering if what I could (or couldn't) do with the stone was the whole issue. "I can touch it again, to show you."

"Then I'll let you walk out of here," Gabriel continued, "and you can take your chances going after it another day. If you just promise to never hurt her."

"I've heard about your race. Are you really so naive, or are you just an idiot?" His accent made it sound like id-ee-ot. I tried to place the accent, but was at a loss. It sounded sort of like Vin's, but monotone, without Vin's melodic inflections. Every syllable evenly stressed, each word delicate and silky. The way he pronounced "idiot" was like he'd learned that word just to taunt us. Toy with us. Just like the lack of urgency in his body language. It was like he planned to take his time.

"Naive? If that's what you've heard, you're in for a surprise," Gabriel answered.

"You? Surprise me? The only surprise is that you are even more of an id-ee-ot than I thought—not leaving now, while I am letting you," he grumbled. "It was not my idea to give you a chance. Not my fault if you are too stupid to take it."

"What?" Gabriel asked almost inaudibly, evidently puzzled by the giant's grudging offer to let one of us go—even if was just… him.

"And no matter how dense the hide, blades are the best weapon against your kind"—he swung his knife out—"and when I hit the right spot, my blade will take you down just fine."

"Think you'll get a chance?" Gabriel shifted, his back broadening in front of me. "I've grown since the last time I faced one of you."

"No matter. You are so inexperienced, you would never have escaped to nurse those scars. My brothers would have survived, not you, if that other bear and your father had not been there. And I made sure to take care of that other bear, when you just left him there afterwards. All alone in the forest." He chuckled. Gabriel's hands clenched, muscles tensing all the way up to his shoulders. "Too bad it is you here, not your father." The giant sighed in regret.

"Leave my father out of this."

"Do not worry, little Cave Bear. That is part of the deal too."

"Deal?" Gabriel's head tilted in puzzlement.

"Yes. But if it was up to me, your father would not be spared. Not after the trouble he caused." The giant shook his head. "The few times your father left the entrance and actually entered the mountain, he moved too quick to follow very far inside. Then some old bears ambushed my cousin—"

"Admit it," Gabriel cut in. "You're not up to the job, just like the rest of your family. And they're dead." His mouth spat out the last word like an attack.

"Not up to the job?" The giant laughed. "We are just careful." He paused, appearing to ponder Gabriel's words. "Like you, there are not many of our kind left." A somber look flashed across his large face. "But at least we do not ask old men to fight, to add to our numbers. I cannot believe your race was chosen as one of the five. Simple-minded Neanderthals," he snarled. The giant lifted his weapon higher, steely glints running along the blade's edge as it reflected the light now pulsing from the stone behind us. "So simple-minded, this morning you left the way in wide open." Gabriel flinched. "You led me straight to the relic, and brought the girl with you for me to kill. Like a present. So... you were asking for this."

My pulse quickened, my body readying for action. Everything—the knife, the giant's position in front of our only exit, his unhurried attitude and rambling talk, to the lengths he'd gone just to follow us down here—signaled deadly, patient malice. And unshakable confidence. He was prepared to hurt us. More than hurt us.

"If you want to fight, fine." Gabriel turned his forearms outward, as if bracing for an attack. "Just leave her out of this." Gabriel suddenly shifted his weight forward, preparing to lunge, reminding me again of the attack outside the cave. My body, already prepared for action, flooded with adrenaline.

Too much adrenaline. My heart pounded too fast. My hands trembled. My body shook.

I tried to stop the small jerky movements as I considered what to do. "Gabriel, maybe you should just gug-go like he said—g-get help," I stammered in a harsh whisper, hoping only he could hear me. It wasn't much of a plan, but Gabriel would be safe, and if help didn't come in time, maybe I could lull this guy into a position where I could surprise him. Escape.

I was so much smaller, light on my feet. Surely it would be easier for me than Gabriel. Besides, the giant seemed willing to let him walk away.

Gabriel glanced back at me, but didn't respond. I caught a glimpse of bare chest, scarred ribcage, a trail of hair leading down… abruptly, I looked away, reminded all too clearly that he was completely naked so he could fight better. *Not the time for embarrassment or nerves.*

The giant smirked, watching our exchange. "What is funny too," he snorted, "is that we did not even know she existed until you brought her here. The Summum Malum had no idea that there were any females left in this area, since the last two we killed. They were yours, right?" The giant's smirk widened.

Gabriel tensed, cords of his neck standing out. "Shut up. You talk too much. Like a monster in a movie. But this isn't a movie."

"This will be whatever I want it to be." The giant's smirk twisted into a sneer. "And with this new female here, this will be exactly what I need it to be. It was risky letting her get so close, just in case she was the Una. But I knew you'd lead me here, right to the relic, and she'll still die in the end."

Die in the end!? Gabriel already told him I wasn't the girl he wanted—nothing happened when I touched the stone. Maybe I really should just touch it again, to show him? I started to back toward it.

The giant's face relaxed into a sickening smile as he leisurely looked me over from head to toe, freezing me in my spot, speaking to Gabriel without tearing his eyes from me. "And if you stand in my way, Cave Bear, I will gut you like the animal you are." He pointed the knife tip directly at Gabriel.

"Why are you doing this?" I shouted, desperately hoping we could resolve the situation without a fight. Because that was not going to go well for us. The giant did not answer, simply staring at me with a sick hunger on his face, refusing any resolution other than the violence he had long planned.

"Why are you helping them?" Gabriel echoed, drawing the giant's attention back to him. The giant ignored him, taking another step forward. "The least your race owes is an answer." Gabriel's statement boomed across the chamber, reverberating and echoing back to us from every corner and recess.

The giant paused. "Why are we helping them?" His expression hardened. "Because after working so long to get back, the Summum Malum can finally do it." The giant swept his free hand in the air, closing it into a huge fist, one of his shoulders nearly brushing a low-hanging stalactite, pointing down like a stone dagger toward the floor. "And then," his voice grew stronger, "when they are back, they bring back the rest of our race with them. That is the agreement." His fist opened, hand hanging in the air before he dropped his arm, an unreadable emotion sweeping across his face. He looked past us, toward the light, and for the first time, the giant's amusement vanished entirely. He had a strange look, not of fear, or uncertainty, but of desperation.

Gabriel and I glanced at each other, acknowledging how this had to play out. The inevitable conclusion. Even if I could understand everything the giant was talking about, there was no responding to it. There was nothing I—we—could say or do. The giant wouldn't be stopped. Not by words. Not by telling him, or even showing him, I wasn't the girl he was after. He wanted to kill me anyway.

"You know the Summum Malum can never bring back the girls who were burned." Gabriel held his stance.

"So what?" the giant shot back softly. He took yet another stride to close the decreasing distance between us. "There are plenty other of our females trapped with them."

"But why now?" Gabriel demanded. "Why would you suddenly start helping them now?"

"You want more answers? Before she dies?" The giant smiled, unshakeable in his belief that there was nothing we could do to avoid the fate he had in store. "The Summum Malum realized that using humans to interact with the physical world is too unpredictable. So we struck a deal."

"You know that before that ever happens, they'll come after your remaining girls, when they're done with the others. Right?"

The giant laughed, a hard, grim sound. "We don't have any left to be killed. Your father got lucky finding that fairy-thing we got rid of," a trace of the prior taunting tone returned, "but you and your brothers won't have anything left but human girls—"

"You don't know what other races are still out there," Gabriel jumped in, "or how many girls remain." Gabriel's bare body stiffened for the first blow even as he spoke. "There could be hundreds, even thousands, left. Even some of your own out there."

"Delusions," the giant snorted, his voice finally betraying a hint of tension. "No more delaying. It's time to make your decision. Do you live or do you die today?" The giant plodded toward us quicker than before, knife in hand. Though he was unarmed and quivering, Gabriel didn't budge, didn't leave me. The giant raised his knife. As I prepared to deliver the best blows I could, I cursed myself for not doing more weapon work in my self-defense training. Target the groin and head.

And stop shaking!

All thoughts vanished as I glanced at Gabriel and saw a furry haunch instead. I blinked several times, fearing I'd fallen into one of my visions, as I watched the fur travel down a bare leg, toward a ripped pair of pants on the stone. Gabriel's shoe burst open, shredded by the clawed foot that formed within. I craned my head up. A huge, unwieldy bear now stood on hind legs in his place. It knocked its domed head against one of the stalactites and roared loudly. I shook my head to clear it, but Gabriel was really gone. What remained was a massive, dark brown bear with bright blue eyes, forearms bent, braced for attack. Fierce. Threatening. My heart pounded.

The bear lunged at the advancing giant. They collided and collapsed to the ground in a tangle of thrashing limbs.

What should I do? What could I do? With flesh and fur blurring before me? They moved so fast. Too fast. Claws, teeth, straining muscles flashing. My heart throbbed in my chest. The giant ended up on his back, struggling beneath the bulk of the bear. The bear had the upper hand, but surprisingly seemed to be holding back in the brawl, simply intent on pinning the giant down.

After several attempts to push the bear away, the giant stopped. Stopped struggling entirely, suddenly accepting his vulnerable position with the animal above. He labored to push his knife into the bear's torso. The jagged, saw-like portion of the blade merely cut away a small mat of fur.

The giant pulled back and tried again.

But the bear's hide acted as an almost impenetrable barrier.

The bear snarled in response, pushing forward to place both forepaws across the giant's shoulders, fully pinning down the giant and his knife. The bear then lifted its head and turned its long neck to the side. To look right at me.

The bear's gaze bored into mine. It bellowed softly, and motioned to the entrance of the chamber with its dark muzzle. It bellowed again.

I wanted to move, but was frozen. Disconnected from my body and everything around me, like the past few moments hadn't really happened. Like I was trapped in some sort of warped horror movie, and, as I watched it in playback, I realized I was one of those throwaway cast members whose purpose was to act helpless and be eaten in the next scene. My voice and body played along with the script, both failing me.

The bear continued to hold my gaze. Its deep blue eyes pleaded for me to go.

I finally stepped forward. To do what? To help the bear, to leave, to do something, I don't know—and in that moment the giant saw his opening. He pulled away from the bear, swinging his arm back to ram the knife's sharp tip into the side of the bear's neck with all of his strength.

The bear yelped, then howled in pain. The blade had finally found its mark, penetrating below the fur, although strangely stopping less than halfway in. The exposed metal of the blade jutting out of the fur shone orange from the light behind us.

The bear's howls turned into agonized roars and it clawed at the giant's body. The giant seemed oblivious to the attack, focusing on one thing. Just one thing. Pushing and sawing the knife back and forth, with great effort, to force the blade all the way in until hilt met hide.

As the knife slid bit by bit into the animal's neck, the bear went rigid. Its eyes flashed rage and something in the animal snapped. The bear growled harshly. Its long claws tore into the giant's flesh in a frenzy. Over and over. Showing no mercy.

The chamber filled with a pink fog, and a pelting of droplets. The bear's forelegs moved in a blur through the spray jetting from the giant. I was so close, the mist enveloped me.

My body shook at a frantic rate. I couldn't even turn away from the massacre, or step back from the warm haze continuing to foul the cold cave air. And through it all, I could see the giant was still intent on driving the knife home. Twisting it. Turning it. Deeper and deeper.

The bear's growls weakened. It gradually stopped clawing.

I tried to move again, but all that resulted was my hand lifted to wipe a smear of copper-smelling paste from my face. I looked down. My hand was slick. Shiny. Scarlet.

The giant heaved at the inert mass pinning him down, heaving again, finally rolling the bear off him. He straddled the animal's body and sat down right on top of it, his legs on either side of the bear's rounded midsection. The giant's chest and arms were a shredded mess, and yet, as he looked down at his captive, he seemed entirely unconcerned by the damage the bear had done. He pulled the blade out of the hide around the bear's neck, watching in apparent triumph as a fountain of deep red spouted from the wound.

The giant then turned his head to the side and looked at me, bestowing a thin smile, transforming into a threatening leer. His gaze ran up and down my body, then over to the mysterious light source still emanating from the pit in the floor. His smile broadened as he turned back to the bear. "You're not going to walk away this time, id-ee-ot Cave Bear," he whispered.

The bear wasn't dead?

Gabriel wasn't dead!?

The giant seemed to be counting on dispatching me at his leisure, hanging exhausted over the bear, intent on its failing gasps of air. Was the giant vulnerable now? Injured enough? It didn't matter. The bear was still alive.

This time, I didn't hesitate. This time, my body seemed to move on its own. Without calculation or plan, instinct asserted itself in its most primal form.

I needed a weapon.

I glanced up. One stalactite was larger, sharper, and hung lower from the ceiling than the rest. As the giant shifted over the bear with knife still in hand, I reached above me and heaved at the stone cylinder, tugging on it with every bit of my slight frame. As I pulled, the stalactite cracked and detached. I was borne down by the full force of its weight, knees bending as it scraped against my chest.

Somehow I kept hold of it and found my footing in my diving boots. When had my shaking stopped? Thankfully the giant hadn't noticed my clumsy efforts. He was distracted, staring down at the bear's torso, seeming to measure it with his eyes. He suddenly fixed his gaze on one spot and lifted his blade over the animal's chest, preparing to puncture its hide a second time, a final time. Though defeated and dying, the bear's hide was still tough, and the giant, visibly weakened from the battle, was unable to muster the strength to sink it in. He leaned down over the bear, ready to add his weight to the force driving the blade. I staggered forward, desperate to keep on my feet, yet fearing I would act too late. The stalactite was far too heavy, wet, and slippery to wield as a club, and I did the only thing that I could possibly do with it, in the instant I had left. I heaved it downward onto the giant's body—just as I held it—point first.

Driven as much by its own weight as any extra force I could impart, the blunt tip plunged downward, cleaving flesh and muscle, separating ribs, impaling the giant through the back.

The giant lurched forward, then slumped against the bear, his blade skidding off the fur as he struggled to reach behind him with his other hand to grab the object stabbing him. I stepped back as he toppled. He rolled off the bear, red blending with brown to paint the bear's fur deep maroon, the bear whimpering as the giant's far leg swept along its neckline.

The giant landed with a thud, and in the next instant was up, rising fully to his feet, yet awkwardly, all legs, not able to use his arms. Still, he kept hold of his knife, and now grasped it in the position he'd held it against the bear.

He turned slowly toward me, making small thrusting movements with his weapon. But he couldn't lift it more than a few inches above his waist, not with the stalactite buried between his shoulders. He stood for a moment, eyeing me keenly, doubtless weighing the changed circumstances. If his confidence was shaken, he did not betray it.

But I saw I might have another chance to shift the odds my way. I stepped in, kicked up, circling my leg in a practiced defensive move. The knife clattered away, coming to rest among a cluster of low stalagmites rising from the floor a few yards away.

I took a step back, preparing for what came next—the risk I might have to touch him with my hands.

The loss of his knife didn't seem to discourage him. He charged, as though the makeshift stake had inflicted no damage, no pain. The giant's hunched shoulders, his inability to raise his arms, were the only evidence anything had happened at all. Though he stumbled as he charged. Thank God. The fight with the bear must have exhausted him.

With the giant's weapon gone, my training took over. Not only the training I'd been taught to deal with the kids at school, but what I'd learned when I truly needed to immobilize a threat. When my life depended on it. And now it was clear the bear's life depended on it too. With the giant's bulk and strength, it was risky, but I stood my ground. As he found his footing and rammed his head down toward mine, I shoved my open palm up under his nose.

Crack. Pain burst through my hand.

Flash! A fragment of a vision shot through my mind. I fought against it and struggled to stay on my feet, ignoring the vision and the burn, shifting my right leg back, building momentum. When he collapsed further, trying to swing his arms out on my level, I stepped in and kneed his groin, pushing my full weight into him. I used his surprise to take us to the ground, turning my torso away, planting my hands as best I could on the slippery ground, starting a series of kicks. He slithered toward me, grasping for my legs with weakened, bent arms, but I pivoted and kept kicking, slamming his head again and again. *Thud. Thud. Thud.* Until finally he stopped.

I jumped to my feet, ready to strike once more. There was no need. Somehow the stalactite had pulled out and he lay on his belly, blood spurting out of him with each beat of his heart. The giant's body quivered and his face, twisted to the side, flashed rage, then disbelief—that I had attacked him. That I had stopped him.

That he was going to die.

Though little blood now flowed, it was apparent the stalactite had done more than limit his mobility. It had left a gaping hole near where his heart should be, if he had the anatomy of a normal man. There was nothing that could be done for him now. He'd never make it out of the mountain alive and the bear was so injured. And I had done this. If only I had acted sooner. If I hadn't been rendered frozen by the bizarre brawl that had played out before me. If only I'd been able to think or react.

His quivering stopped, and his body splayed out unnaturally on the stone floor. His mouth opened and his eyes beseeched me to listen. His breaths came in heavy pants as he struggled to speak.

I knelt down to listen to his final words.

"Just… the start," he gasped. And then his eyes fluttered shut, his labored breathing stopped.

What had just started? I didn't know, though the giant had left me with another final message that I didn't want to know. I'd been fortunate to touch him only that instant. A flash. Of pain. An image. Of darkness. The giant speaking to it. Not seen or heard clearly. Concerning what exactly? I hoped never to know.

I collapsed onto my hands against the cold rock, unable to tear my eyes away from the giant's lifeless form, but thinking of only one thing. Gabriel.

Soft moans from the bear broke the silence.

I stood and turned, and a naked Gabriel lay on his side, curled in a tight ball on the ground, several feet away where the bear should've been.

The bear is Gabriel. Gabriel is the bear. I had known it all along but could no longer deny it. As if I needed more proof, Gabriel's hands were wrapped around the side of his neck, right above his collarbone, where the knife had been lodged in the bear's hide.

My vision suddenly went fuzzy. The chamber was now washed out in a red hue. My eyes struggled to process the color and keep their focus on Gabriel's body, through the moisture now clouding them—*tears*—spilling over and down my face.

There was so much blood. Pools of blood. Everywhere. It spread all over Gabriel's hands and body, covered the cave formations in the middle of the chamber, and ran in rivulets along the ground. A piercing sound startled me. It echoed around the enclosed space.

The sound had come from me. I still felt the pressure in my

vocal cords. Another scream escaped, muted this time by the disgraceful hiccup that choked it.

Gabriel couldn't die. I refused to let him. He didn't deserve to die. I didn't deserve to lose him. If only I could force my limbs to move.

Maybe most of the blood was from the giant? Or maybe from Gabriel's bear-form who had more blood to lose? Hopeless attempts at reassurance. It was clear that Gabriel's own blood seeped through his fingers, pushing past the force of his hands, trickling down his neck and chest.

Gabriel's blue eyes locked with mine. His lips struggled to lift, then moved into a small half-smile. All the tenderness and affection that we shared flowed back and forth between us, tangible like a wave. Back and forth again. The feelings compounded. Building and building through our connected gaze until they punched me in the gut—at my most vulnerable, with all my barriers down.

The freeze response paralyzing my body suddenly lifted. I took a step. Then another. I fought to stop my tears as I used the giant's knife to cut off large strips of the giant's cargo pants, still damp from the stream water but the best I could do since we'd left our day packs back by the first sump and the other gear outside the cave. I grabbed them and rushed to Gabriel's side.

I sat on folded legs and leaned in close. Gabriel uncurled a bit but kept his knees tucked into his chest as if he was in too much pain to move. I laid a cloth strip across his hip in case he wanted to straighten out, wanted some modesty, but he didn't move, clearly in agony. His eyes searched mine and his lips parted.

"Shhh… don't try to talk." I whispered in a breathless voice I barely recognized. "It'll be okay. We just need to keep pressure on that wound. Steady pressure." I wrapped a cloth strip around my burned hand and used it to peel back his slippery fingers, while I reached in with the other hand to press a folded cloth against the slice in Gabriel's neck.

The opening in the flesh was small and deceptively benign, but a torrent of blood poured out. In the instant I switched his hands for the cloth, the blood gurgled and spouted out of him. So much blood. *Too much.* Still seeping from the cloth. I pressed harder. It slowed, but how was I going to get him out of the cave?

His large body shivered, looking so fragile now. Even if I had something to stop the bleeding, he didn't look capable of standing on his own, much less swimming or climbing out of the mountain.

Gram and Bernard knew we were here. They'd send someone when we didn't show tonight.

But could Gabriel make it that long?

No. "Gabriel, I'm going to go get help." His cell phone was back at the cave's entrance.

"No," he moaned, his voice so weak it was barely anything at all. "Don't leave. Too much blood… not much longer—" his voice broke with another shiver.

"There's no other choice. We can do this." I used my cloth-covered hand to place his palms over the makeshift bandage covering his neck and pressed down, ignoring the pain in my palm. His eyes started to drift shut. "Stay awake!" His eyes opened. "I'll have help here before you know it. All you need to do is keep pressure on that wound." I pressed on his palms again with my cloth-covered hand, then slid a heavy slab of rock behind him so he could lean back against it and another in front of him to brace on top of one of his forearms, to keep things in place.

Gabriel's mouth opened again, moving up and down a fraction as he struggled to speak. "Stay," he finally protested, almost silently, on an exhale.

"But—"

"Stay," he mouthed.

I shook my head, trying to keep my face from collapsing and reflecting the anguish tightening in my chest. "I need to get help. Let me do this for you. Let me show you I care. All you need to do is hold on for me." I took a strained breath and rushed on. "Then when you're better, next time we're together… next time, I won't fight my feelings for you anymore." It was all I could think to say, to make him understand how important he was to me. That he needed to find a way to live.

Gabriel opened his mouth, starting to mouth "stay" again, and this time I didn't hesitate in pressing my bare fingertips to his lips. As flesh met flesh, I knew it was as much a means to stop him from wasting precious energy on trying to speak, as it was my own desire to give him a light, tender caress. And his lips. They should have been warm, but they were so cold.

I shook off the cloth wrapped around my burned hand, brushing its knuckles over his jaw, sliding my other hand to cup the scarred side of his face in my unburned palm. Gabriel's eyes opened wide. They blinked once and opened wider as my bare hand pressed into his bumpy, disfigured cheek. His other cheek slowly pulled up and lifted the corner of his mouth into a huge half-smile—the largest and most lopsided one I'd seen from him yet, and I could tell the moment wasn't lost on him.

He knew—he must know—that this was the first time I'd ever touched anyone out of an actual desire to do so. Leaving my hands where they were on his face, I leaned in, huddling as close as I could to his body, and rested my head against his chest, shocked by the iciness of his skin against my cheek.

I wished in that brief moment that I understood more about how people expressed affection. How they did that through physical contact, which seemed to come so naturally to everyone else. Maybe then I could convey to Gabriel through my soft touches all the emotions I felt igniting in my heart.

His flesh at last absorbed some of my warmth. I rubbed my cheek against the soft, textured skin of his chest, then lifted my head. Our eyes locked one final time. His gaze grew focused, searching, determined, as if he was trying to memorize something. His expression softened, looking like it had when he'd shared that moment with Zoe yesterday. His lips pressed against my finger as his smile deepened and widened further.

Then his eyelids closed.

"Stay awake!" I pleaded. His eyes opened a fraction. Oh God, it was past time to leave. To say goodbye to him.

As my finger slipped off his lips, I didn't have more than seconds to appreciate the profound feeling of Gabriel's mouth on my skin— or process the fact I hadn't even had a vision when we'd touched this time. I took one last look at his bloody body, his beautiful smile, his beautiful face, and ran back toward the water to get help.

18
HELPLESS

Somehow I managed to get myself outfitted with diving gear, and into the first stream. I was expecting a slower journey back, without Gabriel's guidance, but my adrenaline kept me fleet and focused as I navigated the sumps, clambered out of the black depths, and ran the last length of dark passage with a burst of energized relief. I'd left my gloves and head covering on, to save time and for the return trip to Gabriel, only stopping long enough to slip on my boots because they'd help me go faster. The sun blinded me. I stumbled toward the gear we'd walked away from that morning. Just hours ago.

It felt like ages.

I managed to find Gabriel's cell through squinted eyes, and searched for his father's number, just barely able to call with gloves still on. My shoulders relaxed a fraction when he picked up on the first ring. "Bernard! Come quick. Bring help. I'm outside the cave, but Gabriel's been injured. He's still inside, in that chamber with the stone."

"I'm coming. Are you okay?"

"I'm fine. It's Gabriel. You have to do something. He was stabbed. And he's bleeding out. Bad. I'm not sure how—"

"Is he conscious?" Bernard cut me off.

"He was when I left." My knees shook.

"Good." Bernard paused, gulping. "Stabbed, you said? By whom? Are they gone?"

"It was this big guy. Huge. He-he's dead."

Bernard didn't pause to digest this news. "Is the relic safe?"

"What? The stone? Yes, yes, it's still there."

"Good. Now, where's Cameron?"

"What?"

"You don't see Cameron? And maybe a bear, nearby?"

I glanced around the clearing. There was no one.

"He said he'd—"

I spoke over Bernard. "I don't see anything."

"Listen, don't worry. I'll be there soon."

"Just send help, quick! I'm going back in."

"No! Stay right where you are. I promise I'll be there before you know it." He paused. "Cassandra, don't call anyone else. I'm bringing all the help we need. If anyone goes in without me, they could end up injuring him worse and then—" Suddenly, the line went dead.

The phone fell from my hands. My knees shook again and I collapsed to the ground.

I understood what Bernard meant about not to calling anyone else for help. Trying to get a police dispatcher to believe or even understand our plight did seem impossible. Relics and giants and bears. All the dispatcher would gather from that phone call was that I was insane and I'd killed someone. I'd have to trust Bernard, for now.

I sagged against the ground, all the energy that had gotten me out of the cave gone. With it left any hope of returning to Gabriel's side right now. Plus, I'd found my way out by pure luck. I couldn't help at all if I got lost.

I pulled my legs to my chest, wrapping my arms around them. My head dropped to my knees. I pictured Gabriel as I'd left him. Blood-soaked. Barely breathing. My hands trembled like an alcoholic's, and I gripped my legs tighter, lost in myself until two truths surfaced.

First, I had left Gabriel. To bleed out. Alone. After he'd asked me to stay.

If he died, I would regret that decision for the rest of my life.

Second, I had killed someone. Without a second thought. Acting on pure instinct. What kind of person did that make me?

Hopefully one that had kept Gabriel alive.

The irony was overwhelming. Every day I walked around thinking I was so much better than the people who touched me. Thinking I had some sort of moral compass they didn't. Condemning them to punishment in my imaginary circles of hell. Picturing them in pain, getting the retribution I thought they'd earned. I got a sick sense of satisfaction from it too. But in the end, what if I was the one who…

"Gabriel." In the cradle of my legs, my forehead pressed to my knees, I invoked his name like a prayer or an apology that bounced back to me off the silent mountain. How had I let this happen? No matter what my mind told me, my heart knew. He was everything I didn't believe existed in the world. Kind. Gentle. Good. So special. More than special. More than I had words to describe… although I didn't know what that meant, and nothing could really come of it. Still, what would I do without the hope of him? Without allowing myself, when things got really tough, to entertain the fairytale dream of ending up with a guy like him? What would I do if I could never again bask in his ridiculously optimistic and beautiful half-smile?

"Stop!" I turned my head from the sun, my voice carrying into the cave and booming back to me—an eerie reminder that none of these silly, sorrowful thoughts helped Gabriel.

And yet I couldn't keep my perpetual self-critic at bay. *Why didn't you act sooner? Why did you freeze, allowing your body to let you down when you needed it most? When Gabriel needed you most!*

My inner voice of censure was right. I should've run when Gabriel told me to, instead of distracting him. Or at least found my weapon and attacked the giant sooner. Or just given the giant that stupid stone Gabriel seemed bent on protecting. It wasn't worth his life, no matter how upset he'd be. At least I wouldn't feel so help-less—so weak, so useless—right now.

Bernard and Cole arrived as I was filling my backpack full of food, water, and a small first aid kit I'd found in one of Gabriel's duffel bags. As they jogged toward me in running shorts, Cole hurriedly pulled a t-shirt on over his head. A leather satchel hung across Bernard's bare chest by a long strap.

I'd only rested for maybe ten or fifteen minutes. But I didn't question how quickly they'd made it up the mountain. Clearly, I had a lot to learn about the Knights.

"Cole's taking you back to Rose," Bernard said as he rushed past me into the cave.

"I'm ready to head back in." I grabbed my bag and hurried to catch up.

"No." Bernard turned. His face was an impassive mask of hard lines and grim determination. "You're going home, and Cole's staying with you there. Sorry, you're in too much danger here. And to be blunt, you'd just slow me down."

"But you didn't even bring help! Can't you call a ranger or something? The Forest Service line? The paramedics?"

"They can't help him."

"But you're going to need more people! You're not even a doctor."

"I got ahold of Cameron. He and Aaron will secure the area. They'll help if I need it."

"But—"

"We're wasting time." Bernard's frustration was about to spill over into anger. "Go with Cole." He disappeared into the cave.

I was useless, again. Bernard was right. There was nothing for me to do here but worry. But I couldn't just leave Gabriel. He would certainly never leave me.

You failed him.

My mind tormented me, still. I had done this. Or at the very least, stood back and allowed it to happen. Would Gabriel even want me around when he realized I'd repaid his selfless protection by getting him stabbed and letting him bleed out at my feet?

"Come on." Cole reached a large arm around my bodysuit-covered shoulder. I slipped out of his hold, emptied my bag, left the supplies, and stuffed my clothes and scarf back in. Only then did I allow Cole to pull me toward the trailhead. After a few moments, I tugged myself free of his grasp and stumbled down the mountain. I could only half-listen to Cole's rambling optimism. Something about how Gabriel would recover quickly, like he had last time, and be just fine after he got the rest he needed.

I was too upset to speak. Definitely too upset to argue, to tell Cole the stark truth: I'd seen Gabriel's earlier wounds from his vision last night, and what I'd seen today was so much worse.

Only when we reached the bottom of the mountain did I reconnect with my surroundings. When we got to Gabriel's SUV, Cole produced the keys from his running shorts and jumped into the driver's seat.

"Dad would want you to drive, but I can do it."

Was Cole mumbling to me or himself? Was he old enough to be driving? He was big like the rest of his family, bigger than Cameron, but had the cherubic face of a boy. I gave him a hard look. He announced brightly that Aaron had taught him and helped him get his permit, and though he wasn't supposed to be driving without an adult licensed driver, he'd gone out on his own plenty, so I shouldn't worry. Cheerful chatter, meant to ease my mind, but it grated on me. I climbed into the passenger's seat, throwing down my bag without a word. Despite the reminder that some, or maybe all, of the Knights broke the rules when it suited them—much like everyone else—I still didn't feel capable of speaking, much less driving, right then anyway. My shaky hands didn't even feel capable of removing my gloves and head covering.

Cole crawled the SUV out of the forest at a snail's pace. He gripped the wheel at each bump in the narrow dirt road, and after only a minute of driving, his knuckles were white. I looked away and tried not to scream with frustration. Everything was moving too slow. Gabriel didn't have time. I was wasting more of it in this barely rolling car. No one had been called. But who could we call? Would a doctor come out and look at Gabriel, no questions asked? Or would he need a vet?

The whole thing was nuts.

I stared out the window. Lush terrain rolled along, framed at the top with a clear blue sky, showing no trace of last night's storm. The tranquil scene eventually quieted my mind, and at last I had a hold on my usual, pragmatic self. None of that overly emotional, frozen, weak, and whiny bullshit from the cave. I'd let Bernard brush me off much too easily. Now that he was there to explain the situation (in a way that didn't sound crazy), it was irresponsible not getting search and rescue and anybody else who could help to come up to the mountain. I owed that and more to Gabriel, and it wasn't too late.

"We need to stop at the police station," I finally said to Cole, while still watching the passing shades of green and blue outside. I didn't want to be blinded by Cole's irritatingly cheery smile.

"Nope," Cole responded in his sunny, singsong voice. "My dad will take care of things. Don't worry."

I side-eyed his gentle features. Was he the dim one in the family? Maybe he was just young and naive. In fact, most members of the Knight family—him, his father, and yes, Gabriel, too—seemed somewhat naive. A bit too innocent and trusting, and expecting too much trust in return. Too well-intentioned for their own good. Had that been what the giant meant, what he said he heard about "their race"? I turned to face him fully.

"I don't think you understand, Cole. Gabriel is going to need more help than your father can…" My voice trailed away. I couldn't finish the sentence even in my mind. "Anyway, the other guy's dead. I stabbed him," I admitted for the first time out loud. "We need to report this. Especially if your father thinks there could be more dangerous men in the forest."

"Nope." He remained cheerful, and unmoved. "My dad will handle it. Cameron and Aaron too."

"But I killed a man!" I shouted, my high voice piercing in the confines of the SUV. *Ahhh,* I let loose in my head, *you're better now. In control. Stop the dramatics.*

"It doesn't matter." Cole was totally calm. "If the guy you killed was the one who hurt Gabriel, it was over you, the relic, or both. He had it coming."

I sat with my thoughts, unsure of what to say or do. I didn't disagree, but even if you killed someone in self-defense, you were supposed to report it. Not doing so made you look guilty. What was Bernard going to do with the body? Dump it somewhere? Let it rot in the cave?

"It'll be fine." Cole's voice was firm, but he fidgeted, nervously anticipating approaching bumps in the road.

"It's just so much to process." My voice was strained.

Cole grunted, almost a sound of sympathy. "Cassie, after everything, haven't you figured out my family's different?"

"Different doesn't even begin to describe it."

"It's pretty simple, really," he said with assurance.

"OK then, explain it for me, since no one else will."

Cole hesitated, slowing the SUV, and peered out the windshield, then the side windows, then out the front again, up at the clear midday sky. "Well, there's a bad group of people—well, not really people actually—that want what my family has. They'll do anything to get it. I thought Gabriel was going to explain that to you, in the cave." His smile dimmed a fraction as the SUV hit a bump. "Anyway, they want you dead too. You could prevent them from getting what they want if you aren't dead. Dead and burned. So we're not going to do anything to draw more attention." He released a hand from the wheel and wiped sweat off on his shorts.

This matter-of-fact yet unease-filled recitation by Cole would've sounded crazy yesterday, but today, not so much. Today, I needed to hear the rest of it. "Attention to what? From who?"

"To us, and you, and the, ah, stone. You saw it didn't you? From the, er…" Cole's gaze flitted around the car nervously, looking everywhere but at me. "From the Shadows. You can never be sure when or where the Shadows might be listening."

"Come on. Is this shadow stuff for real?" I glanced out the windshield. Just the mountains looming and the forest all around us.

"Of course." His reduced smile took on a more confident tilt.

"Then what are they?"

"We call them Shadows as a sort of nickname, since that's how they are supposed to appear. As darkness, voids of light, my dad says. We're supposed to use that nickname here, where it isn't safe to speak, instead of the name Grandpa says the older generations used."

"And you've seen one of these shadow things?" I asked, eyebrows drawing together in thought.

"Well, no, I've never seen one, but that's a good thing. I mean, it's best just to lie low. That's why Mom and Sarah were safe so long. Because we kept to ourselves. Kept quiet…" He trailed off with a rare frown.

"I'm sorry about your mom and sister," I said in a quiet voice.

"It's okay. I'm just glad I had as much time with them as I did." His foot slipped from the gas pedal. "Dad says a lot of other families aren't as lucky. The Shadows have been getting more aggressive." He recovered and hit the gas again. "And then when you came and caused the relic—ah, stone, well, I think my dad said it's okay to say relic since they know it's here now—to reveal itself, that probably got their attention."

Gabriel had said the same thing. That there was some sort of connection between my arrival and the stone lighting up, which led to the attack on Gabriel outside the cave, the same day his mother and sister were murdered. "Come on, Cole. Do you really think my coming here had anything to do with that?" I laughed, trying to seem casual, but gripped the armrest. It was too horrible to think, let alone say, but Cole didn't seem to have any uncertainty about what I was asking.

"Well, yes. We went to the cave to talk about it with Grandpa and the elders, when Gabriel learned about you and your smaller stone. There is no other explanation," Cole said with complete conviction. "You arrived here with your smaller version of our relic. Then our relic showed its powers for the first time, and a few days later, the Shadows sent giants to investigate the, um, power surge, I guess you could call it. No alternates, or anyone they'd sent, had known about our relic before. Or had even been in this area since they'd killed Rose's daughter, who wasn't even an alternate, by the way. They killed her just to be safe because her dad was one of us."

I tensed, my fingernails digging into the armrest through my glove.

Cole seemed to have lost his caution, plowing ahead in his soft tone. "Anyway, they came to investigate, and when they couldn't find what they were looking for, they confronted my dad and Gabriel. They also discovered my mom and sister. They killed and burned them because the Shadows believe any female could be the Un— Oops. Can't say that word here."

I had a feeling his family wouldn't like him talking about a lot of this stuff here.

"They believe any female could be the One. And they can't have the One around if they want to control all the relics' powers, so that they can stop being those shadowy things—so that they can get back to this world. That's basically it," he said with a calm finality.

If what Cole said was true, and he certainly seemed to believe it, then in a way, I was responsible for the violent murder of his mother and sister. The slaughter of Gabriel's mother and sister. Aaron's mother and sister. Bernard's wife and daughter. How could any of them forgive me if they believed that? How could I forgive myself if I believed that?

And Cameron's father, he was part of all that too.

Cole discussed it so easily, but no wonder Aaron was never

happy to see me, and Cameron had been such a jerk. But hadn't Cameron acted that way before he'd known about how I was connected to this? Long before they'd decided I was what awakened their relic thing?

"Why doesn't your family hate me?" I said quietly, gripping the leather tighter.

Cole glanced between me and the dirt road. He quickly pulled over into the weeds alongside the narrow, single lane cut through the forest. He put the SUV in park and faced me with huge, sparkling blue eyes and his gentlest smile yet. "Cassie, I know you've had a bad day, but please don't get upset. You didn't do anything bad, to us or anybody else. You're gonna be my new sister. Why would my family hate you?"

"What is this new sister business? And if you guys really think my coming here brought along the men who killed your mom and Sarah," I said, recalling Gabriel's vision in the tent last night with a shudder, "why pretend to like me at all?"

"We're not pretending," Cole claimed with another easy smile. "We do like you—for so many reasons. Gabriel blabbing on about what a wonderful person you are is only one of them. Gabriel's an expert at that, you know. But there are so many other things that make you important."

"What things? What reasons?"

"I need to spell them out?"

I nodded at him, still turned toward me in the driver's seat.

"Well… um, you're special—like us." He shifted his large body even further in the driver's seat to face me. "There are so few females left, and you came here without any family of your own. So, it's like you were meant to be part of our family. Our new sister." He gave me another soft smile. "Second, like I said before, none of this is your fault. The Shadows are responsible for everything bad that happened. Okay, what else…" Cole paused, and his smile suddenly widened. "Third, you and Gabriel have a special sort of connection that my dad says can happen sometimes between alternates like us.

I remember exactly what my dad said because I've never heard anything like it. He said what you and Gabriel have is more profound than any sort of love. Very rare. Our ancestors called it bonding. It means you and Gabriel are meant to be together. Forever. I think it's really cool." His eyes shone with wonder, and he looked so hopeful—like if he was lucky, he might "bond" with someone too. "And, umm, there's at least one more reason… What was it?" He rapped his fingers on the steering wheel. "Oh, of course, you're the One." The rapping stopped. "And you can take the relic's powers. So that solves all sorts of problems—for my family, of course—but also for everybody!" He concluded his list of praise and shifted out of park, shooting us back onto the road with the spinning of tires, kicking up a cloud of dust behind us.

I turned away from him, toward the soothing colors outside, absorbing everything he'd just said about how I fit into his family's strange existence. Regardless of what I thought, or what made any sense, Cole seemed to believe in it all so sincerely, just like Gabriel. How did I reason against their sincerity? Did I even want to try?

There was a frightening theme to everything the Knights believed. I'd sensed it before, but the scope of it was getting worse and worse the more I learned.

Not only did Gabriel and his family want things from me I wouldn't want to give; they wanted things I couldn't give. They wanted things that weren't possible under any circumstances. Because even if everything they believed existed—and it certainly seemed possible, after witnessing Gabriel turn into a bear—I couldn't live up to the Knights' mountain of expectations.

I wasn't special, like them. I was cursed. I wasn't meant to be anyone's sister. I was meant to be alone. I wasn't meant to be anyone's savior. I was hopeless at keeping my own nightmares and pain at bay. Hopeless at maintaining hope—and my sanity—in the wake of my dark visions.

And I certainly wasn't meant to be "bonded" with anyone. Even though I cherished the feelings I had for Gabriel, even foolishly sharing my hopes that maybe we could make something between us work, I couldn't count on spending forever with anyone.

It was inevitable. No matter how hard I tried, I'd let Gabriel and his family down. I'd already let Gabriel down this morning. How did I explain everything to Cole? At least there was one thing I could clear up now. I turned back to him, catching a glimpse of his boyish, eager eyes as he drove. "I'm definitely not the girl you're waiting for. Whoever or whatever she is. This morning, I touched that stone, like Gabriel told me to. Nothing happened."

The news didn't faze him one bit. "Well, my dad will figure that out too. No worries." Cole smiled. "You must be her."

I sighed loudly, not surprised by his sanguine response.

"Now, no more of this," he said, sunny as ever. "My dad would ground me till the end of time for talking like this. And he would lock you away too, for even thinking about the police or telling anyone but Rose."

I opened my mouth to protest again, but it was a waste of time. Instead, I bit my bottom lip until I tasted blood, watching the first of the large houses by the river crawl past, ignoring everything except thoughts of Gabriel.

19

A MOTH TO A FLAME

WHEN WE GOT TO GRAM'S, VIN WAS SITTING ON THE FRONT porch.

Cole didn't seem to notice him as he focused all his attention on parallel parking Gabriel's SUV along the curb outside. My stomach certainly noticed him, though. Butterflies danced. Vin looked as hot, and as sure of himself, as ever, lounging on the top step of the cottage's small entry in his peach button-down shirt with sleeves rolled up and top buttons undone. He'd swapped out slacks today for clean-cut, olive-green shorts, and his usual shoes for leather ankle boots. Hiking boots. Had Vin been out in the forest looking for us? The question faded away as his smooth skin, more of it on display than ever, caught my eye—beyond flawless in the afternoon sun. I shivered, weirded out by my strange attraction to him. Like a moth to a flame.

Totally inappropriate, too, with Gabriel bleeding out in a cave.

Vin was the last thing I needed to deal with. I'd ask Cole to drop me off at the shelter. I could use Dr. G's phone. But suddenly Vin did something he'd only done once, that night he was up in my room, and I couldn't have walked away if I tried.

He smiled. Smiled right at me.

And it was his warm, genuine smile, not the forced one he used at school.

I was hooked again, pulled more forcefully than ever. Enthralled by its perfection. It was so mesmerizing and electric, entirely different from Gabriel's gentle expressions. I was desperate to get close. Before Cole even turned off the ignition, I leapt out of the SUV and sprinted up the porch.

Vin patted the top step. I sat down next to him. I tried to keep my focus on my hands, resting on my bodysuit-covered thighs. Within seconds my gaze strayed. I couldn't help staring at him.

Vin finally dropped his smile, which seemed to help a bit. The fog effect he had on me lifted, just slightly.

"Cassandra, how are you?" Vin murmured in his smooth accent, as he looked me over with a raised eyebrow.

My mind was a jumbled mess. What should I say? I unconsciously scooted a bit closer to him on the step. I pulled off my gloves and head covering. Vin's eyebrow rose further.

"Hey!" Cole yelled as he rushed toward us from the SUV, no trace of his usual lightness on his boyish face.

"Hello," Vin didn't hesitate in responding, "I'm one of Cassandra's friends—Vin. You must be Cole."

"Yeah, but how did you know?" Cole asked.

"Well, I make it my business to know. I'm her friend, after all."

"Gabriel told me about you." Cole looked confused whether he should be smiling or scowling.

"That's nice that he mentioned me. We only met once," Vin responded with politeness but no sincerity. "And it's nice to meet you too, Cole. Do you mind giving me and Cassandra a few moments?"

"Actually, I do."

"We just need a minute." Vin gave Cole a tight-lipped smile and waved his hand in a shooing motion.

"No," Cole's voice was firmer this time.

Vin tipped his head to the side, surprised.

"Cassie needs to be with Rose right now, and you need to leave."

"But—" I started to protest, wanting Vin to stay. It was the strange look Cole gave me that cut me off. Cole was right. I needed to stop acting silly and go inside to Gram, then somehow distract Cole so I could get more help to Gabriel.

Just don't look at Vin—that will help.

"Vin," I mumbled to the wood planks of the porch, "Cole's right. This isn't a good time. You should get going. I'll see you at school. Tomorrow. I guess that's tomorrow." God, so much had happened in the last twenty-four hours since Gabriel and I'd left this very spot to go camping. My world had shifted so much since I'd hiked up the mountain. I'd gone from cursing Gabriel to letting him hold me in his arms. Then from simple complacency in his embrace to acknowledging how much I wanted to be there. And finally, to wanting so much from Gabriel I couldn't even put my feelings into words. Yet, I'd stood by when he needed me. *Please let him be okay.*

I shivered.

"OK, if that's what you want, Cassandra." Vin rose smoothly from the porch and took a step toward me, before pausing. "Don't forget tomorrow's a holiday. Labor Day. So I'll see you at school Tuesday."

"Oh, right," I said, feeling so out of it. I shook my head, and my hair felt strangely stuck in place.

"We'll catch up later." An odd note strained his voice.

I risked looking up.

He stared at my hair, his brows pinched together, an anxious frown on his lips. He blew out several short breaths and finally turned, striding down Gram's uneven walkway, each step deliberate, like he might change his mind at any moment and turn around. I let myself admire his elegant gait from behind. Halfway down the walkway, he looked back. He scanned my body, from my hair to my bodysuit to my waterproof boots, seeming to make sure I was still okay. His features relaxed. He caught me staring back and his lips lifted, hinting at a smile, this one genuine. He looked away and continued to a muddied pickup truck parked on the street. It looked newer than most in town, but not a bit like something he'd be caught driving. He climbed in, started the engine, and pulled away, giving me one last glance.

The truck disappeared, and my thoughts refocused: get to the phone.

I hurried Cole inside. He leaned back into the front door and exhaled. "Oh man," he looked down at me. "You have to be careful with that friend of yours. He's sending off some pretty powerful emotions. I've never felt anything like it." I gave him a questioning look. He pushed away from the door and looked beyond me.

"Cassandra?" Gram burst into the hallway with flour-covered hands. Zoe hopped along at her feet, snout lifted, sniffing the air. Suddenly, Zoe froze on three legs. Gram froze too, her eyes filling with tears. What was wrong? Was it because I wore this bodysuit? I'd had to leave the sweater Gram had knitted for me in the cave too. Or had Bernard taken the time to call?

Gram's gaze went up and down, from my head to my hands. I lifted my hands. Red, scaly skin covered them. I reached up to feel my face—crusty—then my hair—glued together. No wonder Vin had stared. Dried blood must be globbed in my hair and caked around the edges of the diving gear.

"What happened?" Gram asked. A tear rolled down the wrinkles of her cheek.

"It's okay, Gram. No need to worry." I lied, thinking of Gabriel, but also of Gram's asthma. Zoe hobbled toward me and whined softly. I knelt and stroked her fur. She licked my hand, and I sank closer to the floor.

"Go shower." Cole bent forward and touched my shoulder gently. "I'll tell Rose what happened. As much as it's safe to." He crouched and looped his hands under my arms, helping me up.

"Thanks." I stepped away, recovering a bit. Maybe this was my chance to get to the phone. "But remember, keep it simple. Don't upset her with details."

Bringing the cops into this mess was probably a bad idea. Too messy. Too inexplicable. But a doctor? Gabriel needed real doctor.

Hospitals treated everyone, with minimal questions asked. Surely one doctor could be convinced to stay quiet.

"Yep." Cole nodded, his boyish chin bobbing up and down several times. "And Gabriel's going to be just fine, so there's really nothing to say to upset anyone."

In that moment, I felt decades older than Cole. I didn't care what he said; I had to get to the phone, and Gram's only phone was in the kitchen. (Would she never break down and get a cell?) I tried to give Gram a reassuring smile. "I'll be back before you know it." I just planned to dart to the kitchen first. "And please don't worry."

"Sure," she said, wiping the tears from her face. "Cole, follow me. I'll fix us something to eat."

Damn. Of course she would invite Cole to join her in the kitchen.

I meant to shower quickly, to rush back. But I stood limp, like a ragdoll under the water, staring at the bottom of the tub, the steam rising, the pink water swirling. I'd killed a man, or a man-creature. That was probably not something water or time could just wash away. And Gabriel had become a part of me too. What would I do if—I couldn't even bring myself to finish the thought. Later, I'd think about it again later. I scrubbed at the blood around my fingernails, rubbed my hands up and down my arms, and finally reached for my shampoo bottle and lathered my hair. The sweet scent of vanilla clouded around me. Like it had when Gabriel held me last night.

I needed to be strong for Gabriel.

I changed into a black camisole and a pair of ridiculous pink leggings that were so cheap at the second-hand store I hadn't been able to resist, and hurried into the kitchen.

The bright smell of lemons and chives greeted me.

Cole sat at the table, happily eating Gram's chive, cream cheese, and cucumber finger sandwiches. Gram stood at her wooden pastry table cutting dainty yellow shapes from what must be her lemon tea cookie dough. A lemon, half its peel zested off, sat next to the mixing bowl. Beneath the table, Zoe shifted her weight between her three legs, looking up eagerly for dough scraps. She spotted me and raced over, trying to hop up on her one back leg. I reached down to give her a hug, and she sighed and licked my cheek. I straightened up, watching the rise and fall of Gram's chest. "Gram, how are you doing?" Her breathing seemed okay. I walked toward her, my bare feet absorbing the chill from the cold kitchen floor, then glanced at the phone, resting in its cradle on the counter.

"Good." She nestled a star shape into one of the last open spots on the cookie sheet and turned toward me. "Cole told me someone came after you this morning, and he's gone now. That's all I needed to know. You're safe."

"Umm… yeah, I'm safe. But Gabriel needs help. So, you see," I concluded, without looking at Cole, "we should call a doctor, or the paramedics." I moved to the counter.

"No," Gram said.

I froze.

She carefully lifted the baking sheet, put it in the oven, and set the timer. "Cole said he explained that to you."

"Really? You too?" I sighed, my hand hovering over the phone. I understood everything Cole had said, but what about Gabriel?

"Yes." She untied her favorite embroidered apron, folded it neatly, and draped it over the side of her walker. "You made a promise you'd let the Knights help. Secrecy is part of the deal," Gram spoke in her most resolute tone. "Oh… and don't forget that this would get back to Social Services. I can tell you what they'd say, and it wouldn't be good." Her tone didn't need to be dramatic. Her words were enough.

I let my hand fall to my side. Social Services. How could I forget? For my own selfish reasons, I needed to stay in their good graces. Well, too late for that, but at least I shouldn't piss them off any more than I already had. And Gram was right, spearing a guy in the back—even if I claimed I was trying to keep him from stabbing Gabriel again—wouldn't look good. Especially not with my reputation around town. I couldn't bet on a doctor's silence. If they saw a dead body or suspected foul play, they'd get the cops involved.

"OK, maybe not just any doctor. But don't we need to send some sort of help? Aren't there any, uh, special doctors? Alternates?" I tested the word on my tongue, looking desperately between Gram and Cole. "We've already waited too long. Gabriel was… He was in such bad shape when I left."

"No. We have to trust that Bernard knows best. You have to stop worrying."

"How?" I asked in one sharp breath, rushing on, "If I was hurt, Gabriel would worry. He'd try to help me." There were so many instances he already had.

"I know, angel. Just give me ten minutes." She glanced at the timer. "Warm cookies always make things better. I'll make you some of that hot cocoa you like too, with lots of extra marshmallows, and just a bit of whipped cream." She nodded, her white curls bouncing gently. "You've had such a long day. Rest. What happens now isn't your concern. It's up to Bernard how to handle this. Not you."

I guess Gram was right about that too, when she put it that way. She didn't have to spell out the obvious part—that Bernard was Gabriel's family, and I was no one to Gabriel. Worse, I was the crazy girl who didn't want to be touched, who wouldn't trust him, who'd stood frozen while he fought for her. *Useless. Pathetic.*

"Yep," Cole chimed in. "My dad will handle it. That's what I told you before, Cassie. So just sit down, enjoy a snack with me. Oh man, do those cookies already smell good." He glanced at the oven, then smiled widely at Gram before motioning me to the table. "You've done enough today."

With that final reminder of what had happened, what I'd done (*killed one man, maybe caused the death of another*), I gave up arguing. I'd eat the damn cookies. Drink the damn cocoa. And try to forget for maybe two seconds how much pain Gabriel must be in right now, try to block out the image of Gabriel's bloody body, try to ignore for maybe five seconds the voice in my head that screamed at me to do something, and taunted me over and over again. *You failed him.*

Because as much as I cared about Gabriel, it seemed determining his care wasn't a decision I was entitled to make. If he was even still alive.

I lay in bed, fighting sleep, like most nights. But the nightmare and the pain were the least of my worries when visions of Gabriel still haunted me, pale and cold, sheeted in blood. No, I fought sleep tonight so I'd be awake and ready for when the phone rang downstairs, for when Bernard called with news of Gabriel's fate.

Cole had assured me several times during dinner, and again before he'd collapsed on the makeshift bed of quilts Gram had made for him on the living room floor, "Dad will call."

"But when?"

"As soon as he can." Cole was useless for anything but unreassuring reassurances. When Bernard hadn't called all evening, I'd pleaded with Cole to go back up the mountain with me, just to deliver more supplies and fresh water, and to check on things. Cole refused to leave the cottage, even going so far as to block the door when I'd try to leave, making a prison out of it as well. Gram was his eager warden.

I was trapped in an emotional prison too. Everything reminded me of Gabriel. Just being in my narrow bed reminded me of when he'd been here with me, which of course reminded me of his warmth, the shelter of his embrace, the depth of emotion in his gentle face. And all of that reminded me of the intensity of my feelings for him. The intensity of what I'd felt this morning when he lay curled in a ball on the chamber floor and our gazes locked. Of what I'd felt when my fingers had touched his lips, when I'd touched his scarred cheek. How there was only the glorious feeling of his skin. No pain. No vision.

It all came back to Gabriel. What a kind, wonderful person he was. The frightening force of my feelings for him. The fact that he seemed so good—so impossibly decent and honest—I wanted to trust in everything he said, including that he'd had good reason to search through my things, and had meant no harm by it. And that he didn't have anything to do with my missing locket. Something that was sure to haunt me forever, but in this moment seemed so unimportant. Even his transformation in the cave was something I somehow just accepted, and everything it implied (in the way of weirdness), didn't matter. After all, I was pretty weird too.

Zoe's deep and level breathing next to me reminded me of the steady rise and fall of his chest as he'd held me during the storm. I hugged Zoe tightly. Her body grew warmer against mine. I'd never get the opportunity to be wrapped into Gabriel's warmth again. I would never again experience the comfort and safety I found in his arms. Or have a chance to express my feelings in return.

Because even if he survived, I couldn't be with him. No matter how much I longed for his lopsided smile in my life. No matter how much I desired a taste of his lips.

I brushed my lips with my fingertips. I craved just one kiss. An experimental, first kiss. But if for some inexplicable reason there was only pleasure—no pain, no visions—like with our touches today, I was sure to want so much more from him. An impossible forever. An impractical happily ever after…

I wasn't Sleeping Beauty. I dropped my hand back to Zoe, my fingers sinking into her thick fur, absorbing its soft warmth.

I had too much darkness in my life to count on forever and fairytale endings. To allow someone to get that close to me. To let them in on all my secrets and for them to learn how truly messed up I was. What hurt the most, but was probably for the best, was the realization that once Gabriel recovered—if he recovered—he'd rethink whatever feelings he had for me anyway.

Another vision of Gabriel's bloody body flashed in my mind. I shut my eyes, as if that would erase it. I kept my eyes closed, taking several deep breaths, holding the air in for a count of ten between each exhale, trying to clear my thoughts. Relax my body. I finally gave up. Maybe I was meant to have the image of Gabriel's suffering imprinted in my brain. And maybe I deserved it.

A tapping sound came from the lowest window.

My eyes opened wide as my head turned.

Vin stared at me through the glass. Looking so picture-perfect, his black hair blending in with the night sky, half his sculpted features shaded and the other lit up, the moon glowing to the side of him. Was this how Bram Stoker had pictured Dracula, coming to visit one of his victims at night? I released Zoe, my body tensing.

If Vin wanted something, like Dracula—and hopefully he wanted something other than my blood—I had no energy, nothing left for him. I'd left everything in the cave. Everything with Gabriel.

He tapped again and motioned with his hand upward, indicating he wanted me to open it. To let him in.

My fingers dug into my soft comforter. I shouldn't let him in. Absolutely not.

He smiled through the dirt-streaked pane, and suddenly, I was helpless to do otherwise.

20

AGAPI MOU

VIN SPRUNG OFF THE BLUE SPRUCE, LEAPING TOWARD THE window in a powerful movement but also shifting his weight like a cat, with tremendous grace. He landed on the ledge outside, crouched down, and pulled himself through the frame, moving from the darkness into the soft light of the attic. I stepped back. Momentum carried him forward, he lost his footing, and stumbled to a stop within inches of me, bringing in the scent of spruce and pine, and also his own scent. Clean and fresh. Like lime and something else I couldn't place. He stood to his full height, ethereal in the gentle glow of the reading light affixed to the headboard above my pillow.

He should've looked ridiculous, having just climbed a tree in his peach button-down shirt and the charcoal slacks he must've changed into, biking gloves covering his hands. But with his confident stance, he couldn't have been farther from it. On firm footing now, he stepped even closer. Much closer than I should allow. Instead of fear or distaste, energy I didn't know I had flooded my body. "Vin…" I sighed breathlessly, already feeling butterflies in my belly, and tingles through my chest, from the feelings he generated in me.

He pulled off the gloves and looked down at me warmly, an unguarded radiance in his expression, without a trace of his usual detachment. "Cassandra. Thanks for letting me in. We need to talk."

Neither of us spoke. Or moved. Silence sizzled between us. We finally drifted away from the window, seemingly as one, just a sliver of space between us as we moved into the room with complete awareness of each other. Of each other's bodies. Like an electric connection pulsed between us. How I'd always imagined dancing with someone might be. Though he didn't touch me. Did I want him to? Yes. Oh God, yes, I did, even after everything that had happened today.

Zoe, head up and ears alert, rose from the bed coverings. She barked, jumped off the bed, not even bothering with the ramp, and crouched down to stuff her large body through the narrow opening created by the floor and the bottom of the bed frame. There was a bit of scuffling, then bright eyes peeked out at us from the shadows.

I patted my thigh and called her to come out.

Bright eyes blinked back, but she didn't move.

Vin seemed unfazed by the inhospitality. He broke from our dance, strode over to my small bed, leaned against the edge to remove the expensive-looking sneakers he was wearing, and sat cross-legged in the middle.

Standing away from him, tension built in my chest every passing moment.

He patted the coverings for me to sit down.

I zipped over and hopped up on my mattress. Once again only inches separated our bodies. The nearness relieved some of the tension in my chest. The same tension that pulled me toward him like a magnet. God, I was so, so attracted to him.

I tucked my legs under me and looked up into his hazel eyes. He leaned in, and a sweep of silky black hair fell across his forehead. He brushed it back with long fingers and his lips curved up gently to hit me with one of his miraculous smiles. "So, Cassandra, what happened in the cave?"

Despite Cole's and Gram's warnings from earlier in the day not to tell anyone, I found myself giving Vin an overview of the whole dreadful tale. Of course I left out several parts, like the bit about a glowing stone that looked like my locket, and Gabriel turning into an animal.

Vin didn't blink once. Or speak. He just nodded several times, as if he seemed to understand why something like this might happen. As if, oddly enough, he was filling in any gaps in his head.

"So," I concluded, "it was a long, miserable day. That's why I had to tell you to go earlier. I'm really sorry about that. I appreciated you coming by. Really." I leaned in closer and the tension in my chest eased a bit more.

"I understand." He rubbed his hands along his slacks. "So, this morning, did anything happen to make you feel… different?"

"Different?"

"Stronger?"

"Wait." Alarm bells went off in my head. *Fight against your perpetual Vin-haze!* I pulled away from him. "How did you know to ask about the cave? That was the first thing you asked, and we talked about camping, but I didn't tell you about going to a cave. Not until you asked."

"Oh." Vin took a breath and hit me with another smile. "That's simple. I followed you."

"What? Why?" I straightened, bracing my hands on the comforter, my back tensing.

"Well, for several reasons, I guess. But really, I just wanted to make sure you were safe."

"Safe!?"

Zoe shifted under the bed at the tone of alarm in my voice.

"Yes." Vin's smile dropped. "I assumed you were safe when I left. After the storm cleared, Cameron showed up, I assumed to stand watch. So I thought it was safe, and best for me to go. I also assumed Gabriel explained everything to you." He frowned. "Well, I can say that I wanted to make sure you were safe from Gabriel too—that you kept yourself safe from him. You didn't. I had to keep my distance before the rain, or he would've caught scent of me, but I got close to the tent, saw the shadows from the flashlight. Saw you wrapped in his arms. After I warned you about letting yourself get drawn into something… without knowing more." His shoulders stiffened.

"Oh." I looked down, hair falling along the sides of my face. My cheeks felt hot. "I was cold…" No longer looking at Vin, my thoughts became more clear. What he'd just said about spying on me and Gabriel sounded totally weird. And he was clearly wrapped up in all of this somehow, as was Cameron, who was supposed to have been watching the cave. And of course the Knights were back to complicating my life. But when I looked back up into his hazel eyes, which were staring back at me with accusation, everything fluttered away. All that was left was my self-doubt. "Why do you care?" I shrugged and picked at pieces of Zoe's hair on my leggings.

"You really need to ask?" He reached out with his hand. Before I could pull back, he lifted a thick, red curl of my hair away from my chest. He held it gently in his fingers, staring down at it with an odd sort of longing on his face.

"Yes." Though something in me wanted to beg him to play with my hair all day, I forced myself to reach up and tug the curl from his grasp. *And why is it when Vin's not here, all I can think about is Gabriel. But when Vin's here, Gabriel disappears?*

"You truly don't know—don't remember at all?" Vin pressed roughly. Hurt filled his eyes. "What if I call you Cyndra?"

"Cyndra?" I repeated blankly.

"Sin—dra. C—Y—N—D—R—A."

"That's supposed to mean something to me?"

"I guess not," Vin shot back, a scowl marring his features.

"Are you trying to say you know something about my past? That that was my name?"

His face cleared and the corners of his mouth pulled up tightly. "Just forget it." I could tell this smile was forced, although it had the same effect on me as all the others. I was lost in it for several moments.

"Um, Vin." My mind was finally clear enough to speak, though not processing everything. "I still don't get it. I mean, I appreciate you being so nice to Gram when you brought me home last week, and helping out at school. You didn't have to keep Reese from falling all over me, but you did. And you seem to, um, care about me. Why?"

"Because I like you. We're friends."

"Why?"

A sad look flashed across his face. "Leave it alone." Vin's up-turned mouth tensed further. God, what a forced smile.

"No. Tell me why?" I asked, not able to drop this when it didn't make any sense. "Why are you interested in me? Why do you like me? You could be with—be friends with—anyone you want."

"What's not to like?" he questioned in a mocking tone. Yet the gravity in his expression seemed to proclaim he meant it. "You're strong and determined." His features relaxed a bit. "And stubborn and independent." He nudged my knee with his. "I just wish you'd exercise that a bit more around Gabriel, instead of falling into his arms."

I coughed awkwardly, feeling my cheeks warm again, at the same time my body felt exhausted from such a long day. I yawned, covering it with the back of my hand, then glanced down at my chest. The skin above my camisole was already a deep rose, getting redder by the second, nearly matching the ridiculous pink leggings. The shameful color was probably a combination of embarrassment and the undeniable attraction I felt for Vin whenever he was near.

"I'm pathetic," I muttered under my breath.

"Agapi mou… sweet Cassandra." Vin's accent was particularly thick. I looked up. "Stop being so hard on yourself. You've had a tough day. I'm sorry I gave you a hard time about Gabriel. That doesn't matter right now. And it doesn't matter what happened this morning, so long as you're all right."

"What does that mean—agapi mou?" I asked, giving another small yawn. And where had I heard that phrase before?

"You've had enough excitement. Time for bed." He gave a small smile, somewhat less forced than before. Although there was some-thing stirring in the back of my mind that didn't want me to, I found myself agreeing with him. "Okay," I muttered, sagging over my bent knees, barely able to remain sitting up.

"Good." He leaned in and kissed the top of my forehead, just above my hairline so he missed any skin. Why wasn't I protesting? Well, Vin had never tried to touch my skin or hurt me, and this touch on the hair was innocent enough. Kind of like Gabriel kissing the back of my head in the tent last night. No harm done.

Vin suddenly smiled again, lifting his mouth into a full, natural smile with none of the tension he'd expressed earlier, and I revised my opinion of the kiss he'd just placed on my hair. Actually, the kiss was kind of sweet. I wouldn't mind him doing it again. I was back to wanting him to touch me…

Before I gave that too much thought, he rose gracefully from the bed, put back on his sneakers, and patted the covers for me to lie down. "Get some rest. It's been a long day. You've got a break tomorrow, but then the rest of a school week ahead. I've got a friend for you to meet." Vin frowned and stared out the window, as if his thoughts were somewhere else. With someone else. "But it's going to have to wait. We had some… complications. You'll meet her soon."

"Who?" I struggled to sit up straighter.

"A friend of mine, from before I came here. Hopefully you'll meet her, everything will work out soon."

I opened my mouth to ask more. He graced me with one more smile, even more stunning. My head clouded. My mouth hung open.

"Just sleep for now. Keep up this small-town routine for a bit longer." He held his smile.

"Mhmm," I mumbled as I stretched out on the bed.

Vin leaned over me, smoothed back my long hair, and pressed his lips above my hairline again. "Goodnight, Agapi mou…" He lingered for several moments and slowly backed away from the bed with an odd look of longing on his face. "Sweet dreams."

I knew nothing of sweet dreams and knew I shouldn't sleep when I was still waiting for Bernard's call. How could I sleep when

I still didn't know if Gabriel was okay? But with Vin asking me to, it kind of seemed like I should at least give it a try.

Wait. Why was I letting Vin have influence over me? Gabriel was who I cared about.

Vin paused by the window, slipping his gloves back on, resting a hand on the windowsill, watching me curl up beneath the comforter. His hand fidgeted on the sill, his dark eyes still watching. As I closed my own eyes—just to give them a break and convince Vin he could leave—I willed Gabriel to be all right, and for tomorrow to be a good day. A good day seemed so elusive, but I needed one of them. Desperately. Just a bit of good news that Gabriel was going to be all right. Just a little lighter load. A small break. I rubbed my cheek against my pillow, desperate for the softness of Gabriel's skin. I inhaled deeply, desperate for the wood-laced scent that had surrounded me the night before.

I breathed in again, turning toward my pillow, but of course it wasn't there.

Zoe settled herself back on the bed, snuggling against my side. Vin must have left.

I reached down, and she rolled over for a belly scratch with a grunt.

It struck me that she hid when he came in, and came back out when he left. Why didn't Zoe like Vin? It was odd. Anyway, it didn't matter if he told me to sleep, I needed to stay awake.

I drifted just above slumber, finally jolting fully awake at the sound of a faint ring downstairs. I flew across the attic and stumbled down the steps, my heart racing in my chest. My legs shook like I'd just finished a cross country race. I braced a hand on the wall.

Cole sat on the living room floor, his hand gripped around his cell, pressed to his ear. "I will. 'Night, Dad." He dropped his hand, his expression solemn, but his eyes soft with relief. He stared at his cell.

I couldn't speak, my throat too tight.

He looked up. "It's okay."

I let out a harsh sound.

"He's alive."

I gasped and tried to catch my breath.

"I know." His voice caught. "Dad said—" he broke off and swallowed. "Well, I hadn't wanted to believe how bad it was."

"I know. I know." I bent over, my hands bracing against my thighs. I gripped my quads. But they wouldn't stop shaking. It's okay. *He's okay.* "Thank God." I collapsed to my knees, any remaining thoughts of Vin vanishing. Three images flashing in my head. Gabriel's bloody body. His beautiful smile. His beautiful face.

21
SURVIVING

I WOKE TO THE NIGHTMARE, THE BURN, THE PAIN, STIFLING MY scream into my pillow, slobbering as I bit into the flannel, Zoe whimpering beside me.

Gabriel was gone. The nightmare was back.

At least he was still alive. And there was no school today. Labor Day. I bit into my pillow until I could stop screaming. I pushed myself up, petted Zoe to calm her, and examined the new burn marks covering shoulder to shoulder and down, more of my chest than ever before.

I bandaged them up and took Zoe out to the yard then to the kitchen. I made a pot of coffee, Gram shuffled in and made French toast, and Cole finally woke and stumbled into a chair at the table, the one right in front of the toast. I gave him a hard look. "We need to go back to the mountain." I clutched my mug.

"No. Are you crazy?" Cole plucked a piece of toast off the plate. "Way too dangerous." He tore it in half and popped one in his mouth. "Wait to hear from my dad."

Gram nodded firmly.

If I couldn't see Gabriel, I had to see B.B., B.G., and the other animals. I think Gabriel would want that too.

I left Zoe with Gram and biked to the shelter, Cole jogging along at my side.

Near the donut shop, I spotted Vin on his fancy road bike.

I waved.

He slowed, glanced around, caught sight of Reese, Paige, and Cameron cruising around the corner in Reese's Lexus, and didn't wave back. Had last night never happened? My eyes swelled with tears. I blinked to clear them and kept biking.

At the shelter, as I chained my bike up, Cole pointed out B.B. wandering around the play yard. The only other creature out there was Pip, an old pug with dementia, who clawed furiously at a spot where the fence pulled away from the ground. Pip was digging a hole almost large enough to fit his body through, and fit B.B.'s body through—and B.B. would surely follow if Pip escaped!

I raced inside, across the lobby, bumping into Kaylee as she slid out the door from the dog wing. Our shoulders knocked together. "Hey!" She pulled her cell away from her ear. "Watch it." She lifted her cell back up. "Ree, he's not picking up. And Freakenstein is back. So he must be home." She sniffed. "I'm done logging my hours. Can you pick me up?" A pause. "Great, I'll just check on the cats. I'm done with the dogs."

Of course. Kaylee had clearly forgotten about two of them. Out in the yard, I picked up Pip, who was covered in dirt and dog poo, and Cole herded B.B. back in. Cole gave B.B. and B.G. their cuddles while I bathed the exhausted pug. An image of Gabriel covered in blood flashed in my mind. I was almost too distracted to find Dr. G and tell him what happened, but I did and Dr. G wasn't pleased. He found Kaylee practicing a cheer routine outside and laid into her. She argued that she was all done with the cats and waiting for her friend. Their voices drifted in from an open window in the dog room as I rubbed down Pip with a towel. "Wait. How do you know it was me?" Kaylee's voice rose.

"It doesn't matter." Dr. G sighed loudly, a frustrated sound. "Kaylee, this can never happen again. I'm sending you home immediately. And docking your hours. Frankly, you're lucky I'm going to let you come back."

I turned away from the window, not waiting for Kaylee's

response, settled Pip in his cage for a nap, and went outside to patch up the hole. I didn't have to worry about running into Kaylee, so I stayed at the shelter all afternoon, the time passing in a blur of worrying about Gabriel. Cole and I got home right before dinner, just minutes before someone knocked on the door.

"Cameron." Gram exclaimed as I sliced ham by the stove. Cole folded napkins by the sink. "Come in, come in." She ushered him into the kitchen.

Cameron slid into a chair at the table and smoothed his hands down his shorts. "Hey, Cassie. You doing okay?"

Cameron Knight was visiting me? Who'd have thought it? Though his face was unreadable, as closed off as ever. Wait. Was this about Kaylee and me getting her in trouble today?

I didn't respond to his question.

"I just wanted to say sorry for this weekend." His leg jittered under the table.

I stepped back, hitting the counter.

He gripped the edge of the table, the jittering of his leg slowing. "I mean, for screwing up while keeping watch outside the cave." He glanced between me and Gram, then back at me. "The giant must've slipped in right after you guys in the dark, when I circled around the entrance." For an instant, the closed-off look on his face vanished. He pinched the bridge of his nose, like he was in pain.

The image of Gabriel's body flashed in my mind. I clenched the knife in my hand. Cameron wasn't the only one who'd screwed up that morning. "It's okay." I set down the knife.

"Stay for dinner." Gram opened up the stove, the smell of baked beans wafting out.

"No, thanks." Cameron dropped his hand. "I mean, I've got practice." He jumped up. "Gotta get home. Back to Aaron." He tripped around Zoe, mumbled a goodbye to Cole, and dashed from the kitchen.

"Wait." Gram shut the stove. "I have something for you."

He obeyed her, pacing in the living room while Gram wrapped

up brownies for him. "You're welcome any time you like." She walked him to the door.

"Thanks. Thanks so much." His voice was unexpectedly soft.

At least he was being nicer now. And wasn't here to stick up for Kaylee. Back to worrying about Gabriel.

As I was getting out of the shower that night, Cole's cell rang. I threw a towel around me and slid into the hall. Cole strode towards me, his cell pressed to his ear. "Love you, Dad." He handed it to me, being careful not to touch my fingers.

"Gabriel. How is Gabriel?" I rested my forehead against the cool, rough wall.

"He'll make it." Bernard's voice was polite but rushed.

I straightened up, clutching the towel to my chest.

"Here is what you need to do, for your own protection as well as ours, and for everything that's important."

"I'll do anything." Anything for Gabriel.

He drew in a breath and rushed on. "First, let Cole stay with you and Rose, until you hear otherwise from me. Try to keep it to yourself that he's there. He'll sleep downstairs. Do his homeschooling. But not go outside much. Just keep an eye out for anyone suspicious."

"Suspicious?" I cut in.

"Dangerous. Like the man who found you and Gabriel." Bernard's reply was curt. "Aaron will watch out for you at school. But not be obvious about it. And you can't go anywhere else without Aaron around. Nothing like what you and Cole did this morning. If something happens, Aaron's stronger than Cole." Why wasn't he mentioning Cameron? Maybe he didn't trust him after what had happened on the mountain. "And under no circumstances can you come back to the forest."

"But if I can't go back to the forest, how am I supposed to help Gabriel?"

"You're not. You're helping us all by staying put. For now."

I drew in a deep breath, ready to protest, but Gram peeked out from her room. "Cassandra, no."

I sighed. "OK." I handed the phone back to Cole. My shoulders slumped.

Bernard's instructions amounted to a prison sentence.

And I was so tired, I slept that night. Of course the nightmare came. The pain bubbled to a bursting point, then slowly fizzled out. When I could finally lift my head from my pillow, wet with tears, I stared at the dull pink glow of my silly Sleeping Beauty nightlight. "You can handle this. You can keep handling this for the rest of your life," I whispered, lying to myself. Like last night, I pushed myself up, petted Zoe to calm her, and examined the new burn marks inching further down, toward my breasts. They weren't that much larger than the day before, the blisters weren't any deeper, the red skin wasn't more raw, right?

I was lying to myself again.

I bandaged up the skin and lay awake on the floor of the attic, Zoe joining me with a soft whine. At dawn, I got up to dress. My bra pressed into my burns and stung them. I ditched it. Gram didn't comment on my baggy, long sleeve shirt. The day passed in another blur, nothing could distract me from the image stuck in my head. Gabriel's bloody body. His beautiful smile. His beautiful face. I barely even noticed Vin. Barely cared when he refused to partner me in AP Physics lab when no one else would. He whispered something to Mia about her partnering with me instead, which she did.

Days meshed together. Vin treated me like a stranger anywhere I ran into him, which seemed to be everywhere. Gram and Cole continued to act as jailors at home. Cole worked on his homeschooling books in the kitchen every day, Gram and I taking turns helping him. He slept on the living room floor each night. Aaron managed to keep his distance at school while keeping his eyes on me, his sharp nose turning with purpose as he followed me like a hawk. I had to cut back my time at the shelter because Aaron wouldn't stay unless

Kaylee was there too. And we had to leave as soon as she wanted a ride from him. He called Cole to come get me.

I had to cut back my shifts at Burger Boys because Aaron would only go if he could hang out with Kaylee, Reese, Luke, Mike, and the rest of their current crowd in the front, with eyes and fingers glued to their cells, while I worked in the back. I glanced through the food window to make sure everyone stayed out front, which they usually did when Officer Fry or one of the other policemen were there.

I had to quit cross country completely to accommodate Aaron's afterschool football practice. Coach grumbled. I missed running so much, especially since it helped calm me after thinking about Gabriel all day, that I jogged around the school track while Aaron practiced with his team in the middle of the oval course. At least Aaron kept his distance and gave me space, which I appreciated.

So we wouldn't have to go to the library, Aaron loaned me his old laptop, setting up internet at Gram's too. I was able to look up that strange name Vin had mentioned—Cyndra. It was derived from Greek mythology, another name for Artemis, the Greek goddess Homer referred to in the *Iliad* as the goddess of the wilderness. I couldn't make any sense of Vin calling me Cyndra or asking about it, but I was thankful for the laptop. Though when Aaron had wandered into the kitchen before school the next morning, and his old screensaver popped up—a picture of him as a boy helping a toddler girl with honey-blonde hair and wide blue eyes down a slide—his face held such a hard look, he must've regretted loaning it to me.

Aaron did give me a gift, my very own cell, but it was for emergencies. He kept pestering me about it, making sure I carried it with me, reminding me about the panic button app that would send my location to him and Cole.

To make each day worse, whatever had convinced the other kids during the first week of school to leave me alone wasn't working so well anymore. Every day after History, James Cooper tried to grab me in the hall, smirking at his friends as he said, "Watch out, it's Freakenstein!" Midweek, Paige slammed into me as I was leaving the bathroom stall and smashed my shoulder into the door frame. On Friday, Reese and Luke cornered me in another bathroom between classes. I landed a good strike against Luke, but received a nasty burn to the bottom of my chin and a vision of a near-miss accident involving him texting in his car and a boy playing near the side of the road. I'd barely been able to hide the raw, boiled flesh from everyone, Gram included, until it magically healed overnight.

I skipped sleep that night and the next, over the weekend. But avoiding sleep had its limits. I'd learned on my own, and also had Shakespeare to blame. After reading *Macbeth* last year, speaking of sleep knitting up the raveled sleave of care, and being the balm of hurt minds, I'd read more about why we need sleep. Dreaming sleep, the kind most painful for me, was also the most vital. Lack of it could be fatal, in rats anyway. But still, the less sleep I got, the more I could limit my dreams, and the nightmares. I tried so hard, downing tea, coffee, and sodas, but fighting sleep was so hard when everything drained me, especially thoughts about Gabriel.

Why wasn't Bernard calling more? What else could possibly be going on up on the mountain? Gabriel must still be in bad shape.

I couldn't take it. I had to see him.

School dismissed early on Wednesday. I slipped away from Aaron as he started practice, got on my bike, and pedaled hard in the direction of the forest. I neared the edge of town and spied Cameron alone, shooting hoops in a park across the road to the forest.

He waved.

Dammit. I couldn't get far before he told Aaron or Cole he'd seen me.

He held up his hand in a welcoming gesture and the muscles along his arm stood out. They didn't seem nearly as large or intimidating as the impressive muscles of his cousins.

I shouldn't waste this trip, not completely.

And he had been nicer recently.

I braked and glided over, risking getting close enough to ask a question that had been bothering me since my first real talk with

Mia. I put one foot down as a kickstand, and left the other on its pedal. "So, um, Cameron, why would anyone say that ah, Gabriel, could've been a star, like you?" I pointed to the basketball in his hands.

He tilted his head, his closed-off eyes widening a fraction, revealing their dark depths. "Oh, well, since I won the big championship, I'm the big star around town. That Aaron wants to be." He shrugged. "That Gabriel could've been."

"What?" I shifted on my seat.

"Gabriel played football like Aaron is now, but stuck with JV. Guess he just wanted to be part of the team. Really got into the school spirit, team building stuff too, unlike his brother." Cameron's grip on the ball tightened. "No one could believe how good Gabriel was either. How strong, but of course we both know why, right?" He laughed, giving me one of his closed-off looks, staring at my lips like he expected me to laugh too. "Anyway, after Eddie broke his knee, Gabriel stepped up—varsity quarterback—saved the day. They almost made it to state championships too." He shrugged, but with more tension in his body. "Everyone just loved Gabriel. He really could've made it bigger than me." His fingertips flexed around the ball. "But there was this accident in the final game. Some guy on the other team got hurt tackling Gabriel. Gabriel helped carry him off, and rode with him in the ambulance to the hospital. Our only other QB option sucked. So with Gabriel gone, we lost." He bounced the ball, relaxing a bit. "Of course everyone just loved him for that too."

OK, that just made me think that Gabriel really was good, like I'd thought. "Thanks, Cameron. I, ah, needed to hear that."

"No problem." He bounced the ball again. "We're a good family, you know. Even if some of us are a bit competitive, and well, strange." He grimaced. "I mean, I do appreciate them taking me in after—" His gaze dropped to his sneakers. "And I know why we had to tell the story we did, and why we have to watch out for you now. I know I don't act like it." He lifted his shoulders as if to shrug again, but ended up hunching, looking a bit ashamed. His voice lowered, as if he spoke more to himself. "I've refused Uncle B so many things. Even when he just wanted to make me feel like one of them." Cameron glanced up, to an old, beat-up pickup truck at the end of the paved lot.

His truck. I recognized it from school.

And Cameron probably hadn't always lived by the river. I think I'd heard once his father had been a handyman, working part-time at the school. Maybe Cameron actually had some understanding of what is like to be like me? More than his girlfriend, more than his friends?

And he'd told Aaron and Cole to give me a break, after Cole caught me sneaking back in that afternoon, saying something about how not everyone was raised as strictly as them.

The bell rang at the end of the day Friday and I could take no more of the rules, restrictions, and worry about Gabriel. I prepared better this time. I raced out of my last class, my head whipping left and right to make sure no one got too close, and headed to the locker room to finalize my plans. Aaron had football practice right after school, a warm-up for tonight's big home game. I'd told Gram and Cole over breakfast that I was going to Aaron's practice and staying near him by the sidelines for the game, so they wouldn't expect me back until late. Just a few miles logged around the track, so Aaron could see me from the football field, then I could take off. Aaron should be oblivious with both football and Kaylee there.

In the locker room, I changed out of my best pair of jeans, black and silver striped lightweight sweater, and black ballet flats that Gram had pleaded with me to wear, and into a sports bra (thankfully the burns from last night were almost healed), leggings, a long-sleeved running shell, and my running shoes. I strapped on the waist-pack I'd filled that morning with Gram's dried fruit and nut bars, added my cell, slipped two water bottles into their mesh carriers on the back, then hurried outside and started around the track. Just a light jog. I needed to conserve energy to bike all the way to the forest and run up the mountain. It was too risky to take the VW, with Cole keeping watch over everything at the cottage, and Gram knowing that Aaron followed me on my bike in his big fancy truck to and from school.

After my first lap, Vin took a seat in the bleachers. Several laps later, as I took a water break, Kaylee broke away from Reese and their cluster of cheerleaders at the side of the field. She walked in my direction and called out for me.

"Hey, freak!"

I re-secured my bottle and started jogging.

"Hey, Freakenstein. Stop." She continued toward me. Should I increase my pace? Her scrawny ass wouldn't be able to keep up. Her legs looked like breakable pencils in the shorter-than-short fuchsia skirt all the pom-pom junkies wore. But if she was really intent on talking to me (and from the firm set of her glossy, fuchsia lips, it looked that way), I was just delaying the inevitable.

I slowed, coming to a stop, turning toward her and bracing myself for whatever sort of confrontation she had in mind.

She came right up close to me, her white cheerleading sneakers planted hard in the grass. "So, Aaron says Gabriel's been really sick. He's not even checking his cell."

"So?" Instinctively, I shifted my right foot back, preparing to fight or get the hell out of there.

"Well, I can't go over there, risk catching it. Not with Homecoming." Her eyes widened with a dreamy look. "So I just wanted to remind you Gabriel's going to the dance with me." She eyed me from head to toe, her gaze coming to rest on my worn shoes. She sighed, bending down and wiping a scuff from what was probably last year's pair of shoes for her too. She popped back up. "Got it?"

"Um—"

"Vin wanted to go with me too, of course, but he'll be away with his dad." She shrugged.

I glanced up to find Vin in the same spot in the bleachers, now surrounded by a girl-flock. The cheerleaders had even moved their warmup over to the grass in front of his section. "Why would I care?" I silently wished that Gabriel really was well enough to go to a dance, even if it was with Kaylee.

Kaylee gave a menacing look. "Oh, come on." She tossed her hair over her shoulder. "I know you and Gabriel went camping. That you have a thing for him. That he finds something about you fascinating—more like curious and freakish. Well, you guys are done. It's only right that the star quarterback goes to the dance with the head cheerleader." She swished her skirt back and forth. "I just don't want you messing with our plans."

"Don't worry. I won't," I responded with complete sincerity, though Kaylee wasn't making any sense. Was she talking about Aaron—the quarterback—now? Or, was she really obsessed with Gabriel because of what Cameron had told me?

She smoothed her skirt, straightening the fuchsia pleats so the lighter stripe around the bottom was even. "Good. Because if you get in my way, you'll regret it," she said serenely, then puckered her glistening lips into a distorted version of a kiss. "You can kiss your senior year goodbye."

What kind of messed-up threat was that? Maybe she really had lost her mind.

Kaylee and I stared at each other for several moments. What could I say to convince her I was no competition for Gabriel's attentions—especially not now? Better yet, I wished she'd forget I even existed. The last thing I needed right now was Kaylee Cook making threats.

My focus was finally torn away by Vin walking up behind her. "Hello, Kaylee," Vin said melodically and she turned toward him. "What's going on here?"

"Oh, nothing." Kaylee's expression was pure, fake sweetness. "Just girl talk. Nothing you need to worry about."

"Well, let's get you back to the other cheerleaders then." He held out an arm for her and graced her with one of his rare smiles, before I could think to say anything else.

She turned and gave me one more menacing look, then linked her arm in Vin's and floated away.

The cheerleaders broke for water as soon as the jocks did and swarmed around each other. It was my moment. I darted around the bleachers and slipped out the gate. I biked to where Gabriel had parked the day we went camping, only pausing to gobble down one of Gram's bars, and sprinted up the mountain. Reaching the other end of the trailhead at the top and slipping around the far fence, I stopped and panted hard, trying to calm myself for the next leg of the journey.

The sun threw soft rays over the mountain. The clearing around the cave looked so serene. Except for the large brown bear laying outside.

The animal rested at the side of the entrance, on a small patch of packed dirt surrounded by stone, almost exactly where our tent had been. Its lower back and hind legs were covered with a thick wool covering, almost the exact same mud-brown color as the bear. I shouldn't be surprised about a bear in a blanket, after everything with Gabriel, but had to wonder if I was making it up. Had I not drank enough water?

I forced myself to drink more, then crept out from under the trees.

The bear's eyes were closed, its massive head resting on its crossed forepaws like a pillow. It was a bear tucked into a blanket. And didn't look threatening at all, actually. Just old. Tired. Especially with its drooping features, the white tufts in the ruff around its neck, and grey laced through its brown coat.

A chipmunk chattered on a large rock. I nearly brushed its stone perch with my knee, and it chattered louder, watching me with interest. A hawk shrieked above us. The bear didn't even lift an eye. Gabriel had implied that the old bears around here were friendly, so there was no reason to turn around and run back down, right? I took another step. Then another.

The bear lifted its muzzle, sniffing the air. It raised its muzzle higher and sniffed again. The animal's eyes flashed open, drilling into me. I froze. The animal slowly shifted its legs underneath its body and rose in stages, starting with its right hindquarters, then the left. The blanket drifted to the ground. All the while, the bear's body moved laboriously, like the stiff and awkward movements of a foal trying to stand for the first time.

But this was no newborn animal. It was old, experienced, and huge.

I should leave. But when would I be able to slip away again? I averted my eyes, trying to avoid threatening it with eye contact, and started moving in a wide path around it. The chipmunk hopped off the rock and followed me.

The bear bellowed. The chipmunk scurried away. All my muscles locked up. I took two quick breaths, then turned my head to see if the bear had moved.

No bear. A weathered-looking, naked old man trembled on his hands and knees. He reached for the blanket, wrapped it around himself, then started a slow ascent to standing. He rose bit by bit until he reached his full height, which was not that much taller than me, with his body stooped so much. The blanket draped over his frail limbs, pooling on the ground. He was all brown stubbly wool except for his head sticking out, thinning, light grey hair standing up. Grey hairs sprouted out of his ears and nose as well, but the most prominent thing on his face was a wide, pleasant smile. Why the big smile?

I backed up several steps.

"No need to be afraid, Cassandra." The old man coughed and wrapped the blanket more tightly around his shoulders. "Sorry I didn't turn for you right away. But you know, it gets harder to leave the bear form the older you get, and it took me just a moment to realize it was you."

A bear had just turned into an old man. And Gabriel had turned into a bear and back again. The Knights really were messed up in some wondrous things.

"Um, that's okay?" I said, as more of a question than I'd intended. I sank down onto the rock.

"It's really nice to meet you, my dear, but you shouldn't be here. My grandson wouldn't approve."

I pondered him through slitted eyes. "You mean Gabriel?"

"No. Bernard."

Through all the wrinkles and bushy eyebrows, he did resemble Bernard. "Where's your son—Gabriel's grandpa?" I glanced around the clearing, as if expecting to see another old bear sitting around having tea with him.

"Gabriel thinks of me—calls me—grandpa. My damn hair-brained son. Long gone." He wheezed, then suppressed another cough with his blanket.

"Are you okay?" I sprung up and took a step toward him, concerned he sounded like Gram on her way to an asthma attack.

"Just tired. A bit out of breath from the change, I think. But it's very sweet of you to ask. The bear form is so much stronger than the human form, but I can't talk very well like that." He winked, and as if in slow motion, all of the leathery folds around his eye squished. When they opened, they revealed more of the shade of his eyes. Blue—like all of the Knights except Cameron—just not as deep, more watery, almost faded from age. "Usually us old fellows, the ones that are left, just hibernate a good part of the year. But lately I haven't been able to do that." His voice withered away as he gasped in a mouthful of air. "Have to help out with the crisis, my grandson says. He's right, unfortunately, so I'm a bit behind on my sleep."

"Oh, well, I guess that's good—that you're not sick or anything." The sun dipped, hovering over the peak. How could I wrap this up so I could get to Gabriel? I needed to see for myself he was okay. "I'm just going to go inside the cave now, if that's okay." I inched toward the opening.

"Fine with me, but my grandson would throw a fit if he knew you were here." His wrinkled cheeks plumped with mild amusement. "Never seen Bernard so frazzled. I don't blame him." The grin fell away. "He shoulders the responsibilities of keeping you and the relic safe. Thankfully, he didn't inherit my son's lack of duty." He curled his thin lip. "Quite the opposite, in fact. Bernard overburdens himself. He won't even talk about anything outside of the mountain. Barely uses that cordless phone thing he carries around. I told him there's no need for all the precautions now." The old man chuckled—a light, airy laugh that restored fullness to his face as it picked up in intensity but ended with a loud coughing fit.

I took another step toward him, worried he was choking, but the noise stopped suddenly.

"I told him the Summum Malum can't hear us," he continued in a breathless but sure tone. "The Summum Malum can't get anywhere close to the relic when you're near, so long as you're alive and the relic's powers are locked onto you. At least according to what my grandpap told me. In fact, I can't imagine the Summum Malum have been able to listen in on anything in this area for the last two years now, since the powers of the relic revealed themselves when you arrived. How frustrating it must be! They didn't know anything about our relic being here until it came to life—and now that they know, they can't get close enough to listen."

As much as I wanted to keep him talking, I started to back into the darkness, reaching for my running light. I still had a long way to travel.

"Don't go," he called out. "I have things to tell you. And I don't think I can hold human form much longer."

"Oh. Well." I stopped my retreat into the shadows. No need to be rude. "Maybe I should know your name?"

"I'm Henryk Augustus Knight. At your service, my dear." He paused and hacked into his blanket-covered shoulder several times. "Oh goodness. I swear I'm not as weak as I look right now. I can't believe the impression I'm making."

"You're making a fine impression." I attempted a reassuring smile.

"You really are such a nice girl." Henryk tottered closer on rigid legs. "Just like Gabriel said." His eyes twinkled with warmth and enthusiasm. That kind expression confirmed his identity as Gabriel's great-grandfather more than anything else.

"And it is so very wonderful to meet you after all this time," he continued in a soft tone, his breathing finally calmed. "Several hundred years I've been on this earth, hearing stories about the Una from my grandpap when he was alive, believing I'd live to meet you, and here you are."

"Um, you're saying you're several hundred years old?" I couldn't help asking, out of all the questions circling in my head.

"Three hundred and forty-seven, if I remember correctly."

"Wow. Pretty awesome." I swayed forward, rocking onto the balls of my feet.

His bushy eyebrows twitched. "I keep forgetting Bernard said you lost your memory, and whatever you were taught as a child about the alternate races is gone," he responded slowly, then rushed on. "Well, we don't have time to delve into all the details, but almost all of the races have strong bodies and live at least one hundred good years."

"At least?" My feet planted on stone.

"My race is stronger than most and we live longer, because we hibernate throughout our lives and if we want, can spend the last bit of our extended life in hibernation. It's part of the reason my race was chosen as one of the five."

"One of the five?" There was so much I didn't know.

"One of the five races to guard the relics."

"Um…" I hesitated. "What is your race… exactly?"

"We're called Cave Bears, although the bear part is a bit deceptive. There is no bear alive quite like the one we're related to." He paused with his mouth slightly open. I couldn't tell if he was having trouble breathing again, or if he was testing my reaction. "I have the honor," he continued, "to be one of the few left in a race tied to an ancient cave animal that was driven to extinction over 20,000 years ago. By the Ice Age, you know. The animal spirit gave us our size, bone structure, dense hide, and propensity to spend a lot of time in mountainous regions. As you can see, we like caves." He gave me a gummy, cheerful smile.

That seemed to fit in with everything I knew about the Knights so far. "So could you tell me why your family thinks I'm like you?"

"To be perfectly honest, we don't know what you are. Your natural gift doesn't make much sense either. More like a weakness or curse, that suffering pain thing. But maybe it's a good thing. Maybe it's one reason you've been able to stay hidden longer than most, as they certainly haven't been looking for a girl like you. With an apparent mental or physical issue. Not a strength."

"But shouldn't there be someone else out there like me? I mean, I must have come from somewhere?"

"You could be a hybrid of several races, perhaps. We can't be sure. What I am sure of, though, is that you are the girl we've been waiting for," Henryk said gently, and deliberately, in what could only be described as a humble tone. "I was told I'd be alive for this. For when you finally came for the Fire relic."

"Who told you? Why would I come? Why are the relics so important?" All my thoughts tumbled out.

"Important?" He latched onto my last question. A hand emerged from his blanket and scratched his cheek. "The relics were created long ago, in Ancient Greece. By five Priestesses, closely related, who were able to harness the powers of the five elements and lock them away in stone vessels."

I didn't mean to, but I pulled a face. It sounded like more mumbo-jumbo. He offered a knowing smile, unoffended.

"You see, dear, the earth was once a magical place. The gods of the Ancients could speak to man because the planes of existence, including the afterlife, had stronger connections. It was accepted that some people were just different. They shared a special connection with the elemental magic that existed in all things, allowing them to harness previously untapped potential. Some could heal with just a touch. Some could command rivers to flow where they wished or summon rain. Wonders were performed every day. The alternate races did not have to hide away like they do now."

"So… the relics are supposed to be magic?" I tried not to sound too skeptical.

In true Knight fashion, he grinned again. "Well, what many folks call magic is simply the rules of nature that we don't understand yet. And nature has laws, however odd they may seem."

I nodded, thinking that might be the sanest explanation a Knight had ever given me. "So, then the relics are bad? Because they trap the… magic?"

"No. The Priestesses created them out of necessity, to stop an evil that had grown in secret, undetected until it was too late. The Summum Malum. They started as regular folks, driven to extremism by the desire for power and everlasting life. A cult, if you will."

"I studied Ancient Greece, but I've never heard of them." Not until that terrible day in the cave anyway.

"Many secrets are lost to time and myth. Organizations as secretive as the Summum Malum are even harder to track. But we alternates passed down the tale through the centuries because it is we who they hunt."

I waited for him to go on, curious despite myself.

"The Summum Malum sought to enter the afterlife alive, and in this way, dominate both the living and nonliving realms to cheat death forever. But as often happens when man exploits nature, there were unforeseen complications. They succeeded in entering what many call the limbo world, where newly departed souls coalesce into their true form. There, we are not young or old, we are the sum of our entire earthly existence."

The mere thought made my head hurt. I wanted to ask where he was getting his information about eternity, but he didn't pause to take questions.

"The Summum Malum corrupted and clogged the limbo world. No soul could move on to the next phase of existence, not even the Summum Malum themselves. So, they started coming back into the living world as shadows, wreaking havoc."

I shivered, the mention of "shadows" summoning Gram's warning and Sarah's charred journal.

"Their control in the afterlife allowed them a deeper connection to the elemental magic, and they harnessed it to plunder and devour whatever they wished. Until the sisterhood contained the magic in the relics for someone more worthy to wield one day. A fellow sister. An Una."

"Why does the Una have to be a girl?"

"Well, Grandpap said—he rubbed his chin on the blanket, like he was taking a moment to remember Grandpap's words—"elemental magic is a living thing that must be nourished within its wielder so that it can gain strength as it passes through the body. Only a woman's body can nurture life from within. Only a woman can harness the power of the relics." When I didn't respond, he rushed on. "And it appears this is the first you've found. What an honor for us!" He clenched the blanket to him with one arm and the other swept out from a fold, motioning to the forest around us, like I'd discovered a sacred place. I guessed it was a place the Knights had treated as such for a long time.

"Um, I'm sorry, but I can assure you I'm not who your family thinks I am."

"Well, of course you are." He took a few more rigid steps towards me, wobbling on an uneven bit of rock beneath his feet. "Gabriel told us that nothing happened when you tried to retrieve your powers, but we'll figure that out. You must be the Una. Without a doubt."

"But how can you be so sure?"

"Gabriel told us about your matching stone. That confirms it for me. Although I wish you hadn't lost it. I'd have loved to see it. That was never reported in the scrolls or stories passed down."

I didn't want to get into another argument about my missing locket and the girl the Knights were waiting for, especially with Henryk, who actually seemed kind of sweet. But this was as good an opportunity as any to get to the purpose of me being here. "How's Gabriel doing?" I asked, my voice hardly louder than a whisper.

"Hmm? How's my great-grandson doing?" Henryk coughed. "Getting stronger every day. Hibernating will energize you like nothing else."

Ah. So that's why I was told to stay away and remain patient. Whatever race Gabriel was from didn't heal like regular humans. They went into hibernation to heal. But why couldn't they have just told me that? "So, he's really going to be okay? I mean, he's going to survive, with no damage done? Because you don't need to soften the truth. I was with him when he was stabbed. I saw how bad it was."

"Oh, he'll have another nice scar to add to the collection. Too risky to have him treated by a doctor. Other than that, yes, he'll be just fine. Just give him a bit more time in the resting state and Gabriel will heal. Minus the cosmetic part of it, he'll be as good as new, I think that's the expression people use nowadays." He gave an emphatic nod. "Or is it 'right as rain'?"

I let out a small breath. My body sagged. The stress that had been weighing me down all week eased. There was so much more I needed to know, and I desperately wanted to see Gabriel with my own eyes, but I believed and actually trusted the old man, at least about this. "That's great. Really good news, just the news I was hoping for," I said. And then—even though I still wanted to see Gabriel, I knew it wasn't needed now—so I forced myself to say, "I guess I should be going."

I made myself walk out of the shadows of the cave. Each step felt heavy, strained, and I stopped near where our campfire had been. *Keep going!* I'd come to check on Gabriel and I had, without even having to worry about whether he'd been moved to a part of the cave I could get to before the first sump, or if not, whether there was diving equipment left behind for me to use. It was actually better this way, right? Not to see him. That way I wouldn't risk forgetting when I looked into his eyes, that I wasn't supposed to think of him differently than anyone else.

As if to get me moving again, Henryk called out, "Yes, you should be going." I still didn't budge. "You know," he said. "It's a lot safer around here, since over the last few days we've dealt with the rest of the Jentilak, or Gigantes, I guess you could call them—the ones who came looking for the Jentilak you and Gabriel disposed of. But one never knows who or what is coming next, especially not now that entire races are making deals with the Summum Malum."

I gave him a long, hard look. "What do you mean? More of those giant men came?"

"Well, yes. There's a small group of them left. Or, rather, there was a small group left. It seems like they've finally stopped coming, so they're probably all gone."

"All gone?"

"Yes. But don't worry. They weren't too tough to deal with. They're descendants of the Basque giants, called Jentilak, of that region's lore, but they've mixed their blood with normals and their strength is much diminished. It took us awhile to figure out exactly what they were. Grandpap had it reported in his records that the Basque giants were hairy. But it seems losing their hair was one of the effects of having to mate without nature's magic. They also like to stick to the region they're from, so it's a bit odd to see them any-where outside of Europe. Luckily, they don't have any sort of gifts besides their size, strength and capacity to tolerate a good deal of pain. They were easy enough to handle."

"You don't mean you killed them all?!"

"Why sure." Henryk's tone was tranquil, revealing no trace of his earlier troubles. "We got lucky that they were only sniffing around the cave. None of them seemed to know about you. It appears the one who stumbled upon you and Gabriel hadn't told the others yet. We couldn't risk them finding out."

Oh no. I shivered.

Now the Knight family was taking their obsession with me to an even more frightening degree. Maybe the giants had it coming if they'd been mixed up in the murders of Gabriel's mom and sister, Cameron's father, and if they were planning to kill and burn even more girls—young, defenseless girls, like Gram's daughter—but I didn't want to be responsible, even as their mistaken target, for luring them to their doom. "You killed them because of me?" I asked as calmly as I could, rushing on. "Because it seems to me you did, and I told you before, I'm not the girl your family's waiting for. You have to stop trying to protect me. Or whatever it is you think you're doing!"

"Cassandra, don't you see how important you are?" Henryk questioned gently. I didn't respond. "My dear girl, you're critical to the continued well-being of my family, my race, the others. So much more... you're the key to stopping the Summum Malum. If you can claim all five of the relics' powers, you can control the portals between this life and the next. You can free the trapped souls and force the Summum Malum onward. You can stop them from interfering with this world, keep them from ever coming back."

"What!?" Still I found myself asking, "How?"

"You can send them all to their final resting place. Then, after all this time, humanity might actually have a chance."

Good God. No way. They thought I was responsible for all of humanity too?

"So you must be protected above all else." He stood up tall under the blanket. "You really need to start believing it—believing you're the One—the Una." He paused and his bushy white eyebrows twitched. "Hmm... maybe that's the problem... not believing. Maybe Gabriel will have to talk to you about that."

"Oh, no. No, that's not necessary." I took a step in retreat, back toward the trailhead. "Gabriel and I really have nothing to talk about. Actually, you shouldn't mention I was here." I kept retreating.

"Really? From what I understand of how our boy describes his feelings for you, you both will be vital in each other's lives for a long time to come. I should know. It's a very rare thing, but I was bonded with my wife."

I stumbled over a tree root and paused. "Was bonded?" A chill crept up my spine.

"Yes, for two wonderful years before she was taken. My son never really knew his mother. Perhaps why he had such a hard time of things? Hmm. Anyway, she didn't just pass onto the next spiritual world, which would've been tolerable." His shoulders sank. "No, she's dead—burned—completely dead and gone. I can never be with her in the next life and she can never come back to me here." He looked at the clouds swirling above the mountain, his eyes going distant. "The humans who were compelled to do it returned what was left in a box outside our door." His tone was quiet, practical. He finally looked away from the clouds. "That's my last memory of her. Melted. Mutilated." A muscle ticked at the side of his face. "At least they could have spared me that. But no."

The chill spread, numbing me. I had no idea what to say.

Henryk continued, this time with a determined expression lifting his wrinkled cheeks. "It was only the promise of you—of keeping what we protect safe for you—that kept me going. I fueled myself with faith that you would come. I met a prophetic wanderer, you see, and she foretold I'd meet the Una, that I'd play a role. I prolonged my life by staying in bear form even more than usual. I wanted to ensure I'd remain strong enough to be of some use by the time you reached us."

That information was almost too much to take in. "I'm so sorry about your wife," I mumbled, feeling so unsure of myself and how the Knight family was ever going to accept that I wasn't the savior they'd been waiting for.

"Thank you, my dear." He wheezed slightly and started to sink back into the ground. "Oh goodness, I'm tired. I should really be getting back to bear form. And you should be getting out of here. It'll be dark soon." He stopped his descent, on hands and knees, and looked up. "Just remember what I said. About everything. So of course Gabriel will be disappointed to have missed you. But he'll be back on two legs—rather than resting on four—very soon." The old man's body collapsed further, the blanket covering him completely. "And don't worry about understanding everything. Not all at once." I barely caught the muffled words.

"Huh?" I questioned.

"Cassandra, you of all people should know."

"What?"

"The greater the evil, the harder it is to comprehend."

One second his shape resembled a bag of bones, haphazardly tossed into a rucksack and discarded on the ground, and the next, a large brown bear snored peacefully under its blanket.

22

HAUNTED

HALFWAY DOWN THE MOUNTAIN IN THE DARK OF EARLY night, the crickets stopped chirping, the owls stopped hooting, and the forest fell silent around me.

I slowed my descent down the rocky path, immediately reducing my stride to measured steps. I scanned the dense woods on either side of me, ready for the stare of two sharp eyes to materialize out of the foliage, or for the piercing crack of a snapping twig to shatter the eerie silence. Anything that might indicate I'd run into the most likely form of trouble in the forest at this time of night. A mountain lion on its evening prowl.

All the signs posted at the trailheads warned that fast movements might trigger the big cat's instincts to chase and attack, and jerky movements might make it believe you were injured. Easy prey. I drew in the cool, pine-scented air to my lungs' capacity and forced my feet to maintain their unhurried descent down the steep, unstable terrain. After several yards of unbroken silence, I turned to look back up the mountain. A white streak flashed over a tree top. I blinked.

The light. It darted in the landscape above me.

Oh God. Bright and electric, like a tiny thunderbolt, it dazzled, appearing to shoot sparks into the night sky. Zigzagging forward, moving toward me out of the dense, dark woods.

I flinched, and turned back to the path, reached for my running light, and turned it to its brightest setting. I gave my body one more second of calm. I took one last deep breath of forest air. I then accelerated to a run within an instant, risking a full-out downward sprint. I was flying, almost falling, down the mountain. My knees and ankles twisted on every uneven landing. My feet protested every harsh impact. My lungs burned with each labored breath.

Ignore them! It doesn't matter whether the light, or the fact it was following me, is all part of my imagination. Or if I might make a misstep on the rugged terrain and lose my footing on the way down. Or even if there is a mountain lion lurking in the woods. I had to keep running.

Run faster.

I finally glimpsed the river. My body relaxed a degree. My pace slowed a fraction. My bike was near. Surely everything would be okay if I could just get myself out of here. Maybe Bernard was right. I shouldn't come back to the forest.

I dared a glance behind me. Complete darkness, other than the glow of the moon above the mountain.

I let out a huge breath, but was still too frantic to give my legs the rest they needed. I raced past the river, across the narrow bridge leading to the trailhead parking area, then through the parking area and down the bumpy forest service road, heading to my bike.

I slowed to a jog and glanced behind me again. Nothing but darkness. I huffed twice, and slowed to a brisk walk. I started panting and tried to calm myself. Had I been attempting to outrun something real? Or was I simply outrunning my own imagination? Did I really want to know the answer?

I stopped completely and doubled over, hands resting on bent knees.

I still panted hard, harder than I probably ever had. With the combination of getting up the mountain, the talk with Gabriel's great-grandfather at the top, the dash back down, I was beyond physically and mentally beat. I wouldn't make it home until way past Gram's bedtime. I pulled out the cell from my pack, and actually got a signal—probably thanks to the cell tower the Knights had built—so I texted Aaron like he'd shown me how, saying everything was fine and I'd headed home early. Hopefully he and Cole would do what they normally did: not talk.

I finally got back to the ditch sheltering my bike. Okay, this day was not done testing me yet. A sleek sports car blocked my way. I was no expert, but the tiny two-door car looked way too fancy and impractical to be out on this unpaved road.

I approached with caution, watching the darkened window of the driver's side, thinking of my defensive skills in case anyone wanted to hassle me tonight. My running light bounced gently against my chest and flashed several times on the car's yellow hood. When I finally got within several feet of the driver's side, starting around to my bike, the door opened swiftly with a smooth whoosh.

Vin stepped out leisurely, shut the door, and leaned back against it with all the poise of a model in a luxury car commercial. He crossed his arms in front of his chest. His face had a cool, almost cold, expression. It didn't stop my body from heating and reacting, from yearning for him. It also didn't stop my mind from losing focus, slipping into its typical Vin-haze. *God, girl, fight against the hold he has over you. Remember how much it hurt you the last few weeks when he'd treated you like you had the plague!*

"Vin." My voice was harsh, a mixture of greeting and accusation. Of all the people I had to deal with right now, of course it was the one I couldn't help but want to get close to. "What are you doing here? And in that ridiculous car?"

"Oh, you haven't seen my 911 Carrera yet?" He responded smoothly and tilted his head to the side, causing his dark hair to sweep across his forehead. "You were inside it when I brought you home that first day, but I guess you wouldn't remember."

"No, and what are you doing in it?" I battled the urge to step in closer to the car—to the temptation Vin presented.

He yawned, looking a bit bored by the conversation we were having. "It's a great ride."

"No, that's not what I meant. What are you doing in it here?"

"I have to admit my Porsche is not what I would have chosen for this road. I actually rented something for this sort of thing." He rolled his eyes in apparent exasperation at his choice of vehicle today. "But it's what I had at school when I noticed you'd taken off without Aaron. I finally figured out you weren't at the shelter or back home." He leaned back further against the car, as if he didn't have a care in the world, out in the forest in the middle of the night.

"Ugh," I groaned. "Forget about the car. Would you please just tell me what you're doing out in the forest? So far out of town? That's what I've been trying to ask."

"I'm getting really sick of this." He straightened away from the Porsche. "If you remembered me at all, you'd know that this is me trying to cool my temper right now. And it's not working, so why bother?" He whispered a foreign-sounding phrase under his breath. "Just get your pretty little ass in the car so we can get out of here."

My eyebrows shot up at that choice of words. "Oh really? Why would my, what did you call it, pretty little ass go anywhere with you? You've been such an ass. You don't even like me," I replied angrily, more angry at myself for caring.

"Of course I like you. Enough to say this straight out." He paused before finishing what he was going to say and I'd never seen him look more serious. "You shouldn't be in the forest alone. I thought at least the Knights were watching out for you to that degree. Clearly they can't handle the job. Frankly, they're a bit incompetent." I stared back at him mutely. "I'm only going to say this one more time. Get. In. The. Car."

My nostrils flared at the order.

His head fell forward in a defeated, exhausted way for an instant before he looked back up with pleading eyes. "Please, Cyndra, get in the car."

"But I have my bike," I protested weakly, still fighting my attraction to Vin, actually wanting to get in the car—to be close to him. I just didn't want to be ordered to do it. And of course, I wanted to know why he'd just called me Cyndra again. If he knew me from before Meeker, why not just tell me? Why not talk about it like a normal person?

"Your bike is already on my rack." Vin swept his arm up toward the top of his car. I looked over, and saw that in the darkness, I'd missed the outline of my bike secured there. I quickly lost interest in the sight and sought out his perfect features again. His jaw set suddenly in determination. "Now, please. Get in," he said with a tense smile and shifted forward, directing the force of that smile right at me.

I found myself doing as Vin asked, walking around to the Porsche's passenger side and sliding into the sleek interior.

The car purred to life and Vin handled it with ease on the rough forest road. *Don't look at him.* Instead, I looked out at the hard-packed dirt illuminated by the headlights, and the flashes of thick brush and trees bordering on either side, which seemed to encase us in a dark, hypnotic bubble of tranquility.

I opened my window and looked out at the moon, almost full, glowing above us. Cool air rushed in, tickling my cheeks, rustling the loose curls of my ponytail. I released a small sigh. The air, permeated with all the sharp, yeasty scents of the forest, swirled around the car's interior, caressing me.

After several moments my gaze shifted to the nearest stars, easily visible on such a clear night. The dotted beacons were more than pretty specks in the sky—they were an odd sort of symbol belying the self-centered views I saw in people all the time. They disputed the view that our world is the center of the universe, that human beings are the most important thing in it, that any individual's particular wants or desires are all-important. If the stars could actually speak, what would they say? Maybe that humans are not the supreme species, or the ideal expression of creation, that our egos tell us we are?

Just looking at the sky made my issues with Vin, and all my other problems, seem insignificant and unimportant. At last, the strange feelings that took hold of me whenever Vin was near me began to ease, to the point I almost felt like my normal self. My capable, reasoned self. Not the lunatic girl who was crushing on the new most popular guy in school and acted all stupid around him. And definitely not that weak, teary-eyed girl I'd been with Gabriel, who couldn't take care of herself.

"First, I need to apologize to you." Vin interrupted my thoughts as we reached the paved road heading toward town. He accelerated, speeding us away from the mountain.

"You don't need to apologize for not wanting to hang out with me," I said after a moment's pause, and tried to mean it. "I get it, Vin, I'm not the girl a guy like you should be hanging out with."

He was silent for several moments. "I'm sorry if keeping my distance upset you." He slowed the Porsche to glance at me. "But what I was going to apologize for was the kids at school bothering you again. I thought I'd handled that, but I'd forgotten how obnoxious some teens can be—how stubborn they can be when they want to pick on someone to feel better about themselves."

Wasn't he a teenager too? "What do you mean?" I glanced at him in the dim confines of the car, and was instantly reminded that looking at Vin only multiplied my feelings for him. I turned back to the window.

"Kaylee was bragging after we left you on the track. She said her friends know how to keep you in your place. They've been touching you again. I had no idea my efforts had worn off. Has it been bad?"

"I've been handling it." I continued to stare at the stars.

"That doesn't answer my question, Agapi mou," he admonished gently.

I didn't reply. I was too startled by Vin's calling me that strange, foreign-sounding phrase I now remembered he'd used that night in my room. And I had a vague memory of him using it before, when I'd blacked out at school.

"How often have they been bothering you? Has it happened anywhere else?"

"Not your concern."

"Of course it is." Vin sighed. "And of course you'd say that. Well, I'll take care of it. And I'll make sure it sticks this time."

"Um, thanks, I guess," I mumbled in the direction of the window, the wind brushing my lips.

"Sure. That was the whole point of me not blowing off all the kids at school." Vin cleared his throat. "Now, I have to ask you something. Something I need you to think hard about. Something I need you to answer truthfully."

"Ask anything you want. I can't guarantee you'll get an answer."

He sighed as the Porsche slowed again, almost crawling along the road. "Would you at least look at me? It's important." I risked a glance at Vin and he gave me a tight smile. My head clouded. "I know you've got a stubborn streak, but you need to listen to this carefully. Respond fully. Like I said, it's important."

"OK…" I answered slowly.

"I need to know if you've seen any odd-looking flashes in the sky or anywhere around you. It would almost look like an absence of light. Like a blackness or void. Or maybe a shadow moving quickly by you, that shouldn't be there. Have you seen anything like that?"

"No." I was still annoyed with him.

"Are you sure?"

"Well…" Somehow I found myself wanting to answer, and worse, wanting to trust him. "Nothing black or shadowy."

"Good."

"But I've seen something like flashes of light. Really bright. Like the glare of the sun."

Vin inhaled sharply, tensing in his seat. "That's good too," he finally responded as his hands relaxed on the steering wheel and he accelerated.

"Going crazy is a good thing?"

"Yes, if the light… if it's what I think it is—who I think it is— you're not crazy. The good ones are watching out for you—"

"Cut the crap! I'm not stupid. It's getting pretty apparent you think you know me or knew me, long before you ever walked into AP English."

"I realize that. I'm not trying to hide anything. I'm trying to be careful." His jaw tightened, in apparent refusal to explain himself.

There was one way to learn more without his cooperation. I eyed his forearm, exposed by his rolled-up shirt sleeve, as he drummed his fingers on the steering wheel. Would it be worth it? Yes. In fact, in a way, I'd been itching to touch Vin, just to see…

I reached across the seats.

"No!" He commanded and I froze. He smiled tightly then exclaimed harshly, "Are you crazy!? Drop your arm." I did as I was told, without hesitation. "You want to touch me? You can touch me all you want when things work out, but I can't be responsible for hurting you."

"I just want to know more." I was more confused than ever about the strange effect Vin always had over me. "Why won't you tell me more? More about you?"

Vin slowed the Porsche again, this time turning to the right, half off the road, bouncing the car to a stop. His jaw tightened. "You want to know about me? About us?! We were inseparable. You trusted me. You don't have to trust me now. But I swear I'll earn it if you give me a chance."

Vin's anger vanished. He winced, almost a sound of sadness, and gave me a soft look, filled with that powerful longing I'd noticed in his gaze that night in my room. I couldn't help but yield to the pull he had on me, sink into it. His expression softened further. I sank deeper. He finally eased the car back onto the road. I opened my mouth to speak, but he immediately cut me off. "No, Agapi mou." Vin pushed the speed of the Porsche, as if he was now in even more of a hurry to get back to town. "Just be patient. I hope, I think, I have something that will help bring back those memories."

"That would be nice," I said cautiously, feeling a bit more myself. "And why do you keep calling me aga-pi mou or however you say it? I thought you said my name was Cyndra, as if that isn't weird enough."

"Cyndra is your name. Agapi mou is just an old habit."

"What sort of habit?"

"Just a Greek endearment I used."

"When?"

"When I was searching for you after you left, looking for you… thinking of you."

"Well first, the reason you didn't find me after I left was when I was rescued from White River, one of the rescuers said I said something to make everyone think I could be in trouble and they kept my appearance here quiet." Now I was wondering if that was even true, that I had said those things, but why would the U.S. Forest Service guy lie? "Anyhow, what does it mean?

His jaw tightened. "It doesn't matter," he said. "You wouldn't have been happy if I'd used it before, but I thought things would be different now." Vin glanced at me again. "Maybe they will be."

"I'll just look it up later, if you don't tell me."

"You really are pigheaded sometimes." He scowled, staring out the windshield at the dots of light sprouting in the distance. "I'll tell you what it means, but you have to promise me no more trips into the forest. And you have to stick close to the Knights. Deal?"

"Deal." I agreed easily, thinking of my prison guards at home. "So what does it mean?"

"My love. Agapi mou means my love."

Vin loves me? Or rather, Vin used to love me? Or still does? My hands went cold, even as my cheeks heated. I was so glad it was dark in the Porsche. I pressed my palms to my cheeks to try to cool them. I gulped and pushed back against the confusing riot of emotions, not sure what to do with the feelings other than bury them away. Change the subject. Try to learn more from him.

Vin drove the rest of the way to town in a stony silence, refusing to respond to anything else I asked, silencing me with a strained smile. Maybe because I was so tired, I couldn't fight his refusal or the haze that washed over me each time his lips lifted into a barely-there smile. At least he complied with my request to be dropped off with my bike a block from Gram's.

I left my bike by the porch and Cole appeared none the wiser when I walked into a dark entry and living room, a light from the street casting shadows on the far wall. Zoe's bed was empty. Maybe she was in with Gram? I headed to the kitchen to check for her there, and get a snack.

"Post-game party with Aaron went late?" Cole lifted his head from the pillow on the floor and Zoe stuck her snout out from one of the quilts at his side.

"Yeah, I'm beat. Just need to get something to eat, and collect Zoe." I turned toward the kitchen.

"Food." He rose in a flash. "Excellent idea."

Cole hurried around me and opened the fridge while I grabbed the first thing my hand found in Gram's fruit bowl, and sank into a chair at the table. Zoe rubbed her snout against my leg to greet me, dropped down at my feet, and almost immediately started to snore softly.

"My dad called tonight." Cole set down several plastic containers of different sizes, and slid into the chair across from me. I froze with my apple halfway to my mouth, hoping the news matched what I'd learned from his great-grandfather. "Gabriel's much better." Cole smiled and opened up a container that instantly expelled a sulfurous scent masked with a hint of fresh dill that could only be Gram's egg salad. "He just needs a bit more rest."

"That's fantastic." I set my apple by Aaron's laptop and a copy of *Hamlet* I'd left after working on a paper for Mrs. Merkle last night, scooting my chair back, a bit farther from the eggs Cole shoveled into his mouth.

"Yep," Cole said with a mouth full of eggy mush, then

swallowed. "Gabriel's fine, just like I told you. And my dad says things are much better now on the mountain. Back to normal."

"Maybe things really will get back to normal." I couldn't hold back a small, hopeful smile. "Maybe you can go home."

Cole stared at his egg salad. "Yeah, but hasn't it been nice getting to spend so much time together?" He swallowed hard. Had I hurt his feelings?

"Of course. You've been great. And thanks for being so nice to Gram. I know she's liked having you around."

"Sure. I've loved every minute of it." He looked back up, giving me a small smile of his own. "Rose is like the best cook in the whole wide world and being with you guys here reminds me of how nice it was when my mom and sister—" Cole's smile dropped a fraction. "I'd rather be here, than alone with Aaron and Cameron, anyway. They argue." He frowned. "And Aaron seems upset most of the time."

"Do you think Aaron minds being alone with Cameron?" Maybe Aaron had another good reason to resent me the last few weeks. Until recently, I would've done anything not to be alone with Cameron too.

"Oh, no, Aaron wanted to stay home. He said he'd help watch out for you, so long as he could stay, keep his normal routine, and besides, Aaron's just glad Dad allowed him to attend classes this year."

"What's with all the homeschooling, anyway?"

"Well, it took Gabriel and Aaron some time to get their appearance—their bodies—under control, if you know what I mean." Cole paused to shovel the last of the egg salad into his mouth, then opened up the next container, which thankfully had no odor. "My parents couldn't risk those two being outside the house or mountain for long periods of time."

That made sense. "But what about you?" And Cameron? It hadn't really occurred to me before, but Cameron should be like his cousins too, right? I'd never heard anything about him being homeschooled.

"Oh, me? I got things under control right away, with the help of my gift from mom's family." His chest puffed. "But I liked being at home with Mom, and Sarah too. She had to stay home all the time, since my parents couldn't risk anyone finding out about her. So I never complained."

"Hold on. What do you mean—your gift from your mom's family?"

"Well, it's not nearly as cool as Gabriel's."

"I'm sure it'll sound cool to me." I scooted my chair back in, giving him my full attention.

"Well, I can sense people's emotions." Cole shrugged. "Like any sort of fear, excitement, joy, any feeling at all."

"Are you saying you read people's minds or something?"

"No, no, nothing as awesome as that. I just sense when someone's emotional energies are building. I don't even need to look at them. But if I do, I usually get a sense of what kind of emotion it is. And that's it." His chest sank back to normal, large proportions and he gave a slight frown. "But it's how I got the changes in my body under control so quickly. Because I could feel the surge in myself as soon as it started."

"Does Aaron have a gift from your mother's side too?"

"Nope." Cole laughed brightly. "And he's pretty pissed! He kept holding out hope he was a late bloomer or something, but me and Sarah's gifts from Mom were already showing up by the time we made our first bear shifts. Mom was at least half-human, or more, so it's no surprise that at least one of us didn't get any of her race's abilities."

"So, um, what was your mom?"

"Well." He swallowed a large glob of potatoes. "Mom thought that she came from some Celtic fairy-like creatures, but she really didn't know. Some of her family heirlooms contained Greek so she thought maybe she could be descended from one of the sacred lines too."

"Sacred lines?"

"One of the priestesses who saved everything—everyone—by

locking the magic away, creating the ah, stones, keeping the shadows at bay. Grandpa calls them priestesses. Mom thought maybe she was descended from them, especially with the gift she had—to detect others like us, including their emotions. But like I said, she really didn't know. All the men in her family were normal and the women who would've known were gone. Her mother was killed—car bombing—and her dad sent her away, leaving all her family's money, everything left from their race, in a trust for her. My dad was really lucky my mom found him. I mean, because she was so wonderful, of course. But also, since anyone who's married into pure human blood hasn't been able to pass along the bear gene."

"You've got to explain that too. Bear gene?"

"Yeah, there aren't many of us left."

"How many?"

"Just us three, my dad, and the elders now," he mumbled over another glob of potatoes, then swallowed.

"Cameron too, right?"

"Nope. CJ was Dad's cousin, but Cameron's mom was human."

So that's why they didn't have Cameron watching out for me as much as Aaron and Cole? They must not think he was as strong or capable. "Um, I know what happened to Cameron's dad. But his mom?"

"Cancer. We were kids." Cole dropped his spoon, flinching as it clattered on the floor. Zoe stirred. I reached down to pat her head, and she settled, finally snoring again. "It was a bad time." Cole sighed and picked up his spoon. "Cameron didn't talk much. CJ brought him over a lot. Cameron did seem to like being around my mom, seemed to help. A few years later, Dad even found a woman from another race, so CJ could remarry. Cameron would have a mom again. There'd be more of us kids, hopefully. But Cameron wouldn't accept her. Mom tried to convince him too." He fiddled with the spoon as he nodded. "Said it was for the best. For everyone."

For the best. Where had I heard that before?

Cameron's vision. From the woman with honey-blonde hair.

That's what she'd said to him before he started yelling. It was all coming back to me, coming together, now. They were alone at the cemetery, visiting a grave. It must've been Cameron's mother's. He was crying. "No, Aunt Lillian," he'd said as she dropped a bundle of roses and wrapped her arms around him, pulling him into a hug. He tried to refuse her embrace but she squeezed him tighter. He mumbled he was lonely, he didn't think anything could change that. She'd whispered that his father was lonely too, that this would be "for the best." He looked at his mom's grave and pulled away, yelling awful things at his aunt, that she wasn't loved, not like his mom had been. She was a bitch, brought here for the same reason the other bitch was here. That Uncle B had gotten her trust money for it too. And no one else would ever replace his mother.

None of that had made any sense before.

"Of course CJ had to send the nice woman, Jade, away. Told Dad he had to do it for Cameron, though he knew we needed more like his boys—like us—to keep going, keep our family strong—protect what needs to be protected," Cole continued. "Not more like Cameron, who isn't special." He shook his head. "So see, Cassie, how important you are?"

Oh God. "Important?"

"Yeah, besides you being the girl we've been waiting for."

Oh God. "Besides?"

"Yeah, there are so few girls left of any race, you're the only one Gabriel, Aaron and I have ever met besides Jade, Mom and Sarah. Now Gabriel will be able to keep our race going with you!" Cole concluded with a huge, super-sized smile.

I shuddered. Goosebumps spread down my arms. I grabbed my untouched apple and bit into it, crunching away as fast as I could. Otherwise I'd scream at Cole in response. I had serious doubts about Cole's gift to sense emotions. Because if he knew the desolation that hit me as he'd spoken his last comment, the frost that was still washing over me, hardening my heart, he wouldn't have been smiling so big as he finished his food.

It had occurred to me before that the only reason Gabriel liked me was because he thought I was special, somehow different from normal people, like him. But the situation was even worse than I could've imagined. With Cole's latest revelation, it was clear Gabriel must have only been interested in me because he thought of me as the lone girl left in the world who could help him continue his family line. To give him "special" children. All my feelings for Gabriel, that had been haunting me so, suddenly seemed so silly. I must have dreamt them. Imagined them. Gotten wrapped up in a laughable, girly daydream about a handsome white knight riding into my life to sweep me off my feet and take me back to his castle—to save me from my pain and all my problems.

Because in the last two weeks I'd actually let myself think that I didn't deserve Gabriel. That he was too good for me and I was too messed up for him. That he was something so wonderful that I seemed almost worthless in comparison. When in fact, maybe Gabriel had been manipulating me from day one with his affectionate looks and talk of how we had some sort of connection, so he could get something out of me. Use me. Maybe Vin had been right all along to caution me about Gabriel, without knowing more.

The greater the evil, the harder it is to comprehend.

Gabriel's great-grandfather's parting words came back to me. He said I all of people should know that. But how would Gabriel's great-grandfather know—that I saw so much evil in the world around me? Know about my visions?

Ah. Of course. Gabriel had told him. He was the only one who knew. And after he gave me his word he wouldn't tell. It seemed unfair to be too hard on Gabriel, at this time of all times, but combined with what Cole just told me, maybe things were just as I had suspected all along. Gabriel was still hiding things from me. Gabriel was still spilling everything about me.

I couldn't trust Gabriel.

I still couldn't trust him.

Maybe it was Gabriel who didn't deserve me.

23
SPARKLING

VIN KEPT HIS PROMISE. THE FOLLOWING WEEK AT SCHOOL was better. The other kids stopped bothering me again.

Maybe the kids leaving me alone was due to Vin's efforts, or maybe everyone's excitement about Homecoming this weekend had distracted them. Whatever it was, I was grateful for any part Vin had played in it.

Things also seemed better between me and Vin. While he still didn't feel like a friend—or how I'd always imagined having a two-legged friend who talked in words rather than barking would feel like—his expression turned kind and reassuring when he noticed me glance at him during class. And he checked in with me at least once a day to ask how I was doing. He sat with me during a few lunch periods, climbed up to the attic one evening for a late night visit, and even biked home with me after school on Friday, during a rare 10 minutes when Aaron and Cole let me out of their sight.

Vin also followed me around more, showing up with both Aaron's and Cameron's crowds at Burger Boys, popping up while Cole and I were running errands in town for Gram, even hanging around outside the animal shelter. Although when I'd invited him in to say hello to B.B. and B.G., just up for adoption, he'd given me an odd look and immediately refused. And he still wouldn't talk more about my past or his place in it.

Somehow, when Vin smiled at me, my questions fell away.

When he smiled, I was just happy to have him around.

He even appeared at the craft store on Saturday morning as Cole and I were picking out things for Gram.

As soon as Cole and I got home, he turned to me. "Cassie, has Vin been bothering you?" Zoe rushed from the kitchen and Cole dropped to his knees to play with her. She gnawed at his hand with a soft mouth. He looked up and repeated his question. "So, has he been bothering you?"

"What do you mean?" I dropped two shopping bags full of sewing supplies onto the sofa, and turned toward him, my knees locking up, my body tensing.

"I saw Vin there today. Yesterday at the pharmacy. And I thought I felt him around a few times earlier this week too."

"Vin hasn't been bothering me," I assured him. My knees softened and my lips parted as I remembered the look Vin had given me across the aisles of sewing materials and the small wave goodbye he'd left me with, before leaving. Vin had told me earlier in the week that he was going to be gone most of the weekend, might even miss classes Monday. After one of his mesmerizing smiles, I'd found myself promising him I would stay even closer to the Knights until he got back, and of course, stay out of the forest. "Vin's kinda like my friend, I guess."

"Yeah, but I'm beginning to think there's something going on," Cole muttered. "I've never sensed such strong emotions coming off someone, and it's different than normal. Like he's not feeling the emotion, but sending it out in some sort of weird vibe." He frowned. "And then one night this week I woke up, swore I sensed the same thing, but it was distant. Like he was in the neighborhood or something."

I still had serious doubts about Cole's claimed "gift." There was no proof of it, and he'd seemed so oblivious that night when he'd revealed his family's plan to use me as a bear-incubator for Gabriel's babies. Ugh. "Well, what do you want me to do about it?"

"I want you stop hanging out with him. At least until I can

talk to my dad." He gave Zoe one more pat and stood in front of the TV cart.

"Why?"

"Because even though a few weeks have passed, and Rose and I are letting you get away with things Dad wouldn't—like going outside with me, instead of Aaron—you're still in danger." His shoulders tensed. "I'm supposed to text both Aaron and Dad if anyone comes near who's sending off violent emotions, and get you out of here until they can meet us. But Vin's the only one who's made a blip on my radar—and it's a big blip—so stay away from him."

"Cole." I sighed. "I think your radar is broken."

"Please, just do this. For me," he pleaded in his softest voice, then paused. "You know, I can sense your disbelief right now."

"Really?" He didn't need a special gift to sense that.

"Yeah, really. I sense your emotions all the time. But I try to keep them to myself because Dad told me most people wouldn't like it."

"Fine." I decided to test him. "So how was I feeling in the kitchen that night, last Friday?"

"You were upset. Really upset. It started when we talked about Gabriel, got really bad when we talked about how you guys are supposed to be together." He lifted his chin. "But I figured you were just upset because you miss Gabriel so much. Right?"

My eyes fell to the bottom of the TV cart, Austen's books glaring back at me. "Um, sure," I mumbled, fussing with the bags on the couch, moving around Cole and setting them in front of the cart.

He turned to face me. "Well, you won't have to miss him much longer. You guys will be back together soon!" Cole gave an excited smile, then frowned. "But Dad will probably want Gabriel to stay here instead of me, which will suck."

A sweet smell drifted from the kitchen and thankfully Cole got distracted by Gram's announcement she'd just pulled a pie out of the oven. He dropped the warnings about Vin and the wishful thinking about me missing Gabriel. Because obviously I was not.

He didn't bring up either subject that afternoon, not even when we worked at the kitchen table on his homeschooling curriculum, arguing about the ending to *Romeo and Juliet*. He thought the star-crossed lovers taking their lives showed the power love has to bring us together and make us believe in something greater than ourselves. I insisted Shakespeare was trying to tell us that getting swept away by emotions and fantasies was just plain stupid and deadly.

He whistled a little tune as we cleared the books, set the table, and sat down for an early dinner Gram prepared, seeming perfectly relaxed, although Gram wasn't. Her chair creaked each time she shifted in it. "Cassandra, angel." I looked up from my roast chicken and vegetables. "I heard from Aaron a few days ago that there's a big school dance this weekend. Tonight, actually."

"Oh… um, yeah. I think I saw some signs for it. Homecoming," I responded with fork suspended above my plate, trying to keep two peas from falling off, not sure what Gram was getting at.

"Well, Aaron said he's going," she continued.

"OK." I set my fork down.

"I was thinking." Gram's gnarled hands reached for the small vase of lilies in the center of the table. She fiddled with the arrangement. "Maybe you should go to the dance—"

"No."

"But you've seemed so unhappy recently. A bit of fun might—"

"No."

"Aaron will watch out for you—"

"No."

"But you've been doing so much better with the kids at school, and maybe Gabriel—" she stopped and started again, "or maybe that nice boy that helped you at school before, Vin, will want to take you."

"Whoa." Cole dropped his fork. "Cassie shouldn't be hanging out with Vin."

"But he's been so polite when he's been by." Gram stopped messing with the flowers, and steadied her hands, pressing her palms flat against the tablecloth. "Why shouldn't he be Cassandra's friend?"

"Because there's something weird about that guy. It's like…" Cole paused. His boyish features turned pensive, and he picked up his fork and speared a carrot. "Um, like… his emotions are directed outward, somehow aimed at you, instead of him feeling things like a normal person. Yeah, that's it—manipulative. He's manipulative."

Gram and I both gave him a curious look.

"Why don't you believe me?" Cole huffed. "I sense your skepticism. From both of you, you know." He glanced over at Gram.

"Listen." I'd had enough of Cole's negativity about Vin, one of the few people in town who'd actually been nice to us. "You can stop worrying. I told you, Vin's sort of a friend of mine."

"Yes," Gram jumped in, "and you need more friends, to think about socializing, maybe going to college next year. Once Bernard finally deals with things and helps with your condition, like he promised. So the dance is just a small step."

"Gram," I moaned, "no dance. Vin's not going to be there anyway. He's out of town."

"Well, it's just that I always imagined what it would be like if Bethany had gone to a dance like this." Her voice weakened and her wrinkles tightened into a pained expression. "And I've already fixed up a dress."

Not fair. How could I argue with that?

"You won't say no once you see it." Gram closed her eyes to picture it, and her mouth pulled into a small smile. "The material is so magnificent, a glossy silver-blue silk—it almost sparkles. I bought it after the war, when rationing ended and fashions became indulgent again. When I still had hope Richard might find a way to… to come back." She opened her eyes and stared at the lilies with a distant look. "I was in Denver on the five-year anniversary of the day the War office sent the official death notice, when I saw it in a store window. I knew Richard would love it, or would've loved it, and I had to have it. As a sign of our love and everything he'd told me about finding his way back to me one day. The words he left me." She reached for her watch and took it off, like its weight had become too much. "Of course I never got a chance to wear the dress." She looked back to me, concluding with a sympathetic cough. She then wheezed a bit, which seemed to come out of nowhere since she hadn't shown any symptoms during dinner. When I didn't respond, she wheezed piteously again.

I took in Gram's forlorn expression, her overly wide puppy dog eyes, then shot a glance at Cole. He reached for a second helping of chicken and apparently sensed nothing wrong with Gram. Gram even pulled out her wedding ring from the chain around her neck and laid it over her blouse, making sure I could see. And I asked myself who was the manipulative one now?

Meeker High's gymnasium had never looked so flashy. Or pink. Kaylee and her friends must have run the decorating committee, because the dark school colors had been overlooked in favor of rose, bubblegum, and coral. I never knew balloons and streamers came in so many ridiculous colors. I nearly went cross-eyed following a ruffled, pastel pink streamer trailing across the ceiling, where it joined a waterfall of rosy streamers cascading behind the refreshment table, and then up the strings of a balloon bouquet tied near the giant, tub-like punch bowl.

It was all silly. But the big mirror ball wasn't too shabby. It spun in a spotlight, casting tiny, glittered reflections over the length of the basketball court. I could see how dancing away an evening on the designated polished square of gym floor in the arms of a hot guy, with shimmering sequins of light in your hair, would make a girl feel special. Even if it was just an illusion.

Clusters of dresses and suits littered the floor. Waiting, but there was no music yet. Teachers and other adult chaperones who'd volunteered leaned against the walls or flopped into white plastic chairs wrapped in fake rose stems, punch in hand, looking resigned and weary as they chatted in low voices beneath the rowdy clamor of the students. I took their cue, drifting to the corner with the fewest chairs and tables, and tried not to tug at Gram's dress again. Tugging didn't do any good. The bodice was expertly fitted, the waist tapered to such an extreme, the silky material felt like a second skin glued to my body. The dress was far from immodest, though. From the nipped-in waist a full skirt ballooned out, falling to just above the burn marks on my shins. And though she'd altered the top so it was now strapless, the neckline was perfectly prim—a delicate heart shape, accented with white lace. She'd even added a hidden pocket into the skirt, for my emergency cell.

The dress was beautiful, really, but I didn't feel comfortable wearing something so fancy.

I stuck out like a sore thumb in a sea of slick, metallic, sequined, and achingly bright ensembles, with daring slits, plunging necklines, and ruched butts. Upon closer inspection, I noticed many of the guys weren't even wearing coats or ties. Though I was over-dressed and dressed up more than I ever had been, I might have admitted to liking it, if the tight waist didn't make it so difficult to breathe. At least witnessing Gram's reactions as she'd helped me get ready made the discomfort worth it. She'd climbed the stairs with a spring in her step, humming her favorite song as I dug out the strapless bra, silver hair clip, and dress shoes she'd bought me once—for an outfit to attend a veterans' benefit dinner with her. She'd hurried me back downstairs; I may have left my trunk open. When we'd stood in front of the mirror in her bedroom, Gram had never looked happier, her eyes brighter. Positioning the clip to hold my hair up on one side, she'd carefully arranged my long curls over the opposite shoulder so the red waves cascaded "just so" across the shiny, silver-blue silk.

"A special day," she'd said on a sigh.

I'd only just managed to convince her to leave her pearls in the trinket box, with her watch, which she'd put away as soon as we got to her room. But on my way out Gram had handed me a silver bracelet. Before I could ask where it came from, she'd pushed me and Cole out the door. The intertwined loops were so big, I worried it would slip right off if I put it on, and I'd lose it. Instead, I'd slipped it into my pocket.

A fast beat thumped the speakers, blaring from the ceiling.

Everyone jumped into motion, the adults raising their heads and narrowing eagle eyes onto boys' hands as they grabbed their dates to sway with the beat. I just stood in place, watching everyone and puzzling over the oddity of dancing. Punching fists, flailing arms, turning on your heel, shaking your butt like a cartoon bee about to sting.

Another fast song, and Cameron and Paige danced near, a tangle of limbs and swinging hips. She pulled on his arm, leaning into a backbend, her free hand stretching my way.

I shrank further into the corner.

With a hand on the small of Paige's back, Cameron directed her back out to the basketball court, toward the Bulldogs logo in the center. He looked at me, mouthing, "I'm sorry." I tilted my head. They hadn't gotten that close. "Sorry, for everything." He blinked, looking serious and sad.

What? Was he talking about more than Paige? My eyes tracked them around the floor. But they didn't get close again. At last, I spied Aaron enter with Reese through the open doors. I'd promised Cole, when he'd dragged me in by my gloved hand before stationing himself in Gram's VW, that I'd stay close to Aaron as soon as he arrived, which was Cole's cue to cut out. I'd say hello, then retreat to my corner again, waiting a respectable half-hour before calling Cole back to take me home.

I walked the safe, adult-patrolled edges of the gym toward Aaron, but he was too busy chatting with Reese to notice me coming. She waved her hands around, talking about something, maybe motioning to Luke and Mike, who'd come in right after them.

Aaron's eyes widened. He pulled out his cell, made a quick call, then turned back to her. Cameron and Paige drifted into Reese's orbit, apparently wanting to talk to her too. They started talking to Luke and Mike instead. Mike and Cameron exchanged some words. Mike loosened the tie around his beefy neck, glanced at his phone, and left.

Aaron was still busy with Reese.

I paused. It wouldn't be wise to interrupt him just yet. Aaron always got a bit worked up when trying to impress one of Kaylee's friends. As if impressing her friends would suddenly get Kaylee to start paying more attention to him.

After several minutes, Aaron seemed to sense my eyes on him. He looked my way. His mouth dropped open, apparently in mid-sentence to Reese. She looked to Luke, who shrugged, ran a hand through his gelled hair, and snapped his fingers in Aaron's face. Aaron ignored him. The excited flush on Aaron's cheeks faded away. His whole face went pale.

What was Aaron shocked about? So what if he didn't want me hanging around tonight. I should be the one who was upset after seeing Mike come in right after him. Why the hell was Mike still walking around like he was the king of the world? He bounced between Aaron and Cameron's crowds like nothing could stop him from doing whatever he wanted. Hadn't the police gotten my video? Had they not done anything? I would clearly need to check on Mike, and his young stepsister, again.

Aaron's mouth hung open. He surveyed me up and down. His jaw tightened and his teeth clenched together. He bolted from Reese, marching toward me. I reached into my pocket and slipped on the bracelet—I didn't want Gram to find out I hadn't worn it. "You're not supposed to be here," he said.

"Oh… um, hi." Jeez, what could I do to get Aaron to give me a break? "Gram wanted me to come to the dance. She knew you'd be here. Cole texted. Didn't you get it?"

"No, goddammit, I've gotten a million texts since winning the big game last night. Why couldn't he have just said that was the text he was talking about?" Aaron muttered to himself, then said to me, "You should be at home." Aaron pulled out his cell, checking the time.

I smoothed a hand down my skirt, and sure enough, the oversize bracelet slid off my wrist, down my hand. I caught it and slid it into the pocket in my dress.

Cameron strode up, thankfully without Paige.

"I'm taking you back," Aaron said.

"Give her a break. No harm done," Cameron said. "I'll take her home."

Aaron ignored him, drilling his eyes into me. "You can say hi to whatever friends you think you have, then I'm taking you home."

"I'll take Cassie home." A strong voice materialized from behind me.

Oh God. It was the voice I'd been longing to hear, as much as I'd told myself to stop longing, every single day the last three weeks. "Gabriel," I whispered.

Before I knew it, I'd turned to face him, my body drawn to just the sound of him.

He gazed down at me with warmth. He looked into my eyes, a tentative half-smile lifted his face, and everyone—everything else—faded away. My breath quickened at the same time my heart suddenly felt incredibly full in my chest, as if it wanted to explode out of the tightly-fitted material holding it in.

Gabriel stood tall in a classic black suit, dress shirt, and blue tie. He looked so formal, more formal than the other kids, like me, and also so perfect—a hundred times better than any memory I'd replayed since he'd been sequestered away in the mountain. It was as if the haunting image of his blood-soaked form on the cave floor had been an awful nightmare. There was no trace of what had happened in the cave left on him. Gabriel's cheeks were full of color, his deep blue eyes dazzling, his body strong and commanding. He looked full of life, just like the Gabriel who'd been so patient and polite when we'd met that first day at the shelter, the Gabriel who'd cared for me when he'd found me collapsed on the ground at the cemetery, the Gabriel who'd warmed and comforted me outside the cave, and done everything to protect me inside the next day.

I took a closer look and saw the only remnant of the attack. A new pink scar, to the side of the other on his neck, still slightly bubbled, peeked out of his downturned collar.

"Gabriel." Aaron stomped forward. "You're supposed to be at home. Dad said you still need to rest."

"I'm done resting," Gabriel said to his brother, but kept his eyes on me. "Besides, I called Rose. We agreed the dance would be something nice after everything that's happened, and it's fine with you here too. And Cassie actually came… so where else would I be?"

"Everyone should be where they're supposed to be." Aaron reached for his phone. "Dad won't be happy."

"I agree," Cameron said. "So many people in a tight space. You guys can't control this. Even if you would let me help." He shook his head, expression tense. "This isn't safe."

Aaron frowned.

"I'll get Cassie back soon. Don't worry." Gabriel stood taller.

Aaron turned his attention to me. "Well, do you at least have your cell?"

I nodded.

"Good, I'll update the panic button app with Gabriel's number. In case you get separated."

I dug it out and handed it to him.

"Give me a minute." He stormed away.

"If you stay much longer, I'm calling Uncle B too," Cameron said and his long legs carried him off. So what if they were going to tell Bernard on me? It had been weeks since the cave and nothing had happened. Besides, Gabriel was here. Wasn't he in the best position to watch out for me? Gabriel and I ignored them. Our eyes remained locked, unblinking, for several seconds. Or was it several minutes? I couldn't say.

It was like I'd fallen into one of my Vin-hazes, but this time with Gabriel. And this time the haze didn't feel at all unnatural, or uncomfortable. I stared into Gabriel's eyes and absorbed the warmth reflected there. It was like I was being reunited with a piece of myself. A vital piece. A piece I'd been in denial about missing.

The feelings multiplied as Gabriel reached for my hands, covered by silky, white formal gloves that extended past my elbows, decorated at the ends with tiny pearls. The gloves were Gram's from long ago. She kept them in her dresser and they smelled of lavender. Although slightly dulled from age, they were the nicest pair of gloves I'd ever worn. They didn't look out of place tonight.

For once, Gabriel and I looked like we belonged together.

I pulled my shoulders back, drawing Gabriel's hands closer.

Gabriel gripped my hands and led me toward the middle of the basketball court, where a throng of couples slow-danced to a sappy love song. Reese and Luke rocked their hips, wrapped together, several feet away. Reese lifted her head off his shoulder and turned her face toward his, her lips brushing his in a kiss. And for some unknown reason—maybe the reminder I'd never be like Reese or any normal girl—the spell broke. Doubts besieged me, extinguishing the feelings that had just sparked inside me. I tugged at Gabriel and the short heels of my dress shoes ground against the wood plank floor. He stopped. "Of course. You're right. Let's go someplace less crowded."

Less crowded. Good idea. But that wasn't the only reason I needed to get away. I needed to get away from him. The urge to flee was primal. At least going someplace quieter would allow us to have the conversation that seemed inevitable, now that I'd recovered from the flush of seeing him again. The conversation where I finally got Gabriel to admit he'd only been interested in me from the start because of my peculiarities, the expectations his family had for me, all the things they seemed to want from me. The conversation where I finally convinced Gabriel to leave me alone. Before it broke me for good.

He interlaced our fingers—I didn't seem to have the strength to break our connection yet—and navigated us around the swarm of students circling the dance floor and then outside, into a nearby courtyard.

The music stopped, then started again. A country ballad floated out the open doors of the gym. A gentle breeze carried the sweet smell of the flowering shrubs lining the courtyard. Before I could even think what to say first, Gabriel tugged my hands up to his shoulders, then reached down to circle his forearms around my waist. The full skirt of my dress pressed into his legs. I felt trapped. But I also felt at peace. Like I was exactly where I was supposed to be.

Like after the nightmare of the cave, we were now both awake, ready to live out a perfect, delusional daydream. Happily ever after, together.

But there was no happily ever after for me.

I forced myself to take a small step back, but there was nowhere to go. Gabriel's arms were circled around me. I lost the battle with myself and stepped back in. As if sensing my turmoil, he gave me a solemn look. "You said you wouldn't fight your feelings anymore. Please say you feel the same way now too." He swayed us slowly back and forth to the unhurried melody.

"What are you talking about?" I'd let myself stay in Gabriel's arms for a few more moments—this one last time—before we resolved, and finally put to rest, whatever was between us.

"I'm talking about what you said to me, right before you touched my face." The scarred side of his lips trembled. "Before you left."

"I can't believe you remember that," I mumbled into his shirt front.

"It's all I've been able to think about. For weeks, while I recovered in the mountain—sleeping—I dreamt of you." Gabriel tightened his arms, pulling me closer until our bodies pressed into one, and we swayed together in perfect synchronicity. I could almost feel all the hope in him that had been building the last few weeks. But it had to be because of what he wanted from me for his family, right? "I dreamt of us. Together."

Gabriel kept moving us back and forth, brushing his cheek against my curls, stirring up their vanilla scent. He then rested his head on top of mine, breathing in deeply. For a moment there was no me. No him. Just us. Joined. Our gentle harmonized movements. A lone tree caught in a gentle breeze swirling around its branches.

Gabriel sighed into my hair and moved his chin slightly. He nuzzled into my curls. Several moments later a soft warmth pressed against my head. The spell was broken, again. I stopped swaying, and forced his kiss away. "Listen, I know why you were being so nice to me before—trying to get me to like you." I bit my lip and shrugged. "You don't have to pretend."

"What?" His voice deepened.

"Cole told me that the only way you can continue your family—um, your race—is to find a girl who's different." I bit out the last word, making it sound more harsh, more like how the kids said "freak" than I'd intended. "Like me." I dropped my chin to my chest.

"That's true." Gabriel coughed, a forced clearing of his throat, revealing his unease with the admission. I lifted my chin. His shoulders sank and he shifted back slightly so he could look into my eyes. "But it has nothing to do with my feelings for you." He was so close, I had no choice but to let him stare into me. Into my soul. What did he see there this time?

"I know what you told your great-grandfather too, about my visions."

"God, Cassie—I thought I was dying, I felt like I had to—" He broke off. "I should've known that nothing would be easy once I got back. You're going to keep fighting us, aren't you?" His arms loosened around my back. They trembled and he gulped, a sound of resignation and of pain. His arms released me and his hands fell to either side of my waist. "It's okay. I get it. I do."

"You do?"

"Yes," he exhaled. His hands shook and he pressed his warm palms into my sides. They imprinted into my midsection. The only barrier between us was the silky, skin-tight material cinching me in. "You think you're supposed to be alone."

"I can be alone if I want." My voice sharpened, "I can take care of myself."

"Of course you can. But why be alone when we could have something so wonderful?"

"It's better to be alone than to be with someone I can't trust."

"What can I do to convince you that you can trust me?"

"Nothing. Absolutely nothing." I looked up to his beautiful face and allowed our gazes to connect again. "The sad thing is, I've started to trust you—so many times. And then I always learn something new. Like how you were digging through my things, expecting me to serve as some sort of savior you've been waiting for your whole life, wanting things from me I can't give. And now, trying to make me to like you so I can serve as some sort of mother to your bear babies. It makes me feel pathetic. And it's happened again and again. So you see, I can't trust you. I can't allow myself to—"

"But—"

"Please let me finish." How could I explain things so Gabriel would finally leave this thing between us alone? Leave me alone, so I could get over these strange, strangling feelings I had for him. Honesty might be the only thing that would work.

He kept his eyes locked on mine as I took a deep breath, then spoke from the rawest, most vulnerable part inside me. "Trust is something that has always scared me. I've seen so many visions proving how when people trust too easily, bad things happen. Like an old man opening his door to a stranger, who's just there to rob him. A girl trusting a boy and going into a room at a party, but his friends are waiting there and..." I fell silent and let him imagine what happened next to those people, what I could still see so vividly. "So trust is terrifying. It'll bite you when you're not paying attention. Then before you know it, you're starting to believe in someone— when maybe you shouldn't."

He opened his mouth to protest, but I shook my head and rushed on.

"So that's why I've always been so careful. Not to trust anyone. Besides Gram. But that took time." My hands gripped his shoulders. "And Zoe of course—I know that sounds stupid, but I know Zoe would never hurt me. But I can't trust you. No." I clarified, to both of us, my grip tightening. "I won't trust you. I won't let you, or the trust you think I should have for you hurt me. I just can't." I tucked my head under his chin, my bottom lip trembling.

Gabriel just listened. He didn't try to argue with me or plead his case. He just listened and heard me. He finally spoke. "I'll give you all the time you need. But I'll still be here. I'm not leaving home again, and I hope you'll let yourself trust me. And if you're ever ready to accept our connection, our once in a lifetime connection, I'll be there for that. I'll be there for you."

"I've never had anyone there for me like that before. Like… family. I mean, Gram kinda is."

The music changed to a faster song, and Gabriel suddenly twirled me out away from him. My hair drifted over my shoulder, falling down my back. My dress flared in a large circle, floating around me. Spinning, I stared down at the silver cloud, mesmerized by it for a brief moment. The skirt sparkled in the dim light of the courtyard, the shiny fabric rippling and waving like the currents of White River at night. It was like I was sparkling in that weightless moment too, luminous and dazzling. Special.

Obviously the illusion of the evening, with all its balloons and streamers, had gotten to me too, like every other girl at the dance who'd bought into the Cinderella fairytale. I bit my lip.

Gabriel pulled me back into him, swept my hair back over my shoulder, and pressed me tightly into his solid frame, resting his forearms around my lower back once more. When I looked up, a small grin played on his mouth. He looked silly. Happy. "What are you smiling about?" I asked, my previous moment of lightness entirely gone.

"You—and how stunning you look tonight." His grin widened, before he paused and his expression hardened slightly. His scarred cheek tightened along with the rest of his face, then quivered several times. "I'm always smiling about you." His voice resonated above the music. "I just like being with you."

"You said you remembered what happened in the cave. Don't you remember me just standing there while you got stabbed?"

"What I remember is that you saved my life."

"You clearly don't remember it correctly then."

"Yes. I do. After I was stabbed, just lying there helpless, the Jentilak pulled out his knife. He was going to stab me again. To end it. And I saw you—I saw what you did to save me. How you stopped him and got him off me. And when I would have given up, when I thought I was dying," Gabriel's voice dropped and his arms loosened around my waist, "you told me to keep going. You gave me the strength to do that. You got the help I needed. You saved me, and I—"

"But—"

"No, I need to finish this. Now it's my turn to tell you how I feel. Before I lose the courage." He hesitated, squeezed me in tightly again, then continued in a rush, "I adore you for what you did in the cave. You may think you froze, but you fought when you needed to. You did what needed to be done. I respect you so much. For being so strong. I respect everything about you. Even how stubborn you are." He flashed a small half-smile.

I tried to capture those crooked, upturned lips in my memory, to remember in my most desolate moments—when I was alone and thinking of the worst of everyone around me—as his smile dimmed.

"I will always cherish you, and your stubbornness, no matter what. Even if I have to live the rest of my life without you."

I shook my head, not sure if I was protesting his naive emotional declaration or protesting him having to live the rest of his life without me.

"I know, Cassie. The words are inadequate. But there it is."

I shook my head harder, fearing the words to come.

"I love you."

I stared up at Gabriel for several long moments.

No one had ever said those words to me before. Except Gram. I wasn't sure Gram counted. I didn't deserve her love. Not with all the sacrifices she'd made to bring me into her life.

Love seemed so foreign. I'd only thought about it in terms of my relationship with Zoe. And, of course, that was a different sort of love.

What should I make of Gabriel? His declaration? All I knew was that he was always doing this to me—surprising me with his feelings. His genuineness. His sincerity. How much he really seemed to care for me and want to be with me. It could all be just another manipulation. Or it could be something real—something my body and heart told me I wanted, but that my relentless, overthinking mind still fought. The only thing that was certain was I wanted to be home, with Gram and Zoe, until I sorted things out again.

I started to pull away. His face filled with pain. Hurt. Deep hurt. His arms loosened around me.

"Get off of him!" A shrill voice shrieked from the opening to the courtyard. Kaylee shuffled toward us in a sequined tank top and miniskirt. She stopped a few feet away, teetering on high heels. "Get out of here. He's my date," she slurred in my direction. Someone must've had too much fun pre-partying.

Gabriel dropped his arms, clasped my closest hand in his, and took a step forward. I trailed behind him. "Kaylee, good to see you," he said in a kind voice, but one laced with warning. "I only got your messages today. I'm so sorry I wasn't able to return your calls. I was very sick."

"Not so sick you couldn't come to the dance with her." Kaylee squeaked in her high-pitched voice and pointed at me, then accusingly at Gabriel. "You were supposed to be my date." She teetered again. "What's wrong with me? Why doesn't anyone—" She caught herself before she made too humiliating a confession. "Why don't you want me?" She slurred her words.

"Plenty of guys want to be your date," Gabriel answered softly. Everyone knew about Kaylee's mom—it had clearly left Kaylee insecure. Trust Gabriel to be so empathetic about it. "Including Aaron. I told you he was free. Didn't he ask?"

Kaylee frowned. "I told you. I don't want him. I want you. And you said you'd think about it." She bit her lip. Her chin trembled. "I've always wanted you." She glanced away, back out the courtyard, toward the football field. "The star."

Gabriel's hand tensed over mine.

"I should be with the star." So that was what had prompted her obsession.

Gabriel winced, looking distressed, almost ashamed. "I was never a star."

"You were." Her eyes widened. "Like Cameron, but everyone talked about you different. They adored you. You were different than the others. You still are."

"Stop." Gabriel's arm shook.

"But—"

"The kid I hit was laid up for months."

"Which is why you stayed away. But you still supported us." Kaylee nodded, then grimaced, as if nodding hurt. "God, you must've spent a fortune. All the t-shirts. The boosters. For their team too."

"I was trying to make amends. Because I'd let myself forget—" He didn't finish. His posture sagged, rounding his shoulders, as if trying to make himself small. What had he forgotten? Maybe that he wasn't like everyone else? And he was even bigger and stronger than his brothers.

"Everyone understood, and I—"

"I really am sorry for not calling you back." Gabriel tried redirecting her.

"What does that change?" She put her hands on her hips. "You made it sound like you'd come. I told everyone you were going to be my date. Then Ree tells me she saw you inside with our little Freakenstein."

"Don't call her that." His voice was hard.

"It's too much." She stomped the pavement, and swayed back and forth.

"Don't worry, Kaylee," I finally spoke up. "I'm leaving."

Gabriel tightened his grip on my hand. I yanked away, easily slipping free. Gabriel was left with a long white glove. He looked at me with wide, wounded eyes. The small pearls dangling from the silk in his hand shone in the dim lighting of the courtyard. I'd need that glove back, or Gram would be upset. *Don't worry about that now.* Before I could change my mind, I took off at a run. I slowed just a second at the entrance to the courtyard and glanced back. Thankfully Kaylee had found her moment of opportunity and clung to Gabriel like a vine.

I paused, longer than I'd intended, and shoved my hair off my shoulder, my chest burning with jealousy as Kaylee wrapped a bare hand around his neck. "Wait. I'll get Aaron," he shouted, his voice tense. "You need to be with one of us. He never even gave you back your cell."

I slipped off my heels and sprinted away. I just needed to get to Gram and Zoe. Then surely everything would be okay.

I'd made it just a few blocks from home, when a stocky figure ran toward me on the other side of the street. I would've ignored him completely, as a jogger out for a late night run, but it was weird, because I could've sworn he was running in a light dress shirt, tie, and dark suit pants. Then again, I was running in a party dress, with shoes clenched in my hands and one glove missing, so who was I to judge? *Keep running.*

I turned onto Gram's street, catching a whiff of smoke. The wind picked up. The smell deepened. Who would have their fireplace going on a night like this?

I slowed, taking a deeper draw into my lungs. A thick, acrid odor hovered in the air. Similar to what permeated the neighborhood after a town bonfire. I looked up ahead, to where Gram's cottage was hidden among the larger houses on the street. A soft light arced into the night sky. I stared at it. It didn't move.

A reflection off something? But it was too big, too bright, totally out of place. One loud laugh escaped my lips. I practically skipped the rest of the way down the street, so amused at myself. So the light around town, in the forest, hadn't really been following me. I really was going crazy. Why not find some humor in it?

The light hovering above the middle of the street must be part of my imagination, like the flashes of light that kept popping up everywhere. Vin must've been wrong about them being something good watching over me, because this one was larger than ever and had no interest in me, even as I continued to skip toward it. For the first time in a long time, I felt myself grinning, finding some sort of manic hilarity in my messed-up life.

I slowed to a stop in front of Gram's cottage. A hot gust of smoke-laced air blew away my smile. A bottle of gasoline lay tipped over on the lawn.

This light was not an invention of my messed-up mind. Or unexplainable. Or unnatural. My shoes slipped from my hands, clattering against the pavement.

Fire raged up the right side of the cottage—the side that housed Gram's bedroom. Shooting out from inside her broken bedroom window, it grew from there, edging its flaming fingers up toward the attic.

Clouds of shadowy grey smoke plumed into the night air. Below the smoke, the fire crackled and glittered along the wood siding. Consuming Gram's bedroom. Consuming the whole cottage, building in energy as it sizzled with all the intensity of a fireworks display.

Sparkling.

Burning.

24

INFERNO

I TORE AT THE SKIRT OF GRAM'S DRESS, RIPPING IT OFF SO I could move freely, as I rushed to enter the inferno that used to be Gram's home. *My home.* Scorching heat greeted me as I kicked open the front door and stumbled into the entry.

The hallway leading to Gram's room was ablaze, the flames leaping and lapping out of her open bedroom door, eating away at the baseboards of the narrow corridor and creeping up the walls.

I shivered.

But Gram wouldn't have gone to bed so early on night like this. She would wait up for me, to hear all about the dance.

The heat was unbearable. It felt strong enough to knock me over, billowing out in a continuous blast. Tempting me to sink to my knees.

The heat pulsing into me, I instinctively took a step back. I wobbled, and knocked against the coat rack. Gram's purse swung back and forth on the lowest rung. Each swing a taunting reminder that she could still be in here somewhere, suffocating or suffering an asthma attack. Or worse.

Slowly my body accepted its surroundings. Maybe I could do this. Maybe I could make sure Gram and Zoe weren't still here. Make sure they were okay. As my body acclimated to the heat, the sweat on my bare arm gradually evaporated. Drop by drop. Until, oddly enough, my whole body felt cool and dry. It was as if my skin had accepted the inevitability of the blaze, my flesh deciding that baking in an oven was nothing it couldn't handle, after everything else it had been through the last two years. I could do this.

I wrapped a strip of skirt lining around my nose and mouth and rushed into the living room first.

The fire had spread from the hallway to the wall holding the TV cart. Nothing else—not even the couch—was visible through the thick smoke flooding the room. "Gram!" I forced a muffled shout past the material. I tried to shout Zoe's name too, but choked on the smoke that easily pushed past my make-shift covering, filling my lungs.

I hacked several times and doubled over. There was no air. *No air.* I gasped and gasped, but couldn't get oxygen. The bodice of Gram's dress, the only part of the silver-blue silk still on me, felt tight. *Too tight.*

I held a breath in.

It didn't help. I only tasted bitterness.

Another breath. My lungs burned.

My legs gave out, sinking into Gram's braided rug.

No! I can do this.

For several long seconds I battled against the desire to surrender to the billows of murky smoke rising around me. I finally ripped off the bodice of the dress, found I could breathe a bit easier, and straightened to standing in my strapless bra and underwear. Wasting more precious seconds, I scanned the rest of the dark cloud hovering over the room, seeking anything on the couch, Zoe's bed, the floor.

No Gram. No Zoe.

I hurried into the kitchen. Less smoke. I took several long draws into my lungs.

No Gram. No Zoe.

I raced back to the entry, looking into the flames beckoning me down the hall toward Gram's room, then out the front door, to the temptation of fresh, cool air. Then back to Gram's room.

Forget the fresh air. Gram might only have seconds. And I could handle a few burns. Nothing worse than what I was used to most every day. Oh God. I was probably lying to myself.

Just then, a zip of white light flashed past my shoulder, darted down the hall to Gram's room, and disappeared. Instinctively, I followed it. Stumbling toward the heat, the source of the smoke, into the fire. A splintered floorboard scraped my toes. Within several steps, flames along the floor of the corridor tickled my ankles. The flames grew higher with each step I took down the hall, brushing my legs.

Blistering heat penetrated my skin. But it wasn't so bad. Actually no worse than laying too long in the sun on a summer's day. There was no pain, even as I paused right in front of the largest of the flames billowing out of Gram's room, standing inches from the reddish-orange and yellow, gaseous wave. *Was my mind shutting down? I should feel the burns by now.*

I glanced into the open door of the bathroom, across from Gram's bedroom.

No Gram. No Zoe.

I then willed myself into Gram's room. Into the heart of the blaze.

Please flames, please, subside.

I took another step.

Come on, just break. Let me in. As if I'd spoken my commands out loud—and the fire could actually hear me—it did exactly as I asked. As I stepped forward into Gram's bedroom, the flames parted. With each step I took, the flames nearest me sank down. Fizzled out.

I couldn't help myself. I reached out with my gloveless hand to skim bare fingers through one of the lone flames still flaring near me, like running my fingers through a waterfall.

No pain.

I lifted my hand to my face and stared at my skin.

No burn.

No more wasting time. I dropped my hand, willed the rest of the fire crowding the room to move back. That's when I found Gram.

Collapsed on the floor by her wooden bed frame, which was blazing above her and appeared ready to collapse itself.

I stared at the flames billowing off the bed. *Stop.* The sparks dissolved as if I'd doused them with a bucket of water. The room fell dark. Moonlight streamed in from the window, and the charred hole in the wall next to it, making its presence known as the only light source left. The dimness rested on Gram. Illuminating her stillness.

Gram lay on her side, half curled into herself, facing me. Her eyes were open. Lifeless. Like marbles in her head, they stared down unmoving and unblinking at whatever she clutched in her hands, sheltering against her chest.

Before I could manage to take one step closer, or find the strength in my burning lungs to shout her name, the room flooded with radiant light. I blinked hard against the shocking intrusion. I blinked several times more, this time in complete, absolute disbelief.

A wall of brilliant white light stood before me. Between me and Gram. Like someone had turned a spotlight on, and positioned it right in front of Gram's body. The light was as bright as the flashes and thunderbolts that had been tormenting me, as electric as the flash that had zipped past me in the hall, but so much larger. Concentrated. Overpowering.

I froze. Not even blinking. Was I in shock? Had the fire really gotten to me and this was all some sort of pain-induced delusion? A nightmare?

I took a small, hesitant step forward.

"No," a voice commanded as the light expanded and a blurry form emerged. "You shouldn't see her like this."

I stopped moving.

"You can hear me… finally, finally." The blurry form flickered, then sharpened.

There was no denying who it was. Richard. Gram's husband. Her deceased husband. His ghostly form stared back at me, illuminated in the strange, bright light surrounding him. He looked just like the few pictures I'd seen—young and determined, with a strong jawline, short brown hair cut in military fashion, and as large and muscled as any of the Knight boys. "Can you see me too, Cassandra?" Richard's expression was pained, but oddly hopeful.

I nodded, a tiny movement of my head.

"Good. I'm so glad I can be here for you, now of all times. Your grandparents will be so relieved. You're not alone. You're never alone." He looked at me fondly, like he knew me and liked me, then looked down at Gram. His expression darkened.

Richard's eyes widened with tears at the same time a loving smile lighted his face. "She was looking through a chest of old keepsakes when the fire started." He gestured toward a trunk pulled out from under the bed beside her. "I think whatever happened when the fire started must have startled her, and she had an asthma attack. Or maybe she fell, and the smoke—"

I shook my head, denying that any of this was real—refusing to believe that there'd been any fire. That there was any light. That Richard's ghost-like form was standing in it, right in front of me, speaking to me. That Gram lay unmoving next to me.

I shook my head one more time and opened my mouth, but no words came out. A harsh noise rose from inside me. I quickly closed my lips, choking it back.

"It's all right. You can cry," he said softly, tears spilling over his own lashes. "Remember, she's in a better place now. Truly. I've been watching over her since the war… my presence—I think I was slowly extending her lifespan, selfishly not wanting her to go someplace I couldn't follow. But maybe someday, if you and your sisters can manage to do what needs to be done, I can be with her. I can be with her and tell her all about how you dealt with the monsters who had Bethany murdered." Richard blinked several times and his chin trembled. He struggled to keep smiling.

I refused to accept what Richard said.

Gram couldn't be gone. I raged at him, but wasn't sure I actually spoke. *Gram wouldn't leave me.* Not when I needed her so much. And when I still needed to apologize for destroying her beautiful dress—ruining one of her gloves with the pretty pearls—making life so hard on her. For scaring away her friends. For everything.

I stepped in closer. Gram's shoulders were rounded forward, protecting what she cradled into her chest. Two squares of paper. No, not paper. Pictures. Burned around the edges. One of a young girl in a checkered dress, with pigtail braids. Another of her and Richard, young and happy.

Oh God, I'd missed it before. Gram's chest was motionless. Still. Not one single rise and fall. I fell through Richard's eerie figure, landing on bent knees. I turned Gram's body and started CPR. My palms pressed into Gram's cardigan. I repeated the chest compressions I'd learned as part of the safety section in one of my self-defense lessons. Over and over. Numbly.

Again and again.

The light inched closer. "She's gone. You have to let her go." My body kept moving, continuing the compressions. I couldn't look up, but I felt Richard's eyes on me, searching my face. My bottom lip quivered and I blinked rapidly. "Don't fight the tears," he said, his voice suddenly hoarse. He breathed in sharply, fell silent for a long moment, then spoke in a stronger tone. "Tears don't make you weak. You've been wrong about that."

Richard said more, and spoke of my grandparents again, but I couldn't process it. I couldn't think of anything but repeating the motions that would circulate blood and oxygen in Gram's body.

Richard's voice eventually grew more forceful and the light moved closer, until it seemed to be hovering over me. "Cassandra, you have to go. It's time." Richard's voice rose. I finally looked up through blurry eyes. Richard stood over me, looking down with deep blue irises as bright as any of the Knights, and a face so youthful he could have been a boy from school, yet an expression so impossibly commanding, and full of determination, I instinctively wanted to follow his lead. "You need to get out of here," he said gently. "You have to stay safe. Get to Bernard and his boys. Time is short. I don't know who the Summum Malum sent, but they'll soon realize their mistake. They'll come."

"But Gram." My hands kept moving, doing compressions.

"Cassandra. Look at her."

I didn't answer, looking back down at my hands, just my hands, as they continued their work. I had to keep up. Until help arrived. Had to save her.

"You pushed back the fire and put out the flames, but they'd already gotten to her. She wasn't conscious for long, before the flames got to her. She's on her way to a better place."

A better place? I paused just an instant in my compressions to rub at my eyes. I resumed my work, and blinked several times as the form beneath my hands came into focus.

Gram's body.

My body stilled.

She was hardly recognizable. Her chest, the part showing between my fingers, was mostly undamaged because of the position she'd been in. But the side of her body that had been facing out to the fire was…

Cardigan, blouse, pants in charred tatters. Horrible burns. Blood. Melted flesh.

The image blurred again as my eyes filled once more with tears. I blinked frantically. I kept blinking, even as the dam threatened to burst. All that held it in was a simple truth. Gram deserved better than my tears.

"No time. You have to get out of here," Richard commanded from the light still shining from above. "And you have to stop running from me. I've waited since the disaster, when you first came here, but I couldn't wait any longer. We are still so weak. Even now that we've learned to draw on the powers of your twin, it's still not enough."

"Twin?" I glanced back up. "What?"

"So weak…" The light around Richard flickered several times. Then blinked out.

I was alone.

Wisps of smoke rose from the bed. Cool air swirled in from the window. Dampness spread across my cheeks. More sweat? I wiped at my face with my gloved hand until the streaks of wetness were gone, then pressed a kiss into my palm. I pressed the damp glove to Gram's cheek. "I love you."

The dense, smoke-ridden air quickly absorbed my voice. My three word sentiment sounded small. Choked. Weak. I had never said it before. And now she couldn't hear me. Wouldn't come back.

Oh God. There was one way to confirm if she might be able to come back. I reached out my bare, ungloved hand for one of her gnarled ones. *Please, pain, please come.* I hesitated, my fingers just above her skin. *I welcome you, pain. Out of all the moments I wanted you gone, I need you now more than I'd ever needed anything. Even to be normal.*

I touched Gram's hand.

Nothing.

No pain, no vision, no burn. I waited. None came. Instead my fingertips took in something more awful. Something cold. Wilted. Paper-thin. Gram's flesh.

I'd always thought it would be a miracle to be able to touch Gram's hand and actually feel its gentle warmth through the imperfections marring it, but in that instant touching Gram's skin sickened me. An intense, unbearable pressure tore through me, as if my chest was being shredded inside me. The pressure settled in, tightening around my heart.

I kept one hand holding Gram's, and moved the other to pound on the bare skin above my left breast. Thud. Thud. Thud. My fist struck my torso.

No relief.

I clenched my fist tighter and kept pounding.

Thud. Thud. Thud. I moved my fist higher, then over and across my lungs, hoping for just a bit of release from the tightness that threatened to burst my chest and strangle me.

Thud. Thud. Thud.

Still no relief. I just felt tired. More drained than ever. More alone.

I was alone.

I stopped pounding.

So lightly, I held Gram's hand in mine, lifting its limp weight to my cheek, brushing her fingertips against the side of my face, until I could no longer stand the feeling of holding something that didn't resemble Gram at all. I slowly placed her arm back by her side.

I sorted through her open chest of keepsakes until I found several old pictures still unburned, added them to the two she'd been clutching, tucked them all into a small beaded purse I found at the bottom of her things, and slung the purse over my shoulder. I finally forced myself to stand up.

Shivering and numb, I walked out of Gram's room. For the last time.

Zoe. I stumbled into the hall.

If Gram was still here, Zoe had to be too, right? And where was Cole? Why hadn't he gotten Gram and Zoe out? How had this happened?

"Zoe! Zoe!"

Nothing.

"Zoe-bug."

A soft whimper. Then another. The whimpering grew stronger, floating down from the attic.

Dammit. She'd been doing better navigating the stairs, but she must be stuck. Alone and scared. A few remaining flames smoldered along the walls of the hallway, reaching toward the ceiling, and more now shot out from the living room and wall housing the kitchen. I willed them away. I added a thought for any remaining in the cottage to vanish, and dashed up the narrow stairs.

Zoe was deep under my bed, near the corner of my trunk. Shaking. Still whimpering.

Thankfully the fire had only gotten to one wall in the attic as it climbed the side of the cottage. Smoke swirled around the room and the top of my open trunk, but Zoe was buffered from it. Sleeping Beauty was a melted mess of pink plastic, but the princess and the scorched wall around her were the only signs of real damage. Zoe seemed panicked but okay.

I coaxed her out from under the bed, pulled her large body into my arms, and carried her down the stairs and out the door into the cool night air. I staggered into the yard, my feet shuffling through the grass, directionless, finding myself at Gram's garden. I sank down next to it. Zoe ended up on my lap, still shaking, my arms wrapped tightly around her.

I buried my face in the softness of Zoe's neck and let her thick coat absorb my sobs.

How had this happened? Where was Cole?

Zoe kept shaking. I wailed into her coat.

I couldn't stop.

A siren shrieked in the distance, growing louder and louder.

The unnatural screeching slowly blocked out every thought, and every awful image of the fire that had just taken Gram. Only the sound remained.

25
TORMENT

FIREMEN SWARMED EVERYWHERE. NEIGHBORS HURRIED OFF porches and gathered on lawns. Two policemen approached me slowly, cautiously. Officer Fry, and another. Not his partner. Thinner. That officer stepped in close, his eyes running over me and Zoe. His eyebrows rose, lifting an oval, puckered scar in the center of them. Like a third eye staring at us too.

Third-eye took Zoe, looping a rope around her neck and dragging her to his side.

"What are you doing?" I cried out.

He ignored my question. "You have the right to remain silent."

Instead of helping me, he read me my rights. He was taking me into custody.

He took Gram's purse from me, and spoke into the radio on his shoulder, "I have a canine that needs to be dropped at the shelter."

"No!" I scrambled after Zoe.

Third-eye pushed me back with his foot. "I've heard about you. You want me to touch you? Or book you on obstruction too?" Third-eye tugged at the rope. Zoe pulled back with a whine and looked around, confused.

"It's okay, Zoe. Be a good girl. I'll see you soon." I tried to keep the terror out of my voice.

She let him lead her to a patrol car.

Officer Fry handed me a blanket. "Don't worry, she's going into the overnight pen."

An hour ago, I was at my first school dance, swaying in the moonlight with a boy that scared me to death and made me feel safe all at the same time. Now I was in handcuffs in the back of a police car, under suspicion of setting fire to the only home I had ever known and killing the only person who had ever really loved me. I'd even lost Zoe—again.

They drove me to the station, booked me, searched me and asked me to take out my hair clip, and finally gave me shoes—orange sandals—and something to wear. An orange jumpsuit. It itched. Rough patches covered worn spots. At least it offered protection from the hands that kept reaching for me. After each time I explained I came home to the fire, and didn't stage the whole thing, which is what Third-eye accused me of (saying they had a witness too), he yanked me out of my chair, marched me outside into the frigid night air, told me to clear my head, then shoved me back inside. I could see how it was weird to find a lot of fire damage but no fire to put out—but how could they think I'd set fire to Gram's home? And how could they possibly think I'd start a fire with Gram there?

I kept protesting, declaring my innocence.

Third-eye raised his eyebrows, looked at the others, and whispered, "Crazy."

The social worker arrived, and mouthed, "Crazy" too.

Should I ask for a lawyer? Would they think me more guilty? Where was Cole? Gabriel? Surely the Knights must know what had happened at Gram's by now. Maybe my words earlier had pushed Gabriel and his family away for good. I guessed I should be happy.

The night turned even colder. Third-eye asked me another question, but I couldn't process it, something about whether I'd acted alone or had any friends from out of town?

"She's had enough," Officer Fry said. He handed the blanket back to me and took me to a small, windowless room. A long bench sat against the wall. I spent the rest of the night on the bench, huddled under the blanket, slipping off my sandals and rubbing my feet to stay warm, counting the cracks in the ceiling, catching snippets of conversation outside.

"It's not just the witness. The letter explains it," Third-eye said. What letter?

"I agree… never been right since they found her," the social worker said.

Footsteps. Mumbling. A file drawer slamming shut.

"Commitment?" Third-eye asked. "Heard there's a good place outside Glenwood Springs." My heart sank. I always knew a strait-jacket was coming.

"But she's a minor," Officer Fry said. "Only had trouble at school, not with us."

More indistinct conversation.

"Let's finish our investigation." Another officer's voice.

"For now, commitment, treatment," the social worker said. "Who'll sign?"

I tried to come up with a plan, but could barely think at all, not sleeping, but happy to escape the nightmare—the burns—on this night of all nights.

In the morning Officer Fry gave me a granola bar, bottle of juice, and banana, and a hair band to pull back my hair. I had no appetite, but forced myself to slowly sip some juice. After I finished half, Third-eye's foot tapping impatiently the whole time, he snatched it away and he and another officer bound my arms to my chest with restraints. They loaded me into a patrol car, down the rural, one-lane highway, onto the closest freeway. About an hour later, we arrived at a psychiatric hospital outside of Glenwood Springs.

From my first view, the hospital appeared less a place for treatment and more a place for confinement. A large concrete monstrosity surrounded by a tall metal fence. An angry-looking nurse pulled me by my restraints into a windowless corridor, an abyss of harsh fluorescent lighting and cold concrete slabs. At least despite my previous troubles, they'd never condemned me to this hellhole before.

The nurse jerked us to a stop in front of a placard that read "Chief Psychiatrist & Medical Director." She opened the door next to it.

Tired and confused, I shivered in my jumpsuit, and took the only seat across from the man behind the door. He straightened the collar of his white lab coat and glanced down at an open file, revealing a small bald spot on top of his head, and looked up, frowning across the desk at me. He introduced himself, and uttered a few mindless pleasantries before declaring his plan for me. "We'll keep you here on a 72-hour mental health hold. That should give me time to provide a recommendation of how this case should be handled going forward."

I should focus. I shook my head to clear it.

He continued with a pinched expression, "I have to advise you to be as forthright as you can about your condition."

"I'll try." I forced myself to answer softly, when what I really wanted to do was shout at this whole situation and break free from the restraints forcing my arms down and across my chest, numbing my hands into uselessness.

"Good. Because I've seen the records from your other doctors." He motioned to the file. "And I have to say I don't think they've been aggressive enough."

Focus. "Um, what do you mean?"

"You're suffering from a phobia that is clearly impairing your ability to function normally, and there's no reason for it." He scooted his chair away from me and closer to the file cabinets rising to the ceiling behind him.

"I don't understand."

"You should be cured by now, kiddo." He scooted back another inch, as if whatever was wrong with me might be contagious. "They eliminated neuropathic pain early on, and you don't exhibit the full spectrum of PTSD symptoms. Your lack of response to medication leaves little doubt on that." He pointed to a red circle in the file. "What we have here is a phobia. I understand the problem when you were first recovered from the water, because clearly, that experience must have been painful. But you've been allowed to go on too long without serious intervention."

"Intervention?"

"Yes. Your prior desensitization therapy was too tentative, diverted by too much focus on your amnesia. But your phobia is the key. I expect rapid progress resolving your symptoms, once it's broken through."

"Broken through?" I shivered. The rough canvas of my restraints chafed where the too-short sleeves of the orange jumpsuit ended mid-forearm.

"Think of it as a threshold. Below a certain intensity, exposure and desensitization aren't effective. It varies by patient. We have to reach your threshold. We're going to start with that tonight, after my rounds. A type of shock therapy, if you will. This is the perfect opportunity, since we're equipped here to do that sort of thing." His eyes gleamed, and he scooted in toward his desk. "Don't worry, no matter how much you carry on, we'll keep you from hurting yourself."

I tried to stay calm. "Dr., um, Dr. Ramsey," I said, finally recalling the name he'd given me when I entered, and resisting the urge to call him "Dr. Creepy" instead, "I think what you're talking about is using touch therapy on me. That hasn't worked in the past. So no intervention is needed. Really."

"You just haven't had enough. It's been too mild, too sporadic."

"But—"

"Of course we'll also need to work with you on your fascination with fire."

"I don't have a fascination with fire." Was I lying?

"Of course you do. And you're clearly a danger to yourself and others, so I apologize for the restraints, but they're just a—"

"I'm not dangerous!" My arms instinctively pushed against the bindings holding them in. "I'm not going to hurt anyone."

"There's no sense denying it. It's all reported here in your file. All the fights you've gotten into. The martial arts lessons." He eyed me knowingly, like the file had many more details. "How skilled you are." I couldn't deny that. Self-defense had come naturally, even without the lessons. Maybe I'd learned it before Meeker. "And then, of course, there's also the report from the police that just arrived, from interviewing your principal."

"They talked to Principal Cook?"

He tented his fingertips together in front of his chest like a church steeple. "Oh, yes. Thankfully his daughter called the police, must have been right around the time of the fire, and told the police how you'd just been at a school dance, acting crazy—more than usual—threatening her, threatening to hurt anyone who got in your way." Kaylee was their witness? "It's how they knew to be cautious when a fire was reported at your guardian's. And then this morning, they interviewed her father."

"What? Why?"

"Don't be coy. Just to learn all about how you've gone on and on to his daughter and her friends about your curiosity with flames. Setting fires. His daughter told him all about it after everyone learned what you did last—"

"What!?"

"Come on, kiddo. Stop the protests. You told me you'd be honest with me." He reached for a pen, tapped it thoughtfully, and made a note in the open file in front of him. "I can see treatment is going to take longer than I'd thought. Well, nothing we can't handle. Some patients have been here for years."

Years. My whole body went cold. "But there's nothing to treat." I shifted in my seat. "I don't have a fascination with fire—um, not in the way Principal Cook's daughter said. And once the police investigate, I'm sure they'll figure out that I had nothing to do with it."

"Hmm," the doctor murmured, scratched his bald spot, and made several more notes. "Social Services was right. You're going to be a difficult one."

He slipped the pen into his lab coat pocket, closed the file and called for Tank, a tall, heavyset nurse—or security guard, I couldn't tell which one—to take me to my room.

"Ahhhhh!" A high-pitched scream rang out, followed by another round of persistent moaning.

I sat on a narrow cot—the only furniture I had besides a sink and toilet—and covered my ears against the howls and wails of whoever was kept next door. A young woman, I guessed, based on her high-pitched racket. My troubled neighbor certainly didn't help with my plans. I dropped my hands. Silence would make it much easier to hear when anyone approached the door. But that wouldn't deter me. Dr. Creepy had convinced me I needed to get myself out of this hell-hole, as soon as possible. This seemed as good a time as any since Tank had actually removed my restraints before shoving me inside and clicking the deadbolt in place. I just needed to be ready to surprise—and take down—whoever opened the door next. Would it be Tank? Probably, since Dr. Creepy seemed to think I was so dangerous.

Plan in place, I kept my ears focused on sounds. Beyond the moaning, the creak of a cart being wheeled down the hall. A heavy thump, a door slamming shut. My mind was finally starting to wake from the numbness that had set in after the fire. Was I responsible for what had happened? Had I been the target, as Richard implied? Like Richard and Gram's daughter and the women in the Knight family? Fire had been used there too.

But why had Gram been the one who'd suffered? If it was going to be anyone, it should have been me.

It should have been me. It should have been me.

I shivered. I looked around for a blanket. The cot was bare. Just a stained, canvas-covered mattress. Like the staff was afraid I might use loose material as a weapon. Or a noose. Another howl from my neighbor. I bet she'd wished for a noose long ago.

My shivers shook the bed and I slid off my sandals, pulled my legs up, and hugged my arms around them, dropping my head to my knees. I squeezed my limbs in, curling into a tight ball, thinking of

Gabriel's heat. No! Forget Gabriel. Envision the comforting warmth of Gram's hot chocolate instead, sitting at the kitchen table with my mug, Gram pushing her walker around in her favorite apron. She'd pull out something sweet from the oven, offer it to me as she asked me about my day. She'd say something nice, or maybe something silly. I could almost hear it. *You need more marshmallows in your hot chocolate, angel.*

The thought was too painful. *It should have been me.*

I gulped, taking in a breath. It was barely enough to keep the feeling of misery from bursting my chest. I couldn't succumb to more useless tears, no matter what Richard had said about it being all right to cry. And I wouldn't even contemplate how Richard had appeared above Gram's body. Or how I'd been able to walk through fire.

Was I really the girl the Knights had been waiting for? If so, why hadn't I been able to do anything with the stone in the mountain?

Was Richard one of the "good ones" Vin said were watching out for me? If so, why had he said something about a "disaster" when I first came here?

I shook my head, trying to clear it of the exhaustion and grief making my thoughts so foggy. Well, if the fire was set for me, whoever did it was stupid. I hadn't even been inside to begin with, and there was no way for anyone to know I'd get home when I did, or that I'd be so impulsive as to rush inside. I hadn't seen anyone around watching.

But I had seen someone running. Running toward me, as I was running home. I might not have noticed, or remembered at all, if not for their odd running attire. White dress shirt, tie, dark suit pants. A man. Medium height, maybe shorter. A bulky, muscular frame. The shirt had hugged his beefy shoulders. *Focus. Picture the memory.* I zoomed in on the details, searching for anything, no matter how small, like the way the runner carried himself. The man's features, which were washed out in the muted streetlights, but round, soft.

Mike.

The runner looked like Mike. I'd certainly seen him enough to know.

The fluorescent bulbs in the ceiling flickered, and a dark spot flashed across the sheet.

I jerked up.

The lights flickered faster. I jumped off the cot and pressed myself against the back wall, squinting at the long bulbs. Three dark clouds swirled across the ceiling. *Shadows?* My scream came out a whimper when they zipped toward me, as though checking me out. I flinched, anticipating pain, but they drew back and vanished through a crack in the concrete.

My neighbor's howls grew sharper, then stopped completely. Silent. For the first time since I had been here.

What was going on? A hallucination brought on by sleep deprivation? I held my breath and approached the adjoining wall. I pressed my ear against it, rallying the courage to say, "Hello? Are you—"

A piercing scream sent a chill down my spine. "Shadows!" my neighbor shrieked. "Shadows!"

More silence.

"Burn her?" The question echoed through the concrete, lifting the hairs on my neck.

A single dark spot appeared on the wall in front of my nose, and I staggered back. A tiny absence of light at first but growing larger as the lights flickered wildly.

What the hell!?

I backed away from the darkness and hit the cot, falling back against it as the dark cloud took a new shape. It stretched, growing lanky limbs and an elongated, crooked neck. Empty holes for eyes revealed the white paint behind it. Claws the length of my forearm sprouted from its slender hands. I scrambled to my feet, making useless fists as it peeled itself off the wall and took a more solid, billowing form. Its feet were bent outward, its elbows twisted forward, claws trailing the ground soundlessly as it took two shuddery steps.

Head to the fire. My breath caught. The thought came from inside me, but the voice sounded… wrong.

You love the fire.

My arms lowered, body warming. The shadow took another step.

Embrace it. Become it. Leap in!

I shook myself, banishing the grogginess. That final growl was definitely not me, not my voice. It was the shadow! Whispering to me.

"No!" I hissed through clenched teeth.

I had to get away, but I had nowhere to go. Four walls. A locked door. I rushed my attacker with a strangled cry. I plowed right through, fist first, and nearly rammed the wall. I whirled to find the darkness gone. The fluorescent lights hummed, strong and bright once more.

I gasped for air, my heart thumping in my ears.

I wasn't hallucinating. And memories or not, embedded deep inside me was knowledge. Whatever I'd just seen was bad. Worse than that. Evil. Something to fight. Powerful. Something to run from.

I struggled to breathe, to calm my racing pulse.

Footsteps approached, fast and determined. I jumped to attention. The deadbolt clicked back. I positioned myself behind the door with raised arms. The door latch lifted. I prepared myself for pain, just in case.

As the heavy metal slab opened, I visualized Tank's height and the location of his solar plexus. Right around the middle of his uniform. I let him push open the door, then struck my right arm out and around the edge. My fist connected with something surprisingly supple, for how muscled Tank's chest had been. The thought vanished as a shot of pain went straight to my head.

A raging burn bubbled in my hand. The heat quickly spread up my arm. A split-second later, fire consumed the entire right side of my body. I fought against the pain pulling me to the floor as I forced myself to step around the door and get in position for my next strike.

A knee to the groin.

The vision started as I moved. I could only see the vision, not what was right in front of me. I tried to kick up with my leg, but wasn't sure anything happened between the haze of pain and the image starting to take shape.

The picture slowly focused on a large, fancy rug, then up a wall lined with built-in wood shelves overflowing with rows of books and a scattering of framed pictures. Dammit. I was seeing the vision through someone's eyes—definitely an actual memory, not even tampered with. I struggled to ignore it as I blindly kicked and thrashed to connect with whoever had come to get me, striking out with my left arm, clawing with both hands between blows. To knock them out, incapacitate them, before my body was rendered useless from the pain. I continued my efforts as the vision shifted. Away from the books and across the room to a girl.

My clawing, my whole body slowed.

The girl in the vision had a serious, yet exotic look. A pale face set in confident repose, framed by a tremendous mass of red hair. Her features were washed out by the wavy curls' vibrancy.

The color of flames.

My body went limp. I felt myself sinking to the hospital room floor, losing focus on everything except the unbelievable sight in my head. *Me. It was me in the vision.* I was the girl, half-leaning against a large bed.

Useless on the hospital floor, escape on hold, I absorbed every detail...

I was dressed in a slip dress I'd never seen before. The silly thing looked new and like I'd thrown it on with no care for the fact just two small straps held it up, exposing so much skin. Laying against my skin was my locket—my missing locket.

"You know how I feel about you," a male voice, thick, with a melodic accent, whispered in my head. "You have to. You felt it, didn't you? I mean, you kissed me."

"Okay, I admit, I thought maybe..." My fingers tightened into claws around the plush comforter. "But I shouldn't have done that. The kiss. I just thought—But I don't want anything to change our friendship." I pushed away from the bed, my stance turning defiant. I gulped. My face softened. "I couldn't bear that, Vin."

Vin?! Vin's vision? Why would he be in a mental hospital? How had he gotten in? *Wait, I kissed him?!*

"Cyndra, I love you."

"I love you too. As friends." I strode away from the bed, away from Vin. "Best friends."

"We're beyond that." Vin held out a hand. "I mean, you're the only girl who's been able to resist my appeal, when you try."

"Well, that's true." I took several more steps, but this time, toward Vin.

"It's how I know you care about me," he said gently. I moved even closer to him, the dress floating around my knees. "It's how I know you aren't like all the other girls"—Vin's tone iced over—"who hang on my every word. Because of my unnatural appeal. My poisonous smile. My damned predatory body, making me look twenty from twelve to forty."

"Don't think of yourself or your gifts that way." I stepped within inches of him, reached forward, and pulled his hand into mine. The vision focused on our clasped hands. Our bare hands. Touching. Vin slid his other hand up my arm, his fingers skimming my bare bicep, cupping my shoulder. I disappeared in the vision as our bodies came together and pressed, chest to chest.

Vin shifted back in our embrace and looked down. "What did you see?"

"I try not to look."

"What did you see?"

"I always see good things in you." I smiled up at him. "Every time we touch."

"I know I've hurt people. Hell, my whole genetic makeup is designed to lure people I don't care about."

"You can't help that, but you never take advantage and you're always kind. That's what I see."

"I think maybe we were meant to be together. You and I. Bonded, even… perhaps." He pulled me closer. I sighed against him. "I know that doesn't happen much anymore. But in all these years, everywhere I've been, you've been the only girl I've met who can resist my pull."

"Yes, I can resist it. When I think about it," I whispered into him, "and of course I like you for you. You're like the best guy I know."

He pulled back just enough to look down at me.

"I'm not just saying that because I know so few." I blushed. "Or because you're my friend. Or come across as being so damn refined all the time." I grinned.

"See, I knew how much you liked me."

"But that doesn't mean we should be together. Like boy-friend-girlfriend, or anything." I shook my curls into a raging bon-fire—licks of reds and oranges. "Hey," my tone brightened, doing a 180 like I was desperate to turn the topic. "Let me change. We'll spar."

"Again?" He laughed.

"I'm not you. I can't get by on charm." I poked him in the stomach.

He leaned into me, and my hand flattened against his chest.

"Come on. Time to fight." I jabbed him playfully.

"Fine." He sighed. "But this isn't going to change things." He brushed his lips across my brow. "I can't say it enough. I love you."

"Vin." I ducked out of his hold, danced over to a dresser, and slid open a drawer. "I didn't want to say this. But it's Alanna who cares for you that way."

"I know."

"You do?" I pivoted toward him.

"How could I not? It's creepy."

"Creepy?"

"Very. The past few months, she stares at me. She has this weird look too. At least other girls have the gumption to flirt a bit, annoying as that is. But Alanna—not a word."

"She can't help it." I whirled back to the drawer and yanked out a pair of leggings. "She's shy."

"I could never care for her like that, even if I thought she really liked me. Not just how I make her feel."

"Give her a chance." I turned, my expression pleading.

"No." He shook his head and a fall of black hair swept across his eyes.

"But—"

"No. I never will. You're it for me. When you kissed me, I finally had to admit you're not just my friend. And definitely not my kid sister. You light up my day, Cyn. Just by looking my way. Before I met you, I wandered this house and helped Dad pick out artists' depictions of love and beauty for his collectors. But you made me understand them. You brought the art to life for me and then put it all to shame."

"Vin—"

"Alanna may look like you, but she doesn't have a speck of the fire you have." Vin paused to take a long breath and brush back his hair. "I hate to say this, since you're both always lost in a book, but Alanna has nothing but the make-believe. No life of her own. No spark. She couldn't be more dull if she tried. I couldn't be attracted to that. No guy could."

A soft gasp caused Vin to glance behind him.

A girl—a mirror image of me, except for her shock of dark brown hair, librarian-like cardigan, and pleated skirt—stood in the doorway on shaky legs. She opened her mouth to say something, then quickly closed her rosy lips as her face crumpled and her cheeks burned red.

"Damn it. Alanna," Vin snipped, then softened. "You're so quiet. I didn't hear you."

The tremors in her legs grew so violent I thought she might fall over. Instead, she spun around and vanished in one hurried step.

"Alanna! Come back." My voice called out as the vision faded.

The next moment I was back in my concrete cell, Vin struggling to pull himself up to a kneeling position over my sprawled body, huffing heavily through his mouth, his ripped shirt revealing a smooth chest and red scratch marks.

26
FACING THE PAST

"Really, Cyndra? Was that necessary?" Vin wheezed, rubbing at his throat with one hand, laying the other across his chest. Blood oozed from one of the scratches. "What a way to greet the guy... who came... to rescue you."

I couldn't open my mouth or I'd scream. My whole right arm was still on fire, the skin below my right wrist a quivering, bubbly mess. My left forearm throbbed too, but I didn't have the strength to turn my head. Inspecting the damage would have to wait. Vin and I stared at each other for several moments while the pitiful howls of my neighbor reverberated through the wall. I almost howled too. But luckily the pain progressed beyond cognition, to the point it was almost mind-numbing, shutting down all sensation and instead focusing my thoughts on basic survival. Getting the hell out of here, like I'd originally planned.

"I'm sorry," Vin spoke again, his melodic voice almost back to normal. "I came to help, as soon as I got back and found out what happened." He dropped his hands to his lap. "I certainly didn't mean to hurt you." He looked down at my right hand, and grimaced. He looked over to my left, and grimaced again. "Agapi mou. I'm so sorry."

At last I felt strong enough to move my head. My left forearm looked just as bad as my right hand, a mass of blistered and burned flesh. Vin's face fell at the sight. The emotion on his face seemed real. Made it seem like the thing from the vision about him being my friend—"my best friend" and "the best guy I knew"—was real.

"It's okay." I managed to get out. "You did get the door open. And it'll heal in no time." I found myself reassuring him, hoping I was right. If the burns kept getting worse, how much longer until my body was too damaged to heal?

As he kept looking over my burns, the smooth lines of Vin's face fell further. A pained expression settled over his features, like knowing I was suffering hurt him worse than anything he felt. For now, I'd reserve judgment on the things Vin had shown me—all the things he must be keeping from me. "I'm sorry if I hurt you too. Obviously I thought you were someone else."

"It's okay. Just a sore throat." He glanced at his ripped shirt. "Some scratches. But we need to get you out of here."

My blood chilled as I remembered. That creature. That voice.

"Vin, the shadow things. They're here! I saw them. One of them talked!"

He shook his head, his face paling. "Even more reason to hurry. But you're in no fighting condition." He leaned in, examining my burns, which had healed just the tiniest bit. "And I'm a bit drained."

"Drained?" I gave a weak laugh, my back spasming against the concrete. Had he never been in a fight?

"Yes." He pulled back, looking like I'd insulted him. His chest broadened. "I mean I'm fine—physically. But between my wasted efforts this weekend, then the effort it took to track you here, on top of the persuasion it took to get inside this place, I'm pretty useless. At what would help us the most," he clarified quickly.

"OK…" Unfortunately questioning him about all of that would have to wait. I lifted my head and shoulders and fell back down. "You'll have to carry me. Put my shoes back on first." Maybe I'd be able to walk soon.

Vin nodded, slipped on my sandals, and looked around the room. Suddenly, his head jerked up, eyes wide. "Do you smell that?"

Oh God. I did.

Gasoline.

Smoke.

"Hurry!" I yelled over the howls of the girl in the next room, pulsing through the concrete, louder than ever.

Vin pulled out a small pocket knife from his pants, cut off a length of canvas from the covering of the cot's mattress, and wrapped it around my torso. A foul smell rose from it, even more sour than the smoke. We both gagged. He heaved me up into his arms. As we turned down the hall, Tank shot out from my neighbor's room, charging us.

"Stop!" Vin commanded, and Tank slowed, but did not stop. "Dammit. I'm too weak," Vin cursed.

But whatever Vin had done to get Tank to hesitate gave me just enough time to will strength back into my legs. As Vin turned me away from Tank's grasping hands I kicked both feet into his face. The bottom of my sandals struck his jaw. Tank stumbled back into the room he'd emerged from, right into my neighbor, who appeared with a banshee scream in a halo of flames.

Her hospital gown raged with fire, burning right off of her, melting into her skin. Her gown quickly spread the blaze to Tank's shirt as they both righted themselves with crazed looks in their eyes, and rushed toward us.

"Burn her!" my neighbor screamed, reeking of gasoline and burnt flesh.

"Kill her!" Tank echoed, his words slurred, showing no concern as the blaze spread down his uniform.

Without thought, I simply willed the flames away.

The fire devouring them both fizzled out. Tank and the girl stopped moving, in utter confusion. As the flames vanished, Vin's body tensed, but he seized the opportunity to rush us down the hall. He glanced down at me with puzzlement, stumbled, then found his footing. Neither of us spoke. I peeked over his shoulder. Tank and my neighbor stood in a puddle of water; the overhead sprinklers had finally kicked in. Both looked distant and dazed.

Vin didn't carry me as securely as Gabriel would've, and his bouncing clacked my teeth, but he raced us down a corridor, pushing through an emergency exit, into a brilliant afternoon. Behind us, the distant din of fire alarms echoed. Vin turned toward a parking lot, but he looked back over his shoulder. I squinted, struggling to get my bearings in his arms when he stopped and muttered, "Damn."

He followed something up, into the sky, and I craned my neck to locate an abstract shape flitting past the edges of my vision. At the peak of the asylum roof, I saw them: a flock of large birds of prey spinning together in a windswept dance. No, not birds. Not really. Just their shadows.

An idling engine hummed nearby. A door whooshed open.

"We'll talk about that thing with the fire when we're alone," he whispered. What did he mean—alone? Besides, we had other things to talk about first. To begin with, how the hell could he control people like he had Tank? And had he ever tried that on me? Later, when we were far away from here, we'd talk about the Shadows.

Vin set me down onto a leather bench seat, arranged my orange jumpsuit-covered legs so I lay across it, and pulled away the foul-smelling strip of canvas before closing the door.

The vehicle immediately enveloped me in a soothing, unmistakable scent. Cedar. Cloves. Gabriel's face appeared around the driver's seat. His driver's seat. His SUV.

"Why was he carrying you?" Gabriel's bottomless blue eyes searched mine, then quickly moved over me, coming to rest on my right hand, then my left forearm, his mouth tensing as he saw the burns.

The front passenger's door opened and closed as Vin slid in.

"What happened?" Gabriel roared at him.

"Get moving, bear boy." Vin rolled down his window and shoved his head out, eyes skyward. "Fast. Take backroads if you can. Question and answer time will have to wait."

"You're going to answer for every burn on her body." Gabriel slammed his foot down on the gas. He shot us out of the parking lot, then turned down a dark, one-lane road at the last second. We cut back on to the main road at the next opportunity, then flew onto the freeway ramp and cruised into and around traffic.

"I think we're clear," Vin said, checking the sky again, "but don't slow down."

A cop car, sirens blaring, shot past us on the other side of the freeway, racing to the hospital. Gabriel took a deep breath. "Were you touched before or after Vin found you?"

"Listen," I spoke up before Vin could answer, managing to lift myself to sitting without using my hands, "it was me that hit Vin. I thought he was the guard, and anyway, Vin still got me out. That's all that—"

"I have a first-aid kit in the back." Gabriel cut me off, but his glance in the rearview mirror was not angry. Not at me, anyway. "I'll pull over a few exits down, once we're within the relic's radius. I don't think anyone from the hospital's following. I'll look at those burns, we can take a quick breather, talk about what happened last night."

"No!" I protested, the SUV's confines amplifying its harshness. Gabriel's expression in the rearview mirror closed up into self-consciousness. My heart constricted at the sight. Why did I have to care if I upset Gabriel? "Isn't it safer to keep driving?" I used safety as an excuse, when my outburst really had everything to do with not wanting to risk a moment with him alone. "I mean, how fast can those shadow things move?"

Gabriel startled. "You saw a Shadow?"

"Shadows," I said, putting emphasis on the plural. "One of them turned into this boogeyman-looking thing, and it was like it was talking in my head, telling me to do things."

"It tried to compel you, like its friends did to the orderly and that poor patient," Vin said. Then he turned to address Gabriel. "My father heard from an alt clan in Africa that they've started breaching the living world in greater numbers and taking to the sky in the form of birds to avoid detection. The clan leader thought the influx was because of an ancient portal there, but it's happening here, too. I just saw the proof with my own eyes."

Gabriel's brows jumped, and he bent over the wheel to peek up through the windshield at the clouds. "Once we get closer to Meeker, they shouldn't be able to find us in any form."

"Good," I said to Gabriel, then frowned at Vin. "You and I need to talk." Vin turned to look back at me. "And turn back around, dammit. I can't think straight when I'm looking at you."

Vin faced forward again. "My persuasive energies are really weak right now. It's perfectly fine to look at me."

"We're not taking any chances," I said, shifting on the bench seat, my strength returning. "You've got just this once to explain—to tell the truth. Have you been manipulating me all along, doing whatever it is you do with that smile of yours. From day one?"

"I have to admit," Vin answered in barely a whisper, then coughed and started again, "I have to admit, there have been a few times since I found you when I've felt like I had to use my skills—my smile—on you." Vin cleared his throat, turning toward me, then remembering my wishes, turned back once more to face the front. "But other than that, I've tried to keep my distance. Tried not to influence you. Or your feelings for me. I knew you'd hate me for it, so I tried to avoid it."

He'd made me pretty miserable in the process too. But he was right. I would've hated him if he'd turned me into a girl like Kaylee and Reese.

"But unfortunately there's not much I can do about the energy I send off, even when I'm not smiling. The response people have. Especially girls. I'm sorry, Cyndra. All I can say is before you lost your memory, you used to be able to resist my appeal. When you tried."

I had been able to resist the last few weeks, when I'd thought about it. At least I was still strong enough to do it. "What do you want from me?"

"Nothing." Vin said simply. Gabriel grunted, a disbelieving

sound. I shifted on the bench seat. Vin released a long sigh as he turned his head farther from me, to look out the side window. "Well, actually, I do want something. For us to be friends again."

I didn't have to look in the rearview mirror to know Gabriel was rolling his eyes.

Friends again. In a strange way, I wanted that too. The memory Vin had shown me—it made it clear I'd once actually thought of him as a good friend. A best friend. Something I'd never thought I had before.

"Actually, I think it's obvious I want us to be more than friends," Vin continued. Gabriel shot him a hard look before turning back to the road. Vin glanced back at him with a resigned expression on his face. "But all I really need is for you to be happy and safe."

"In the hospital, when we touched, you showed me a vision. A memory of us together. We were in a bedroom. It had a wall lined with books. Our skin touched." An edge of excitement crept into my voice. "We actually held hands, you touched my bare arm. You hugged me, and I let you." Gabriel drew in a sharp breath.

Vin responded with a stiff nod as if recalling what I spoke of.

"It didn't look like I was in any pain. How?"

"You weren't seventeen yet," Vin said simply.

"Seventeen?" Gabriel accelerated and swerved into the next lane, cutting off of a small sedan, and the driver honked. Gabriel tugged at his shirt collar.

"What does being seventeen have to do with anything?" I asked the question Gabriel seemed to be wondering too.

"Right around your birthday, everything changed."

"Everything?" Gabriel dialed up the air conditioning, and pointed the closest vents right at his face.

Vin ignored him and responded to me. "You'd always been able to see inside people's minds when you touched them. What you inherited from your parents. But you saw mostly what you wanted, whatever it was you wanted to learn, you could control it. And then suddenly you couldn't." He shook his head, and scratched his forearm, where his sleeve was rolled up. "And the pain started." His nails dug into his arm. "We thought maybe it would make sense—things would get better—when you found the relic you were destined for. And then you left us. Not long after your birthday."

"But didn't I just turn seventeen?"

"No. You're nineteen now."

Nineteen. I let that sink in.

Vin pushed up his sleeves, then pulled them down quickly as if he was cold. "It's freezing in here, bear boy."

"If you call me that one more time," Gabriel growled.

Vin ignored him. "You'll age even more slowly from here."

"Okay." I acknowledged, eager to get to the next part, "and then in the vision you hugged me and you were saying we should be together, as more than friends."

"What the hell!" Gabriel looked at me in the rearview mirror with a stricken expression.

"And a girl walked in. She looked just like me, with brown hair?"

"Alanna," Vin said softly.

"Where is she?"

"I don't know how to say this."

"Spit it out. Then we can get to whatever else you've been keeping from me."

"Alanna's dead."

Like an ocean wave crashing against the shore, the fact my twin sister was dead hit hard, scattering my thoughts. Finally the sound of Gabriel whizzing us through traffic pierced through the void, filling my ears with noise again.

I pictured my twin again in my mind. I tried to feel some sort of connection to her, but nothing, not even her name, sparked any familiarity. Just an ache in my chest.

"She died before you left home. One of the reasons you left." Vin spoke at last. "My father and I promised we'd keep you both safe. We didn't. I'm so sorry, Cyndra."

I rubbed above my heart with my left hand. "What are you apologizing for?"

"For being so arrogant." Vin dropped his head. "For costing Alanna her life," he whispered the words towards his chest, his accent heavy. "Alanna was sensitive. We all knew that. She left because of things I said, things she overheard. Ran right to her death. I was trying to make up for it now that I've found you. I was trying to bring Ellis here. You and Ellis need each other."

"Ellis?"

"Your younger sister. Well, one of them. You're the oldest, even older than Alanna. And you have four younger sisters. Well, three younger sisters, now—"

"Dammit, Vin!" I shifted on the padded bench, unable to control the rage building with every answer he gave me. The fury exploded inside me, my right arm shot out, hitting the back of his seat. Pain exploded in my hand as the blistered skin absorbed the blow. "Damn. Damn. Damn." I winced.

Vin's head dropped lower. "I'm sorry."

"You can take your sorries and shove them up your—" I didn't finish, but his defeated expression told me he'd been speaking English long enough to understand. I lifted my hand to my mouth and blew on the blisters. "Tell me why I'm not supposed to hate you for keeping all this from me."

"How could I explain before?" His chin lifted a fraction. "So much pain. Your parents are gone. Your twin is gone. Your two youngest sisters are gone. Well, we think they are at least alive, but we don't know where they are. Ellis is all that's left." He exhaled hard, like holding his breath in was causing him pain. "And Ellis, she would've helped explain things. I'd even hoped you seeing her might bring back memories, since obviously seeing me hasn't brought back a thing. But we can't get to her."

"Get to her?" I shook my hand, still trying to relieve the burn my outburst had inflamed, and held it in front of the cold air blasting between the seats.

"Ellis was taken. Just months ago. While we were waiting for her to connect with her relic. She's been held by the people who took her ever since."

I dropped my hand. "What people?"

"There's an underground division of the government, we don't even know what to call it. They seem to know all about special races like us, what we can do. We found out about them when they came for her." Vin straightened in his seat, his usual confidence back in full. "We don't know what they want. They haven't killed her. Haven't burned her. Haven't chosen a side."

"You're trying to help her, right?"

"Of course. My patera—my father—finally located the facility they're holding her in. That's where I was. But there were too many guards, too many barriers, to get past. We got just a glimpse of her on a security camera"—he shuddered—"and it was like they expected us to use compulsion. It was the dead of night, but they were ready for us. We had to turn around."

Gabriel gave a grunt of disgust at that, but kept his eyes on the road.

Vin gave him an icy look. "Hey, bear boy"—Gabriel snapped his teeth and looked like he wanted to devour Vin—"at least it meant I got back to Meeker sooner than expected, which turned out to be a good thing. After what your family allowed to happen."

Every bit of hardness in Gabriel's features vanished. A look of guilt flashed across his face. "We were doing our best."

"No you weren't." Vin shot back.

"Describe her." I interrupted, redirecting him from more sniping at Gabriel.

"I'll do better than that." Vin reached down to the floor of the SUV for his messenger bag. He pulled out a small photograph, handed it to me, and quickly turned back around.

I focused on it, hoping the photo would immediately trigger a memory of something. Anything. But a stranger, an entirely unfamiliar-looking girl, stared back at me. This girl Vin called Ellis sat on an elegant, mosaic stone tile border at the edge of a pool, her legs dangling in the water, her upper body tipped back on braced arms behind her. She was half-turned toward the camera, a playful smile lighting her face. She was captivating. So beautiful. So delicate. She looked like one of Kaylee's friends.

Only more stunning.

And what was most stunning was the color of this girl's—my sister's—hair. The shade was even more striking than my own. Deep black, almost blue tresses flowed like a waterfall, straight down to the tile behind her. Even in this photograph, her sleek strands glowed like the iridescent heart of a storm cloud. Only more electric. Had she'd dyed it? The bluish-black seemed so bold, especially next to the sheer, light pink covering she wore over a matching pink bikini, a hint of pink eye shadow glittering around her eyes. Kaylee and Reese would surely want to be her friend.

"I'm not sure she'd like me," I blurted out.

"You were close." Vin turned to look out the window again.

"Really?"

Vin thought for a moment. "OK. I'll put it in language you'll understand. You were as close as Jane and Elizabeth Bennett. And just as different from each other."

"How did you know Gram asked me to read her Jane Austen?"

"She did? I didn't know that. You used to be crazy about that stuff."

"No way. I liked that happy-ending garbage?"

"You loved anything written by women who defied stereotypes of their day. And even though Ellis wasn't book-crazed, like you and Alanna, you were actually closer to her than your twin. Alanna was… more the sort to keep to herself." Vin's voice changed as he spoke of my twin, tinged with an emotion I couldn't read.

I refocused on the photo. "This girl in the photo looks superficial to me." Between the pink bikini and glitter, I was done looking at it and tossed it onto Vin's lap. Not before registering that Ellis also wore a strange necklace. A brilliant blue stone, shaped like a tear drop.

"Ellis isn't superficial." He picked up the photo and frowned. "Well, maybe she'd seem that way to someone who doesn't know her. But when you finally meet her, if you don't remember her still, you need to give her a chance. You leaving was hard on her."

I straightened up in my seat. "I'm sure I left her behind for a reason." If I'd really had a sister, I wouldn't have parted from her so easily, right?

Vin continued to stare at the picture and didn't answer. He finally closed his eyes and forced back whatever memory he wasn't sharing. "And now, after what we saw this weekend." Vin's eyelids clenched. "I can't imagine what Ellis is going through."

Vin stopped talking, and avoided answering any more questions about her on the drive back to Meeker, mumbling something under his breath about how I had enough troubles of my own. The only other thing Vin would say was not to worry, that his father was watching over the government facility night and day looking for an opportunity to get her out. That he spoke with his father often and would let me know when things changed.

Seemingly, as a way to stop talking about Ellis, Vin talked about himself. He was trying to distract us both. But I played along. He didn't want to talk about what he'd seen last night, and besides, learning more about him was long overdue. According to Vin, his skills at compulsion worked against nearly everyone when he used his smile. But for the most part only females felt the intense attraction, just being near him. He was only nineteen, like me, but girls, even older ones, had been being unnaturally drawn to him for a long time, since his race grew up fast, maturing quickly. And he confirmed what I suspected—that his skills worked best when someone looked at him. Vin admitted he'd used them to get the other kids to leave me alone. To hide his unnatural abilities from everyone, he'd actually allowed Mike to punch him after the choking incident on the first day, so it would be appear his fists were his only defense. That'd been smart. Though I still wasn't happy Vin hadn't been more open with me from the beginning about our history together.

As the miles stretched on, Vin told a sad story. I'd lived with him and his father since I was nine, when my parents were murdered. My mom reached out to Vin's father for help when she realized she'd been discovered by the shadows—the Summum Malum—the darkness I acknowledged to Vin and Gabriel I'd seen for myself today. My mom knew she'd been discovered during a trip off our farm. She tried to keep her girls safe by staying away, hiding in a location Vin's father arranged. Only everything went wrong. Vin and his father arrived to find her dead, burned, and a hidden message she'd left. Two words. "Home." "Traitor." They raced to our farm, arriving in time to get me, Alanna, and Ellis to safety. They found my dad dead and strangely, burned too. My two youngest sisters missing.

I absorbed this, numb, still feeling so disconnected from my past. All I knew was that there was so much death in it, and the present. I changed the subject. "Where the hell was Cole last night?" I asked.

"It was just a tragic mix-up," Gabriel answered softly, all his anger at Vin gone after the exchange he'd just listened to. "It was all a mix-up." He tightened his grip on the steering wheel as he sped us closer to Meeker. His nails bit into his palms, as if his anger was now directed at himself. "When Rose heard I was back, she got the idea of you going to the dance—of us both going to the dance and I was so excited about being down from the mountain, nearly recovered, I encouraged her. Even away from the forest, in town, I should've realized the danger." I inhaled sharply, but didn't say anything, waiting for him to get to the part about Cole. "And I guess there was some sort of confusion… everyone thought Aaron was watching your place. Cole thought he was supposed to go home, to stay with me. See, Cameron was going to an after-dance party, spending the night with a group at Paige's. I would've told Cole to stay at Rose's, but he didn't think twice because he couldn't reach me, my cell was dead." He shook his head. "I'm so sorry."

I couldn't keep count of the number of times Gabriel said sorry during the drive back, for encouraging Gram to send me to the dance, for Gram being left alone, for not coming by himself. "Again, I'm so sorry, Cassie." Gabriel glanced at me in the rearview mirror. "When you ran away, I thought I'd give you space. I thought you might need time to process everything, the talk we had, the feelings we have." Gabriel's voice deepened on the last words. Vin shot him a sharp look. Gabriel looked directly back at him, challenging him without saying a word, not ceding an inch. But that look of guilt flashed across his face again and he refocused his attention on the road with a long sigh. "Of course, now you must think I abandoned you when you needed me most. But I swear I knew nothing about the fire till this morning. Later I learned Aaron had partied too hard, asked Cameron to help."

I shook my head at the Knight family's typical behavior.

"Ended up at Paige's too…"

Vin had called them incompetent. But that wasn't it. The bear members of the Knight family were just too trusting, too well-intentioned, for their own good. If Gabriel and Cole thought someone else was supposed to be at Gram's, they didn't worry. But I couldn't blame them, or even Aaron, who just seemed to want to be a normal kid. No one else was responsible for this. I was the one who should've left town long ago. Gram had been my responsibility.

I remained silent during the rest of Gabriel's apology, as did Vin.

"Zoe?" I asked.

"Cole picked her up from the shelter."

I sighed, grateful she was not back at the shelter, thinking she'd been abandoned. My mind numbed, my ears shutting off.

Gabriel's mouth kept moving in the rearview mirror. I caught a few more words, something about how Zoe and I could stay in one of their guestrooms.

Who would have ever thought I would sleep under the same roof as Cameron.

But things were different now. He'd even apologized—for

something—at the dance. He'd seemed so much nicer since that awful morning in the cave.

I turned away, thinking of Gram and Mike, and stared out the window.

Gabriel slowed to pull the SUV into the garage, and I jumped out, took a step to get steady on my feet, and ran up the Knights' porch. I burst into their foyer, ready to call out for Zoe, but she was already there, pacing awkwardly across the floor. The door swung wide, banging against the doorstop, and she looked up, scrambled on the hardwood, and raced over. She showered my hands with kisses, licking my fingers frantically.

I knelt and she kissed my face again and again. When we finally parted a few inches, she gave a low howl. She howled again, and excited yips rang from the back of the house.

B.B. and B.G. bounded from a hallway by the stairs, two black and grey balls of fluff floating over large white paws. They climbed all over me and Zoe, panting and yipping.

Cole appeared from the same spot, shifting uneasily. "They were in the shelter yard, curled up around Zoe. I couldn't leave them behind." He swallowed. "If it's okay, I thought I might call them Richie and Rosie."

I nodded, and swallowed too, trying to give him a reassuring smile.

I sat on the floor, surrounded by wiggly warmth, soft fur, and more licks. Soft yips from the pups. Quiet sighs from Zoe. One happy moment in this awful day. I actually started to feel hungry for the first time since dinner the day before.

Zoe suddenly stiffened and Vin strode into the back of the foyer, biting into a peach. He must've gotten the fruit in the kitchen, where the garage connects through. Peach juice ran down his chin. Before I could ask if he'd get me one, he slipped up the stairs. Gabriel hurried in devouring a turkey sandwich. Richie and Rosie sniffed the air, jumped off me and Zoe, and darted over to beg at his feet. Zoe hopwalked over too and he gave them each a small bit of meat. Zoe wobbled on her back leg. Gabriel gulped down the rest of the sandwich. "Cole, take the pups out." Cole corralled them, guiding them out the door, and Gabriel picked up Zoe, turned with purpose, and carried her up the stairs.

I followed and by the time we reached the top, where a landing separated a wing to one side of the house and matching one on the other, Zoe's eyes were half closed from being so tired. Gabriel strode down the left corridor and stopped by a door. "This is my room." He swayed forward and back on his feet, hesitating. He rocked Zoe against his chest. "You can come in if you want. Maybe we can just… be together?"

I dropped my gaze.

"I'll just"—his voice was raw with pain—"I'll just be a sec."

I waited outside, staring at my sandals. I didn't trust myself. Something in me wanted to run after him, bury myself in his arms, ask if he'd hold me for a few minutes or more, like that night in the tent. But I couldn't just "be together" with anyone. Especially Gabriel who created such frightening feelings in me, making me doubt the parts of me that trusted him, making me want to run towards him and run away from him at the same time. I forced my eyes to stay down, mentally tracing the orange plastic around my feet and not peek into his room.

He returned with a first aid kit, and without Zoe. "She was already half-asleep. I left her to nap."

"Thanks. She needs the rest. Last night was…" I couldn't finish my thought. I turned.

He stepped ahead of me, leading me silently back down the hall. Right past the stairs, he opened a door to a room in the other wing. Vin popped his head out from the door across from it.

"Hey," Gabriel said. "You're supposed to be down there." He pointed to a room at the end of the hall.

"Better if I'm closer. Safer." Vin gave him a tight smile, causing

Gabriel to grimace, and Vin's smile widened a fraction before he shut his door.

In my room, an antique chandelier hung from the middle of the ceiling, a delicate nightstand held a dainty lamp with a rose-patterned lampshade, and floral wallpaper decorated the walls. At the end of a huge bed, my trunk waited for me.

Gabriel saw me staring at it. "Cole picked it up."

I kept staring at my trunk and Gabriel set the kit on the white bedspread and left without another word.

Alone for the first time since my concrete cell, my shoulders slumped.

My throat swelled with all the emotions I was trying to keep down.

I swallowed and tried to regroup. I lifted my arms. The burns were already healing nicely. They didn't stop me from stripping off the horrible orange jumpsuit. I walked into my very own bathroom, with the largest shower I'd ever seen. The air conditioning blasted in my room. I still turned the shower to its coldest setting, the water both stinging and soothing the damaged skin, both shocking and calming my nerves. I stayed under the water a long time, letting some tension wash away.

I hopped out and opened up my trunk, the smell of smoke drifting out, quickly overpowering the faint scent of roses in the room. I grabbed a pair of full-length black leggings, a long-sleeved blue shirt, and my spike-heeled boots. I shut the lid, dressed, and bandaged up my burns with gauze from Gabriel's kit, then covered my good hand with a glove and my bandaged with a mitten, the only thing that would fit over it.

I quickly went back downstairs and searched the foyer for the way to the kitchen and the Knights' oversized garage. Hopefully, along with Zoe, the pups, and my things, Cole had brought Gram's VW back from town too. It was time to find Mike before exhaustion, grief, the police—or something worse—caught up with me again.

While the fire at Gram's might have had something to do with the mysterious shadows, like what happened at the hospital, would that really excuse what Mike had done? I wasn't sure. And I wasn't sure exactly what I was going to do about Mike, but had at least dressed to interrogate him.

"Cassie!" Cole smiled brightly as he rushed back in the front door. Richie and Rosie scampered after his heels. "You're looking so much better." He opened up his arms.

"No hugs!" I stepped back, lifting my covered hands.

"Sorry." Cole's face fell as he stopped mid-stride. "Forgot." His arms dropped to his side. "I meant to say before. I'm so sorry about last night." Cole's tone instantly changed from sunny to doom and gloom. "Not being there."

"It wasn't your fault." No matter what I thought about the Knights' over-trusting optimism spilling over into everything they did, I couldn't blame Cole.

"And I'm so, so sorry for Rose." Cole's voice wobbled.

"Yeah." I scooped up Rosie, cuddling her under my chin, hoping we could stop talking about Gram. Cole's eyes fell as he sniffled. Was he crying? I cleared my throat. I had to find Mike. Maybe Cole would at least help me get out of here? "Um, Cole—"

"Cyndra." Vin's melodic voice floated over us. He strode down the wide staircase in his usual perfect attire. Damp black hair fell stylishly across his forehead. "It's good to see you out of that orange monstrosity." He paused halfway down, a picture of unhurried elegance, and looked me over from head to toe. His eyes narrowed in on Rosie in my arms, then surveyed my going-out attire and narrowed further. "I got cleaned up too. Thought I'd better find you."

"Why?"

"I realized our talk earlier might not have been enough to convince you to stay put."

"Stop." I twisted my head away, dropping my gaze to the floor. Rosie whimpered and I set her down.

"I'll just, um, go to the kitchen," Cole mumbled and backed away.

Richie and Rosie each gave a frightened yip towards Vin and dashed after Cole.

"Cyndra, please." Vin descended the bottom steps. I backed up, bumping into the large stone sculpture. "I don't want to compel you, but you need to stay put until we figure out why you weren't able to take the relic's powers. I'm hoping what you gain from it will help stabilize your own abilities. Maybe you'll be able to touch people again."

I glanced up. "Really?"

"Really." He stopped a few feet away. "Bernard and I talked, and while he's not convinced of it, I think it's because you need your guidestone for the relic to release everything to you. Then, along with a whole bunch of other good things, you can touch people again."

"Guidestone?"

"Your matching stone. You wore it around your neck. My father always thought the guidestones were simply that—to bind you with and then guide you and your sisters to the relic they are bound to themselves—so I hadn't been worried about it before. But it seems they're more than that."

"OK, good. But I don't understand how or why I had a guidestone in the first place? Was it like a family heirloom or something?"

"No. The guidestones weren't your family's. There are five, and they were guarded by my family. We were the keepers of the guidestones like the bears are the keepers of the fire relic. You and your sisters were each given a guidestone because my father received a sign."

"A sign?" I gave the word a ghostly "woo" quality and snorted.

He pulled a "Really, sassy pants?" face and powered on, "My family was given a scroll with the guidestones. We're talking ancient history here, but recent generations of my family believed the creators of the relics and the guidestones could communicate with us through this scroll. But maybe they could only use it once because it had always stayed blank. Until your youngest sister was born. Words appeared, telling my father that chaos and darkness were coming.

The Malum's evil could no longer be contained. It was time to risk utilizing the relics. And a powerful alt woman had just given birth to her fifth daughter. Those sisters would be perfect candidates for bonding with the relics. It was an opportunity that alts hadn't seen for centuries. With the scroll's guidance, my father tracked down your parents, and he says the moment he saw you, he just knew. Even as toddlers, you guys seemed to be connecting with the relics. You each had different hair colors, as if to match your elements."

I blinked at him a minute while all that info rattled around my skull. But, hey, weirder things had already happened. Who was I to doubt anybody's wild stories these days? I puffed my cheeks and blew out an exhale. "Okay, so, how do we find my guidestone?" Right now, I had to focus on what I could control and nothing larger.

"Based on when Bernard said it went missing, I'm guessing it was a prank. Maybe one of the kids at school. I'll work on it. And in the meantime, Bernard will continue to guard the relic, while the rest of us stick together. Here."

I shifted, unease making me indecisive. "I'd certainly like my locket back, and I know there's something going on with me and the stone in the mountain." Putting out a fire, twice in the last two days, seemed to prove that. "But I have somewhere to be." I pressed against the sculpture's base, moving around it.

"I saw what you did with that fire today. It wasn't the sprinklers that put it out."

Part way around the sculpture, I paused.

"And I suspect you were the one who put out the fire last night?"

I gave a small nod.

"Your abilities." Vin inched toward me. "They're growing. Touching the relic probably brought it on. And who knows what you'll be able to do when you finally have all its powers." He sniffed, probably taking in the bitter odor that was rising from my chest, which I was trying to ignore, and grimaced. "Goodness, we'll need to get you new clothes." He took a breath and stepped in close, leaning in. "But you shouldn't tell anyone what you can do."

"Not even the Knights? Not even Gabriel?" I looked into Vin's warm hazel eyes. Why wasn't I moving away?

"Not anyone." He didn't smile, not a bit, as if he was hoping he could trust me to do as he asked, without compelling me. "Gabriel and I might have our differences, but it's not that I distrust him. I just think the fewer people who know, the safer you'll be. And anything you need, anywhere you need to go, I can help with it. But you have to let me help. Because now we need to be more careful than ever."

"Why now? Why not before?" Why didn't I feel trapped? With Vin so close in front of me, the stone at my back, with him telling me I had to let him help me. Strangely, I didn't feel trapped a bit. Now that I knew for sure about Vin's unnatural appeal, I sensed myself resisting it. But rather than thinking of him like most anyone else who got close to me, I actually felt… at ease.

"It's clear the secret's out about you." Vin took a small step back, his smooth brow puckering as he frowned. "I don't know how the Summum Malum found out, based on what one of the old bears—I think Bernard's grandfather—said. But somehow, it seems quite recently, the Summum Malum discovered you're here."

"Well, your dad's scroll did say they're getting stronger, right?" I asked, chewing the inside of my cheek.

Vin nodded. "Yes, and I think we've seen the proof for ourselves. The fires last night and today, just the first attempts."

"But last night, the fire wasn't set by anyone weird-looking. It was Mike, from school."

"I know. Someone like Mike can so easily become a tool of the Summum Malum. They put him up to it. A clumsy attempt to get to you."

I shivered. "Why didn't you tell me about them before?"

"It wasn't safe. At home, we'd talk about them, but my father was assured of our isolation there. Here, as soon as I found you, I realized the Knights had finally come across your connection to them, were watching out for you. I hoped the Knights would take care of explaining things, transferring the relic's powers to you. So we could get the hell out of here." Vin paused, his frown deepening. "But Gabriel and his family seem a bit… well, clearly their race was not chosen as one of the five relic guardians because of their cunning or guile." He sighed. I couldn't say I agreed. Yes, Gabriel and the bear members of his family didn't seem conniving, but they seemed primal, powerful and wild, innocent and trusting of their instincts, like animals often were, maybe in a way Vin or I couldn't understand. "Anyway, today Bernard's grandfather convinced me we can talk a bit more openly because the Fire relic's powers have developed fully with you here—expanding the range of protection it provides, blinding the Summum Malum to most of what's happening near Meeker. Whether he's right or not, we can at least say their name. Because the Summum Malum know you're here."

I tensed, recalling the darkness I'd seen hours ago. "Hold on," I protested. While there was a lot I didn't know, we'd skipped over the most important part. "How exactly did they get Mike to do anything? They compel people—like you?"

"No, no. It's often said the Summum Malum can compel humans. But that's not the right word."

"What is the right word?" Was Mike responsible for what happened or not?

"Influence. Influencing humans is one of the few ways they're able to reach out. They've been able to do it for as long as they've been trapped, still tied to this world. As revenants. Spirits is the word humans might use. As revenants—spirits—they influence humans by planting suggestions or ideas in someone's mind. It is usually the sickest, most perverse minds, those people who seem to find pleasure in doing wrong, who most consistently follow through on their prompts. The Malum's evil has always been at work in this world, and if that scroll and my dad's intel from his alt contacts are right, that evil will only continue to grow in unimaginable ways. I'm not sure how they're doing it—tapping into the old-world magic said to still exist in parts of this world and especially in the afterlife or somehow stealing powers of the alts trapped in the afterlife with them would be my guesses. But no matter the method, influencing Mike was nothing."

OK, scary stuff. And maybe the fire hadn't been Mike's idea to begin with. But he'd gone along with it just fine. "Mike is certainly sick, that's for sure."

Vin nodded. "I ran into him at your place when I got back, admiring his work, and it was easy enough to figure out what happened. And also, he is one messed-up guy. I want you to stay away from him."

"But not after what he did to Gram."

"Mike will have to answer for his crimes."

"But there's a girl…" I hesitated, inching my way to the side until I was free of the stone behind me, finally creating some distance from Vin.

"I've already made sure he'll leave her alone." His hands tightened into fists at his sides. I opened my mouth to speak, but he rushed on. "And I'll deal with Mike from here on." He released his hands, smoothing them down his slacks, and gave a determined smile.

I quickly turned, in case the effects of that magical smile spilled over to me.

"Don't worry, I've got this," Vin said, more to himself.

Zoe's bark echoed from upstairs. I circled back to the stairs, climbing, calling for her. Several moments of silence. Then Gabriel's voice floated down from his bedroom, "Zoe-girl, you should go."

She barked louder, clearly wanting him to come too.

I called for her again, trying not to be jealous of her and Gabriel's bond. And Zoe must've had a tough time after the fire. All the more reason we should both get outside on a nice day. Zoe could use the distraction of sniffing all the scents in the grass. I could use the quiet to clear my head.

Maybe, if my mind was clear enough, I could figure out if Vin had somehow manipulated or compelled me to walk away from a confrontation with Mike, or if I'd decided of my own volition to do as Vin asked.

I stumbled on a step near the top, reaching for the banister. Oh God. I already knew the answer.

As impossible as it seemed, I'd just accepted Vin's help without questioning his motives, or his intentions. And I'd done it despite facing my past with Vin and knowing everything he'd done since arriving in Meeker.

I reached the landing, stopping in a pool of dim light streaming in from a domed skylight, and Vin hurried past me, striding down the corridor and slipping into a room right across from mine, like he had things to do and think about, and trusted me not to go after Mike now. When Zoe arrived, Gabriel trailed behind her. She gave a yip, and I ruffled the fur behind her ears. I helped her down, and we headed out toward the river, Gabriel following.

We wandered past the patio's overgrown rose bushes—only a few blooms hanging on into fall—and a butterfly leapt off a bloom. Zoe chased it, trying to sniff it with her nose.

"Zoe-bug." I laughed.

She let the butterfly be, glancing back at me.

A look of peaceful contentment passed between us. A silent understanding. An unspoken friendship.

And, oh God, Vin incited similar feelings inside me.

Despite everything Vin had done—or maybe because of it—I believed in Vin. And I believed in our friendship. Past, and present. Zoe and I kept strolling along the lawn, toward the water, Gabriel following us, but I knew. I already knew.

Vin's vision from our past made it so clear. I wasn't alone before. I used to have him as a friend, and he insisted I still did. If that meant staying at the Knights' home with Vin, because Vin thought it best, I'd give it a try. And if that meant letting Vin have the first crack at Mike, I'd do that too. I'd even keep what I could do with fire to myself. I wouldn't tell the Knights like Vin had asked. Because Gram said I needed to open up—to start believing in people when my instincts told me it was right—and my instincts told me I believed in Vin, despite the confusing feelings he could create inside me, which would always complicate things with him.

In fact, I believed in Vin enough to have instantly felt at ease when he got near, even knowing what he was capable of.

Because Vin would never hurt me.

I glanced back at Gabriel, his shoulders tense, his face pensive. Gabriel would never hurt me, not intentionally, either.

But with Vin, it was more than that. Not only would Vin never hurt me, it was the complete opposite. Vin would be the one to help free me from Mike's hands, like he had that first day at school, or anyone else's, and he'd do it a thousand times over if I needed him to. And if Vin thought I was in danger, he'd continue to watch out for me. Unlike the Knights, he'd do it in a way that didn't make me feel smothered or useless, incapable or incompetent.

I believed in Vin.

I trusted Vin.

In spite of everything I'd said to Gabriel about how I always kept my guard up, I'd done the unthinkable. I'd turned my back. I'd allowed Vin to sneak under my defenses.

I'd been bitten.

Oh please. Please don't let this blow up in my face.

27
CHANGE IS THE ONLY CONSTANT

L ATE THAT NIGHT, I PACED MY ROOM. MY EYELIDS BLINKED shut, I stubbed my toe, and fell on something hard. My trunk. I pushed myself up and opened it. The smell of smoke tinged with cedar rose up, stinging my nose worse than the molasses cookies I'd burnt to a crisp when Gram was recuperating from that incident at Betty's (*don't think about all the sacrifices Gram made, don't think about why she died, don't cry*). I held my breath, grabbed my black knitted scarf and cross-country hoodie, and dropped the lid before the smell filled the room. I shook out the scarf, trying to rid it of the odor, folded it in half, and wrapped its thickness around my mouth, tying the ends behind my head. I slipped on the hoodie, flipping up the hood against the blast of air conditioning from the ceiling, and collapsed onto the large bed. I curled around Zoe, sharing her warmth, and stopped fighting sleep.

I woke within hours to my screams. The scarf muffled the noise. My shaking shook the bed. Zoe woke and whimpered. I lay helpless, burning patches of skin spreading along my arms and chest, reaching deeper into my skin and farther down my chest than ever before.

Zoe trembled with me.

"Zoe-bug, it's okay," I murmured. But it wasn't. And not just because the pain kept getting worse. Even if I would've called out for her, Gram wasn't there, just steps away, to tell me everything would be all right. It didn't matter that I wouldn't have believed her, I just needed to know she was there.

I finally got up to turn on the chandelier. The tiny bulbs pulsed gently, casting soft light on the walls. I bandaged up the burns, climbed back into bed, and petted Zoe, staying awake till morning, imagining Gram in a place just like this. A light, peaceful place. If she really was in a better place, like Richard said.

I pulled on a loose-fitting t-shirt over my leggings—no bra—and was the first in the kitchen, sipping on coffee when Cole entered, yawning. I forced myself to nibble on berries while he wolfed down a bowl of Cheerios. "Want to go out?" He dropped his bowl and spoon in the sink with a clatter.

"Sure." I left my half-eaten fruit.

We walked Zoe, Richie, and Rosie to the river. Halfway there, Vin caught up with us. When we got back from walking several miles along the river, he made us an elaborate salad of baby greens, green beans, eggs, tomatoes, tuna, and olives. He insisted I finish my plate. Aaron and I helped Cole with his homeschooling that afternoon. Cameron made lasagna that evening, using a recipe Lillian had taught him, and everyone sat down in the dining room to eat. Gabriel took the farthest seat from me, at the other head of the table, and tucked into his food with shoulders hunched over his plate. Richie and Rosie, on the other hand, rushed my chair, their paws on my thighs and their noses wiggling closer and closer to my plate until Zoe let out a sharp bark that startled them back onto all fours. She was already taking them under her wing, keeping them out of trouble. They still swiped the spatula Cole dropped a few minutes later, licking off the cheese, but they were too cute to reprimand.

After dinner, Gabriel showed me a door hidden in a panel in the kitchen. He slid part of it away to reveal a keypad, entered an eight-digit code, and backed up as it beeped. The door sprung open. "Only my family knows the code. Now you. The elders say it's safe to talk, so—1390 1771. Can you remember it?"

I repeated the numbers.

"It's easy for us to remember. The year we fled the Carpathian Mountains in Romania when women from alternate race groups were being hunted, followed by the year my great-grandmother and Cameron's great-grandmother were murdered."

I gasped. Of course they'd remember those dates. And they seemed to like reminders of what they were fighting for. Like the spot in their lawn where the remains of the fire still stood.

"Cameron's great-grandfather died in the attack in 1771 too. My great-grandfather got what was left of the family to move into the wilderness of Poland, not far from where his mom's family was from, to raise what kids were left—my dad's dad, CJ's dad, Richard's dad, Cousins Everett and Otto, and Uncle Gus. Later, after the kids grew and the next generation was born, they immigrated to the U.S. Unfortunately, they were discovered on the journey. Lost my grandmother and the other women and girls." Gabriel looked down at his large hands. "With only men left, they roamed around, discovered Spring Cave, settled here." His hands pressed into his sides, his jaw quivered, seeming to hold in a storm of emotions.

My mouth opened and closed, struggling to form the right words. My body swayed forward and back, wanting to move closer to him, wanting to comfort him. I gripped the side of the door. "That's all awful."

"So awful. Even after they settled into a quiet life here, in case part of the family was discovered, some of the men pretended not to be related. Like Richard. Rose's husband." He looked back up, his blue eyes abnormally lackluster. He didn't even try to look into mine. "Eventually my great-grandfather built this house. We lived a normal life. Mostly." He swallowed hard. "Well, we tried."

I nodded, taking in this bit of history. He stepped around the door and disappeared down a set of narrow stairs. I followed. "Our safe room." He moved to the corner of the concrete basement and watched me circle around a row of bunkbeds, shelves of freeze-dried food, medical supplies, bottled water, water purification tablets, and toilet paper, and a desk set up with monitors and panels with switches and buttons. I stopped in front of a wall of screens, flashing images from throughout the house and grounds.

He stepped to the side of the desk, leaving several feet between us. "Come here if the alarms go off. Or if you feel threatened at all. The house ventilation system emits a gas knocking anyone out upstairs." He pointed to the gas switch and directions next to it and moved to the far side of the room while I read them.

He shifted uneasily as he watched me. As if unsure of what I might do or say next. Did he think I was upset at him?

I followed him back up and Cameron passed by us, heading into the dining room after Cole, Aaron, and Vin with bowls of ice cream in each hand. "I've got yours." He nodded at me.

I turned to Gabriel. "Join us."

"I have to rest. Um, get ready for watch later tonight." He turned and escaped to his room.

A while later, when I retreated to my own room after ice cream, a knock came on my door. "Hey." Gabriel stepped inside the door frame. It was the closest he'd been in days. My heart beat faster. My throat constricted. He held up the sweater Gram had knitted for me, the one I'd left behind in the cave. "I thought you'd want this back."

I reached for it, my hand inches from his.

He quickly dropped his arm. My shoulders fell and the sweater dangled loosely at my side. Zoe hopped over from a blanket on the floor, burrowing her snout into it. She sniffed it, whined softly, and I set it on the dresser nearby.

"And this," he said, reaching into his jean's pocket. He pulled out a strip of white satin, decorated with small pearls. "I'm sorry, so sorry," he mumbled, pushing it toward me. "I hadn't been able to give it back before. I can't image what you think of me. For encouraging Rose to send you to the dance, for her being left alone, for not being there after the fire." He did think I was upset with him.

"What happened—it's not your fault. Don't be hard on yourself." I cleared my throat. I accepted the soft satin. Gram's glove. I lifted it to my cheek. A faint lavender scent tickled my nose. I inhaled deeply, rubbing it against the side of my face. My chin trembled.

Gabriel's eyes widened. He looked away. "I've gotta head out. Goodnight, Cassie." His heavy boots thudded as he fled from my room on the hardwood. The thudding faded as he reached the paisley hallway runner and dashed down the stairs.

I stared out into the empty corridor, glimpsing Vin's door cracked open across from mine, and I breathed in the scent again. I knelt to my trunk and slipped the glove into a plastic sleeve my last store-bought pair had come in. Maybe it would help keep the scent from fading away to nothing.

I found Gabriel's sister's diary tucked under clothes at the bottom. I'd almost forgotten about it. My fingertips brushed over the blackened pages, their rough, fragile, edges. So much life had been destroyed in the pursuit of some sort of power. Dark forces, literally, seemingly willing to destroy anyone and anything. For the relic? For the power it was supposed to contain? For what purpose, ultimately? For the sheer delight in doing evil? There was more to it than that. I didn't understand everything, but if I could take some of that power away, like everyone claimed I could, I'd do whatever I had to in order to do it.

I wanted Gabriel to know that.

I couldn't fight sleep again. Again, the scarf muffled my screams. The bed shook more violently. I needed Gram. Oh God, I needed Gram. More tears escaped.

The next morning, I knocked on Gabriel's bedroom door, holding his sister's notebook. The door swung open and my breath caught at the sight. He wore only a pair of boxers. The creases of his face were heavy with exhaustion. I risked a peek around his bare chest. The covers on his bed—the largest bed I'd ever seen—were pulled back, like he'd been about to crawl in.

"Cassie." He sounded startled, his eyes wide in surprise.

I held out the notebook. "I know Gram hasn't been the only one who's been lost because of all this." My hand shook. "I'm truly sorry about your mom and sister. Especially if me coming here led to what happened."

"Don't be hard on yourself." He inched closer. "It's not your fault either." He accepted the notebook, running a hand over the cover. His jaw muscle twitched, and he stared at the burned edges. "She wouldn't want you to feel guilty. She would have liked you—called you a kindred spirit or something. Her ability hurt her too." He looked up at my questioning stare. "Not the shifting. The one she got from our mom. Mom could only sense alternates' emotions. But in alternates and humans, I sense good, Cole senses all emotion, but Sarah, she only sensed people's fear. It took a toll, especially in this paranoid family." His smile didn't reach his eyes. "If she were here, she'd plead with us both to think about something happier." He thumbed through the pages and was quickly lost in her words.

I turned for the door but paused with my hand on the knob. "She seemed like a great kid. Kind, like you." I cleared my throat. "And for what it's worth, from what I read in there, you made her feel safer than anything or anyone else."

He looked up at me, eyes glossy, and I fled to find Vin in his room. He'd promised to take me into town so I could get Gram's affairs in order. I needed his ability, what with being an escaped mental patient and all. I hadn't known Gram had written a will, or a new one anyway, but she had. I'd gotten a voicemail summoning me to her lawyer's office for the reading. The message had sounded stiff, rehearsed, and I'd told Vin I had a feeling it was some sort of ploy. Sure enough, when we arrived, a police officer paced the lobby. Vin saw him first, through the windows framing the front door, and stopped me by grabbing my coat sleeve.

"I'll take care of it," he said. "Just stick close."

When Vin opened the door, the cop rushed forward, but Vin hit him with a dazzling grin, slowing his footsteps.

"We're here to read her grandmother's will," Vin said, his hand resting on my back. "She's been invited. She's entitled to be here. You can let us upstairs."

"Oh, uh, of course," the cop said, stepping aside.

"No need to stick around," Vin told the officer, smiling over his shoulder.

Stomach fluttering from the residual effects of his charm, I followed him to the lawyer's office, where he flashed his pearly whites again to get the bird-like, elderly gentleman to read the will without a hitch. Gram had named me executor, which would make things easier. The less important things, the material things.

When we left, the policeman was nowhere in sight, and I breathed easier.

"Well, that was interesting," I said.

"Too close for comfort is what that was. We have to clear your name, and soon." When he looked over at me, his expression softened. "I'll bring you into town again tomorrow to make the funeral arrangements."

"Thanks. For everything."

Back at the Knights' house, I settled into the living room to read a book, feeling more at ease than I had in a while. I wouldn't have expected it, but besides Zoe, the one thing keeping me going was being surrounded by a makeshift family. Over the next few days, Cole and I fell into a routine, walking the dogs each morning. Aaron and I helped him with his homeschooling each afternoon. Cameron made sure everyone who was in the house—usually everyone but Gabriel—sat down for dinner, preparing more meals Lillian had taught him. Bernard even took Cameron up on his offer to help with the patrols.

Cameron went out each morning with one of the elder bears, Cousin Everett, who was his great uncle and in human form, looked like him too.

Though Gabriel took most of the shifts, especially at night. He even took to surveying me from a distance when he was technically "off duty," though many times I was already protected by Vin or Cole. I was rarely alone anymore, but the person by my side most often, helping to sort through all my most pressing problems, was Vin.

At first, I was annoyed Vin handled everything so easily. On our second town outing, I almost protested I could take care of myself. But Vin wasn't trying to interfere. He was just showing me what friends do. Friends help. Friends rely on each other to be there. Friends give of themselves, and don't expect anything but friendship in return.

It rendered me speechless—I hadn't yet told Vin how much his presence meant to me—but there it was. Together we saw to all Gram's affairs, and he used his gift to keep the school and the police force off my back.

Gram would be laid to rest in the cemetery next to Richard, wearing her special occasion skirt, her fanciest blouse, and her wedding ring around her neck. I picked out a small marker. Vin and I agreed just to inscribe her name on it, not any dates drawing attention to how old she really was. But I promised myself someday I'd get a larger stone—like Richard's—and find the perfect words for it. With what little money was left, I set some aside for the college fund Gram said in her will she wanted me to start. Adding to it what money was in my trunk in the savings envelopes I'd labeled Gram and Future. It was what Gram would've wanted me to do. Then I made a donation in Bethany's name to a charity that assisted child burn survivors.

Vin wanted to buy me a cell, but Aaron had given mine back that morning, handing it to me with unfocused eyes, cast down, staring out over his nose. He'd looked so hawk-like and sad, I'd given his arm an impulsive squeeze. So instead of a cell, Vin insisted on paying for new clothes for me, neither of us able to stand the odor lingering in the fabric even after several washings. Except for the scarf Gram had knitted for me, two pairs of gloves, and the hoodie Coach had given me, I said goodbye to everything, including my work shirts. "You're not going there again," Vin grumbled. He picked out my new clothes at a boutique in town, not even looking at the price tags of the dresses and pretty shoes he grabbed, or flinching at the number of shirts and leggings I threw in. I barely had time to thank him before he was off to run another "errand."

The next morning Mike turned himself in to the police.

Vin, Aaron, and I went to the police station. Vin made me wait by his car with Aaron, but Vin compelled the police to allow him into the interrogation room to make sure Mike gave a full confession.

Left behind, Aaron slouched on the hood of Vin's car, eyes cast down over his sharp nose, staring at the Bulldog in the center of his shirt. I kicked at the pavement. "So, I'm sorry you haven't been able to go to school as much, with the patrol shifts."

"Yeah. I've made most practices. So it's okay." He shrugged.

"And I'm sorry for not being able to return your laptop."

"Don't worry about it." His spine straightened. "I've been meaning to talk to you. I wanted to apologize for the night of the fire." He shifted on the hood. "All the confusion. It shouldn't have happened." His hand tapped on the hood, a staccato sound. He looked down again, unable to meet my gaze. "She deserved better."

"I know." I cleared my throat.

Silence buzzed between us, filled with everything we weren't saying: about Gram, that night, her death. I paced around the car, trying to ignore it. Finally, Vin exited the station, smiling. He gritted his teeth, forcing his cheeks to relax as he approached. "Mike confessed everything." The start of a smile formed. "Not just setting the fire, but the abuse of his young stepsister, all the bullying at school. All of it."

Aaron jumped off the hood. "That's great. What did he say?"

I looked Vin in the eye. "What did he say about the fire? About Gram."

"Cyndra..."

"Please."

"He said the idea came to him in a daydream. And sounded... well, he said it sounded fun."

Vin winced at the sight of the emotions on my face that word set off. "But don't worry. He didn't leave out anything that might reduce his sentence. He admitted to hearing noises of movement in the cottage, even as he doused one side with gasoline and wiped the bottle for prints. But told the police he'd set the fire anyway. Because he knew who lived there."

Vin didn't have to say it.

Me.

My eyes clouded and I crammed myself back into the Porsche's almost non-existent back seat. Aaron and Vin slid into the front. Vin sped us out of the parking lot.

"Tell me what Mike said about me." I blinked hard.

"Cyndra."

I ignored the note of warning in Vin's voice. "Tell me what he said about me. How he described me to the police."

"He said you're a—listen." Vin tightened his grip on the gear shift. "Apparently Mike hadn't liked how you'd warned the school counselor about him and started standing up for yourself and others at school. No surprise."

If there was no surprise, I could guess how Mike had described me to the officers. *Bitch.* The awful word rang in my head as we sped out of town. I bet Mike had called me a bitch. It wouldn't have surprised me if he had, and it seemed silly to even think about it with everything I knew of human nature, but I wished I lived in a world where that word didn't exist.

Vin glanced back at me in the rearview mirror. "There's more. I wasn't prepared for it, all of his confession. He told the cops he didn't act alone that night. Someone knew his plans. Supplied him with the gasoline. He said it was Cameron."

I gasped.

"Cameron?" Aaron jerked around in his seat to face Vin.

"I didn't believe it. I still don't believe it. So I didn't mention it right off. But apparently Cameron emailed an anonymous note to the police. They traced it to his IP address. Accusing Cyndra of starting the fire. He sent it that very night. It helped build their case against her." Vin pulled something out of his shirt pocket and reached back, keeping the other hand on the steering wheel.

He handed me a folded piece of paper. My hand shook, fluttering the paper, as I tried to calm my nerves and prepare to see what Cameron had to say inside.

28

BETRAYAL

I SAT UP IN THE BACK SEAT, UNFOLDED THE PAPER, AND READ the words out loud:

Meeker Police Department:

In investigating who set the fire that took the life of Anna Rose Merritt tonight, you need to question her ward, Cassandra Merritt.

Cassandra appeared at the school dance earlier wearing a vintage dress, gloves, and bracelet, almost certainly taken from her guardian. She's never worn such fancy things. In fact, Cassandra's a loner, never attending social events. But strangely, tonight, she came to one. Her cheeks were flushed. She made an embarrassing play for the attention of a boy, pulling him outside. It was the eldest son of the wealthy Knight family. When his date appeared, she fled. This could not have been more than a few minutes before the fire.

I suspect she may have returned home and taken her frustrations out on her guardian or set the fire in a psychotic break. Everyone knows her history. She keeps claiming her skin feels like it's on fire. You'll be able to verify what happened at the dance from witnesses.

This is all I know. Please follow up on it. Holding the person responsible for the death of a beloved community member is at stake. Thank you.

Sincerely,
Citizen of Meeker

"Cameron wrote that? I don't believe it either!" Aaron postured in the passenger seat, leaning his large body closer to Vin.

"It's true. Or at least Mike says it is." A wild turkey darted out of a bush and onto the road ahead of us. Vin braked sharply, swerving, and jerked us to a stop. He hit the emergency lights button and turned to me with a frown. "Cameron was supposed to have been his alibi witness too."

"But why would Cameron do all this? Be involved?" Blood drained from my face, my whole body turning cold, numb.

The turkey strode back into the bush, and Vin turned off his emergency lights and sped up again. "The Summum Malum make strange bedfellows."

"Let's not jump to conclusions." Aaron's voice was hard but contained now. "Not till we get home."

"I'm not jumping to conclusions." Vin focused on the road, pushing the Porsche faster. "I think it's hard to believe too. I interrogated Mike pretty well after the fire. He didn't mention Cameron. But we'll have to get back quickly if we're going to hear what Cameron has to say. The police believed Mike. And I didn't do anything to deter them. They're coming to pick up Cameron for questioning."

Vin didn't waste time parking his Porsche in its usual spot near the Knights' garage. Instead, he left it by the porch and we burst through the front door.

Gabriel rushed down the stairs to meet us. "Cameron's gone!"

"What?" I slid to a stop. Aaron and Vin fell silent to either side of me, the sounds of our breath unnaturally loud in the huge foyer.

"He left a note." Gabriel handed it to me.

Vin and Aaron read over my shoulders.

Cassie,
I can't apologize enough for what I did. There is no excuse.
I just don't belong here.
But things will be better now. I'm leaving.
~Cameron

"I'm calling my dad." Gabriel stuffed his hand into his jeans pocket for his cell. "Dad, you've got to come quick." He spoke in clipped words, nothing specific, just confirming Bernard would hurry down from the mountain. "Yes, yes, Cole should stay out patrolling with one of the elders."

Feeling even more numb than I had in the car, I went in search of Zoe, Richie, and Rosie. I heard Vin compelling the police to leave as I found them in the living room next to the huge fireplace, curled up together in one of the many extra-large dog beds Cole had bought and scattered around the house. Zoe stirred first, reluctantly followed by the other two. Richie picked up a ball, and all three ambled out to join us. Aaron and Vin paced in circles around the foyer, lapping the sculpture, their footsteps striking the hardwood harshly in the silence. Gabriel bounced the ball for Richie and Rosie. I sat on the bottom stair and scratched Zoe's favorite spot behind her ear.

Bernard made good time. The sound of the back patio door whooshing open broke the silence. He rushed in, hunched and out of breath, his beard grey and scraggly, eyes bloodshot, deep grooves replacing wrinkles that had been barely noticeable weeks before.

Vin spoke first, explaining about Mike's confession and handing over both notes.

Bernard read them quickly. "Cameron couldn't have been involved with the fire. With Rose." He handed the papers back to Vin and rubbed at his temples. "It's simply not possible." He rubbed harder. "I doubt he had anything to do with that email." His hands fell. "But even if he did, it doesn't prove a thing. What I don't understand is this note. It's his handwriting. But what does it mean? Why did he leave?"

Gabriel went to his dad, appearing so much taller than him today, and placed a hand on his shoulder. "And more than that, where could he have gone?"

"Cameron does have some distant family." Bernard seemed to be talking to himself. "I'll send Cousin Everett to track him down. Don't worry. Whatever this is, Cameron would never betray us.

Everything is okay." His weary look said otherwise. "Everything has been quiet at the cave."

"Dad, maybe you should take a break. Eat something."

Bernard nodded. Aaron excused himself to work out in the Knights' gym on the third floor, and the rest of us moved to the kitchen. Gabriel pulled out a casserole dish from the fridge, filled with leftover lasagna Cameron had cooked. He heated up servings for himself and his dad while Vin threw together a salad. Vin and I picked at the lettuce, tomatoes, and cucumbers as Bernard and Gabriel inhaled their pasta. Bernard scraped his bowl clean and rushed off for the mountain. Gabriel left to check in with Cole. Vin and I cleaned up the dishes then wandered across the Knights' lawn, down toward the river, Zoe watching Vin with cautious eyes, but following us regardless of her faint distrust. Richie and Rosie followed her without question, but like two rambunctious children became distracted, chasing each other, bounding around her in circles.

"There's something I didn't tell the others." Vin stopped, his leather shoes sinking into the grass. "Mike told the cops that the day before the fire, someone had whispered in his ear that you'd recorded him in his stepsister's room weeks ago." His hands clenched at his sides, his expression turning stormy. "Mike claimed he couldn't remember who told him, but he knows you were responsible for the investigation the police had started, for his parents being notified, and for him being interrogated the week before."

"Well, at least the police didn't ignore my video," I said slowly. But how had Mike or anyone else connected it back to me?

Gabriel approached and we fell silent. "You guys were talking about Cameron?" Gabriel looked between us.

"Yeah, sort of." I flushed.

"Oh." Gabriel slipped his hands into his jean pockets. "Well, I'd better get a nap in, before overnight watch."

I couldn't sleep that night. Didn't want to sleep. I knocked on Vin's door. "It's me. Cyndra." The name rolled off my tongue with surprising ease.

"Come in." Vin's voice was smoother and warmer than it had ever been.

His guestroom was dark where mine was light. Somber-toned oil paintings hung on the walls, heavy curtains falling to the floor in shades of deep red. He wore loose pajama bottoms and nothing else, sitting on the bed, propped up by pillows against the headboard, a book in his hands. I walked inside quietly, my bare feet sinking into a plush rug, so soft, it was like I was walking across my old pillow. He dropped the book to his lap.

"Got a minute?" I traced my finger along the carved shapes of the mahogany four-poster bedframe. His chest was lightly muscled, almost no hair, just an expanse of what looked to be silky skin.

I forced my eyes to the book. Before I could make out the title, he tucked it under the edge of his pillow. "I always have a minute for you." He scooted over and motioned for me to sit down on the maroon duvet covering.

I did, relaxing on his bed, fighting the urge to close my eyes. "So, how do you think Mike found out about the video?" I yawned.

"The Summum Malum must have given Mike the idea you were responsible."

"But why?" My throat swelled with another yawn and I covered my mouth.

"They hoped it would fuel his desire to start the fire." His hardened expression slowly softened as he yawned too. He slid his legs under the maroon duvet cover, looking ready to call it a night.

But I forced myself to keep interrogating him because that wasn't a good enough answer for me. Vin couldn't explain how the Summum Malum had known about the video or gotten to Mike at all, since Gabriel's great-grandfather kept insisting that the powers of the relic extended for miles, keeping them well away from Meeker. Vin finally pulled the cover higher and fell asleep, and I slipped out of the room.

Cameron really must have been involved, because when I walked Zoe to the river the next morning and stopped to question

Gabriel who had trailed behind us on his patrol, he admitted Cameron had been there with the rest of the Knights when he'd told everyone what a "good person" I was, mentioning the video as proof, and to watch out for Mike.

I reminded myself I shouldn't jump to conclusions though, not until we tracked Cameron down. But how else could the Summum Malum have learned about the video, if they could only send people in but couldn't come near themselves? And everyone they sent, all thuggish-looking humans, Vin easily spotted and compelled to return to whatever hell-hole they'd come from.

One silver lining amid all the craziness came in the form of Betty, of all people. I received a handwritten invitation to a memorial service Gram's old friends had organized for her at the library. More surprising, it began with an apology and ended with, "Now that that monster has been caught, we want to move forward with a celebration of Rose's life, and I would love for you to join us." I knew I needed to go.

The day of the service, I wore one of the outfits Vin had bought me, a violet wrap-around dress with long sleeves and matching ballet flats. Vin and I walked side by side into the library and slid into the last row of folding chairs, peering over heads and around people still standing as Betty gripped the edges of a podium up front. "Welcome, everyone. Thanks for coming. You have a few more minutes to get settled."

Everyone found seats. A few people chatted in hushed voices. Sprinkled among Gram's older girlfriends were Dr. G, his sister, Mia, Mia's siblings, Coach, Officer Fry, Mrs. Merkle, the retired owner of the bakery, the ladies from the craft store, the organizers of the veterans' benefits, and so many more people from town, filling the room.

Betty cleared her throat, a harsh sound through the microphone, and the room quieted. She took a deep breath. "When I first met her, I thought that to Rose, Richard meant everything." She drank in air through her thin lips, as if she couldn't get enough. "He'd died, but she still wore her wedding ring and the watch he'd gave her, just like he was there to see it. He was gone, but she spoke of him like he was there. She visited him at the cemetery but spoke of him like he might come back. Some might have thought, and I thought at first, that she gave so much of herself to Richard, that she had nothing left. No love for anyone else." Her voice was crisp, tightly controlled, as if she were fighting to control her emotions. "But that's the mystery of love. The more one gives, the more one has." Her tone softened. She searched the audience until her gaze found mine. "The love she had for Richard didn't mean she had less love to give. It expanded her capacity to love, to be the best version of herself." Betty looked at me for another instant then dropped her head and wiped a tear from here face. "And she proved that in every way. She was a dear friend. I hope she knew that in the end." Her voice faded and cracked, and she hurried back to her seat in the front row.

More friends stood and spoke of Gram. Her work at the bakery, volunteering with veterans' support groups, dropping off meals for anyone sick in town, knitting scarves for the shelter in Glenwood Springs, bringing anyone who was going through a tough time flowers from her garden. They said so many kind things about her and her positive influence around town. How much she'd done for people over the years. What a great friend she'd been.

Betty walked slowly back to the podium and dabbed her eyes with a tissue. "Thanks for coming. Thanks for honoring Rose." Betty paused and looked around the crowd. "Would anyone else like to speak?"

Vin leaned in, his shirt-covered arm resting against mine, his lips brushing my hair. "Cyndra, you should say something."

"They wouldn't want me to." Though Betty had extended an olive branch, I wasn't sure the town majority had changed their opinions of me. It was now common knowledge I'd been involved in the incarceration of their star wrestler.

"Even if that's true, it doesn't matter." He reached for my gloved hand and pulled me up. "You should still do it. For her."

My legs wobbled. They moved out of sync with my body all the way to the aisle and Vin slowed his pace at my side, reaching for my hand again, his thumb rubbing circles into the back of my glove. When we reached the podium, he released my hand and we turned together.

Gabriel appeared, tall and solemn-faced, in the doorway at the back of the room. My mouth fell open as he slid into the back row. He sat in one of the chairs Vin and I had abandoned, seeming to fill the space that both Vin and I had taken together.

Someone cleared their throat. A chair squeaked. Someone muttered, "Is that her?" and two women near the front ducked their heads together with sideways glances at me.

"Hello," I stammered. Vin gripped my hand, and the two gossiping women parted beneath his smile. "Hello." I managed again, glancing at Vin for reassurance. He nodded.

I turned back to the crowd and found myself focusing on Gabriel's face. He gazed steadily back at me, his expression both grim and reassuring. Solemn and thoughtful. And loving, like when he looked at Zoe.

Gazing at Gabriel, words poured out of me. "Anna Rose Merritt was the best person I knew. She was everything you said." I was able to pull my gaze away from his face and sought out the faces of her friends. "And you're right, there was so much more than her work around town, her volunteering, everything she did for others. She had an energy. A special energy about her. Kind. Giving. So hopeful. A friend to so many people. A friend to me." I gulped. "More than a friend to me." My words started to slow. "She was the only mother I knew." My voice wavered. "She kept me going when I thought I couldn't. Kept me believing in myself, my future." Tears clouded my eyes. "I hope she knew, knew that—" My voice cracked.

Vin squeezed my hand.

"Hope she knew how much I loved her." I could no longer blink back the tears.

Vin squeezed my hand again.

"Thank you, everyone." I leaned toward him. "It's time to go," I whispered and pulled out of his hold. I flew down the aisle.

Gabriel jerked to his feet.

I swiped at the tears in my eyes and held up a palm, warning him to stay back. If he came any closer, I'd sob.

His eyes followed me all the way to the door.

Vin caught up to me in the lobby. We didn't say anything, didn't touch, as we passed a long table being set by two library staff members with a tea service, dainty teacups, and all of Gram's favorite sweets. The largest platter held dozens of Gram's lemon tea cookies, cut into tiny yellow stars. The familiar sight stopped me dead in my tracks. Just as pretty as if Gram had made them. My ballet flats glued to the floor, I finally forced my eyes from the platter, forced one foot in front of the other, and hurried to catch up to Vin.

"Cassandra," Betty called.

Vin and I stopped and turned in the parking lot.

She rushed over. "Here. Take this with you." She handed me a bag full of the star-shaped treats with a sad smile. If Gram was looking down, surely this would make her smile too.

I walked out lighter, bolstered by a sense of accomplishment and closure, until I spotted a familiar white coat across the street. "Vin!" I shouted, though he was standing right next to me on the sidewalk.

"I see him."

Dr. Creepy lurked around the corner of a building, looking out of sorts, still wearing his lab coat, flapping in the wind. The doctor was so out of it, he must've hurt himself. A bandage clung between his eyes.

"Can you watch Cyndra?" Vin called back to Gabriel, who'd just walked out behind us, and raced across traffic. After a few of Vin's tight smiles and carefully chosen words, Dr. Creepy was on his way back to the hospital in Glenwood Springs.

Was sending Dr. Creepy and some random thugs the best the Summum Malum could do? Thank goodness the Knights had gotten rid of the giants sniffing around the mountain. They seemed much more of a threat, especially because they'd seemed totally committed to their mission. But it appeared the Summum Malum were at a disadvantage because they couldn't even watch as Vin easily dispatched whoever they sent, none of whom seemed to have any real allegiance to their masters. It wasn't lost on any of us that now that Cameron was gone, the Summum Malum really seemed to be flailing.

One of the elder bears, Cousin Simon, speculated that perhaps the Summum Malum were blind to their blindness.

"Blind to their blindness?" Vin asked him when we ran into him in human form on patrol.

"Yes." He clutched a blanket around his shoulders, which were surprisingly broad but rounded with age. "Not only did the relic's awakening cause a disturbance, it may have also caused this area to be invisible to them in a more profound way. Making it hard for them to keep focus."

"Well, I'm not sure I believe that, but I'll take any advantage we have," Vin said.

That night, Gabriel was out on patrol. Aaron and Cole watched *Batman v Superman* in the Knights' movie room on the third floor. Vin and I sat side by side on barstools in the kitchen, far away from the noise of the movie, surrounded by silence. He sipped coffee. I stuffed cookies into my mouth.

When only two of the dozen cookies I'd set on the plate remained, he pulled the plate toward his side of the counter but didn't take one. "The fire marshals finished their investigation." He traced a long, elegant finger around the rim of his mug. "I can bring back what's left of Rose's things. I just want to warn you—there's not much."

A bit of cookie caught in my throat. My eyes watered.

"Do you want to come with?"

I coughed, a strangled sound.

He slid my mug of milk closer to my hand.

I clutched it, chugged half down, and shook my head.

The next morning Vin returned with a single box. I scooped out two rag-wrapped bundles at the top, set them on the floor of the Knights' foyer, and unraveled the rags to find two of Gram's mom's teacups, both chipped.

"The cabinets in the kitchen collapsed." Vin reached for my shoulder, then let his hand fall. "Not much to save there. But elsewhere I found some knitting. Jewelry. A few photos." He pointed to what was left in the box.

I rewrapped the teacups and dug under two half-knitted sweaters, finding the framed wedding photo from Gram's dresser and the photos from Richard and Gram's youth that had hung on the living room wall. Finally, I pulled out Gram's pewter trinket box. Her gold watch and strand of pearls lay inside, unharmed.

"Thank you, thank you, Vin," I whispered.

Back upstairs, I buried the photos, trinket box, and pearls in my trunk. But I set the pretty teacups out on my dresser and kept out the watch. I read the words around the inside of its bracelet: *No matter the time, my love will be with you. I will always find a way back to you.* I snapped it on, knowing what I needed to do with it. But not yet. I couldn't do it yet.

The next day I mentioned to Vin Gram's beaded purse that Third-eye had taken and my hair clip. Vin showed up with them that afternoon. But there was one thing Vin couldn't retrieve for me: my missing locket.

The elder bears' insistence that the Summum Malum hadn't been able to come anywhere near the mountain since right after I arrived convinced Vin more and more that the Shadows hadn't had anything to do with the theft. But Vin had no luck finding it among the kids at school, forcing him to expand his search in town. My only guess was that Cameron must have taken it, after Gabriel had told the Knights he'd seen it that night in my room.

"He had good reason to be working against me," I pointed out to Vin. "Cameron probably blamed me, my coming here, for the death of his father."

"I'm still not sure of Cameron's involvement in the fire," Vin said. "Or that he had anything to do with the Summum Malum."

Explaining how the Summum Malum had found out about me and gotten to Mike in the first place—unless it really was Cameron who'd helped them—were the only loose ends Vin couldn't solve. Vin spoke with the police again and they sat Mike's parents down for a serious talk about parental responsibilities, warning them they'd be interviewed further to make sure they were providing a safe environment for their daughter. The police's victim services employee also discussed the therapy and help the young girl would need going forward.

Vin had the police sit Kaylee down too. They lectured her on the consequences of interfering with a police investigation and cautioned her about harassing me, or anyone else at school, ever again. Her online posting and boasting was all the evidence they needed to unravel everything she'd been up to. They discovered she was just as much a bully as Mike; she just had more subtle methods. After Kaylee's latest lies and run-in with the authorities, it seemed Principal Cook finally understood how misguided his daughter had become since his wife had left. His first step was to insist Kaylee write a note apologizing to me. She agreed to put in more hours at the shelter, and after some earnest promises from her father that he'd address her behavior, the police let her off without a permanent mark on her record for it.

At the end of the week, Gabriel finally took a break from all the day and night watches and patrols. He called out for me and found me and Vin in his mom's sitting room. I was working on calculus problems—Gram would've wanted me to keep up on schoolwork even if I wasn't going to school—and Vin was reading news on his cell as he sat on the loveseat next to me. Gabriel strode over and glanced at the small space between our legs. I dropped my text book to the cushion and stood.

"Cole's been begging to go out, practice driving." Gabriel

nodded toward the front of the house. "I'll be back by sunset." He stared hard at Vin. "Don't let Cassie out of your sight."

Vin rolled his eyes, as if he obviously had no plans to.

"There are two elders on the lawn, if you need help."

Vin rolled his eyes again, but nodded.

Gabriel and Cole came home as the sun started to set; they'd brought back Burger Boys' hamburgers, fries, and milkshakes. Vin, Gabriel, Cole, and I sat around the Knights' massive dining room table in an awkward silence, Vin half-heartedly picking at his burger, Gabriel inhaling a second serving of fries, and Cole slurping down the remains of his chocolate milkshake. Zoe, Richie, and Rosie lay snuggled up in one of the extra-large dog beds in the corner, so tired from play, they weren't even whining for a bite of hamburger.

One of the elder bears had gone back to the mountain. It was Aaron's turn for patrol with the other. Aaron burst in. "Who got Kaylee in trouble?"

"Calm down for a sec," Gabriel responded with an uneven frown. "What are you so upset about?"

"Kaylee's grounded, for like forever. All because you're"—Aaron looked from Gabriel to Vin to Cole—"so overprotective of her." Aaron stared at me, the subject of his scorn. "I finally thought you were cool. But you're just our resident princess." His cell buzzed in the background. "Kaylee was just talking. There was no real harm done. You couldn't just leave things be, could you?" Distracted from his rant by the incessant buzzing, he pulled out his cell and checked it.

"I think if you just call Dad, get another elder to take over your watch, have some dinner, while we talk this over, you'll calm down." Gabriel reached over and pulled out a chair. "In fact, Kaylee's still getting off easy."

"Whatever." Aaron snatched two hamburgers out of the bag Cole had left on the side table. "I have to go." He stormed out, his cell buzzing again. The front door slammed shut. Gabriel's frown deepened.

Vin glanced at me across the table, the corners of his perfectly formed mouth twitching and curling upward into a slight smile. I couldn't help but smile too. Aaron's outrage on behalf of Kaylee, who didn't seem to be at all interested in him in return, was a bit funny, in a ridiculous sort of way. When I didn't turn away, and silently held Vin's gaze across the length of the table, Vin's features softened further, and gradually changed from suppressed amusement to wide-eyed, open amazement to a soft look of sincere contentment.

Vin looked more relaxed than I'd seen him in days. Since before he'd left the weekend of Homecoming, before I'd confronted him when he got back about all the things he'd kept from me. In fact, Vin's warm gaze—now set off by a hesitant smile—was more than just relaxed. It was so full of relief, it was almost as if he sensed I'd forgiven him for keeping all his secrets. And I had. Vin had even reminded me before dinner not to say anything to the Knights about my new abilities. But no need. I wouldn't say anything. I trusted him. I still trusted him…

We continued to stare at each other. I felt for Gram's watch on my left wrist under the table, twisting the smooth gold in my right hand, imagining what it would be like to touch Vin's skin. The corners of Vin's mouth gradually lifted higher, his smile broadening to stunning effect. A flickering of warmth stirred in my belly in return. The warmth grew hotter, flaring like it usually did, but with an ease I'd never felt when looking at him before, with every second we silently communicated across the room. My breath quickened, my heart beat faster. My body quivered with a restless desire to get out of my chair, walk around the mahogany slab separating us, and join him on the other side. But I didn't do anything. I didn't say anything. I just let myself enjoy the moment, appreciating the understanding passing between us, before our eyes dropped and I released Gram's watch—I hadn't yet found the strength to take it off and leave it where it should go.

I lay in the middle of the big bed in the Knights' guestroom that night, Zoe curled into my side, and fought both sleep and thoughts of Vin. Was the warmth I'd felt for him at dinner due to his unnatural appeal, our friendship, or something messier? Something more complicated? I reached for the final book on Mrs. Merkle's syllabus from the pile on my nightstand—*The Grapes of Wrath*. The answer to those questions didn't matter right now. Vin was certainly my friend. Figuring that out, and actually admitting it to myself, had been challenge enough for one week.

The next morning, Vin appeared in sweats, something I'd never thought I'd see him in, and we practiced Krav Maga, the self-defense training he and his father had taught me, Ellis, and Alanna. No wonder self-defense had come naturally to me. We advanced, dodged, and landed light blows, our bodies circling and weaving like our moves were choreographed, as if we'd rehearsed this hundreds of times. I felt more and more like myself.

The final part of Vin's ingenious work, the part that truly put to rest any doubts about him being my friend, was what he did that afternoon. This time I went with him into the station, watching as he ordered the police chief to delete all records of me being in their custody. On the way out, Officer Fry gave me a wave. Third-eye glared but didn't try to stop us. He must remember me, but however Vin compelled the officers worked like magic. Vin seemed so relaxed after, he even agreed to stop by the shelter, actually getting out of his Porsche to walk in with me. He waited just outside the room, in the hallway, while I said hello to the animals.

"Oh, um—hey, Vin," Kaylee called from the corner where she was mopping out a dog cage. "Didn't see you there. You were looking for me?"

I stopped petting one of the new arrivals and looked back at him. Vin stepped just inside the door. Several dogs jumped up in their cages.

"Actually, I'm here with Cassandra. And you must have some things to say to her. I mean, about what you did after the dance?"

"Not really."

Vin gave a tight smile. The nearest dogs whimpered. "But—"

"Drop it," I cut in. "If she leaves me alone, that's good enough for me."

"So Kaylee"—his features relaxed, but I could still see the humor in his gaze—"you must be enjoying all the attention from Aaron recently?"

"No way!" she exclaimed. "He's been chasing after me for ages. Now, it's like, he won't even return a text." Had Aaron finally realized Kaylee wasn't worth the bother? Or that he'd have better luck playing hard to get? Maybe whatever friend had been calling or texting yesterday gave him good advice? "He just left me here yesterday. I deserve better than that." She pouted prettily. Vin took another step forward, and whimpers turned into growls. The closest dogs started clawing at their cages.

I pulled Vin away, said hello to Dr. G in his clinic, and waved to Mia, who was filing papers outside his office. I turned to leave, but Mia called out for me. I froze.

"Wanted you to know, there's talk around town," she said.

I stiffened, and my face must've looked stricken.

"No, no. About Kaylee. People are waking up to who she is. Finally." Her dark eyes lit up with amusement. We exchanged a smile.

It felt like a moment of friendship.

Vin laughed on the way home about what fitting recompense he could compel Kaylee to make.

"Just leave her be," I said as we cruised into the Knights' driveway. "You could compel her all day long, have her tattoo 'SORRY' across her forehead, clean a million dirty dog cages, and show up in her pajamas for the rest of senior year—that's not going to change who she is." Kaylee would have to do that on her own.

As it turned out, it was Kaylee's father, not Kaylee, who had a change of heart. Without any prompting from Vin, Principal Cook erased the fight reports from my school records, apparently realizing I wasn't the one who'd been instigating them all along.

As a final, mind-blowing wipe of the slate, Vin drove into Denver bright and early the following day to speak with the head administrator at the Social Services office. He wouldn't tell me his end goal, but I'd seen him in action enough at that point to expect some razzle dazzle. He'd told me about other alternates, all with various mental and physical abilities, but emphasized that his power of persuasion was pretty unique. But I still wasn't ready for him to hand me that single piece of paper when he returned to the Knights' house late that afternoon.

I stood in the middle of the foyer, holding the letter proclaiming my fate with my gloved hands, reading it three times. The words blurred. My breath quickened. I finally closed my eyes as I took a deep inhale, opened them, and read the letter once more.

I couldn't believe it. I was free.

Social Services had closed my file.

Then somehow—I don't know quite how, since I don't remember Vin smiling at me—the paper fell from my fingers and my legs carried me across the middle of the foyer, around the sculpture of Apollo and his river nymph, and to within inches of Vin's tall frame. The letter floated across the floor, and I floated too, as if in a trance, ending up with my arms cinched around Vin's waist. What I was thinking in the moments leading up to my body reaching for his? I had no idea. I certainly wasn't thinking about protecting myself from pain.

I was just lucky I was wearing elbow-length gloves with the sleeveless, flowy dress Vin had bought me. He also had the wherewithal to lift his arms as I tackled him, so my upper arms wouldn't make contact with his hands or the exposed skin of his forearms below his rolled sleeves. Vin kept his arms lifted to the crystal chandelier twinkling above us, and I wrapped myself tighter around him, pressing my cheek into his crisp, button-down shirt.

"You're welcome, Cyndra," he chuckled melodically. "Who knew this is what it would take?"

"Take?" I mumbled.

"To get your attention."

I didn't respond. I pressed myself closer, until our bodies

perfectly aligned, sticking like magnets. My chest meshed into the top of his abdomen. My hips pressed against his firm thighs. My legging-covered knees, just below the bottom hem of the dress, bumped into the tops of his slacks-covered shins. I released a small sigh, not understanding myself at all. My only explanation was that I wanted to thank Vin for everything he'd done. My body trying to squeeze itself into his lithe frame made it clear that wasn't the complete answer. This hug was more than a simple thanks. Because I'd certainly never thanked anyone else this way. If I was being honest, this hug was also about a suppressed longing to be close to someone—someone I cared for. Because being close to Vin sparked all sorts of hidden desires. For closeness, companionship. That basic need I'd tried to convince myself I could live without; not even letting myself get close enough to Gram to tell her I loved her. And now, after realizing what Vin and I shared, it felt easier to be near him than it had felt to be near anyone the last two years.

It felt familiar. It felt right.

Vin slowly dropped his arms around me and wrapped them around my shoulders. He carefully rested his chin on the pillow of curls on the top of my head and sighed into my hair.

I breathed in Vin's clean scent. That was familiar too. Like the crisp aroma coming from the kitchen when Gram made her key lime pie, but familiar in a more distant way. As if the scent had fished around in all the lost memories floating adrift inside me and hauled in something fantastic, and my body responded instinctively, melting into his.

I couldn't say how long Vin and I stood, joined together, in the middle of the Knights' foyer, soaking up the emotion passing between us. I only knew that minute by minute, I felt lighter. Happier. More positive about everything in my life. With my arms still around him, I reached for the bracelet of Gram's watch, clasping my right palm over it on my left wrist, creating a lock at the base of Vin's low back. I felt so much better than I'd felt in such a long time, and certainly more grounded and hopeful than I'd felt since Gram's death.

More settled too, with not knowing what was going on with things here, Cameron's disappearance, the burns that kept getting worse.

A whimper from the sitting room, like the soft shriek of an alarm clock, jarred me. I loosened my hold, turning in Vin's arms.

Gabriel stood in the doorway of the sitting room, the source of the whimpering at his feet—Zoe perched awkwardly on her three legs, her head cocked to the side, her ears tucked back. Zoe whimpered louder. Gabriel's face tightened. He looked almost as uncomfortable as Zoe, with his smooth, unmarked cheek pulled as taut as the flesh on the other side. His hand flew to his upturned polo collar.

I immediately let go of Vin.

"Sorry to interrupt." Gabriel coughed and forced his face to relax a fraction. "I was reading in the other room, thought I heard something going on out here. I guess congrats are in order. On the trip to Denver?"

"Yeah, isn't it great?" I pulled myself out of the circle of Vin's arms, something that for some reason took me much longer than necessary.

"Maybe when you guys are done…" Gabriel let his hand fall and glanced down at the floor, then after a moment's pause, looked back up at me. "I can take you into town. There's something I thought you'd want to see."

"Sure. Now's good." I stepped away from Vin with an apologetic smile, before refocusing on Gabriel and the unceasing whimpering at his feet. "Let's take Zoe too." I petted her, and she quieted.

"Good. Um, just give me a sec. I'll meet you in the garage."

When he arrived, he carried several roses it looked like he'd cut from the bushes outside. "They were my mom's," he said. "Didn't want to cut them before, in case somehow she is able to look down and still see her garden. But these won't make it much longer. I think she'd understand."

I nodded, not sure what to say, and climbed into the passenger side of the SUV, helping Zoe up and onto my lap. Zoe relaxed her weight across my legs, closed her eyes, and nodded off with her large head resting on my forearm, spilling over onto the armrest.

Gabriel laid the roses—five of them—on the dash and drove toward town without saying a word, not even bothering to tell me our destination. I didn't mind the lack of chatter. I was afraid if Gabriel started talking, he might end up asking me why I'd been hugging Vin. An even better question, one that would've been much more difficult to answer, was why I'd been hugging Vin so long. So tightly.

And why I hadn't wanted to let go.

29
TWISTED UP

As Gabriel drove, I turned away from his pensive face. I glanced down at Zoe, resting peacefully. I looked out the side window, seeking a bit of my own peace from the autumn colors beginning to blend the landscape into bronze and gold—feeling so twisted up inside.

The silence built inside the SUV, until it thickened like a dark cloud about to burst, as Gabriel pulled up to the back entrance of Meeker Highland Cemetery. He took the roses off the dash, opened my door and helped Zoe down, and headed toward the cemetery's back gate, Zoe at his heel.

I hurried to follow. With every step I took behind them, my eyes collected a bit of moisture. Was I having an allergic reaction to something in the air? But the brilliant blooms of spring and summer were long gone. I couldn't blame the pollen. I couldn't even blame the late afternoon sun. The long days of summer were gone too, the sun already setting, casting more muted pink and orange reflections than bright white light all around us.

I stumbled around a low grave marker, and reached out for a gravestone next to it. The fabric of my glove snagged on its rough surface. I straightened to standing and rushed to catch up to Gabriel and Zoe walking single file ahead of me. Dog dutifully following its master. Catching up, joining the procession, I realized it was time to acknowledge Zoe was as much his dog as mine.

My eyes finally welled to their bursting point.

This time, I didn't fight the tears. I let them spill. It was all I could do to keep one foot in front of the other. If I'd tried to keep the tears in too, I'd probably collapse to the ground and completely embarrass myself.

We walked silently through the back of the cemetery and reached our destination. A new gravestone stood beside Richard's—much nicer than what I'd ordered—pristine and unweathered above a freshly dug plot. Gabriel walked up, set one of the roses on the ledge across the top, and returned to me. We stood side by side facing the narrow stone. So close, I could feel his body heat radiating from the length of bare arm beneath his short-sleeved polo. It warmed my upper arm.

Zoe lay down at our feet, dropping her head to the grass with a little whimper, her nose touching the fresh dirt of the plot that hadn't yet been covered with sod. She whined, a high sad sound piercing the uneasy silence. Gabriel didn't say anything as he reached his arm around my shoulder, being careful to grasp my glove-covered elbow, pulling me into his side. My bare shoulder rested against his polo-covered chest. In that moment, I was too weak—too raw and vulnerable—to resist my body's desire to soak up every ounce of comfort he offered. And I couldn't deny that having Gabriel standing next to me made me feel stronger. Safer. Less alone.

Warmth seeped through the thin layer of clothing separating our skin, soothing me, even as new tears formed. When my vision cleared, I finally made out the inscription on the new stone.

Here Lies Anna Rose Merritt, devoted wife to Richard, loving mother to Bethany, proud grandmother to Cassandra. Rose's kind and giving nature never faltered with the challenges life gave her. She was a light among so much hidden darkness, and she will live on through her granddaughter, who will carry her Gram's memory with her always.

Gabriel must have done this.

Of course he had. This was exactly the type of thing someone like him would do.

Oh goodness. Another stone, a smaller one, had been laid between Richard and Gram's graves. The shiny marble lay flat in the grass, its delicate engraving depicting a small angel and below:

Bethany, Beloved Child.

My eyes swelled. I had no idea how to tell Gabriel how much this meant to me. I started blinking, but my eyes kept filling with tears. I lifted my hands to swipe at them, thinking I'd been weak enough for one day, but then I remembered what Richard had said in Gram's room, when I'd fought tears over Gram's body. I stopped blinking. I dropped my hands.

Maybe Richard was right. Maybe I didn't need to fight my emotions. Because maybe, just maybe, strength and sensitivity weren't incompatible things.

New tears spilled down my cheeks. They ran down my neck and chest, wetting the edge of my dress. When there was nothing left to let go of, I read the inscription Gabriel must have written for Gram's gravestone one more time, wanting to come up with something to say to thank him—"But she wasn't my real grandmother," was all that slipped out.

"But—" Gabriel hesitated, then dropped his head near mine. "You were a granddaughter to her."

"I don't know…"

Gabriel dropped his head closer, his lips nearly brushing my ear, as if the words coming were too precious to trust to the late afternoon breeze. "You were Rose's family. The only family she had left. She'd want you to have a reminder of that."

Gabriel straightened but didn't move away.

I leaned into his side, letting my weight rest into his, and his arm tightened around me. We stood together in silence over Richard and Gram's graves as the calm of the early fall evening settled around us. The sun slowly set over the cemetery grounds. We only separated for a moment, when I knew it was time for me to take off Gram's watch. For the final time, I read the words Richard had engraved around the band—*No matter the time, my love will be with you. I will always find a way back to you.*—then rolled off one of my gloves, dropped the watch in, and wrapped it up.

Gabriel helped me bury the bundle in the soil above where Gram lay. He placed another of the roses on Bethany's marker. A streak of light flashed among the nearest rows of gravestones, bobbing back and forth as if trying to get closer. But I ignored it, not fearing it now. I leaned further into Gabriel's side. When all that was left was the hazy purples of nightfall, Gabriel pulled back slightly and looked down at me. I stared back up at him, trying again to come up with the words to thank him. I opened my mouth.

Gabriel pulled away completely, clearing his throat with a loud cough. His whole demeanor changed so abruptly, I closed my mouth, my words forgotten.

He coughed again. "I just want you to know. Vin's a good guy."

"What?"

"Vin's a good guy." Gabriel stepped away, paced back and forth, and turned toward me. "I've forced myself to look into Vin's eyes quite a bit, to see exactly how good of a person he is, because people can trick me at first. I mean, everyone's done something really good in their life once or twice. And then, if there's nothing else, it's like watching a reality show on repeat every time I look at them. It gets boring and stale. You realize there is nothing else to the person. They're superficial, selfish, and self-interested at best. At worst… well, you would probably know something about that." He frowned. "But Vin's done a lot of good things. So many, really good things. Vin's a lot like you, looking out for people who might need help, including you and your sisters. I just wanted you to know that." Gabriel's frown disappeared, but at the same time his face looked darker than ever.

"Yeah, Vin's a good guy. A friend. From way before I ever came here." I crossed my arms, feeling the evening chill with one glove missing and Gabriel gone. "I just wish Vin and Zoe got along."

"I'd wondered about that." Gabriel knelt down to pet Zoe, looking up at me on bent knees. "But Cole thinks Zoe picks up on Vin's unnatural energy and is a little frightened by it. She'll probably get used to him as she sees how much you trust him. Animals are more intuitive, more aware of their surroundings than people."

"I know, it makes sense." I shivered. "I just care about them both so much, I want Zoe and Vin to get along. Now, more than ever." The words came out before I could even think how they must sound.

"I can only imagine how hard this has all been on you." Gabriel rose. He started to reach for me again, then stuck his hands in his jeans' pockets, the remaining roses he held sticking out awkwardly. "I just hope having Vin back helps. You guys really seem to share something… special. I hadn't realized that, until now." He looked away.

We lapsed into silence. Unlike before, this silence felt strained. And Gabriel looked so uncomfortable with his hands stuffed in his pockets, his bulky shoulders bunched up around his ears. I was avoiding the conversation Gabriel really wanted to have, the one where I told him exactly how I felt about the hot, picture-perfect guy from my past. But how did I tell the guy who said he loved me whether the other guy in my life was just a friend, or maybe meant to be something more? When I didn't really know myself?

I looked back down at Gram's grave.

This had to stop.

If Gram was still here, she'd sit me down at the kitchen table, make me a mug of hot cocoa, drop down a plate of something sweet, and tell me to stop twisting myself up in knots. I wasn't an indecisive person. I was capable of figuring out my feelings. And now, standing in the middle of the cemetery—above where Richard and Gram lay—I knew what she'd say. She'd say to stop hiding. Stop doubting.

"Kiss me."

"What?" Gabriel looked astonished, like the skies had just opened up and started raining down frogs.

"Kiss me. Right here. Right now. I need to know."

"Really?" He glanced uneasily at my remaining glove, then my lips.

"Kiss me. Don't worry." I stepped into the shelter of Gabriel's body, raised my arms, took hold of the sides of his upturned polo collar with both hands, and pulled his face toward mine.

30
MEMORIES

I TILTED MY FACE UP. TIPPING ONTO THE BALLS OF MY FEET, I stretched tall, my lips seeking his. Deep down my mind and body—my entire being—had finally accepted a most unlikely, yet elemental, truth: Gabriel was safe. His touch would always be the one that would not hurt me.

Pain didn't seem a possibility.

His lips touched mine, soft and gentle, warm and weightless. He pulled back, as if worried he might hurt me. I tugged on his collar and he tentatively leaned into the kiss. Gabriel's top lip pressed above mine, his bottom lip full and slanted on one side, rested against me. A soft sound of contentment hummed in my chest.

He responded with a hesitant pressure, as if still uncertain whether I might pull away or not. I couldn't have pulled away if I tried. Sensations of such pleasure, like I'd never experienced before, blossomed where the delicate flesh of my mouth met his. How could I have ever imagined such satisfaction—such peace and contentment—was possible? I gripped his shirt tighter. I needed more of this. I needed as much as I could get. I reached up to clasp my hands around his neck, pulling the softness of my chest more firmly against the hardness of his.

A small sigh escaped my lips. Gabriel's tongue brushed across the parted seam of my mouth. Once. Twice. My heart pounded. Heat flared between us, energy flowing where we touched, like we were creating something. Passionate. Intimate. Safe. All our own. I unclasped my hands and worked my fingers under his collar.

One strong arm wrapped around my waist. His hand skimmed along my hip where the dress flowed out from my side. What would it feel like if the material wasn't there? His warm palm cupped into my side, pulling me closer. Petals brushed my cheek, falling away as he dropped the roses, reaching his other hand up, threading his fingers through the curls behind my neck. His fingers flexed.

The pressure fitted me even more securely against him. Our lips moved instinctually, melding together, exploring the heat, the intensity, the sensations surging between us. His fingers rubbed above my neck, tangling in my hair. I moaned deep in my throat, struggling to get closer.

"You're going to be the death of me." Gabriel pulled his head back, catching me unprepared.

I stumbled and fell into him.

His fingers untangled from my hair. His arms gripped me tighter, steadying me. But a look of pain flashed across his face. His scars appeared more puckered and wrenched than ever. His eyes sought mine—neither of us breathed—then his eyelids flinched shut.

I gasped for breath. "What's wrong?" My heart raced with so much passion, so much emotion, for him. And I knew. It was so obvious now. No matter how much I tried to fight it, I couldn't escape it. It would always be Gabriel in the end.

Yes, I trusted Vin. Completely. I wasn't sure I could say the same of Gabriel, yet. But that was because I think I'd known all along I was going to trust Gabriel with something so much more frightening than friendship. While Vin was my friend, someone I obviously cherished from my past, Gabriel was meant to be something more, if I could only find a way to...

"I can't take it any longer," Gabriel whispered. His eyes were still closed, his expression tightened. "Now that I see what sort of connection you and Vin share, I don't know why you'd choose me. Why you'd settle for something so… when you could have so much more. Something perfect." His scarred cheek quivered and he opened his eyes, connecting my gaze to his with only inches between us, and looked into me—into my soul. "Maybe you should be with him, but I'm not so selfless as to step aside. And you have to choose. You have to do it right now. I know I said I'd give you all the time you need, but—"

"You"

"What?"

"I'm saying…" I leaned in. "…I've already chosen. You."

A flush swept over his face. His beautiful features beamed and the tension in him eased. But his arms loosened around me, as though he wasn't sure I meant what I said.

"I'm sorry it took me so long. Sorry for all my doubts." I paused. While I couldn't force the walls I'd built to crumble entirely, not with every experience that had built them up, brick by brick, I could at least give him the reassurance he deserved. "I'm ready. More than ready. For us. To see where this goes."

"Really? You mean it this time?" His hold tightened.

"Really." I laughed.

"Finally." The last bit of tension fell from his body. The corner of his mouth pulled up into a wide, silly half-smile. He leaned in and down, kissed me one more time, and rested his forehead against mine. There was still so much left unsaid, but he seemed okay with that now.

I slipped off my remaining glove, dropped it to the ground, and brushed my fingertips over both sides of his face, absorbing the warmth, the prickle of his stubble, the contrasting textures of his skin. We stood together for a long while as the sun sank low, wrapped in each other's embrace. The cemetery darkened. Zoe, sprawled patiently at our feet, made a little grunt, as if bored. Gabriel sighed, bent down to rub her head, and picked up the roses and my glove. He clasped the roses in one hand and tucked my glove into his back pocket.

Without a word, we moved quickly in the little light left, visiting the graves of his mom and sister, and Cameron's mom's too. Gabriel knelt by each to leave a rose. We left hand in hand, I couldn't stop rubbing my palm against his and interlacing and re-interlacing our fingers. We walked with just enough distance between us for Zoe to amble along under our joined hands. When we got to the back gate, the light reappeared, zipping closer in the dark.

Zoe barked. Gabriel froze, tightening his grip.

"You see that too?" I whispered.

He nodded, releasing my hand, and started to pull his shirt over his head, preparing to change into bear form to protect me. "Cassie, whatever this is, let me—"

"But it's Richard."

The light came to a stop in front of us, sharpening and coming into focus, showing I was right. "Wow," Gabriel said, looking at Richard's ghostly image in awe, their gazes level. "I've seen pictures, but it's really you?"

Richard smiled. "Nice to finally meet one of Bernard's boys, but we need to be quick. I'm doing this with the help of Cassie's twin. I can't sustain it long."

"Um, my twin's dead." I bit my lip. What did my twin sister have to do with this?

"Alanna's dead. Not burned. So she's with us. And her gifts are very unique. When she was alive, she could connect to the place we're both in now, and I'm using it a bit in reverse since we figured out how. Listen, we—"

"Wait," Gabriel interrupted. His hand found mine again and gave it an excited squeeze. He looked intently at Richard. "Your mother, her race could shape people's memories. Dad said it helped a lot with keeping the bears hidden when she was alive. Dad said you could do it too."

"Yes." Richard's chin lifted. "Just not as well." Anguish reflected in his eyes.

"Well enough to help Cassie?"

"No." His image wavered. "I can't help." He hesitated. "I'm the reason her memories are gone. And they're really gone, with what I did."

"What did you do?" I asked, needing to hear confirmation of the pieces—the light, what Richard could do, my missing past— that were falling into place.

"When you came, trying to find the relic, I had to do something. I sensed the Summum Malum getting near, coming to investigate the disturbance created, but you couldn't find the relic, just wandering the forest and deciding to camp for the night."

"What did you do?" My voice was stronger this time. Insistent.

"I drew on my own abilities, trying to show myself, to warn you, but I did too much."

"Too much?" I needed to hear him say it.

"It—I—wiped out everything—all your memories. It was awful." Richard shuddered.

"How awful?"

"The shock. You stumbled into your campfire, your hiking trousers caught fire. You found your way to the river… Yes, I threw them off your trail, but with a price."

I drew back, tugging against Gabriel's hand, not being able to recall what Richard spoke of, but remembering the agony of when I woke in the water.

"I'm so sorry I didn't find a safer way." Richard's expression was haunted. The light around him dimmed. "All I can say is that when Rose took you in, I was so relieved. After everything you and your sisters had been through, you and Rose connecting—" He gulped back a harsh sound, but hope lit his face. "Well, it made me think fortune had not entirely abandoned us, and our cause. I waited for when Bernard would discover you. I can't tell you how many times I wished I had the power to talk, to help, to explain. Finally I do." The light flickered. "But before it's too late, I need one of you to tell me why Cassie doesn't have the relic's powers."

"We think maybe she needs her matching stone," Gabriel answered, "we're trying to—"

"Yes—" Richard's image flashed in and out "—why has no one… to her?"

"What? Where is it?"

"—what do you mean," the light shrank, "right at… home…"

"Home? Whose home?" I asked in a rush.

The light flickered again, and went out.

When we got back, rushing in from the door between the garage and kitchen, savory aromas of meat and oregano greeted us. Aaron and Cole stood over containers of reheated leftovers, Greek dishes Vin had cooked for me and him last night after the others kept picking up burgers, the tubs spread out on the corner of the counter. Zoe, Richie, and Rosie pranced eagerly for scraps.

Gabriel's eyes drilled into Aaron. "Why aren't you out on patrol?" Gabriel asked. "It's your turn."

"A break, is that not allowed?" Aaron straightened, puffing his chest, as if trying to match Gabriel's size, then snatched up a lamb shank and tore into it. "Besides, Vin's out, said he'd walk the perimeter."

Gabriel shook his head then explained about Richard. I told them straight out about the last thing Richard had said, then asked flat-out, "Do you guys have any idea where my locket might be?"

"'Course not," Aaron mumbled as he chewed. Cole looked dumbfounded.

"But why would Richard think it's at someone's home? Asking why no one's given it to Cassie?" Gabriel wondered.

Cole shook his head with wide eyes.

Aaron swallowed hard, shaking his head too. "Maybe he meant it was lost somewhere, in Cassie's old home. Someone will have to dig through what's left. Before they start demolishing."

"Vin went through it already." I leaned into the counter. "Recovering what he could. Besides, it was taken. Not lost."

"Maybe he didn't look well enough." Aaron bit off more lamb.

Gabriel gave me a reassuring look, eyes still bright with emotion from before. "I'll talk to my dad."

"Talk to Vin too," I said.

"Why?"

"Because he's here to help." I was too tired to argue about it. Vin and the Knights would probably never see eye to eye, but the growing tension had to stop. Vin and I would have to talk too, but not yet. First, I needed to figure out how Vin and I could talk about those last few moments in the foyer, when we'd found something I didn't want to lose, even now that Gabriel and I were… together. It seemed so strange to think it. That I could—or should—be with someone.

But I was.

My temple throbbed. Gabriel and Cole headed off to circle around the grounds. "Check in with Vin too, tell him about Richard," I called after them, then forced myself to eat a bit of rice. Aaron texted on his cell and I washed the dishes. "Aaron, I'm heading out with Zoe and the pups for a walk by the river."

He followed behind us as the sun set. Richie and Rosie scampered in circles as if playing tag. Zoe hopped along on her three legs, stopping now and then to mouth a few blades of grass. I tried with every step not to sink down, close my eyes, and fall asleep.

On our way back, Gabriel and Vin appeared out of the forest. "Where's Cole?" I asked.

"He offered to take the overnight watch." Gabriel closed his eyes briefly, clearly tired, probably relieved to have a break.

"And we're searching Cameron's room. In case that's what Richard was trying to tell you guys." Vin gave me an intense look, as if he and Gabriel may have talked about more than just Richard. Had Gabriel told him what had happened between us at the cemetery?

"Damn right we're searching Cameron's room." Aaron huffed.

It didn't seem the time to ask them about it.

We tromped back to the house and searched Cameron's room. His closet and dresser drawers were mostly full. He must've left most of his things behind. But it wasn't there. Aaron shrugged. "How about a movie? Might take our minds off it." We climbed up to the third floor and he picked out an *X-Men* film. It looked like most of their DVDs were superhero films. He plopped on the floor and called over Zoe, Richie, and Rosie, who nestled against a pillow near him. Zoe settled her head over Aaron's thigh so he could rub her ears, and with Aaron and the dogs on the floor, it left several recliners and a small couch empty. Tired, I sank into the couch. Vin and Gabriel sat on either side of me. I yawned, trying to keep my eyes wide, staring at the screen. I felt myself drifting off. I woke suddenly, sideways. Credits rolled down the screen. A warm weight nudged my knee. My side was pressed against Gabriel's, his knee rubbing against mine, trying to rouse me. My head rested on his chest, Gabriel's arm was wrapped around me, and as I straightened, his hand cupped my bare arm.

Vin stared at us and flinched away from us, as if in pain. Oh no. Without thought, I jolted towards him, trying to make this moment okay.

Gabriel's hand held me back.

Vin stared so hard at Gabriel's hand, there was no way Gabriel had told him he could touch me. Vin was learning that fact right now.

Vin rose. His mouth twisted into a grim expression, and he stalked out, his movements quick and stiff. I slipped out of Gabriel's embrace, dashed after Vin down the hall, down the stairs, trying to catch up to him on the second floor. He disappeared into his room. "We need to talk about this," I called out.

He slammed his door shut with a bang.

I went to my room, wrote him a short note—*I'm sorry. I should've told you. Yes, he can touch me without pain or any vision. Please talk to me.*—and slipped it under his door. "Vin?" I called out.

He didn't answer.

My heart raced, my palms grew damp, and I knocked on his door, but he didn't answer. I turned away. Gabriel stood in the hall. "If he'd answered, what would you have said?"

"I—I'm not sure. But he's my friend." And hurting right now, so I'd have said something to try make him understand, make him feel better.

"I get it." Gabriel's voice faltered. "I do. Um, goodnight." The corner of his lips quivered and he pivoted sharply on his heel to his room.

"Goodnight," I called after him. Why did I feel like I'd said the wrong thing?

Sometime after midnight, forcing my feet to walk back and forth the length of my guestroom, I tripped over a stack of books Cole had loaned me. I'd run out of room on the nightstand. A book fell and slipped out of its cover. I tried to slip it back on, but my hands fumbled the flap. I was more drained, my head more cloudy than ever. And if I couldn't talk to Vin and I was going to sleep again, like I had those few moments on the couch, I had to admit it to my-self: I wanted to sleep with Gabriel's arms around me.

I wrestled on a short robe, covering up my camisole and under-wear, petted Zoe when she looked up, and helped her off the bed. With every other step down the hall her snout pushed at my heel, nudging me along. When we got to Gabriel's door, I hesitated. Zoe's softness brushed past my leg, heading for the opening between the partly open door and the wall.

She entered the dark room.

"Who's there?" Gabriel called out.

Zoe answered with a soft woof.

"Why aren't you with Cassie, girl?" Gabriel shifted at the far side by the window. The bed creaked. "Come on, Zoe-girl, you should be with her. What if she has one of her nightmares?" In the darkness I could just make out his large form as he started to rise, his outline eclipsing a tree outside the window.

"I came too," I said, so faintly, I barely heard it myself. I tried again. "I came too."

He inhaled sharply, surprised. "Then come here." Gabriel sank back down.

I entered, inching past the door until I reached Zoe. I slipped off my robe, letting it fall, and shifted on my feet uneasily. Zoe had no such reservations. She circled once at my feet, made a bed out of my robe, and within seconds her soft snores broke the silence.

"Come here," Gabriel urged, his voice low.

I didn't move.

"It's okay." His voice deepened. "I know it'll take some time for you to get used to this, when everything has taught you to stay away. But I think you want to be with me, as much as I want to be with you."

He was right. And while I still didn't like the feeling of dependency my desire for him created, my feet carried me forward.

Gabriel lay still, sprawled across the bed. He was in the middle, and all exposed flesh except for a pair of boxers riding low across his hips. Feeling his eyes on me, I slowly crawled onto his plush comforter, joining him. On hands and knees I reached for him, my fingers seeking his warmth. They found his chest, splaying across it. I soaked up the feeling of him. Smooth. Yet firm. Silky. Yet textured. There weren't enough words to describe the pleasure of touching his body. His bare skin. He tried to keep me away from his scars, guiding my hands back to the other parts of his face and chest. But even his scars had a texture that were all their own. Like mine. I tugged up my camisole to right under my breasts, to show him the scars on my stomach.

In the dimness, his eyes focused on the rippled marks. He winced. "The campfire?"

"Yeah." I dropped my camisole back down. "They're just a part of me now. No different than any other part. Nothing to feel self-conscious about." Gram had taught me that. "If we're lucky, the other scars, the ones you can't see"—I tapped above my heart—"will heal too. Don't get hung up on the ones that don't matter."

I laid a hand across his abdomen and kissed the trail of scars from his chest, his neck, his cheek, his temple, and back again. Not too much. Nothing we weren't ready for. But enough for now.

Gabriel let me explore, finally reaching for me and pulling my face down to his for a long kiss. I settled into his arms, and stayed awake for as long as I could—enjoying the feeling of our bodies together. The heat. The safety. The lengths of our bare limbs. Entwined and entangled.

Touching as we melted into each other's embrace and dropped into a deep sleep.

I slept past sunrise in Gabriel's arms, waking to find him staring at me. He brushed the hair back from my face. "Why now?"

I got what he was asking, without him saying more. Why was I finally coming to him now, trusting him now? I snuggled deeper into his hold and tried to open up about my insecurities. I started with what he already knew a bit about—my pessimism about life, human nature, the people around me. Then I shared my worries for the future. "I worried for so long I could never have one. But Gram would want me to try." I breathed the words against his skin, barely audible. "I'm coming to you now because you make me hope maybe I can have a future, a happy one."

He gulped and squeezed me against his chest. "Me too." The words poured out as he shared about his own insecurities. More than his physical scars, which I kissed again. He was sensitive about his unnatural strength, how he'd injured that boy because of it. And he was still coming to terms with the death of his mom and sister, his reaction to it, and how if he'd stayed in Meeker I might never have been without him so long.

That night Gabriel asked Aaron and Cole to share the overnight watch and we slept in each other's arms again. Again, the nightmare did not return. On our third night together, I curled deeper into his side, inhaling the scent that was entirely his, trying to work up the courage to bring up the strangest part of our connection. Zoe snored at my feet, her new spot, where she'd taken to sleeping after Gabriel installed a ramp. She stopped snoring, looked at me, and rested her head on my foot. "So, why do you think I can touch you and no one else?" I traced the lines slashed across his abdomen with my index finger. He didn't flinch or try to cover them. In just days, he'd gotten used to me exploring every texture of his skin.

But at my question, Gabriel's breath caught, he stopped breathing, and his large room fell silent. Zoe snored again. "Well," he said at last, "maybe it's all the goodness I see in others, the small bits of positive energy they share me when I look into them. It might balance out all the darkness you carry inside you."

"The darkness inside me?" Maybe the visions did leave a bit of negativity inside me. Leaving me with more than just my distrustfulness. The tiny hairs on my arm prickled.

"Yes, that must be it. It makes so much sense." Gabriel squeezed me into his hard frame.

I rubbed against him, trying to shake off the cold feeling that still caused my arms to prickle. I lifted my head to find his expression looking serious, yet gentle, in the dimness. "How does it make sense?" I rested my cheek back down on his warm shoulder.

"Just like how you suffer pain, I get sensations too—of joy—happiness—things I haven't felt as much since you've been touching me the past few days. It's like you're actually drawing on my unnatural energy, to balance out your own."

"I'm not a parasite!" I protested against the heat of his skin.

Gabriel laughed. "No, you just need me as much as I need you—and that's okay." He tightened his hold. "I see the light and you see the darkness. Together we pull each other back from those extremes." He kissed my forehead, his lips lingering against me, and I softened into his hardness, and for once, welcomed my dreams.

The next morning I walked down the hall from Gabriel's room, back to my own, as Vin trudged up the stairs with a mug of coffee. His clothes were rumpled, his sneakers caked with mud, his eyelids drooped. He glanced up, saw me, and quickened his steps, slipping into his room. At lunch, he darted to the coffee pot in the kitchen. Cole and I looked up from his geometry, watching Vin fill his mug in a rush, like he couldn't wait to escape me again. And more coffee? Was Vin out at night patrolling too?

Leaving Cole to his math, I followed Vin out onto the back patio at a distance. He sat on a bench facing the river, the mountain towering in the background. He raised his mug, blowing gently as steam rose out, and took a sip. I approached behind him, the earthy smell of coffee mixing with the sweet smell of grass. I kept walking, but not quietly enough.

His back tensed. He dropped the mug to the bench. Coffee sloshed over the side. I sat next to the spill, risking a hand on his sleeve. "So, um, it's been a few days... maybe we can talk?"

"Give it a rest, Cyndra." Vin gave a tight smile, then immediately grimaced and relaxed his features. "I just need time. I knew that night on the sofa. But I really know now." His voice lowered. "We're just friends." His eyes squeezed shut and he shook his head. "This isn't like me." He shook it again. "Normally I can talk about these things. I just need time." His eyes shot open, he pulled his arm away and practically sprinted off the patio, circling around the house. I started to follow, but the sound of his Porsche's engine revving, tires screeching as he peeled away, stopped me.

Time. That was the problem. Time had changed nothing for me. I was still torn between them. Not romantically, but Vin was still my friend. Now that Gabriel and I were talking again, Vin and I weren't. I still abided by Vin's one request though, and didn't tell any of the Knights about how my abilities had developed since the fire. It seemed such a simple thing to do for him, when I didn't know how to erase the strain the past few days had put on our friendship. Vin was apparently patrolling at night now and still questioning more people in town, trying to find any clue of what happened when my locket went missing or where Cameron might've gone, in case he was involved—but how much longer would he stay? With all this tension? When the Knights didn't even seem to want him here? When he wouldn't even look at me now?

Vin walked into the dining room that evening, the first time he'd come near me and Gabriel together since that movie night, and my mouth fell open in mid-chew.

I dropped my half-eaten piece of pizza, the thick crust plopping to my plate.

He nodded at Cole and Aaron, sat across from Gabriel, and looked him dead in the eye. "I don't think it's safe for Cyndra here anymore." I was sitting right next to Gabriel, but Vin ignored me like I wasn't even there.

Gabriel's arms tensed. A piece of pepperoni slid off the slice he was holding, landing on top of his other slice. "OK, this is about the hikers?"

"Yes, partially, but it's also a bit strange that—"

"Wait. What hikers?" I swallowed the bit of cheese in my mouth.

"He didn't tell you?" Vin glanced at me.

"No. What's he talking about?" I looked at Gabriel.

He set his slice down. "I didn't want to worry you. It's probably nothing." Gabriel shot Vin an annoyed look.

No matter what I felt for Gabriel, that was not an answer that made me happy. "Explain."

He rubbed his fingers on a napkin. "Well, two days ago an elder spotted hikers on the mountain. No big deal, right?" Gabriel's hands twitched. "They looked normal enough. Vin's just upset because he overheard the elder saying they had a strange scent."

"And…" Vin prompted.

"And it was warm, but the elder said they were wearing gloves," Aaron offered.

"And?" Vin demanded, glancing between him and Gabriel.

Gabriel's hands seemed to move without thought to one of his slices. He raised it to his mouth and half of it disappeared. Aaron answered. "They met up with a police officer. Some guy with a scar on his forehead."

"There was an officer like that who wanted me sent to Glenwood Springs." My stomach tightened.

"But what does it all mean?" Cole asked before I could.

"What it means," Vin answered, his voice turning icy, "is that this has all gotten too easy. Way too easy. The Summum Malum are waiting for something, not even sending any real threats—waiting to strike. Cameron went missing and though I don't think he's involved with them, he could be. And in the meanwhile, we're, what? Playing house. Hanging out. Eating pizza!" Vin shoved his hair out of his face in an angry gesture. "And a strange scent? Odd attire? Meeting up with a cop who wanted Cyndra away from Meeker? And you say nothing's going on? That's crap. I'll tell you what's going on. New alternates are in the area. We should leave." Vin's eyes flashed at me and he even tried smiling. "Once we—"

Gabriel jumped up. "Cut that out!" His chair skidded back across the floor. "She's not going anywhere with you. We have a plan."

"Moving the relic out in the open when we don't even have the guidestone is not a plan." Vin rose to his feet, but unlike Gabriel, he moved slowly. Deliberately.

"What's Vin talking about?" I pushed back my plate and rested my hands on the table.

"Dad was going to tell you tomorrow." Gabriel remained standing, but reached down for my hand. "Aaron and Cole went through all our family's records, and we now believe you couldn't connect with the relic before because it needs to be out in the open. Under full sunlight."

"What she needs is the guidestone." Vin's voice was still hostile.

"You don't know that," Cole piped up. "You're guessing, like we are. And you didn't read what we did." He glanced at Aaron for reassurance. "It's like Dad said yesterday—the sun is, after all, the unfailing re-spectacle—oops!—I mean the unfailing receptacle and source of fire." Cole smiled awkwardly. "So with the sun never dimming or becoming consumed, why shouldn't the fire relic reach its full power under that influence?" He looked to his oldest brother to back him up.

Gabriel returned Cole's smile, then turned to Vin. "You're right about one thing." He acknowledged Vin with a look—or more like a glare. "We need to try something before more alternates are sent. Until we can't control the area anymore. So all the bears agree, we move the relic, and once we know it's safe, we have a secure place, we bring Cassie, and try it again. Outside."

Vin's hand clenched.

"I'll try what Gabriel said." I decided everything quickly, looking back and forth between them. "But if this new plan doesn't work, then we listen to Vin, even if it means I might leave for a while."

Vin's hand relaxed. Gabriel shook his head. "I just don't understand why I can't find your stone," Vin said, looking at me, then at Gabriel's and my hands clasped together. "I've asked practically everyone in town, anywhere near town, except..." He looked from Gabriel, to Cole, to Aaron. His expression went dark, his lips tightening into his special, powerful smile. "Where is the guidestone?" He glared at Gabriel.

Gabriel's eyes went distant. "I don't know."

He turned to Aaron, repeating the question.

"I don't know," Aaron echoed.

"Hey, cut that out!" Cole exclaimed. "We're all on the same side here!"

"You're right, you're right..." Vin pinched the bridge of his nose, closing his eyes. "Sorry." He took a deep breath and looked up at Cole. "And I keep forgetting you seem to be immune to my abilities." He gave a small grimace.

Cole beamed like he'd been praised. And maybe he had. As far as Vin had let on, it seemed the only other person who'd been able to resist his compulsion was me.

"I know it's frustrating you can't find it, but maybe we don't need it anymore." Gabriel lifted his chin. "Besides, you know what Richard said. It's at someone's home, so it'll turn up once we figure out whose home he meant."

"You know, I was wondering the other day, could he have meant Cassie's home?" Aaron offered. "I know you were in there, but couldn't Rose have moved it or it got lost or something, and it's been there all along?"

"You may have a point," Vin said slowly, his tone no longer harsh. "It sort of makes sense. I went through after the fire, but it was so dark. I guess it couldn't hurt to check again."

"Yeah, I'd search tomorrow," Aaron said. "Better chances with daylight."

"OK. And I'll stop by the station to try to question that officer."

I sighed, happy that the peace between Vin and the Knights would last one more day. Gabriel finally released my hand, and gave me a crooked smile. After Gabriel righted his chair and sat down next to me, without thought, I shifted in my seat, closer to him, and pressed the length of my bare arm below my t-shirt into his. Our skin touched, forearm to forearm, and I leaned into his warmth. Vin winced, jerking back from the table, and I cursed myself. *Stupid. Stupid! Why did you just make things worse!?*

What must Vin have been thinking the last few days? Not just about me choosing Gabriel, but about me not being able to touch anyone but Gabriel? I moved my arm away, but Vin stalked from the room. If he didn't want to talk before, he definitely wouldn't want to talk now. I sat, quiet and still, as Cole, Aaron, and Gabriel finished dinner.

The next morning, I meandered along the riverbank with Zoe, Cole, Richie, and Rosie, Aaron and an elder bear out somewhere on the grounds, patrolling. How had I reached this odd equilibrium? My condition was still worse than ever, but out here in the sun and in Gabriel's arms every night, I could almost deny it. In contrast to the recent fires and violence, the relative quiet of the last week had created a false sense of safety. Sure, Mike was in no position to hurt anyone, and he'd implicated Cameron, who had apparently fled without a trace. Everyone who'd wandered into town since hadn't proven much of a threat. But Cameron's note sounded more like an apology than a confession, and now there were odd strangers in the forest. Vin must be right. The calm of the last week gave me a foreboding, an unease that wouldn't subside. Something was up.

Something else was off now too. I'd seen more flashes of light in the last few days—Richard apparently watching over me or trying to talk to me like before—but now when the light got close, it quickly went dark from the outside right into the center. I'd never seen it do that before.

Richie and Rosie ran in circles, chasing their own then each other's tails, and Cole threw a stick a few yards out for Zoe, giving her a pat each time she brought it back, tail wagging. Cole rambled on about everything we'd get to do when all this was over. If Richard did appear again, he'd need to explain what he meant at Gram's about how maybe he could be with her again one day—if my sisters and I managed "to do what needs to be done." I'd do anything if it meant Gram and Richard could be together again, though there was no imagining how I could make it possible.

Zoe dropped the stick and hobbled happily down to the water's edge, placing her two front paws in where the current gurgled at a slow, calming pace. She lifted her head and looked up to the middle of the river where something glinted, sending off bright flashes, lighting the water to a crystal blue.

Richard, again. I willed him to come near, but just as it had since after the cemetery, the light faded from the outside in, the water going dark.

We kept walking. After several more paces the light reappeared, streaking across a cluster of trees only to darken, collapsing into itself. "What's going on with that light?" Cole asked. "Gabriel said it's Dad's friend. I keep seeing it, but nothing happens."

"I'm not sure." It raced toward us once again, this time with so much force it appeared like a small supernova bursting, then quickly fading away. It was like Richard was trying to make contact with us again, but couldn't.

Maybe whatever my sister had been doing to help him appear before wasn't working so well now? Or something stopped him?

Oh God. I froze in my tracks. Cole was now several steps ahead with Richie and Rosie, still rambling on about how perfect life would be when all this was over.

Oh God. So stupid.

Not Cole. Me.

I started shaking.

What if Richard was trying to tell us something—and couldn't? And Richard had seemed so anxious about my locket. He said "yes, yes" and then "why has no one… to her?" and "right at…home…" Then Gabriel and I went home, and asked Cole and Aaron about it. And if Cameron had taken it with him, or a kid from school had it, it wouldn't be "right at home"—the Knight home.

My body shook harder, my thoughts racing.

What if another Knight was involved? What if a Knight had been involved in the fire, but Mike had pointed the finger at the wrong one? What if Cameron hadn't written that letter to the police, getting me sent off to Glenwood Springs when the fire had taken the wrong life?

As if Richard could read my mind, the light appeared again, flashing up from the ground several feet ahead. The closest it had been in days.

It disappeared just as quickly, but left something behind. A small patch of light shimmered in the grass. No, not light. A silver loop. Intertwined loops.

The bracelet Gram gave me.

How had it gotten here? If Richard could transport whatever he wanted, he would've brought my missing locket or left a note— maybe the bracelet was special? I'd forgotten about it, but Richard hadn't and must've recovered it outside the cottage, in the skirt of Gram's dress. What did I know about it? Nothing. And I'd only worn it for a moment on the way to the dance and then for another at the dance, before Cameron walked up. With Aaron there.

And the bracelet had been mentioned in that letter…

My body shook even harder. Somehow I managed to walk over and pick up the jewelry. I slipped it on, clasped my hands behind my back, and turned to Cole, who still meandered along and didn't seem to notice anything. "Cole, why did you come home from Gram's that night, leaving her alone?" I asked in a casual voice.

"Hmm? Oh, Aaron told me to. He said I was supposed to—but Dad's not sure why, he didn't tell him to. I'm so sorry." Cole stopped. "You know I'm sorry, right?" His shoulders collapsed, his large body shrinking into itself. "It's my fault—" his voice broke.

"But if Aaron told you to leave that night, how could it be your fault?" I asked as gently as I could, the shaking swaying my body. I widened my stance in the grass.

"Because sometimes… sometimes I don't pay attention to Aaron like I should. Even though he's been a good big brother, teaching me how to drive, taking me to get my permit when Dad was too busy. He's just so depressed—so angry—all the time. And just, you know, jealous. Of normal kids, kids like Cameron, because they can go do whatever they want. It makes me sad." He curled in on himself further. "So I must have not been paying attention. Aaron said I misunderstood when to leave Rose, and you'd forgive me. You've forgiven me—right?"

I didn't answer.

"Right, Cassie? You've forgiven me? Aaron said you would."

Oh God. It all fell into place.

Aaron. His clear dislike of me. I'll give him this—he never really tried to hide it. And how different he was from the rest of the bear part of his family. How he seemed to want different things. How Gabriel had told his whole family about my locket the day before it went missing. He didn't just tell Cameron. He told everyone.

Would Aaron really deceive his dad and brothers though? Betray them?

Want me dead?

"Cole, we need to get back to the house." My arms fell to my side—the bracelet barely staying on. I rushed us back to the house, Zoe struggling to keep up. Cole followed with Richie and Rosie, the pups trying to play tag with me, Cole looking confused. As quick as I could I left him in the kitchen in front of the fridge, and settled Zoe in his room with Richie and Rosie. Next, I hid the bracelet deep in Cameron's closet. If it was important, it seemed the last place Aaron would look, since we'd just searched it days ago. Bracelet safely hidden, I knocked on Vin's door. But of course Vin was out looking for my locket at Gram's, regardless of what the Knights said about not needing it anymore. Gabriel was gone too, helping Bernard move the relic out from the cave. Gabriel was supposed to come back and get me when they were done. Although it would be just like last time. I'd just disappoint everyone.

But that wasn't what I was worried about now. Now I was mad at myself. For once I hadn't been distrustful enough. I ran back to my room and grabbed my cell. No signal. Odd. Or intentional?

I raced back down the hall and stood in front of Aaron's door. I hesitated, took a step back. If he'd taken my locket, he was smart. It wouldn't be in there. Especially not after we'd told him what Richard said. He'd probably moved it. And when he'd told Vin last night he didn't know where it was, that could've been true if he'd given it to someone else to hide…

I shouldn't waste time in his room, but I couldn't sit still. Aaron might've helped in what happened to Gram. Maybe Mike had been lying, or he'd been influenced again by the Summum Malum. Maybe, as Vin suggested, Cameron wasn't involved at all. And Aaron was still here. *Somewhere.* Should I tell Cole about his brother? Would he believe me?

A car rumbled outside, looping into the drive. I darted to the window. Steps from the porch, a monster pickup truck I'd never seen before idled, half the truck bed loaded with wood—long logs, like they used for the town bonfires.

Suddenly, I didn't feel safe. Not in the slightest.

I burst into Vin's room and scribbled a note. All I wrote was "Aaron." If Vin found it before I found him, he'd understand. Once you got past the impossibility of such a betrayal… he'd understand. I raced down the hall, stumbling down the stairs, through the kitchen—not finding Cole, bypassing the safe room with its keypad—and into the garage, grabbing for the VW key hanging on the wall. *Get to Vin. Get to Vin. Or Gabriel, up on the mountain.* I fumbled the key, knocking it to the floor, not hearing the sound of movement behind me until it was too late.

I turned around.

Aaron stood there, towering over me.

"You have good timing." His chin lifted. He looked pleased with himself.

A pounding echoed from the house.

"That would be our ride." He smirked.

It was my hesitation that did me in. Aaron reached for the flesh of my face fast, so fast. Before I could even think to move, he cornered me, pinned me. His hands brushed past my cheeks, wrapping around my mouth. Silencing my screams.

31
THE PYRE

I WOKE SLOWLY, TO PAIN. CONFUSION. THE SMELL OF PINE SAP. Cold air swirling around me. Fragments of a memory taking shape in my mind: smothering hands, searing burns, a glimpse of the past for a moment before I lost consciousness…

"I'll take care of her," Aaron's voice echoed. "Just remember our deal." He stared into a sprawling shadow. In its depths, something shifted.

"Just remember to break her bond with the relic first," a reedy voice hissed.

Aaron laughed. "I'll break it—it's only like the whole reason we've waited since the fire. Good thing Mike messed up, huh? After all the crap you gave me."

"That boy… was not right. Too wicked a soul cannot be controlled. Only through blind luck did his failure work to our advantage. Next time, you listen."

"Yeah, but good thing the bitch lived, so you got to see what she did at the hospital, or she'd already be dead and burned—part of the relic still tied to her."

"Follow instructions, that will not happen." From the shadow's heart, a hooded silhouette took a threatening step toward Aaron, who shivered. "The relic is her weakness. Yet only so long as she does not access it fully. Bring it close, it pulls in, diminishes her strength.

Burn her then, throw it into the flames, the bond is broken. But too close, a touch… a mistake… all might be lost."

"There'll be no mistake." Aaron's voice wavered. "It was me who came to you. Me who put the guidestone out of reach."

"You made your point. We have an understanding. Now go." The unnatural gloom lifted, revealing a clear night. Silence gave way to the splash of water, waves striking boulders looming in the darkness. Aaron stood on a high bank above. It must be the river, but far from town. Downstream of where I'd lost my memory. Far enough away…

My body pitched to the side, bringing me back to present.

Bang. Pain shot through me, focusing my eyes. I'd hit the side of a truck bed. I lay half facing it, half facing up, my arms pinned under me. I struggled to sit up, and fell back down, my arms useless, imprisoned. Tree tops passed above in a blur. Bundles of wood jostled next to me. And a large body lay unmoving on the other side.

Oh no. Cole!

I rolled onto my belly, my arms pulling at clinging restraints, my legs yanking at the restraints at my ankles, scrambling to my knees. As if tossed in a hurricane, my body moved forward, smacking against metal, knocking into wood, flailing in the wind, until finally I reached him. "Cole." My lips stung, barely parting, trapping the sound. I forced my burned mouth to open. "Cole!" He didn't move. "Wake up."

No movement.

There were no wounds. No signs of trauma. No blood. But the skin around his eyes was red, swollen, bubbled. Traces of a yellow and green ooze leached from the closed lids. What could have caused it? Why wasn't he moving? I rested my ear right below the pocket of his t-shirt. Nothing. Then I heard it. Almost nothing at all.

thud…

Then nothing.

The pause between heartbeats was too long. My hands strained behind me. I needed to start chest compressions.

thud…

I sighed at the faint echo of his heartbeat.

"Cole," I pleaded again. I needed him awake. For his sake, and mine. I needed his help, though his wrists and ankles were bound like mine, with several strips of duct tape, that wouldn't hold him long. I butted my head against his side. Again, harder. Why wasn't he waking up? If Aaron was actually responsible for this, he wouldn't hurt his brother. Right?

The truck stopped. My body flew forward, hitting the cab, bouncing back and crashing into the pile of wood, pain exploding at the base of my skull, spasming down my spine. An instant later, the pain disappeared. My eyelids fell shut.

So… sleepy…

"Oh look, she's moved. Maybe she's up," Aaron chuckled.

I tried to shake my head, fighting off the blackness.

A hawk shrieked in the distance. Familiar scents of the forest surrounded me.

I forced my eyes open.

"Looks like she'll get to enjoy the show." Aaron dropped the tailgate, towering over me. Raising a tire iron, he pressed the hooked end of the metal bar into my head. "Don't cause any trouble, or you'll miss out on the fun."

Fun? My head pounded. I fought to get to my knees, to get to standing, but it wouldn't have made any difference. Even if my legs were free, *my head…*

I'd lose any race. I couldn't outrun them.

Aaron seemed to know I had made the calculations and realized this. He lowered the tire iron, scooped me up with one arm, and tossed me over his shoulder, pinning my legs to his chest. He stomped away, my torso flopping behind him, compounding the pressure in my skull, blurring my vision. He stopped by the side of a narrow dirt road. The pounding eased, and two spots of movement flickered into my vision.

Forming shapes… colors… around the truck.

Two men. Looking ordinary enough. Human enough. Medium height, medium build. Dark hair. Not bald, not creepy, like the giants. Yet, without doubt, part of the *fun*. Aaron must be waiting for them. Well, they weren't much bigger than me. I'd take one of them down if I had to. Maybe even both, if I could get back some strength, get my vision to clear, and get all this damn tape off. It was Aaron who worried me.

The men climbed up the back, reaching for something. Not the brown heaps. There was only one other thing in there. "No!" I screamed. Whatever they wanted with Cole, it couldn't be good.

Aaron turned. "Leave him out of this. We only brought him so her tight-ass boyfriend wouldn't get back and figure things out. She's been stringing him along while she gets cozy with my brother."

They shrugged, and one of them hopped off the back, grabbed a green covering—a tarp?—from the truck cab, and tossed it over Cole, loose enough I had to believe he could still breathe.

The tarp was caught on the wood, but the men pulled it back around Cole and began throwing the wood bundles to the ground. Landing with heavy thuds, the wood rolled this way and that in the dirt. But the men organized them, making several piles. Now that they were away from Cole, I tried to block the men out. Whatever else they were doing wasn't nearly as important as thinking of a way out of this. But I couldn't focus. It was the pounding, still lingering between my ears. More than that, the men. Something wasn't right. Each one's dark head and denim-clad bodies hovered over a wood pile. I squinted. They were securing the bundles, which were already tied together, to each other, with more rope. They were getting them ready to carry? So? I squinted harder. Oh. Oh no, something really was wrong with the picture. Because the men were struggling to tie the rope with chunky, blue fingers. Sunlight pushed through the trees—a warm fall day—yet the men's hands, peeking out from their long denim jackets, were covered with blue gloves. Thick, like a skier's, but shiny, rubbery. These must be the hikers the bear had spotted? But what did that mean? Couldn't be good. Why the gloves?

Maybe it was for handling the wood, but I had to think that probably wasn't good either.

No time to learn more. Aaron launched us up a steep, narrow path, kicking dust in my face. The men marched after us, arms loaded with wood, backs weighed down with bound bundles strapped behind them. With every step, my stomach churned. They clearly intended to burn me, which wouldn't go so well for them if I was awake. But if I wasn't, well, I couldn't put out fire if I was unconscious, and I was pretty sure my body would burn eventually, if my mind wasn't telling it not to. My stomach somersaulted.

Those thoughts don't help! Figure a way out of this. Concentrate. You're smart. Smarter than them. You'll come up with a plan. Better than theirs.

The pep talk wasn't working. Bile rose in my throat. I swallowed it down, but the foul taste shot back up, like so many things shooting through my mind. Hanging upside down and banging against Aaron's back wasn't helping with either problem.

Aaron's vision. That made me the most uneasy. The part about "diminishing" my strength—throwing me in flames—could I do something before they tried? The tire iron at Aaron's side. If I got my hands free, could I use it? Turn it against him? How? With Aaron and his buddies, it would be three against one. *Three against one.* At school, I rarely got out of a fight with those odds without being touched. If they touched me, more than a few times, even once firmly, it would be over. I'd have no chance then.

For now, stay calm. No throwing up.

Pay attention. Learn something. Aaron's plan had to extend beyond the burning, and I had to get past it too, to think beyond it, if I had any chance of escaping. Somehow he'd gotten the better of Cole, but there was the rest of the Knights, the bears, Vin, a host of other details he must have anticipated. Plans that I might be able to take advantage of—if I could guess them.

"Why are you doing this?" I shouted, my mouth feeling like it might be healing a bit.

Aaron slowed, glancing over his shoulder. "So many reasons. Just think about it half a second, you stupid bitch." *Oh Aaron, I am. Trust me.*

What had made me suspect Cameron? His motive. Losing his dad. And Aaron's? Dust stuck in my throat and I coughed. "You, ah, blame me for what happened to your mom and sister…"

"Well, isn't that a nice way to put it? You show up one day, no warning, with your little guidestone, and put even bigger targets on my family's heads—so yeah, you are to blame."

"But, um, what was I supposed to have done?" Maybe I could reason with him?

"You're the miraculous one. You figure it out." He crushed my legs between his arm and chest. A small whimper escaped me. "I can tell you one thing. You weren't supposed to screw up! Do you know how many damn times I had to listen to stories about the Una!?" He squeezed harder. "And you turn out to be a dipshit." He accelerated up the path, knocking my head harder.

His strength was not a good sign for getting the tire iron away from him. "I'm sorry," I mumbled. "I'd change everything. If I could." The pounding was so much worse. I felt light-headed.

"I could almost forgive you—for showing up how you did." I tried to focus on his words. "It was innocent enough. Something Cole would do. I tried to forgive you, you know. More than Cameron."

More than Cameron? What did that mean?

And how this helped, I had no idea, but at least he was talking and seemed happy to continue. "We were there, you know, when you were pulled from the river." *What?* "I was out patrolling, and Cameron tagged along, like he liked to, pretending to be one of us." He laughed. "We saw you floating. You were just this naked, possibly dead, girl. But I had a bad feeling." He ground out between clenched teeth. "Just in case… I called a U.S. Forest guy I'd been bribing for years to be a lookout. I told him to rescue you. But, just in case you were alternate race, I bribed him to tell that story, keep the news about you quiet, find any supplies you'd had around your campsite and destroy them." *Oh god.* Aaron might have been responsible for finding me, getting me rescued, but he was also the reason Vin didn't find me for so long? "Then when the relic lit up, I knew it was trouble. After years of guarding some dead stone, things had finally settled down. Mom and Dad were letting me out more. Life was just getting bearable." He shrugged, his shoulder pressing into my belly. "After what happened to Gabriel, to Mom and Sarah, Cameron's dad, Cameron and I really put the pieces together. Cameron wanted to test our theory, pulled that crap in the gym your first week. Then made it his mission to torture you. Me, I figured you'd caused all the damage you could. And things were okay, for a while."

So they'd known about me all along and Cameron was involved in this too? His touching me that one time hadn't been an accident? "Why didn't you and Cameron tell… your family… about me?" How much longer till I blacked out? Using what little strength I had, I twisted my head, looking around him. Through the trees, something shimmered. A tightly woven pattern came into view. A fence. I sank back over his shoulder. Whatever was on the other side, that had to be it… wherever our destination was. Then he'd stop.

"That would have just made things worse for everybody," he snarled. "Cameron agreed. He didn't really get it; he just wanted to see you suffer. I told him having his friends jump you all the time would only draw attention, but he's as dumb as you are."

He paused and his tone changed back to satisfaction. "And there's also the matter of leverage."

That brought me back.

"Huh?"

"I was always thinking bigger than Cameron. For me, you were leverage."

"What?" *Focus.*

"I knew long before you showed up that we were fighting a losing battle. All to protect some silly stone. For the Una. For you. And you're not strong enough or smart enough to go up against them."

"So?"

"So I waited to use you. For when the stalemate ended, for when it was time to play my hand—and I could finally put an end to this pointless stupidity." Aaron spat out the words. "Of course, I had to ditch Cameron. He couldn't see the bigger picture. He's not special, like us—hasn't made the sacrifices I have—so how could I expect him to understand what needed to be done? I had to deal with the most powerful beings out there, manage Mike for them, send the letter to the police, everything. But when Cameron started going soft and talking about running his mouth… I got him out of the way."

What was Aaron trying to say? What had I learned? Not the details. The point. *Think.* He had a boiling resentment against all the sacrifices the bear members of the Knight family had made. He'd made a deal? Like the giants had? In the beginning, he and Cameron had been in on it together, but Cameron had just been looking to get back at me at school. Cameron was gone because of Aaron. Aaron was the one working with the Summum Malum. He hated me.

What could I do with that?

Aaron halted, shifted my weight, easing his grip, and pulled something from his pocket. A lock clicked, and a wide gate swung out, then back again until it got hung up in some brush. Aaron hesitated before passing through, glancing down one side of the fence. A tall wooden post—a telephone pole? Silver mesh-work of wire, cutting through a sea of green. We were deep in the forest. On one side of the fence-line, rough grass with patches of bare dirt and rock. On the other side, low brush, brown and dead along the fence, as though it had been sprayed with something. Out in the live brush several yards away, brown spots.

Aaron called over his shoulder, swinging me slightly. "Pull the bear in. Toss the wood with the rest of it." As he swung me back, the brown spots resolved themselves into a heap of brown fur laying behind bushes and low branches. Turning my head, I glimpsed a narrow dirt road in the opposite direction through the forest. Another thick wooden pole, and a set of wires crossing high above the road, emerging from the trees down the steep slope. A small power line. He walked several paces past the gate, and dropped me. I wasn't sure how much time passed before I realized I'd landed. But I was sure I was still stuck at step one. *Stay calm. Learn something.*

I had. More than just Aaron's resentment and jealousy, and the depths of scheming and betrayal he'd embraced to revenge himself and reorder his life. I'd learned he had a plan and it involved more than me and a bonfire. Sweat broke out on the back of my neck, dampening my ponytail as my dread increased. They were on a schedule, and this place hadn't been chosen by accident. There was a road up here, to whatever was beyond the fence, and a power line. There was a bear outside. The gate looked wide enough to fit a vehicle, but maybe not their monster truck. Still, why had Aaron parked on a different road, taking a path from the opposite direction?

I watched from the dirt, unable to feel my legs, as the two men did as Aaron directed, chucking the wood bundles on top of a large mound of logs to the side of the gate, then struggling with their gloved hands to heave the bear out from the undergrowth. They grumbled and cursed, but it didn't sound like English. When they rolled the bear over a bush and onto the path by the road, I got a better look. I didn't recognize the animal—it certainly wasn't Gabriel—although it resembled his great-grandfather, but with different white markings. As the men labored to move it, finally each grabbing a bear leg and pulling it past the gate, and then past me, several feet away, I prayed for it to wake. To show it lived. That it might help us both. But its eyes stayed shut. The fur around its face was wet. Matted. Revealing red, bubbled skin. Traces of yellowish-green against the dark coat.

Their grumblings quieted by a harsh rebuke from Aaron, the men dragged the bear in sullen silence, all the way across the expanse of fenced-in clearing. They labored up the slope just inside the gate, along the road up a more gradual incline, to the door of a small building at the foot of a tall antenna tower, planted firmly on a slight rise near the back of the clearing. The power line came over the fence just left of the gate, crossed the clearing on two poles, and disappeared into what looked like a thick pipe jutting out of the flat roof of the little building.

The two men didn't waste any time resting from their exertions with the bear. One of them unlocked the door with a code Aaron called out, a security panel beeping with each number he pressed, and then they lugged the animal inside. Aaron stomped up behind them, brandishing his tire iron. Pounding and a loud crash echoed down from the building. Moments later, all three emerged, minus the animal, and Aaron directed the same man to lock the door again. It was their bothering to lock the door that gave me hope the bear was still alive, and Aaron's knowledge—of the code—that made me realize our location.

The Knights' cell tower, the one they had had built.

Aaron taking the back route here… that would make sense, if he was trying to keep his presence hidden. From who? Slowly the pieces from Aaron's vision were fitting into what was going on. Aaron needed me and the relic together. So it must be on its way. This must be where Gabriel and Bernard were bringing it… they'd be here soon!

I relaxed into the ground, taking a deep breath, hope building, the start of a plan finally forming as Aaron and the men raced around me. They worked silently, gathering up armfuls of wood by the gate, moving every last bundle to a spot up near the building, cutting the ties, then stacking the logs methodically on a strip of flat earth where the slope up from the gate to the building leveled out. They slowly formed a platform several feet high, several feet wide, and what looked to be the length of a body, and finally, doused it in gasoline from two plastic bottles the men fetched from outside the gate, where the rest of the wood had been mounded when we'd arrived. They'd clearly been up here earlier, preparing for this.

Preparing to build a wooden structure much larger than any bonfire I'd seen in town. Double the size. And not built in a dirt perimeter, far from flammable materials, with water nearby. They'd built this one near patches of grass and weeds, not far from the building, with no sign of water.

One of the men stepped back, swiping at his brow, jostling his bottle.

"Hey," Aaron said. "Be careful with that. It's leaking."

"So what if it's leaking?" The man's voice carried a faint, smooth accent.

Before Aaron could answer the other man stepped in, speaking in a similar tone. "Yeah, so? Let the whole place burn." He tossed aside his bottle, sending it rolling into a patch of weeds. Aaron protested, but the first man flung his bottle too. It landed in the same weeds. Aaron glanced nervously at the distance between the gasoline-drenched platform, the weeds, and the building, but seemed to decide it was not worth agitating the men further over. He stepped away from the platform with them, moving to a patch of grass to survey their daunting construction. A funeral pyre. I'd read about pyres—structures for burning a body, used from early times as part of a funeral rite. But I'd certainly never seen one. And this one was obviously intended for me.

For an instant, all my attempts at bravery failed. Terror gripped my heart.

One of the men pulled off his glove and pulled out a lighter from a small pocket on the front of his jacket. He drew a small cloth from his jeans, dropped the lighter in it, rubbed it off, and slowly handed it to Aaron, being careful not to touch him.

Why all the caution? Did these guys have issues with touching people too?

They were talking again, but not loudly enough to hear. When the man stepped away from Aaron, something in his hand caught the sunlight. In his ungloved hand. Gleaming. But not something he was holding at all. It was his hand itself. It was shiny and spotted, with yellow splotches, bright, almost fluorescent. The rest of his dark flesh, face and neck, looked normal, but his hand—his entire hand, up to the wrist—caught in the light, looked more and more like the smooth, wet skin of…

A frog.

What the hell!?

Frog-hands pulled off his other glove and threw them both down by the building. The second man did the same. Even from the gate, with half the width of the clearing between us, it was clear. These men—these frog-men—their hands weren't right. What did their frog-hands mean? Why had the one been so careful not to touch Aaron? Did it have to do with whatever had happened to Cole? And to the bear?

Now, gloveless, they seemed to be readying themselves for something. They moved together to stand shoulder to shoulder to the side of the pyre. Aaron slipped the lighter into his pocket and moved over me. *Don't struggle. Follow the plan. My plan.* I had to save energy, get back more strength, get myself ready for when Gabriel and Bernard arrived. So I let Aaron drag me by my shirt all the way across the clearing, up the incline.

Trying not to flinch as he tossed me onto the wood, I let out an intentional high-pitched scream instead—as pitiful as I could make it—and watched the satisfaction flash across Aaron's face. Let him think me weak and defeated. Because surely my best play, possibly my only one, was to wait until Gabriel and Bernard arrived. And if anyone could convince Aaron to back down from this, it would be his father. I could only hope, from what I guessed Aaron must have been doing in the building—knocking out the cell signal—that he'd acted too soon and the missing signal would be a warning as Gabriel and Bernard approached. If they picked up on that, they'd be prepared for the possibility something wasn't right, even turn around. Call more bears. Who else would they call? Even if they picked up another cell tower? They'd never call the police. But maybe Vin?

No. Yes. Equal parts of me warred. I did and didn't want Vin involved. I didn't think Aaron would hurt his father and older brother. But he'd already allowed Cole to be drugged and bound, done something to get Cameron "out of the way." How much mercy would he show Vin? No, I couldn't—wouldn't—think it.

I wasn't sure how much time passed. Only that the sun beat down, roasting my skin. The noxious smell of gasoline rose, dulling my mind. It didn't matter. I focused on one thing—freeing myself from the tape binding my hands. The tape had picked up some gasoline from the wet logs. It was slick, and seemed to be stretching and softening. Keeping as still as I could, I rubbed my wrists back and forth against the wood beneath me, ignoring stabs of pain as the rough bark cut into the surrounding flesh. Gasoline seeped into the wounds, stinging and burning. Maybe it would act as a disinfectant? That wood must be filthy. *Get a grip*. Not a good time to fall into a delirium.

Aaron moved to stand in front of the pyre, gripping the tire iron. The two frog-men flanked him on both sides. Facing the gate. Waiting.

Finally the faint sound of an engine hummed through the woods. It hummed louder, approaching us. Soon it was joined by the distinctive crunch of gravel on the dirt road outside. The engine shut off. A car door squeaked open. At last, a voice. "Dad, where's Uncle Gus?" It was Gabriel. But I probably shouldn't anger Aaron by speaking yet.

"Maybe a nap?" Bernard answered. A car door slammed shut. "But not on such an important day. You look that way. I'll look over here."

The rustle of bushes being pushed aside.

"Son, he should be here. Something's wrong." Bernard breathed heavily. "Why's the gate open? Aaron? What are you—what is that? Son!?"

I lifted my head from the wood.

Bernard stood by the gate, his gaze taking in the pyre, the frog-men, one of the bottles peeking through the weeds. Gabriel rushed past him, and Bernard lunged, grabbing his arm, pulling him to a stop.

"Cassie!" Gabriel shouted, his eyes locking on mine across the 20 yards that separated us.

He stood so tall and strong, looking so fearless. He hadn't hidden his scars, his polo collar was down today. I'd never seen him look more confident.

But concern and gentle emotions for me were reflected on his face.

I held his gaze and tried to express how I felt. How my pulse had quickened at his voice. How my heart wanted to burst from my chest. I mouthed three words to him—words I hoped he could see from this distance—words I hoped, but couldn't be certain, I'd get another chance to say. I love you. *He must see.* I love you, I mouthed again.

His face lifted with emotion.

Elation. Relief. Worry.

Then he broke from his dad and charged.

"Stay back. No need for this to get messy," Aaron said. The frog-men stepped forward.

Bernard raced after Gabriel, and snagged the back of his polo. They slid awkwardly in the dirt, kicking up dust. Gabriel staggered another step. "Stop," Bernard pleaded, "Gabriel, she's okay. Talk first."

I nodded down from the pyre at Gabriel, still needing more time to free my hands and force myself into action. He gave no acknowledgment, but his eyes focused on my face, which was probably still burned enough for him to see, if the pain in his expression was any indication. His gaze moved along the length of my body, checking for damage. I started to twist and make small movements behind Aaron, working harder at the tape at my back. Would Aaron wonder about the noise behind him? Would he even hesitate before using the tire iron?

Gabriel seemed to sense my fears that Aaron would turn around and see what I was up to, and drew Aaron's attention to himself. "What are you doing?" Gabriel roared.

"What needs to be done," Aaron said. "What no one else would do." He shot Gabriel a defiant look.

Gabriel pulled out his cell and stared at the screen. The twitch of his mouth told me I was right. The signal was gone.

"Explain yourself." Bernard demanded across the clearing.

"Dad." Aaron's features softened. "We have to protect what's left of us. We have to save and worry about our own." He clutched the tire iron to his waist with a hand and a forearm and rocked in place. He no longer looked like a boy on the brink of adulthood, but like a child asking for something. Something he wanted desperately. "It's too late, too far along in the battle. We can't worry about everything—everyone—else."

"Son." Bernard's shoulders sagged. "I think I know what's going on here. And I understand what you're feeling." He hunched forward, looking almost as stooped as his grandfather had that day outside the cave. "But you're going to have to say it—say what you intend before you go through with it."

"I, um, I've made a deal." Aaron kicked at a rock in the dirt. "The Summum Malum will leave us alone, and they'll bring back what's left of the bears. You just need to give me the stone."

Bernard glanced up at me. "But that's not all, is it?"

Aaron looked over his shoulder, at the rows of logs stacked under me and stepped back, until he was standing by the pile, right next to my head. I froze, trying to look as pathetic as I must have when he'd first brought me here. "I'll take care of the rest," Aaron called back, then whispered down at me, "I'll do it quickly."

"Quickly?" My voice sounded higher pitched than Kaylee's.

"You won't have to suffer." His hands shook and he tightened his hold on the tire iron with one while reaching into his pocket with the other. I whimpered, a totally involuntary sound of pain. "You won't be awake." He glanced at me with what passed for sympathy and gripped the lighter in his pocket.

Bernard tilted his head and extended his left hand, palm forward, inviting Aaron to walk across the clearing and take it. "Aaron,

taunt me before I died. Without it my punishment wouldn't have been to the leg.

Aaron shot a glance at the frog-man standing over Gabriel, "Keep an eye on her. Make sure she cooperates."

The frog-man nodded.

Aaron ripped off the remains of his shirt, bunched it up, and wiped his face. Tossing the bloodied rag aside, he walked up toward the building, pulled out of the grass several lengths of rope left from the wood bundles, and compared them, until he found one he liked. It was the longest one. He strode back down, past the front of the pyre, and stood over me, in the middle of the wood stacks. "Unless you want more pain, you'll sit up."

I obeyed, pushing my way to sitting, gasoline stinging my abraded hands. I wouldn't risk anything more happening to Gabriel. And one bad knee was enough. I let Aaron wrap the rope around me. Each length of coil he pulled around my back and chest forced my arms further down, pressing them into my sides. Taking his time, tying it in several spots, Aaron seemed careful not to touch me now that he had human hands and fingers again.

He caught my calculating look. "I don't need you in my head again, witch. Cameron and I suspected you might have special skills tied to touching people, since you made such a big deal about that. That's why he only touched you the once, and then left that to others. But I know exactly what happens—how you get into people's minds. Grandpa told me." He smirked. "He heard it from Gabriel."

Of course he knew. The rest of the bear members of the Knights had no secrets from each other. I realized now that Aaron must have wanted me unconscious quickly when he'd found me in the garage. But at this moment, with the hard look in his eyes, I could tell he wanted me awake.

As Aaron pulled tight the last knots tying me, the frog-man at Gabriel's side finally turned his attention from me, looking around for his... friend? Brother? He glanced all around, finally spotting the other frog-man by the gate. He cried out and ran down the clearing.

He knelt down and tried to close up the openings in his friend's chest. He pressed them together with his hands. Blood continued to run out. He pulled at the shredded denim jacket, trying to cover or bind up the claw marks. It was no use.

"He's dead." The frog-man's voice barely carried up the hill. He touched his friend's shoulder, dropping his head. "They killed my brother." His hands shook.

Aaron shrugged.

The frog-man looked at Aaron, pain and defiance in his eyes, then at Bernard lying near his brother. "No foolish mercy now." His yellow fingers splayed, his hands spreading wide.

"No!" Aaron bellowed. "You promised. Only enough to knock them out."

The frog-man hesitated. But only for a moment. "The deal's changed." He lunged, reaching for Bernard.

"Bernard!" I shouted, but he didn't move.

Aaron hurled the tire iron. For an instant he was the starting quarterback, and it was a good throw, striking the frog-man, sending him stumbling off balance. Aaron sprinted down after him, but before Aaron could get there, the frog-man scooped up the metal rod, grabbing it by the bent wrench end, and thrust the pointed end through Bernard's eye.

A sickening squelch of flesh and crunch of bone rang across the clearing. The frog-man raised a fist. "There! I won't overdose him with my toxin, just like I promised, and we can call it even."

"You maggot!" Aaron raged, knocking him in the face with an awkward blow.

"I'd be careful." The frog-man held up his hands, flashing his yellow palms in the air. "You know what I can do with these." He staggered back, leaning against the fence.

"Dad…" Aaron knelt by Bernard's body. The metal rod jutted across his bear snout, still protruding from his face. Aaron examined the wound closely, before slowly pulling the metal out. From what I could see, little additional blood came out after the rod was removed. Aaron stood. With a tremendous heave, his upper body contracting in a spasm, Aaron flung the tire iron far into the trees beyond the fence, so far that no sound of it landing carried back. He collapsed back to the ground. "Don't worry, Dad." Aaron's body was racked with a sob, then he shook his head, trying to regain control of his emotions. "This is all for the best. All for the best."

A long moment passed before Aaron turned, and spat at the frog-man, "You. Go look for the stone."

The frog-man scowled. "When this is over, we're having a talk. About who should've been in charge here." He rubbed his shoulder where the bent side of the tire iron had struck, and shuffled alongside the fence, sliding a yellow hand against it for support, then pushed away, swaying on his feet through the gate, disappearing into the forest outside.

Aaron trod slowly back up to the pyre, shooting a dark look at me. "And you. This is all your fault." Nearing my side, he grabbed the lighter from the dirt with his left hand, pushing it into my face, nearly touching me. His right index finger waved next to it. "I was going to spare you some pain, but now…" His face was hard, eyes alive with malice, like seeing his father hurt had flipped a switch. Not only was every bit of sympathy gone, his expression held pleasure in what he was about to do. "Now I'll make sure you feel every second as you burn."

The tip of the lighter hovered above me, and I shuddered, knowing with certainty now what the strange conversation from Aaron's vision meant. They believed if the relic was close enough, without me touching it, that it would actually draw something from me, take something back. Like it seemed it already had. Although, perhaps Aaron didn't know that yet—that it had already connected with me, taken something. But it didn't matter, he'd find out eventually, and I couldn't escape the truth.

Aaron knew what I'd been able to do with fire before—he'd said as much. And he wouldn't be worried about me being awake for the fire, if I couldn't put it out, or withstand the flames. My body went slack, going limp against the wood behind me.

"So many innocents have burned in your place, but this time it will be the one they've always sought. Your sacrifice will put an end to the slaughter." Aaron squared his shoulders, shaking the lighter slightly, taunting me deliberately to see the fear flash across my face.

I struggled to stay calm.

"I just need to toss the stone in, and this will be done!" Aaron drew himself up tall like a warrior on the field of battle, proud of himself. He pulled the lighter away and reached into the pyre with his right hand to pull out a tapered section of log. It was a larger and better balanced makeshift bat than the one I'd used on him—more like a club. It fit his hand perfectly. He hefted it, gauging its weight, then placed it gently against the side of my head, drawing it down my cheek in a parody of affection, rough bark scraping my face, until the sawed end rested by my ear. He allowed it to linger there. A warning.

It reeked of gasoline, but I had to breathe. Just when I thought I'd be overcome by the acrid fumes, he graced me with a sneer, and pulled it away, leaving it on the corner of the pyre by my head along with the lighter.

Breathing heavily, Aaron dropped down onto a patch of grass a little away from the reeking pyre, not far from his brother. When his breathing calmed, he pushed up the bottoms of his jeans, examining the welts I'd left. Waiting for the frog-man.

A small breeze brushed my face. Grateful for a few breaths of cleaner air, I scanned the clearing, looking for hope. There was some. More than just a bit. Gabriel's chest still rose and fell—slowly—nearby. He'd fallen near the patch of the weeds where the gasoline bottles had rolled, but with luck, he was far enough away. No matter what happened. Even if there was a fire… Gabriel would be okay. *He had to be okay.* Bernard would be okay too, I hoped. I'd make sure he was. Because while I might be injured, and on my own now,

Aaron and the remaining frog-man were injured now too, and down one man. If I could get my arms free again, maybe I'd have a chance.

But in a straight-up fight, how could I defeat Aaron, who was both stronger than me and more mobile? He was injured, but not enough that it was slowing him down much.

How could I get an advantage in what Aaron had planned?

My eyes were drawn to the lighter, glinting in the sunlight, only inches away. By the way the frog-man had produced it, there was a possibility it was their only one. Foolish of them? Maybe. But Aaron had made other mistakes. If I could somehow get to it, get rid of it, damage it…

I had to try.

I worked my back slowly against the wood, letting the rope eat through my shirt and into my skin, realizing from its thickness it would take much longer to break through than the tape had. Several minutes of rubbing passed, the rope feeling much the same, pressing just as hard into my back. Was it not working?

I rubbed harder.

Then I realized the truth, and my heart sank. The rope. All the coils Aaron had wrapped around me, tying it several times. It wouldn't just take longer than the tape had. It would take all afternoon.

I gave the lighter one last futile glance as my body sank back against the wood.

Aaron, who had been watching me more closely than I had expected, smirked. He shifted lazily to one side and slipped a hand into his jeans pocket. He pulled out a bent book of matches, held between his first two fingers, and waved them at me. Taunting me. He rose to his feet, sauntered over, and scooped up the lighter, tossing it into the air and catching it with one hand, like a kid playing with a ball. Satisfied at the stark expression of despair on my face, he turned on his heel and returned to his resting spot.

After pulling off his cruel joke, meant to raise my hopes and then dash them, it was clear what Aaron was telling me. Whatever

I did would make no difference. Because I had no hope of freeing myself.

I have to try. I have to try. A litany inside my head. I had more hope unbound. The rope had to go. I had no hope, wrapped in it. I moved back and forth, even as dampness spread along my back. *I have to try*, I thought over and over until I no longer felt the wetness. I knew what it must be.

Blood. Soaking my shirt.

A long while passed in silence. I tried to make no noise and to hurry, but failed at the second part. My upper body slowed. I forced it to keep working as it became more numb than my legs, which were flopped awkwardly on the pyre. Aaron ignored me, fiddling with the lighter in his hands. He finally stopped, tightening one hand around it. "Where is that greasy toad?" Aaron muttered. Then louder, in the direction of the fence, "What's taking so long?"

No response.

"Do I have to do everything!?" Aaron shifted his legs under him.

No response.

"You'd better have found that stone by the time I get out there!" Aaron shouted.

Then finally, "You're looking for this?" A familiar, melodic voice called from the gate.

Thank God. Vin. I rolled my head toward his voice.

His lithe frame was poised at the bottom of the clearing, one hip jutted out casually, both hands grasping a canvas bag slung over a shoulder. "Yoohoo. Hi, Aaron."

32

A FIRE SACRIFICE

Vin swung Bernard's bag out from behind his back, clutched it in his arms, and smiled.

I smiled back, although Vin's smile wasn't just for me. He looked at Aaron and his smile widened. Aaron scrambled to his feet, deliberately casting his head down, refusing to meet Vin's gaze. I started to speak, wanting to warn Vin of so many things, but stopped. Aaron would just silence me if I tried.

Vin winked at me, heaved the bag higher, and dropped it. The relic pounded into the ground, sending an eerie vibration across the clearing, and Aaron flinched, but didn't look up. "It won't work," Aaron said. "I'm not going to look at you. You damn cheat!"

Vin shrugged, flicking a leaf off his shoulder. "You've got to look at me to fight me."

"Maybe." Aaron considered it. "But I know another way to ward off your charms." One arm rippled into bear form, the other still held the lighter. "Animals aren't as susceptible, that's what they said. So just try anything. I dare you."

Vin tensed, but his tone stayed calm. "I sent away your friend. I'll do the same to you. If you're lucky."

"You think you brought the stone to save her, but you just made things worse." Aaron stared at the ground. "You're not getting past me, and it's exactly what I need."

"Then come and get it." Vin puffed his chest, but it was forced—his face turned ashen.

"I'll toss it in, right after I'm done with you." Aaron glanced at Vin, turned and flicked the lighter.

The pyre exploded. I rolled away from the flames, managing to move my body, wincing with every bump of my knee, until I fell off the far side, my arms straining, my legs pulling, my body struggling to break free. My chest hit the ground, the impact knocking the breath from me.

"Cyndra! Put it out!" Vin shouted.

I inhaled—*smoke*—and coughed, my throat burning, and tried to do what Vin asked, willing the fire away. But nothing happened. And I couldn't see past the pile of logs. The flames. Where was Aaron? Was Vin okay?

"Stop!" Vin yelled, "Stop!" Then in a different tone, "Cyndra! The fire's spreading. Toward one of the bears."

"Gabriel," I coughed out. "I can't put it out!" A moment passed while I lay on the far side of the pyre, helplessly watching it burn, wondering if I could make my way to Gabriel in time. And if so, how would I ever move him?

Then finally, Vin's voice again. "Here. The guidestone! Connect through it!" A soft thump sounded near my head. Red and orange swirls flickered—*my locket!*—mere inches from my nose, rolling by me, then away, toward the bottom of the pyre. My arm instinctively strained toward it, not able to do a thing as the wobbly sphere kept rolling, trailing its chain, slipping between two logs, disappearing into the rows. I squirmed after it, praying that if I could reach it, it would somehow help. I pushed the questions—*what could it do?*—*without the relic?*—*where had Vin found it?*—out of my mind, focusing on one thing. Time. Vin had taken time to throw it. I needed time to get to it. How long did Gabriel have? Until… the gasoline bottles! I turned onto my belly, searching the wood for my locket. Flames billowed out between the logs. I looked into a gap, heat flashing across my face, the smell of singed hair mixing with the smoke.

There it was, lodged several rows deep. Too far to reach with my immobile arms. In desperation I rolled over onto my back, the rope fighting me, and pushed at the wall of logs with my bound feet. A top log rolled back, out of sight.

"Aaron, back up!" Vin commanded over the crackle of the fire. "Now walk away."

I pushed with my legs again. A log fell forward, next to my shoulder. I thrust my legs harder. Two logs fell onto me, one ablaze, the other smoldering. I squirmed and they rolled off, one still blazing next to me. Flames assaulting from both sides, I twisted around. I wormed my way under a log, back first, pushing my hand in, raking the earth. Burning logs on both side of me, the smoke choked me. The top of my hand heated and blistered. The burn swept up my arm. When it spread, swelling to my shoulder, to my head, I knew time had nearly run out.

I squirmed and pushed harder. A log dislodged from the top of the pyre and smashed down onto my shoulder amid a tower of stinging sparks, knocking the wind out of me. It rolled off, joining the others blazing on the ground. Just a bit further. The flames lapped closer… and finally I felt it. Rounded and smooth at my fingertips. I strained closer, inching my palm over, brushing the hot chain, grabbing the locket, lifting its weight. Energy surging up my arm, I willed the fire away.

It didn't work. The fire flared. *All around me now.*

But my body no longer burned. My flesh no longer felt pain. The flaring fire seemed to be pulling in some air I could breathe. Instinctively, I swung my legs over the flaming log in front of me, melting the strips of tape. I scooted to a sitting position, leaning into the pyre, letting the rope catch fire.

Over the roar of the strengthening fire, Vin shouted, "Gabriel!"

Finally I felt the ropes give. I pulled off my flaming bindings, slipped the locket over my neck, pulled myself upright against the stacked logs, and rose to my feet. My body free, full of new energy.

My skin burned, but no longer suffering damage. My clothes almost scorched off me.

On the far side of the pyre, a puff of flame rose skyward with a whoosh. That patch of weeds, the discarded bottles with their dregs of fuel and vapor. So close to Gabriel. *Please, no.*

I hobbled painfully past the scattered logs, toward the end of the pyre.

"Cyndra," Vin wheezed from the other side. "We have to… Gabriel—"

"I'm coming!" I limped, reaching a hand into the fire, leaning on the top row of wood, staggering forward.

Vin made a strangled sound, horribly audible over the crackling blaze.

I turned the corner and froze. Vin was bent over near the flaming, incinerated weed path, pulling a bear away from it, clutching the animal's foreleg to his stomach with shredded, bloodied arms. His body was frozen, but it was clear he'd been dragging Gabriel away from the spreading fire. Aaron stood over Vin, a smirk on his face, a hairy forearm locked around Vin's neck, a set of claws piercing through the side of Vin's white button-down shirt, their shiny black tops showing. The rest of his claws were embedded.

For a moment I couldn't breathe. Or move. I just stared at the blood spots forming above Vin's ribcage, in circles around Aaron's claws, trying to figure out how bad this was. It was Vin's left side. Below his heart? I tried to gauge. A bit, and to the side of it. Vin's arms—they looked much worse—but they would heal. Surely this would too?

"I told him it wouldn't work." Aaron's voice trumpeted over my thoughts. "Not enough to keep me away."

"It was me." I gulped. "Me you wanted." My voice barely carried over the popping and hissing next to me.

Aaron laughed. "It is you, and you'll be doing what I want now." His claws flexed as he pulled at Vin. Vin's face tightened with pain, and after a final tug, he dropped Gabriel's leg.

My heart raced. Fire raged around me. The locket pulsed against my chest. And I did the only thing I could think of. Something that felt natural. In that moment, instinctual. I looked at the pyre, honing in on the sparks rising from the flames, then directed them up—pulling them off the fire with my mind—and, as they sparkled in the air, pushed them out and over, into Aaron's face.

Aaron released Vin and stumbled back, swiping at the sparks with his paws. For an instant, Aaron paused, looking between me and Vin.

Then he charged Vin again.

Did Aaron not get the message!? I picked up the nearest thing to my hand, one of the shorter lengths of wood, burning in the pyre, and slung it at his face. "He was saving your brother!" I shouted, unable to control my rage. Aaron's head turned toward my shout.

The log spun slowly through the air like an awkwardly thrown knife, giving Aaron no clue how to duck or dodge. There was only a moment for his eyes to widen before it turned to strike his forehead end-on. His neck snapped back. His weight tipped toward his heels, and Aaron fell, collapsing near the foot of one of the power poles.

Vin smiled at me, his smooth lips lifting weakly, then folded at the waist and collapsed over Gabriel. I lunged through the blazing weeds where Gabriel had lain, kicking a blackened and ruptured plastic bottle. If Vin hadn't pulled Gabriel away...

No! There was no time to think those things now.

Stumbling and falling to my knees, I took in the damage. Aaron was still breathing, but out cold. Good. I'd make sure he stayed that way. Vin was still breathing, but blood leached from the punctures in his chest, widening circles of red, soaking into Gabriel's fur. Vin needed help. More than me. I'd get him all the help he needed. But first, I had to do something about the blood. I struggled to remove Aaron's jeans, yanking them down his legs, and wrapped them around Vin's back.

As I shifted Vin to the ground, side by side with Gabriel, he shook his head. "Can't breathe... sit up." Vin nodded at something.

A chunk of cement not far away, round with a large hole through it, perhaps a failed attempt to set the nearby power pole in the rocky soil. I slung the jeans over my shoulders and ducked under Vin's arm, supporting him as he shifted over to it. I placed one length of the denim over Vin's side, the other over the worst openings on his arms. Vin's wounds covered, I examined Gabriel. "Hey. Wake up." I ran my hand along his muzzle. He didn't move. "Gabriel, wake up." His eyes stayed shut. He looked better, his breathing no longer so shallow. Patches of fur were scorched off along his chest, his legs, revealing so many burn marks along his hide, but he should be okay. But if Vin hadn't been there...

No. I willed my thoughts to turn away from what might have happened.

"Cyndra," Vin mumbled. I scooted closer to him. "The relic. Go."

"But—"

"The fire." It was out of control. Almost on top of us. A crackling wall behind and to the side of us, it shot sparks into the air. While we'd fought Aaron, it had rocketed from the pyre, spreading out into the weeds, from one grass patch to another, toward the cell tower and nearby bushes. It was on its way down toward Bernard, too. I hadn't felt it. I didn't feel it now. But Vin did. Sweat ran down his face.

Scrambling onto my good leg, I pulled him back to the far side of the cement. But I couldn't move Gabriel, and I had no time to worry about Aaron. The fire was coming. Vin was right. Putting it out might be the only thing that could save everyone. I hobbled frantically down the hill, one leg dragging behind me, finally hopping the last couple of yards, collapsing on my side, reaching for Bernard's bag, still laying where Vin had dropped it. Ties secured a flap. I tore at them and one side pulled loose. I pushed my hand inside.

This time had to be different.

Whether it was the sunlight, my locket, me now wanting so badly to get whatever was inside, I might never know. But with one touch, I felt not only the stone's heat, but its energy, pouring into me. Pain stabbed through me as I fell back completely, turned, and sat up, my injured leg stretching out stiffly. I pulled the bag toward me and the glowing orb slipped out.

I rolled the relic onto my lap, feeling as if at any moment it might take everything away, absorb whatever power it had given me or I had naturally on my own. But I was in control now. Its bright light faded.

Blazing heat spread up my arms, warming my whole body, but in a glorious way. Not painful. Exhilarating. Empowering. Its energy entering me. Filling me with a positive force at the same time that something deep inside me rose up to meet it. For an instant, whatever was inside the relic and whatever was inside me clashed, ripping at my chest, right at that spot that so often ached with loneliness, with not understanding my place.

Then that spot lightened. My heart relaxed, my spine straightened, and all my memories from the past two years, everything in me, focused and illuminated on a single thought, as if the relic was sending me a message.

Don't be afraid to feel deeply. Don't be afraid to be yourself. Don't deny who you are.

A sense of peace and calm settled over me.

When the stone appeared entirely transformed and I no longer felt a connection, I let it fall back to the ground. Cold and colorless.

I looked back across the shimmering clearing, up to the halo above—what must be the pyre—flames dancing everywhere. Streams of fire spreading out. From their depths, a charred log rolled out, hit a large rock, and snapped. Everywhere there was crackling and hissing. And then, with just a single thought, I put the fire out.

An eerie silence descended on the clearing as the sounds of burning abruptly ceased. Smoke billowed down the hillside, rolling waves of black and grey sweeping the landscape, rising up from everything that had blazed just moments ago. I willed it to dissipate, but either

I couldn't control this by-product of the flames, or it was too late, now that the fire was out.

In seconds a smothering sea of smoke isolated me, washing out everything but the ground in front of me and my burned arms, resting on my clawed-up legs.

One arm—the arm that had reached for my locket—was so disgusting I could hardly stomach the sight. The hand more leather than skin, the wrist a blackened red with oozing blisters. But I still felt no pain. And as I continued to stare, transfixed, at the damage, I could see it was changing, receding, *healing*. The burns I'd suffered before—from being touched, from my nightmares—had never faded this quickly. All along those burns must have been connected to what I could do with fire, because with the blaze I'd just put out, and my arms entirely healed, it seemed everything I could do before the relic had drained me was back. Working better than ever. With my own abilities, and the relic's energy coursing through my veins I wondered what else I could do. But what good did it do me now, when I needed to help others?

"Vin?" I called.

Several moments passed. As thick as the smoke was, was I the only one able to breathe in it? And it wasn't easy for me. My worry grew.

"Vin?" I said louder, and dropped my head. "I did it. I did it, Vin."

"I know." I barely heard his reply.

I scrambled to my knees. I had to get back. Then I'd get help. For him. And for Gabriel. For Bernard, the other bear, and Cole too. But first I'd make sure Aaron was still out. "I'm coming!" I struggled to stand, and fell back down. "It might take me a minute." I warned.

My bad knee failing me completely, would crawling work? I pulled myself through the nearest cloud of smoke. Yes, crawling. That was the way to go. The other knee could support my weight, dragging my bad leg behind me. I avoided the largest rocks, but every smaller one bored painfully into my good knee. It would be a long journey. "I can't walk. I'm crawling. Still there, Vin?" I asked, making my way through another wave of darkness.

"Yes."

"I can't see anything." The smoke was thick around me, stinging my eyes, burning my throat as I tried to breathe.

"Over here."

I changed my course.

"Cyndra… you know…" He sounded distant. Was I farther away? "You know I—how much I care for you, right?"

"Keep talking," I answered, needing to judge my direction. Then I registered his question. "What are you talking about?"

"Just letting you know…"

His tone didn't sound right. Not right at all. "You're going to be fine. I'll be there soon." I forced myself to crawl faster, refusing to let Vin make a deathbed confession. Because he wasn't going to die.

"You know what needs to be done now?" he asked.

"What?"

"Ellis."

My sister? In the government facility? "Yes, yes. We'll get to Ellis together." My hand landed next to a bear paw. Bernard. I must be at least 30 degrees off course—but at the moment, every direction felt like up—and it was good to find him. I leaned in close. His breathing was weak, slower than Gabriel's, but he was alive. His eye… I leaned in closer. Yick. He'd lost it for sure. Maybe worse. Hard to tell through the blood-matted fur. There was nothing I could do for it now. Except hurry, find a way to get help. Using a cell wasn't an option, but Bernard and Gabriel had a vehicle outside. I could take it and head toward town. If I could find the key. If I could drive, with one knee out of commission and both legs mangled.

Don't worry about that now.

I patted around Bernard's bear form. Nothing. No key. Maybe in his clothing? No sign of it either within the few feet I could see through the vast wall of smoke. I brushed off the grit and pebbles trying to embed themselves into my hands and knee, adjusted my direction, and kept moving.

"How'd you know I was here?" I asked, more sure of my direction, but needing to hear Vin's voice again.

There was what felt like a vast silence. "Your note. And Kaylee. And the tracking I put on all the Knights' phones."

Despite everything, I had to smile. Trust Vin to trust the Knights just enough, but not too much. "Wait—Kaylee?" Somehow talking made me feel normal again, and forget about the pain in my knees and hands.

Vin seemed to sense that. "She had the guidestone"—he gave a weak cough—"for a few days. Aaron. Told her to… hide it. She called. Couldn't find that officer. But spoke to her"—another cough—"But next time… next time… need help. Do it when I've left my Porsche at home."

A small smile lifted my lips. God, Vin was so Vin. And so trustworthy, and smart. "Vin, you know, I couldn't have picked a better best friend." I said it lightheartedly, but my voice caught at the end.

"Whatever happens, Cyndra"—the odd tone was back—"you have to get to Ellis."

"We're getting to Ellis together."

The fence rattled.

"Who's there?" I stopped, looking over, but not seeing anything through the murky banks. The slowly rolling masses of smoke. They seemed greyer now, less black, but still an impenetrable curtain. "Is someone there?"

No answer.

A crackle of leaves. Footsteps? Maybe.

Then another rattle, fainter, back toward the gate.

"Vin!?"

"I'm here."

I jerked forward, trying to gauge where he was in the darkness, the furtive sounds throwing me off.

You know how much I care for you, right?" he asked again.

I changed course slightly. "Right."

"Agapi mou… you know…"

I did. I did know. But he shouldn't be saying it now. Like that. I wouldn't let anything happen to him.

"And Ellis. You have to get to her."

"You said that already."

No answer.

"You already said that," I repeated. No answer. "Vin?"

I kept crawling. Finally his light-colored shirt appeared several feet away. A low moan sounded. From farther off? I was almost over Vin when a weak, husky voice startled me. "He's in bad shape." Through the haze, I just made out the shape of Gabriel's large body.

I crawled to it. My eyes strained, trying to focus in the smoke, taking in his bare chest and uneven expression.

He lay not far from Vin, his head hanging at an awkward angle, nose smeared with yellow and green. His eyes were fixed on mine. "Gabriel! I—" My words turned into a gasp as he twitched, shuddering with pain. My hands reaching for him, I stopped myself, bending over him—over his burns—instead. The damage started with a deep red line running from bicep to bicep, quickly turning into bubbling flesh around his elbows and stomach, worsening from there. *Oh God.* It was bad. In spots, along his legs, burns much worse than mine had been. We had to get him out of here, get something for the pain. Guard against infection, which was highly likely. There'd be scars. More scars. But he'd heal. Get him to the cave? "Gabriel, you need help."

"I'm fine," he said, though clearly he wasn't. "But Vin. I just heard it. It's not good."

I called out again. "Vin?"

No answer. I didn't hear anything else either, at first—or I did, but I couldn't register it. What was it? Vin's eyes were closed. He was slumped over by the block of cement, Aaron's jeans no longer covering his wounds. His palm rested below the punctures in his side. It slowly slipped, falling to the ground. Scooting closer, an odd whizzing sound whispered from his chest. It almost sounded like air passing through.

"It's a sucking wound." Gabriel answered my unspoken question. "He must have been holding it, but when he stopped talking, I heard it. We patched one up in paramedic training, but—"

"No," I whispered. No buts. We had to do it. If Gabriel had patched one up before, he knew what to do. "What do we need?" Careful not to touch his skin, I eased Vin to the ground, laying him down as gently as I could on his back.

"Plastic, if you can find it. Something to seal the wound. Block the air. I'd do it but…" He didn't have to say it. Whether it was the pain, or the lingering toxin, Gabriel couldn't move. I revised my plan—patch Vin up, check on Aaron, then get help, then everyone would be okay. Everything would work out.

"Let me see." I scrambled back in the direction of the pyre. A fleeting breeze pushed back the worst of the smoke, and a jumble of partially burned logs came into view. Pulling my way through ash and dirt, I finally found what I searched for. The discarded tape. Bracing myself on one arm, I stuffed the melted remains into my mouth, bit down, and hurried back. "Got it."

"Seal any wound," Gabriel said. "Do it after he exhales. Keep more air from coming in."

I tried my best, ripping away Vin's shirt—being careful, not to touch him, risk getting distracted with a burn—pushing together gooey strips of tape, covering all of the holes, even the smallest, which didn't seem to be the problem. It was a makeshift attempt, really. But the sound stopped.

"Keep it in place," Gabriel said. "Keep it tight. If pressure builds, allow air to escape."

"But…" I took a gulp of smoky air, preparing to acknowledge one worry out loud. "He's not waking up." And how would I ever get help—for Vin, Gabriel, everyone else too—if I had to keep the tape in place? One more worry I had to share out loud. "Where's Aaron?"

"I thought—by the way you guys were talking when I woke,

that—um—no one else was left. Maybe Aaron and Dad were gone…"

I quickly explained to Gabriel what he'd missed, including what Aaron had revealed to me before they'd arrived—that he'd done something to get Cameron out of the way—only slowing to assure him that while his father was injured, it wasn't fatal. I'd just seen him alive. "So Aaron should be around here somewhere." I twisted my head, keeping my hands pressed over Vin's chest, looking around in the haze. "He was near the base of a power pole." If it ever became visible with all this damn smoke. "Do you see him?" My voice had a shrill note, as fear surged again.

"Don't worry." Gabriel paused, as if struggling to find more re-assuring words. "I can't believe Aaron betrayed us. Our entire family. Our ancestors. But it's over," Gabriel said uneasily. "This is all over." God, I hoped he was right, but I don't think he believed it either. He cleared his throat, then cleared it again like he still didn't know what to say or think. "Grandpa's patrolling, he'll smell the smoke. He'll come. I'm not sure it rose high enough to be seen from town."

"But Aaron—"

"What could my brother want now? What could anyone want? You got the relic. It worked. It's done," Gabriel said, more firmly this time.

Was Gabriel right? Even if he was, what about Vin? Was waiting our only option? Because I could see how bad Vin was. He needed help *now*. But Vin was strong, and I was selfish. After Gram, I needed him so much. What was so awful was that I was the one who'd brought trouble to them both. I pressed my hands more firmly over the tape, focusing my thoughts on getting Vin out of here. If only I could leave Gabriel in charge of Vin, I could make a go for the gate. But could Gabriel keep the bandage in place? His burns weren't just bad. They covered so much of him.

Gabriel had already raised his head. He shifted toward me with a long moan, finally unable to hide how much agony he was in. I shuddered, knowing how much those burns must be overwhelming every other sensation—creating such pain—almost feeling it myself.

I wanted to tell him to stay where he was. To not come closer and cause himself more pain. But from his furrowed brow, the determination in his expression, I could see he needed to be close to me, and I needed to be close to him. His eyes went to my knee, clearly mangled, and already freakishly swollen. Part of the story I'd left out. "Aaron did this?" he said, more as a statement than a question, but I nodded anyway, and his face twisted with an unreadable emotion.

"Don't worry about that." I tried pulling my knee away. My whole leg seemed to have stiffened up. It didn't move. "Let's just worry about you… and… and Vin." A small shiver raced through me.

Gabriel inched closer with another moan, bracing his weight on one side, reaching a hand for my face. I caught a glimpse of a blister, then his large palm cupped my cheek.

I couldn't help myself. I leaned in, seeking his comfort.

Ow!

I almost said it aloud. I forced myself not to pull away. For the first time in what seemed a long, long time—since the day we first met—Gabriel's touch held pain. Not sharp, but agonizing in its way. Like the pins and needles after a foot has gone to sleep. Slowly it faded, and I pressed into his warmth, only to quickly draw away. "I'm sorry—your burns…"

"No," he said. "It didn't hurt at all. It's not even stinging anymore." He turned his hand around to show me, and his palm didn't look burned at all. But that wasn't what I remembered. And there was a bubbled spot by his wrist. More along his forearm.

A wild idea entered my head, and I adjusted my hold on Vin's bandage to cover it with one hand. "Can I touch your arm again? I'll be careful."

Gabriel seemed to sense the intensity of my intuition and shifted to place his arm near Vin's side. I touched a fingertip to where my cheek had pressed. Just the warmth of Gabriel's skin. Then up a little. The same. "This may hurt," I said, and very carefully laid my palm across the edge of the burn on his wrist.

Gabriel didn't blink, but my entire hand tingled unbearably. I fought the reflex to pull away, and the tingling slowly subsided. So did the bubbling near where I held my hand. Gabriel looked up. Our eyes met. "Did you see that?" he asked. "And the pain is gone…"

I gripped his wrist. "Remember how my burns from being touched used to go away so quickly? Right after I made contact with the relic, my burns from the fire went away… but much faster."

Gabriel looked at his arm in wonder as the burn receded further. "And it works for other people, too! On me, anyway. But I saw your face—you were hurting."

I thought I'd hidden that. "Just a tingling. It went away. Let me do the rest." I convinced him to lean in and I slowly ran one hand along his other arm, torso, then each of his legs, while I kept the other pressed down on Vin's chest, sealing the sucking wound shut. I did my best not to discourage Gabriel by reacting to the sensations, and soon he had only a few fading spots to show where the worst burns had been. And nowhere we touched tingled now.

If only Vin had simply been burned. Healing him would be so easy.

Gabriel wiped a hand across his face, then onto the ground, then again across his face. Though his cheeks were now begrimed with soot and dirt, the yellow and green was gone. He shifted to his hands and knees. "That was amazing. I feel so much better." He pushed up to kneel beside me. "I think I can go for Dad's jeep. We can get Vin out of here." He looked around us. "Just keep an eye out."

I almost laughed. The area was still blanketed with smoke. We could barely see our own hands in front of our faces. "And watch Vin," Gabriel said, so anxiously, I knew I was right—Vin was in bad shape. "If things don't sound right, you might need to take your hands off, allow some air to escape, maybe blood too. Then cover it back up."

I nodded.

He leaned in. For an instant over the acrid smell of smoke, the scent of cedar and cloves surrounded me, and everything in me calmed. Gabriel looked right into my eyes, into whatever he saw in their depths, and his lips parted. "And I love you too."

So he had seen what I'd mouthed to him across the clearing.

He smoothed my hair away from my face, then cradled my head in his hands. He looked deeper into my gaze. I couldn't believe I'd almost lost him. I couldn't believe all of this had happened. My eyes filled with tears.

He wrapped his arms around me, acknowledging our love, but also simply comforting me in his embrace. All the while my hands pressed into Vin and even though I couldn't touch him, I tried to send comfort to Vin too. Gabriel's arms shook against my back, lacking the confident strength I'd grown used to—only the tenderness was the same. I rested my cheek against his shoulder. A tear slipped out, running toward my temple and into the crease where my face pressed against his collarbone and met his skin.

He trembled. "I'll be back soon." He was up, stumbling into the smoke, grabbing Aaron's discarded jeans, slipping them up over his bare legs, before I could say anything else.

Several minutes passed, my arms slowly losing feeling as I held the improvised dressing in place. More precious seconds slipped by, and in the quiet, in the gloom, I waited for Gabriel to make his way across the clearing and kept pressing the bandage to Vin's chest, as if through sheer force of will I could make everything okay.

"I'm at the gate!" Gabriel shouted through the smoke, then his voice rang out again, quieter this time. "Where's the jeep?"

"What?" I shivered.

"It's not here."

My heart sank. How would we get Vin out of here?

"Aaron must have taken it," Gabriel said. "It's okay. I'll walk. Call for help as soon as I get a signal. Our cells must be around here somewhere. Let me just…" The sounds of Gabriel shuffling. Then, "I found my dad!" Another pause. Gabriel must be taking in the same sight I had, of Bernard's mutilated eye and prone form.

"Gabriel, are you okay?"

"Dad, can you hear me!?"

"He's awake?" I called back, hoping he was.

"Starting to. Just came out of bear form. That happened to me too."

At last a real breeze swept past me, pushing back more smoke. Finally, some better air for Vin, and a much needed good omen. I could make out the mound of ashes that must have been the pyre, blackened logs poking out, and beyond that and to the side, the building at the foot of the cell tower came into view. Looking toward the fence, the nearest power pole came into view, with nothing around it. Aaron was nowhere in sight. He really must have taken the jeep. "So you'll walk toward town—go quickly?" I remembered how fast Gabriel had made it up the mountain before—surely getting down wouldn't take him long now that his burns were healed?

No answer.

Vin struggled to breathe. I let go of some of the pressure, allowing some air and bloody froth to escape, and pressed back down. Vin kept struggling to draw a full breath.

"You should go. Call for help!" I shouted toward the gate. Why was there no answer? Had Gabriel left already?

Vin gasped.

"You really need to go!" My voice rose.

The wind swirled around the clearing, pushing back more of the haze. It rolled back slowly, down the hillside, lingering a moment around the gate, before retreating into the underbrush outside the fence. As the curtain of grey withdrew, two bare legs came into view. Then a pair of boxer shorts, a bare chest, and Aaron's smirking face. The smoke cleared completely and the whole picture emerged.

Aaron stood over Gabriel's sprawled body. He had one foot planted against Gabriel's throat, keeping him in place, while holding the dull, lifeless stone at his waist, right above Gabriel's head. Bernard lay naked on the ground to one side, helpless, unmoving.

My eyes met Aaron's across the clearing, and his smirk widened. "Bet you thought you won," he said.

"I did, if you hadn't noticed." I tried to stay calm. I purposefully turned my head, casting my gaze all around, deliberately eying all the areas that were now coming into view as the smoke lifted. Not a spot of fire in sight. I smiled at him.

"Doesn't matter." Aaron shrugged, but I could tell he wasn't as relaxed as he was trying to appear. "I'm not stupid enough to go back to these people empty-handed. You and the stone are coming with me."

"You can have the stone." I grinned, sensing his anxiety. He didn't need to sense mine. And as for the stone, there seemed no reason to care if he took it now.

"Nope. You too." Aaron nodded, hefting the relic's weight up to his shoulder over Gabriel. "You're coming with me."

"Why would I do that?" What I didn't say was that I *couldn't* do that. I glanced down at Vin. At my hands on his chest.

"If you care about my brother, you will." Aaron left the relic where it was, but pressed his foot further down on Gabriel, pushing out a strangling sound.

"He won't do it," Gabriel choked out. "Don't listen to him."

Aaron scowled at his brother. "She'd better. Because I'm not sparing you this time."

Gabriel moaned. "This time?"

"You really don't know what lengths I've gone to try to keep this family together."

"What the hell… you talking about?" Gabriel answered, and I hoped this was buying some time. At least until Bernard woke. Bernard had no luck reasoning with his son before, but was Aaron really so far gone he'd hurt—risk killing—his brother?

"You might be the oldest. Bigger. Even stronger. But I was the one trying to keep us safe." Aaron looked down, then away, toward the peak in the distance—the entrance to Spring Cave—his expression falling into one of pain. He winced, his eyes turning glassy. His chin trembled. "I made a deal that would keep us safe." He blinked several times and his shoulders sagged.

Gabriel stared up at his brother. "What have you done?"

For the first time all afternoon, Aaron looked utterly exhausted. "Do you think I wanted to do it? Do you think I want to do this now?" He lowered the relic, lessening his weight on Gabriel.

Gabriel shook his head, the movement so small, but Aaron must have felt it.

"You're right. No." He sighed. "And this should've been taken care of weeks ago." He glanced toward Spring Cave again. "I left the entrance unguarded for the Jentilak. Got Cameron distracted too. I told them they could do anything they wanted inside. But they had to promise to give any bear a chance to go. You were supposed to go," Aaron said to his brother, his voice low and flat. He looked up at me, his voice turning angry. "Of course, she screwed things up. But I tried. I'm still trying."

"I know." Gabriel's voice was weak. "Let me up. We'll figure this out."

"I can't. It's too late. I—" Aaron flinched, as if warring with his own emotions, and his face hardened again. "She brought this on us." Aaron glared at me. "She brought this on herself, showing up like she did." He lifted the relic back up to his shoulder. "Enough of this." He nodded at me. "You, come here."

I trembled, and struggled to keep my hands firmly over Vin's wounds. "You really want to mess with me?" I asked. "You don't remember what I just did? What I just did to you? What I can do now?"

"I don't see any fire." Aaron laughed. "It's just you and me. And you don't look so good. In fact, you look pathetic."

"I'm not pathetic." I knew it was true. All those times I'd thought myself weak or useless were behind me now. I was strong. I'd made it this far. Fought so hard and done so much.

But was Aaron right about one thing? Was I only able to control fire so long as it was already there? Hmm… I stared at a small bush growing through the chain-link fence near Aaron, and gave it a thought.

It burst into flames.

"Put that out!" Aaron screamed, shifting the relic's weight. "Come over here!" Aaron was enraged, and maybe frightened too, his eyes flashing wildly, his foot pressing harder on Gabriel's throat. My options narrowed, to one terrible, impossible choice.

A loud roar sounded from beyond the gate. Aaron turned his head, but kept his foot over Gabriel. An old bear lumbered into the clearing. I recognized the white markings—Gabriel's great-grand-father, *Aaron's great-grandfather too.* Cole staggered in behind him, then leaned heavily into the animal's side. The bear and Cole scanned the clearing, taking in the scene. Cole stared at Aaron's foot pressing into Gabriel. "Aaron!" He cried in disbelief. Cole pushed off the bear's side, stumbled forward a step, and paused, his mouth working, unable to speak, then finally, "You wouldn't hurt him."

Aaron's chin trembled, but he quickly shook his head and stood taller. "Wouldn't I?" Aaron lifted his foot from Gabriel's throat for an instant and stomped on Gabriel's elbow.

The crack resonated all the way across the clearing.

Aaron jammed his foot back down on Gabriel's throat. Gabriel's face tightened in pain, his other arm flailing against Aaron's leg.

"No!" Cole stumbled forward another step, started to fall, and the bear moved to his side. "How can you do this?" Cole rested on the bear again. "How could you've done any of it? It wasn't a misunderstanding that day. The fire. You deceived me."

"Yes. And now I'm getting what I want, again. Because I know what needs to be done. I'm the strong one. And I know which boy she'll choose in the end." Aaron lifted the relic higher. My heart ached. But what could I do? Was there some sort of choice to make, that I couldn't… I looked down at Vin.

Gabriel's great-grandfather roared, bellowing around the

clearing. His gaze moved from Aaron, holding the leaden, lifeless relic, to Gabriel in pain beneath, to Bernard, his son, still unmoving and injured next to them. He shook his head then nodded at me. The old bear gestured with his snout toward the burning bush, then dipped his head toward me again.

"You won't come with me? Then watch me crush him." Aaron heaved the relic up to arm's length over his head, ready to throw it down on Gabriel. Was Aaron crazy!? Had he completely turned to darkness? The fire leapt, inexplicably, to another nearby bush, and flared. *Did I have no choice?* Flames billowed suddenly skyward in a tower of writhing orange tongues, like a living thing. *Was I doing that?* Yes.

Gabriel's great-grandfather nodded at me one more time—the old bear, and the old man inside, having weighed the choices of the moment—and I couldn't mistake his conclusion.

Willing the flames to surge to life took a tremendous amount of energy, but in that moment it felt as effortless as lifting a feather. The tower of flames tightened, intensified, and drew back, then lashed out like a whip, cutting across Aaron's chest, lapping over his shoulder, onto his back, circling around, reaching up his neck. Then, as quickly as I'd lashed out, I pulled back, extinguishing the flames.

Though still in the form of a man, Aaron's roar was that of a beast. He was thrown backward, his foot lifting from Gabriel's throat. The relic slipped from his grasp, falling harmlessly behind him.

Aaron lay sprawled on his back, his howls of pain taking on a human timbre, then the rough tones of rage. He scrambled to his feet, taking a step in retreat toward the gate. "This isn't done." His face contorted in a mixture of distress and pure menace. "You've chosen the wrong side," he shouted at us. "The wrong side!" He took another step away.

I stole a glance at Vin. In that instant Aaron was back on the ground, on his hands and knees, scrambling around, stirring up dirt. He was only a few feet from Gabriel, and not much farther from his father. What final, desperate attempt was he making? Did I have the strength to lash out again to save them?

Did I have the cruelty?

Then I saw what Aaron was doing. He already had the bag, and was reaching for the lifeless relic. He lifted the side of the bag and rolled the relic inside. The next instant, Aaron changed into bear form. He dropped his head and backed away with a soft whimper of pain. A wide streak of cauterized flesh cut through the fur on his back. The red circled under his body, up the left side of his neck, ending at his nose. He paused by the gate, his jaws clenched together. His face twitched. The straps of the bag stretched taut to one side of his muzzle.

The relic must be there, lodged under his neck.

He lifted his head and the canvas-covered relic swung out. He turned and raced away.

Nothing I knew suggested the relic meant anything now, but I knew so little still. Gabriel's great-grandfather watched his great-grandson flee, an impassive look in his watery blue eyes. So I let Aaron run. Although I wasn't sure I had a choice.

My shoulders collapsed. My gaze dropped.

Exhausted beyond measure, I laid my head down, forehead resting on the backs of my hands, which had never faltered, still pressing down on Vin's wounds.

33
STRONGER

BLEEP... BLEEP... BLEEP...

Vin's hospital room was cold, dark, and silent except for the slow beat of the machine next to me. Its flickering light jumped in the corner of my eye, and I scooted my chair away from it, and closer to the bed, moving my hands within inches of Vin.

Gabriel shifted uncomfortably in the chair next to me. His movements became more jittery, finally drawing my gaze. His beautiful, full lips parted, and I knew he spoke, but through the deep tenor all I heard was *bleep… bleep… bleep…*

I returned to watching Vin sleep.

Words had lost meaning over an hour ago, when the hospital had let us in. The doctor's eyes skipping around the cold white walls, to the window, to the night sky beyond—to everything but Vin's ashen face and the tube feeding him oxygen through his nose—conveyed exactly how the surgery went, without actually telling us a thing. She wanted to speak to family. We were just lucky they'd let us in. Visiting hours were long over. Her words vague, her voice droning on—"a lot of damage"—"done our best"—"the next few hours are…"—I embraced the only other sound in the room. The heart monitor. Willing it to continue was all I could do. That, and waiting for Vin's cell to ring.

My shoulders sagged. The phone felt like a ten-pound weight in the chest pocket of my borrowed scrubs. There'd been no answer from Vin's father no matter how many times I tried. No call back no matter how many messages I left. And having his father here would help, surely—I read once that even in sleep, people in pain can sense the presence of a loved one near, having their hand held, and find it comforting. But there were so few numbers on Vin's cell, other than Patera, the listing for his father, and what few names were there meant nothing to me. And none of them answered—who else would come to let Vin know how he was loved? My elbows sought armrests, but found none on the chair. Leaning further into the bed, my hands sank into the bedding by Vin's gauze-wrapped arm.

Bleep… bleep… bleep…

Vin… wake up.

His father wasn't coming. He might even be in trouble. The call history showed they hadn't spoken in a week. Vin's calls since hadn't been answered. I had to be the one to show Vin he was loved. But I couldn't even touch him. Did he have any idea how much he meant to me? Had my words in the clearing been enough?

… bleep… bleep…

God, I wanted to show him. Push back his hospital gown where it ended at the tube sticking from his arm, and grip his flesh farther up, where the gauze covering Aaron's claw marks stopped. Slide my hand up and over, to where the gown gaped over his chest, and rest my palm there, above his heart. Maybe then he'd know I was here. That his best friend was here. That he needed to wake up, and be okay.…

Nothing but the sound of machines beeping.

Gabriel reached over my fresh white cast, drawing my nearest hand from the bed. I pulled it back carefully, not wanting to risk knocking his bandaged arm, hanging in a sling in front of his chest. Once free, I glanced at him, holding Gabriel's wide eyes for a moment, hoping he'd understand as I crept both hands even closer to the fingers, reddened from the fire, curled loosely on the blanket. As close to Vin as I dared.

I perched one hand on Vin's sleeve. Frost nipped my fingers. I gripped Vin through the gown. My whole hand went cold. I clapped my palms together, rubbed them, then placed them back down, wishing I could impart the same warmth to Vin. And then a crazy, impossible (*preposterous*) thought struck me. Maybe I could touch Vin now, without any pain. I had the relic's powers. Maybe I was better. And I'd healed Gabriel's burns. Maybe I could heal Vin too.

At least a little. Perhaps enough.

I'd been so careful on the way down the mountain. Not to touch Vin. The surviving frogman must've stolen Bernard's jeep, but Gabriel returned the favor when I told him about the truck hidden off the main road. It had been a better option to transport Vin than the Porsche—with Vin's cell inside—Gabriel found in a ditch near the gate. Cole needed to stay behind to help move Bernard and the other injured bear, his great-uncle, to the cave, and Gabriel had to drive because I couldn't, so I was alone with Vin in the back of the same truck I'd come up the mountain in. Wind whipped through my hair and fragments of pine bark blew up in my face, and I struggled with every jostle to hold the tape in place. I'd been alone and so scared. So afraid of messing things up. With a slip. One touch. Pain. A distracting vision. But maybe touching Vin now was okay. Maybe touching Vin now was what I needed to do.

Both arms shaking, I felt Gabriel's eyes on me. He might have said something, but I couldn't hear him. And this was no time for caution. I glanced at the clock above the door. The night nurse wasn't due back yet. We were alone.

I went all in, clasping Vin's hand in both of mine.

The cold perished, sensations of fire flaring. I started to scream. Biting my tongue, I turned the sound into a whimper. I bit harder. The whimper stopped. But there was no denying the pain, and I knew what it meant. Nothing had changed. Touching Vin was like reaching into the heart of the burning pyre. And yet, I couldn't let go. Not until I was sure it wasn't helping.

Blisters sprouted, spreading up my arms.

I lost sight of them, of the real world, as the vision flooded into my perception. Me, back in my old room. Wearing another silly, revealing dress. Sobbing as Vin wrapped me in his embrace.

I leaned into him, as if on instinct, then stiffened my shoulders and struggled to get free. "Don't."

"I know." His arms fell. "It's all my fault."

"You made a promise."

"I know."

"You and your father said if I convinced them to stay, you'd keep them safe."

"Yes."

"But your words. Your hateful words. Alanna really cared for you, and what you said. If you hadn't... she... she'd still be here."

"I know." Vin reached for my shoulders.

I stepped back. He stepped in, wiping a tear from my face. I turned my head. "They stabbed her," I droned in a lifeless voice. "Stabbed her to death."

"I know—" His words broke off. "It's all my—Please. Please don't hate me." He gasped. "Please say you don't hate me." His voice dropped. "Cyndra?"

I didn't answer.

"Please. I'll do anything." His fingers dug into his thighs, bunching the pant fabric. "You have to forgive me," he choked. "You know me. You always understand. My agelessness, what I do, everything I hate. You make it all right."

"Nothing's all right. She's dead." My voice hardened, frigid and sharp. "You can't fix anything."

God, make it stop, I thought, watching the vision unfold inside my head.

He gasped again, sinking to his knees, circling his arms around my waist. "Cyndra?"

I wrenched away. "She adored you." I jabbed a nail at him. "But you wouldn't give her the time of day because you thought that silly kiss meant something. Well, it didn't." He sagged over his lap, hugging his middle, so I couldn't see my own face. "The second I did it,

I knew it was a mistake. All the stuff people talk about—the spark, the chemistry, the world fading away—it wasn't there. But I never would have told you. Never would have hurt you. But she cared for you that way, Vin, and you knew it, and you still hurt her. So now, you're going to feel it, too."

I can't take any more. I can't watch my former self push him away. Couldn't hear myself tear him down and rip out his heart. He's my best friend.

A warm grip tugged at my wrist, bringing me back. An arm reached around me, pulling me from the bed. "Cassie, let go!" Gabriel's voice broke through. "Let go!"

Finally, I did, the momentum propelling me into Gabriel's chest, each of us turning in our chairs. He pulled me close, rubbing my back as I trembled.

He inhaled sharply, a sound of pain. Gabriel's fractured elbow was bent between us. I tried slipping from the circle of his strong arm, to not cause him more pain, but he squeezed me in, one large hand guiding my head to rest on his shoulder. His body curved over mine. I wrapped my arms around him, my fingers pressing into the soft skin at the base of his neck.

Curling into Gabriel's warmth, I realized the fire had died as soon as I'd let go of Vin. I looked at my arms over Gabriel's shoulder. The welts started to subside within several *bleeps* of the monitor. So I really could heal myself faster now. But after the pain, the burns, the vision—*the horrible vision*—making it clear why I'd ended up in Meeker alone, yet seeing that Vin still wasn't awake, the cadence of the bleeps unchanged, I could forget my silly hope about helping him.

It might even be too late to forgive him and ask for forgiveness in return.

To give Vin the peace of mind he deserved.

I found the strength to unglue myself from Gabriel, inching my hands close to Vin again. If the vision told me anything, it was that Vin felt responsible—perhaps entirely—for everything that had happened when Alanna ran away. I knew he wasn't, really. He'd never meant her to hear those words, spoken thoughtlessly in a moment of inexperienced passion. And he certainly hadn't stabbed her. But my words, equally thoughtless and spoken in the raw pain of grief, had helped convince him that his guilt was valid. We could have shared the pain, found comfort in each other, and instead, I'd built a barbed wire fence between us.

Of all the sins and guilt-ridden moments I'd seen in people, both of Vin's had been tied to him driving Alanna away. It spoke to his character, sure. Though it must also prove that sometimes we are the harshest judges of ourselves. And Alanna, in whatever place she was with Richard, wasn't here to ease Vin's pain with forgiveness. Cyndra wasn't here to take back those vengeful words and put the triviality of his transgression into perspective. But I was, and I had more to be grateful to Vin for, than to forgive. As much as I wanted to show that, to brush back Vin's long hair from his face, to let him know, somehow, what I felt for him. Even though his eyes were shut, maybe he'd feel how much I cared.

It seemed there was only one conclusion.

One inevitable answer to the equation of my life—the last two years. From near-death in the river, to a life of pain and isolation, to stumbling onto my past, or it stumbling upon me.

I thought of what I'd done at the clearing.

My body had been preparing itself for this role all along. And there was no going back to normal. No going back to touching Vin like before I'd come to Meeker. I dropped my head.

"Look!" Gabriel straightened in his seat. I glanced up. "Vin's hand." The red faded, leaching from Vin's fingers until they were the same ashen grey as the rest of him. Gabriel pointed with his uninjured arm. "Cassie—you healed him! Just like me."

A minor burn gone. So minor, we hadn't even noticed it at the clearing. What good was that? The bleeping was the same. Too slow.

Too long between beats.

Now that I could hear more than just the bleeping, I wanted

to ask Gabriel what we were going to do about Vin. About Vin's eyes, which were still shut, the lids sunk, dark hollows in his face. About Vin's father not answering. And yet, his excitement about Vin's healed skin fading, Gabriel seemed focused on me. Staring at my arms, he cringed.

Why? All that were left were a few pink patches.

When Gabriel looked up, and into my eyes, there was sadness.

"So I guess…" His lips trembled.

"Yes?" What was Gabriel thinking?

"Even with the relic, you can only…"

"What?"

"Touch…only…"

"You." I finished his thought.

He looked away. "I thought—I mean, I'd hoped that now…"

Of course.

I'd hoped that too. Hoped that I could touch people again. Not be afraid that one accident could leave me in horrible pain.

Sure, in a sick way, the experiment I'd just conducted confirmed what Gabriel and I had both suspected—but never really said—that for the rest of my life I might not be able to touch anyone but him. That Gabriel and I were "meant" to be together, "fated" in a way, because he was the one exception to the rule of my existence. But at this moment, sitting next to Vin, unable to hold his hand, all I could think was, what kind of existence was that? What must Gabriel be thinking… about us? Would we even work out? Forever? Because how could Gabriel ever be sure I truly wanted to be with him, when he knew I couldn't be with anyone else?

My hands turned cold again on the blanket next to Vin.

Then I remembered Gabriel's most characteristic trait.

Innocence wasn't exactly the right word.

The right word was goodness. Gabriel saw it in others and kept what he saw within himself—carrying that energy, letting it influence how he saw the world, letting it make him a better person. Looking at the sadness still reflected in his gaze, his deep blue eyes flickering between me and Vin, I knew Gabriel wished I could touch Vin and other people for myself. Not just for his reassurance.

Whatever the future held for us, I'd find a way to show Gabriel that I loved him for who he was. Not just because it seemed he'd always be the one person I could touch without pain.

I clutched Vin's arm through his gown. "Gabriel. He's so cold."

Gabriel reached past me, touching Vin's hand, covering it with his larger one. He frowned, then stood, scooting around me, putting an ear to Vin's lips. A faint gurgling sound emerged from the cracked skin. Before I could blink, Gabriel braced his good arm on the side of Vin, wincing as his injured elbow lay against Vin's stomach and took weight, almost laying chest to chest, trying to warm him. "Cassie, go get the nurse."

I grabbed my crutches, finally getting to standing, hurrying but taking too long.

Gabriel shot an arm out, hitting a red button on the wall with his fist. "Cassie, forget the—" His eyes welled up. "Just go. Please. You shouldn't be here." The bleeping picked up. Vin's heart was beating faster.

Vin's eyes fluttered open.

He was awake! What would I say?

He spoke first.

"El…lis." Vin mouthed the syllables.

"You told me already," I whispered, swaying forward, trying to catch his gaze.

"El…lis…" His hazel eyes were empty vessels.

"I know. We'll get her out. And… "

What to say next? There was so much.

Vin mouthed two more solitary words. "Dream. Land."

Dream Land? Or maybe Dreamland?

His eyelids closed.

The bleeping went wild, ending in a flat, piercing sound. Gabriel jerked up, slamming the red button again. Before I could take a step to get help, doctors and nurses swarmed the room. "He's crashing!"

Gabriel stepped back. A smocked body swooped in, hands and metal reaching for Vin. Someone bumped into me. Gabriel steadied me. Someone bumped back. "Clear the room. Both of you. Outside! Now!"

I would have moved. I'd have done anything if it would help. But I couldn't get the crutches under my arms. Gabriel tore off his sling, picked up my crutches, and swung me against his chest. He slowly backed us away. A nurse waved us out and slammed the door.

Gabriel released me and held me up as I struggled to see through a glass panel. The glass was narrow, just a sliver in the door. Hands worked frantically over the bed. More metal. Paddles over his chest. Yells and then breaks of silence while they waited for something—his heart to start—staring at the monitor.

"Vin!" I cried.

Gabriel's warmth circled around me, trying to turn me toward his chest.

I pushed back. "Vin!"

"It'll be okay." A soft voice floated down from above. A speck of yellow light flashed over us, from a corner just outside the room, floating closer to the door. To us. The light was dim, not as bright as I'd ever seen around Richard. Hesitant. "They can't save him, but it'll be okay," a girl's voice whispered.

"What?"

"I can feel it. He's on his way." Her voice carried over curt orders and the sounds of the commotion within the room.

Gabriel's arms tightened around me. "Who is this?"

An answer drifted down, little more than a whisper. "Alanna." The light floated closer to the glass. "Don't worry. I'll find him."

"Please," I pleaded. "Bring him back."

"Don't worry. I'll take care of him." The yellow swelled, filling my field of vision, then faded away.

I pressed my forehead against the cold glass. More words seeped through from the room in which Vin lay unmoving. "I'm calling it." Everyone pulled back from the bed. The room fell silent.

A smocked man dropped orange paddles onto a cart. "Time…"

An unendurable pause as he looked at the clock.

"Time of death. 11:55 p.m."

I woke in pain. The fire burned bone-deep, blazing around my heart. I tried not to cry out. I couldn't—*wouldn't*—wake Gram again.

Find the light. Sleeping Beauty must be here, somewhere in the dark.

Missing her, my eyes shot up, to a twisted silhouette. A tree, its branches casting reflections on the ceiling. The smooth, flawless ceiling… *this wasn't Gram's attic.* The realization made the pain worse. And the pain, it was different. Consuming not my flesh, only my heart.

Slowly the lines blurred, soft light filling the room. It was almost morning.

Morning!

I jolted out of the embrace in which Gabriel's good arm held me, pushing at my leg cast and scrambling off the bed. The doctor's words—the few hopeful ones I'd caught—came back to me. She said they'd be back in the morning, to see if Vin was ready to be moved to another, bigger hospital, to perform the next surgery, something involving one of his wounds, his bile duct, that they couldn't fix here. Even though no one could reach his father, they'd let Gabriel fill out the forms. The Knights were paying for it. I had to…

… *bleep… bleep… bleep…*

Then I remembered.

The sound had stopped hours ago. It was just an echo in my head. We were at Gabriel's home. I'd barely slept a wink.

Vin was dead.

I stumbled out the room and down the hall on one leg and my crutches, trying not to wake Gabriel or Zoe, Richie, and Rosie, curled up together in Zoe's spot.

Nearing the stairs, I swung past them, gliding over the paisley carpet, not wanting to see what stood below. As I passed the top step, heading toward the opposite wing, I tripped and my supports jammed into the floor. The rubber tips skidded across the silky surface, and I paid my penance for trying to avoid the sight of the foyer's sculpture—Apollo and his river nymph. His hopeless love.

I fell. Hard.

A soft whimper shot down the hall from behind me. Adjusting my cast on the silky rug, I sat, turned, and opened my arms.

From the dimness Zoe wobbled forward. She paused below the landing's domed skylight and, still stiff from sleep, stretched in the middle of streaks of sunshine slanting across the corridor. She turned her head over one shoulder, glancing back toward Gabriel's room, then back to me.

"Oh, Zoe-bug." My shoulders trembled.

She jerked forward, and crawled as far as she could onto my lap, pushing her snout through my hair, nuzzling closer, sighing softly.

When we got to Vin's room, I propped the crutches against the footboard, lifted her up, and settled her at the end of the bed. She pawed with her two front legs, the third dragging, crawling across the maroon covering and up the perfectly-made bed. She sniffed Vin's pillow several times, pausing over the rounded indentation in the middle, then sank down, curling up next to it. I stifled a gasp.

Soon her soft snores filled the room.

I hopped over to the dresser, pulling out the drawers. Then to the closet, throwing it open. When I finally tracked down Vin's father, I wouldn't be empty-handed. I didn't know what Dream Land meant, but I'd figure it out. Because those words, they must be about Ellis. Vin was always so practical. Those last words must be too. So not about Ellis, but where she is, the government facility. Where Vin's father was watching—waiting—for an opportunity to get her out. That must be why he hadn't returned any calls.

I had to hope.

Because wherever or whatever Dream Land was, I'd find it. There were people there who I had no living memory of, but who

I was still tied to. And to one—Vin's father—to whom I might owe great debts. Loyalties fresh, and loyalties forgotten, I'd see them honored.

I found a duffel bag under the bed and started to fill it. First with a stack of journals buried in a bottom drawer. Then with books scattered around the bed, all in Greek except for one peeking out from the pillow by Zoe's head.

Wuthering Heights.

I saw it first, but reached for it last.

Sliding out the thick book, hesitating with it in my hands at the edge of the bed, I finally flipped through the worn pages. My good leg gave out. I leaned into the bed and struggled to get back to standing. But Vin's words about Catherine and Heathcliff from the first day of school came back to me, his gaze connecting with mine.

"Tragic love… yet so enduring."

I slid back down to the mattress.

Vin may have seen himself as the love of my life once. But he had been my best friend twice, in two lives. I rose, stumbled forward, and slipped the book in the bag.

Finally, I gathered photos, all unframed, most in Vin's messenger bag, a few tucked away here and there around the room. Several of Vin and a man who must be his father. Although the trim figure in a fitted grey suit looked too young, he had Vin's black hair and such a proud smile. One of me, in a bright pink dress. Another of me, gazing up into Vin's hazel eyes. The photo of Ellis, radiant by the pool. Another of me and Vin, playing soccer. I looked like an awkward preteen, but Vin looked like the same teen heartthrob I'd met just months ago.

He hated his agelessness but kept this photo.

He'd lived in suspicion of all his relationships, convinced his abilities sabotaged them, made them fake. All except ours. He'd let me in because I could resist his smiles, and that made any smile I returned feel more genuine. At least, after all that had happened, maybe I'd managed to give him that back. That genuine connection we both craved and feared was impossible for different reasons.

We'd come to think that sort of bond was absent, unattainable for us, but the last photo in the bunch said otherwise. All of us sat together by a fireplace, stockings hung, Vin and his father shoulder to shoulder, Vin's arm around me, Ellis' elbow hooked with mine, and Alanna, standing off to the side. I couldn't put that one down. I knew what it was.

A family photo.

We'd been a family.

I ran a fingertip over the glossy paper. Vin. Alanna. Ellis. Time slowed. My mind went blank, unable to process any more.

A soft voice startled me. "He loved you unconditionally, you know."

I turned, my eyes darting around for the intrusion.

"He always loved you with no strings. Like you loved me. I see that now," the quiet voice echoed around the room as staticky sparks appeared by the closet.

The photo slipped from my fingers and floated to the floor.

My twin stood materialized from the sparks, her brown hair bathed in a muted yellow light. She made no movement, but the light pulsed around her. Zoe woke, whimpering. I sank to the bed, and petted her, and gazed in wonder at someone I only knew from a few painful visions and a photograph.

I couldn't quite believe it. As though she'd stepped out of the late afternoon glow of a sunlit meadow, and into Vin's dark room, my twin was here.

She had something to say. Her brow furrowed, her lips pursed. She pointed to the floor, motioning to the photo but staring at me. "I'll find him. You find Ellis."

I rubbed my forehead. "You can find Vin?" My hand fell. "You can—" my voice cracked. "You can bring him back?"

"No. I can't bring him back to you." She twisted her head away, brown curls escaping from her pinned-up hair sweeping her shoulders. "But I can feel him on my side. He's wandering. I'll find him. Before they do." She turned back. "I won't let anything happen to him." She lifted her chin, determination in her gaze, her green irises focused on me.

I didn't know what she meant, but I nodded, realizing I trusted her to help him.

"You find Ellis." Tears welled up in her eyes. "Ellis needs us, but I can't find her. You have to do it."

"I will." I stood, settling my weight onto my good leg. "I'm leaving today. Vin left me some sort of message, to figure out how to find her."

"Good." She sniffed, a tear running down her pale face. "It's so hard to see sometimes. I lost Ellis. I can't find her. But I knew Vin would."

I wrapped my arms around myself. "I think Richard's in trouble too."

"I know." She squared her shoulders. "I'm working on it." She said it so firmly. Did she think I would doubt her?

I rubbed Zoe's head, wishing I could move closer to my sister—my breath caught at the surprising sensation—but sensing she didn't want me to approach, I remained where I was. "Why have I never seen you before?"

"It was easier with Richard." Her bottom lip trembled. "I mean, when Richard and I figured out how to connect back, we thought it would be easier. For you. You knew who Richard was, and nothing about me. And it's, um, hard." Her eyes filled again with tears.

Hard to connect back, or hard for her to be here? "Are you okay? Is there anything else I can do?" I hopped a step forward, struggling to stay on my feet.

She blinked, inhaling deeply. "Just find Ellis."

I hopped another step, and she looked around the room.

"And be careful." She wiped a tear from her cheek. "Now that you're connected with your relic, it won't be able to ward off the Summum Malum. There's something different about you now. But

I can't be sure how strong it is, how far it extends. All I know is, their blindness in this town has ended." She looked around again, appearing to search the light around her. "It's risky to connect too long. Make sure you wear Richard's bracelet. It'll help us find you. I'll find you again soon." Though tears still stained her face, her lips formed a tentative smile as she melted into the yellow haze.

The light flashed and went out.

I hugged Zoe, trying to process the fact I'd just had a conversation with my dead twin. She couldn't have looked more like me, and I couldn't have felt more disconnected from her. Whatever sympathy I might have for her story, it was just that, a story to me. Her death, and the death of my memories, had torn me apart from her. And her from me? Or, was our relationship broken before that?

I finally picked up the picture from the floor and slid it into the front cover of a book in the duffel bag. I pulled back out the photo of me and Vin, deciding his father wouldn't mind if I kept it. I set it on the dresser.

Suddenly, the hardest part was over.

I moved to Vin's clothes, making stacks of them on the bed, finding more bags to put them in. I'd leave these with the Knights, but cleaning out Vin's room felt like something I had to do. Something I shouldn't leave for someone else to do. I slipped Vin's shirts off their hangers, bundling them together. *Almost done.* Then it would be time to leave. Time to tell my best friend's father his son was dead.

But, apparently, Vin wasn't gone completely. He was in the same place Richard and Alanna were—and maybe my parents?—the place Gabriel's great-grandfather said so many like us were, trapped between this world and the next. Was that like heaven? Would Vin be in heaven someday?

Zoe lifted her head from the pillow, giving a yip toward the door.

Gabriel stood in his boxer shorts, one foot still in the hall, the other planted in the doorway, looking unbalanced. His toes gripped the floor, tension running all the way up his large body. His bandaged arm shook. His scarred cheek quivered.

I froze with the tangle of shirts in my arms. One slipped out and Gabriel watched it fall, brushing past my cast and settling to the floor. He lifted his eyes, resting them for a moment on the locket around my neck, then to what I held in my arms, and shivered. He braced himself against the doorframe with his uninjured arm. "I woke up, and you were gone, Zoe too, and I thought…"

Tears filled my eyes. I hopped toward the row of open bags on the floor. Would Gabriel come with me? Could I ask him to leave his family right now?

No. I loved him too much to ask that.

Gabriel moved into the room with unsteady steps, stopping when he got to the bags. Cedar and cloves mixed with crisp lime from Vin's shirts in my arms. He looked from me to Zoe, who laid her head back down on Vin's pillow, to the clothes and books overflowing from the bags, then to the photo on the dresser. "Cassie, I'm so sorry."

I couldn't talk about that now. All I could think about was getting out of here. To Vin's father and Ellis. Vin's father. I didn't even know his name. My head fell with the weight of that thought, my chin trembled.

Gabriel gently lifted the pile of shirts from my arms and set them aside. "I've been thinking about what happened. About Vin. Me. Where I was, by the burned area from the fire." He moved to the bed, and started folding the rest of the shirts, moving awkwardly with his bandaged arm.

"Yes?"

"You didn't say how Aaron got the opportunity to get to Vin."

"It doesn't matter," I whispered hoarsely, when it really mattered more than anything. I owed Vin so much.

"It does to me. I have to know. Was Vin helping me? Is that how Aaron…"

I couldn't talk about that either. Not yet. Hugging my arms to my waist, I said what I could. "The fire. It was spreading too fast."

"Oh. Vin—" Gabriel's voice thickened. "Vin saved me?

"He saved us both." I wouldn't have made it out of that clearing without him. And it was surprisingly hard to acknowledge. I wasn't different than anyone else. Everyone wants to believe they can take care of themselves. But it doesn't always work that way, even in the movies. Sometimes you need help, and it's a debt you can't repay. All you can do is hope that you'll be there in your turn, when someone needs you. And I would. I'd be there for Ellis.

"How can I ever repay him?" Gabriel gasped. He teared up.

"We just have to remember him for the friend he was. The person he was."

Gabriel nodded.

I tried to refocus on getting to Vin's father. "Do you think the police will believe our story?" I asked, needing to know that when I left, trouble wouldn't follow, or bother those left behind.

Gabriel wiped the corners of his eyes and finally shrugged. "They seemed a bit skeptical, but Vin's injuries could've been from a knife. We could've run into copper thieves. They could've set fire to the clearing."

"If you think it's a good story, I trust you." I needed to believe Gabriel was right. And his story of how we ran into drugged-up thieves breaking into the cell site was believable enough, especially with the evidence we had. The frog-men's truck, for one. It was handy that it had turned out to be stolen.

Only one more thing to worry about before I left, making sure the Knights were okay. My leg itched in my cast. Okay, make that two things. I couldn't drive Gram's VW with its clutch—I needed to find a car I could drive with one foot. But first, the Knights. "Have you heard from Cole?" I asked.

"Yeah." Gabriel's expression lifted. "He said Dad's in a deep sleep. Great-uncle Gus too."

I sighed, a bit of stress melting away.

"And Cole got the dead frog-guy to the cave too. He'll bury him deep. With the Jentilaks. No one will find them."

So it would be like none of this ever happened. "Aaron?"

"He's gone."

"What I did…"

"You did what we needed you to."

"Do you think he'll come back?"

"I don't know. My father's hoping."

I guessed Bernard hadn't seen the look in his son's eyes. Gabriel must have read my thoughts.

He frowned. "I'm not sure what to hope." He cleared his throat. "Dad doesn't know about how bad Vin was injured yet, but he said he just doesn't know if Aaron could've done it… if he would've gone through with it."

"It?"

Gabriel glanced at my locket and shuddered. "Everything."

"He came close."

"I know." Gabriel rolled his neck as if trying to release a bit of his own tension. "And Dad knows about Aaron getting Cameron out of the way now too. But Dad thinks Aaron just did something to make Cameron go, and Cousin Everett will keep working on finding him." His head jerked almost imperceptibly toward Cameron's room then back to me, as if his thoughts were pulled in different directions. "Dad said Aaron's on the wrong path. But if he comes home, we can't turn our backs. If we push him away, that will just push him closer to them."

"And when your father returns to town, his eye… won't that raise questions?"

"They've already turned his cell phone on in a couple of places, and left things in remote spots consistent with him being held captive with Aaron. When he wakes up, and shows up without Aaron, he'll come up with a good enough story." Gabriel gave me a crooked grin. "We bears aren't as simple as we sometimes seem."

"Are you worried that Aaron took the relic?"

"Well, no. I mean, you got everything from it. What use could it be now?"

I shrugged. "It just seems Aaron wouldn't have taken it without a reason."

"Not sure what it could be." Gabriel stepped closer. "Don't you feel different now? Stronger?"

I shook my head, suddenly unable to speak past the lump in my throat.

Did I feel stronger? Vin had asked the same thing that night in my room after the cave. I didn't feel stronger from touching the relic then. I didn't feel stronger now. Not in the way Gabriel meant. Like I was some sort of superhero. Because touching the relic hadn't changed who I was—either time. If anything, it had shown me to accept who I was, accept all my strength with all my vulnerability. Because the vulnerability didn't make me weak, and I was so much stronger than I'd thought. I'd made it through this. And I hadn't done it alone. "I'm leaving." I looked into Gabriel eyes, realizing I was stronger with Gabriel than without him. But I still wouldn't ask him to leave his family right now. "I have to find my sister. And Vin's father."

"I know," Gabriel said.

"You do?"

"Yes." In several powerful steps Gabriel stood in front of me, holding his injured arm with his other, bent across his chest. "You have to find your family."

I nodded, a tear escaping.

Gabriel inhaled deeply. "I talked to Cole. He'll stay here. I'll go with you."

Of course. Gabriel loved me. I loved him, for so many reasons, but especially the person he was. He knew I had to leave and had already made plans to come with me. "What about your dad?"

"He doesn't know yet, but he'll understand."

"You're injured."

"So are you."

"But—"

"We'll heal together."

I took a breath, letting that sink in. I didn't have to lick my wounds alone anymore. And neither did he. Still, I pressed on, if only to talk the decision out fully.

"You just got home."

"Me leaving before was a mistake. Me leaving now is everything." He stepped in close, but didn't touch me.

"Zoe?" I glanced at her. Her eyes were closed, her snout twitching slightly as she snored on Vin's pillow.

"Cole will take care of her. Keep her safe."

If I left, would Zoe think I'd abandoned her? Maybe. Fresh tears sprung in my eyes. But Zoe knew I loved her, and it was for the best. She'd have Richie and Rosie too. I blinked several times to clear my vision. It would be too risky to take her, especially with what I had planned. I could never put her in danger. And Cole adored them all. So I had to trust Cole, and I didn't doubt for a moment that he would take good care of my friend.

Plus, no matter how long it took, I'd be back for her.

"I'm not stopping at Ellis. I'm going to find my younger sisters too."

"We'll do it together." Gabriel's features relaxed, eyes soft and gentle. "I'll be with you every step of the way." He dropped his arms and extended his good hand to me.

I took his hand and held on tight. Because while I'd never believe in fairytales, once upon a times, or perfect endings, and it seemed I'd never be normal—always living with the fear of pain—I had to admit the truth.

It was nice, at long last, to not be alone.

END OF BOOK ONE

Want more Cassie and Gabriel? Head over to www.cherylkahn.com and follow them on their mission to find Ellis in a free complete scene from Gabriel's perspective. While you're there, sign up for my newsletter to receive more bonus content, including another Gabriel POV scene, this one retelling his and Cassie's night on the mountain through his eyes. Newsletter subscribers also receive exclusive updates and first access to everything in the Five Senses Series. Thanks for your support!

ACKNOWLEDGEMENTS

This book wouldn't have gotten this far without the wisdom of my dad, who's guided me through many rough patches in writing and in life, the love of my dogs, and the support of my husband. I also owe much thanks to friends, beta readers, and critique partners, including: Lauren, Mel, Christiana, Nick, Tasha, Norm, Krissy, Nicole, Alexa, Addie, Kendall, Amy, Ezra, and Phoebe. I was fortunate to find fantastic editors in Janna Balthaser and Hannah Sandoval. Finally, I owe so much to my own Gram, who passed years before this book began but who I imagine is looking down like Cassie's Gram, knowing how much I love her.

ABOUT THE AUTHOR

Cheryl once worked as a corporate attorney and yoga instructor, but when the pandemic scaled back her yoga teaching, she reassessed her passions. Following a dream that began in 6th grade when she and her best friend penned a story in a spiral notebook during recess, Cheryl now spends her days crafting stories with care and a lot of heart. When not at the computer, she can be found sweating at the gym with friends, walking her rescue pup, and glued to her Kindle. She lives in California with her college sweetheart, now husband. Connect with Cheryl and receive exclusive Five Senses Series material by signing up for her newsletter at www.cherylkahn.com.

www.ingramcontent.com/pod-product-compliance
Lightning Source LLC
Chambersburg PA
CBHW031236310726
48971CB00004B/1040